The 1960's Cult British Television Gu

I was looking around for a factual indexed reference book on 1960s British Cu
not find anything. I started digging in my own collection and compiling my ow
was missing or had not seen and thought there may be others like me who may
chosen twenty nine shows and included a surviving episode list plus any up to (
soundtrack releases available for purchase. As history seems to have forgotten t
members, directors and writers I have included a section on each but please bear in mind they are not
career retrospectives or biographies, just their involvement in these particular shows. It is worth noting
that colour television did not reach our shores properly until 1969 and then the coverage was patchy,
the Americans had been watching 'Color' since 1954. Virtually all the episodes made in colour were
aimed at overseas markets and over here we watched them in black and white, indeed the fist time I ever
saw a colour TV was in 1970 when our neighbour bought one for the Mexico World Cup and invited us
round to see it.

I have had to use my judgment and opinion to decide what constitutes Cult Television and the themes I
have chosen are Science Fiction, Undercover Agents, Private Detectives & Action Hero. I did not
include anything with puppets so I am afraid no Thunderbirds. I also had to set some boundaries and as
this book is a reference companion to the shows for the arm chair viewer I have decided not to include
shows which no longer exist as I could see little point if you cannot watch them. I also have excluded all
non UK made shows and with programs such as Interpol Calling which started in 1959 I have included
all the episodes in the series, the same goes for Department S which ran into 1970. The Callen series
which went on until 1972 series 3 and 4 are not included. I plan to write a follow up book to this
covering the 1970's which will dovetail this book and maybe join them both one day. The Third Man
has the ten surviving episodes on DVD so are included although it is an import to the UK. Alas the third
series of Ghost Squad called GS5 no longer exists. Many episodes listed in the book are available on
YouTube, just type in the title of this book and don't forget to subscribe. There are also many episodes
on the Network On Air and Amazon or via IMDb.

Finally as this book is about British culture there are no 'seasons' or Americanized dates, Danger Man
is not Secret Agent and no I do not have shares or get freebies from Network DVD.

This book is dedicated in loving memory to my dad, Jim Sellen 1933-2021.

James Sellen, London, October 2021.

Series Overview Guide

Adam Adamant Lives!

The series starred Gerald Harper and his (usually unwanted) assistant, a young mod called Georgina Jones played by Juliet Harmer. Jack May played Simms the butler and appeared in a supporting role in all but two episodes. For car fans Adam drove a Mini Cooper S of unknown colour (B/W TV) registration AA 1000. Released by the BBC in 1966 it ran for 29 episodes, the first series consisted of sixteen episodes, and the second for thirteen, one episode of series one called Ticket To Terror is missing as are all but two episodes of series two. The remaining episodes were released on a five DVD set with any remaining material in 2006 by 2entertain. The theme tune was sung by Kathy Kirby and a single was released on Decca (F.12432) in 1966. It is available on the Ace Records Compilation: Don't Blow Your Cool (More 60's Girls From Decca) (2020)

The Andromeda Anthology

The Andromeda series was made by the BBC and ran for two series, the first called A For Andromeda (1961) and then The Andromeda Breakthrough (1962). The series is set in the far future (1970) and each series contain six episodes. The first series only one episode remains and features a very young Julie Christie. The premise of the story is aliens send radio signals to earth on how to build a computer, the then send signals on how to create a human to operate it (Andromeda) and the second series stared Susan Hampshire. The program spawned a book titled The Andromeda Anthology written in 1964 by Fred Hoyle and John Elliot who also wrote the television series and is available in the SF Masterworks series. The series was remade in 1972 and 2006. All the remaining materials was released by 2entertain in 3 DVD box set in 2006.

The Avengers

This is the longest running show of any of the genres listed and what began as an ABC Television series ran from 1961 to 1969. The only consistent was Patrick MacNee as he appeared in all but two of the 161 episodes which ran for 6 series. Only three episodes of the first series now survive and the lead role was shared by Ian Hendry and MacNee as John Steed. Honor Blackman (Dr Cathy Gale) joined Steed in partnership in series 2 and 3 although alas Ms Blackman and her leather suit did not appear in all the episodes. Ms Blackman left the show in 1964 and in the following year became Pussy Galore in Goldfinger. In 1965 Diana Rigg joined the show as Mrs Emma Peel (so named as the producer wanted m(ale)appeal) and Mrs Peel became Steed partner (not his assistant) and the shows formula was set. The show switched to colour in 1966 and in 1968 Diana Rigg left the show and followed in Honor Blackmans footsteps to become the lead Bond girl in On Her Majesty's Secret Service in 1969 starring George Lazenby. In the 6th and final series singer Canadian singer actress Linda Thorson took up the role of Steeds partner as Tara King. The last series was hit by financial problems production was suspended at one stage, the series re-emerged as the New Avengers in the mid 1970s but that's another story. StudioCanal currently have a five DVD box sets available covering all the available shows called The Complete Series 2 (and surviving Episodes from Series 1) (8 DVD's released in 2009), Series 3 (7 DVD's released in 2010), Series 4 (8 DVD's released in 2010), Series 5 (7 DVD's released 2010) Series 6 (9 DVD's released 2010). Oddly for such an iconic show there is little stand alone soundtrack material currently available, the 3 x CD box set The Music Of Laurie Johnson Volume 1: The Avengers (Edsel 2007) only CD 1 actually contains Avengers material, there is also The Avengers: Original Tara King Season Score by Howard Blake which was released on Silva Screen in 2011.

The Baron

This 1965 ITC Production in many ways set the established blue print for many other shows in this genre we know and love today, it was made in colour, had 30 stand alone episodes, was 50 minutes long (an hour including adverts) was made at Elstree and in the Hertfordshire countryside and had an American lead actor and was tailored for the American market. The Baron was an antiques dealer played by Steve Forrest and he was assisted by his P.A. Cordelia played by Sue Lloyd. The Baron who was ex-military in his spare time helps solves crime and unofficially assists the British Intelligence via their head of operation Templeton-Green. It was based on a series of novels by John Creasey and his car was a Jenson CV-8 Mk2. An 8 DVD box set called The Baron - The Complete Series was released in 2006 and also a CD featuring soundtrack music by Edwin Astley in 2019 both on Network.

The Champions

The term Spy-Fi would apply to this 1968, 30 episode ITC production more than any other. The trio comprised of Stuart Damon as Craig Stirling, William Gaunt as Richard Barrett and Alexandra Bastedo as Sharon Macready who all work for an agency of the UN called Nemesis. The trio return from a mission in China in the first episode with strange powers which they keep secret but help them solve future cases. The episodes are stand alone but their boss played by Anthony Nicholls becomes more and more suspicious so there is a thread which runs through the series. There is a 9 DVD box set available released in 2010 called The Champions: The Complete Series and a 3 CD soundtrack box set released in 2009 both by Network.

City Beneath The Sea

City Beneath The Sea was a six part mini series released in 1962. It is a sequel of sorts to the Pathfinders series in personnel (Gerald Floods character) but not in content, once again it was primarily aimed at children but and there is enough Science Fiction involved to hold my adult interest. There is a two DVD release containing this and its sequel Secret Beneath The Sea released by Network in 2013.

The Corridor People

Weird is an understatement, this four part mini series was broadcast by Grenada TV in 1966, the series combines all of the genres listed in this book plus modern art, slapstick humour and actors sprouting monologues in period costumes and sometimes all at once. It all combines into an oddly interesting as a piece of TV history. The series stared the beautiful Elizabeth Shepherd as the evil Syrie Van Epp as a master villain and John Sharp as Kronk who is the head of some kind of MI5 organization. A DVD of all four episodes was released by Network in 2012

.Danger Man

The series officially ran for four series but as the 4th series had only two episodes I have amalgamated it into series 3. The first series were released in 1960 and is known as the half hour series and series 2 and 3 were the hour series, all were black and white. The lead role was played by Patrick McGoohan and he's characters name was John Drake, Drake was an American secret agent for NATO in the first series but later became a British agent working for M9. The series had 80 episodes and was released by ITC. The show was an international hit and was released in the USA as Secret Agent. Network released a 19 DVD set the Complete Collection in 2019. There is a CD titled Secret Agent/The Saint by Edwin Astley released 1992 on Retro-sound which still can be picked up second hand.

Department S

This ITC show ran from 1969 to 1970 for 28 episodes, The S stands for special and the Department consisted of Joel Fabiani as Stuart Sullivan, Rosemary Nichols as Annabelle Hunt and they are assisted by Peter Wyngarde who plays playboy author Jason King. The trio work for Interpol out of their office in Paris. This was a big budget production on the scale of The Avengers and was created by Dennis Spooner and Monty Berman who also previously created The Champions. There was a spin off series called Jason King released in 1972. Network released an 8 DVD box called The Complete Collection in 2008, the same year a 3 CD soundtrack box set was released and in 2009 a single CD was released featuring soundtrack highlights composed by Edwin Astley, both were released by Network.

Doctor Who

Out of all the shows this as the one I was most nervous of compiling, the good Doctor has legions of fans and there are tons of material in print and on line and I am just an armchair fan. I will keep things pertinent to the book and please remember this is aimed at the modern viewer who may not have seen the original show yet. Doctor Who began in 1963 and ran until 1989 and was then resurrected in 2005. William Hartnell played the part from 1963 until 1967, Patrick Troughton then became the second doctor until 1969. The sixties episodes were in six series, the six series were subdivided into stories and the stories subdivided into episodes. To try to keep things simple I have listed the shows by story and not series, to confuse things even more there are 97 episodes missing so some stories are incomplete or missing all together. I have only listed the stories which have existing episodes. The Doctor Who theme song was recorded by the BBC Radio Workshop and written by Roy Grainer, it was released in 1973 BBC Records RESL 11 and there are a plethora of DVD's available.

Ghost Squad

The Ghost Squad was a series made by ITC and ran for 52 episodes between 1961 and 1964 for three series. The third series was re-titled GS5 and has been lost. The Ghost Squad was shadowy non defined organization which seemed to be able to operate across borders with impunity to catch British criminals home and abroad and so could do the jobs the normal police could not do. There was in fact a real life Ghost Squad in Scotland Yard but they never operated abroad. The first series stared American actor Michael Quinn as Nick Craig, the second series the lead role alternated (not strictly) between Quinn and Neil Hallett (Tony Miller) and Sally Lomax (Patricia Mort). The lovely Angela Brown was the secretary in the first series. The was a book called Ghost Squad by John Gosling which provided inspiration for the series. There is a ten DVD set of all the 39 existing episodes released on Network called Ghost Squad The Complete Series released in 2008.

Interpol Calling

This 39 half hour episode ITC series ran between 1959 until 1960 and stared Hungarian Charles Korvin and Edwin Richfield and they were supposedly based in Paris. The series was very cheaply made and Interpol seemed to consist of only two operatives Korvin and Richfield and where-ever they went the police force had the same police car and one policeman. Despite this it is well worth watching as shows this of this era, complete and in such good condition are a rarity. There is a 5 DVD box set available released by Network in 2012.

Man In A Suitcase

The series is said to be a continuation of the Danger Man franchise after Patrick McGoowan left but I never picked up that vibe myself. This 30 episode series was released by ITC in 1967. The lead role was played by Richard Bradford in the role of McGill an unlicensed, homeless private detective whose entire possessions are in one suitcase. The show was made in colour especially for the American market as was the choice of Bradford who was American. The show was released as an 8 DVD set and a 5 CD soundtrack box set were both released by Network in 2008. The theme tune was recorded by Roy Grainger and released as a single in 1967 on Pye 7N.17383.

Man Of The World

This series was released on ATV in 1962 and during the second series in 1963 there was an actors strike and the show was halted and never resumed. One episode was filmed in colour (which doubled as the pilot) and other 19 were in black and white. The show featured American Craig Stevens in the role of Michael Strait a famous conscientious globe trotting photographer.
A 5 DVD set of all the episodes were released by Network.

Out Of The Unknown

This BBC 2 Science Fiction series ran for four series from 1965 to 1971. The fourth series are horror stories so the date and subject matter put it outside the parameters of this book. Each of the episodes were stand alone and mostly featured short stories written by golden age Sci-Fi writers and would have appeared in magazines such as World Of IF and it was interesting to see stories I know well such as The Machine Stops were bought to life, a few stories were written especially for the series. Only 16 episodes from the first three series exist and some are poor quality which is a real shame. Apparently Peking is just like Shrewsbury in the future.

BFI released a 7 DVD box set in 2014 of all the existing episodes plus incomplete episodes.

Out Of This World

There were originally 14 episodes of this 1962 ATV Weekend series but sadly only one survives called The Little Robot which was an adaptation of an Isaac Asimov story. The format of this show seems very similar to the BBC's Out of the Unknown listed above where they adapted short stories by prominent writers to make one SF episode. BFI scraped together a 52 minute DVD of this episode plus other incomplete material from the show in 2014.

The Pathfinders

The three mini series named Pathfinders In Space, Pathfinders To Mars and Pathfinders To Venus were follow ups to the ABC series Target Luna released in 1960 which now is lost. The first two had six episodes and the third eight episodes. The show was big hit at the time and was primarily aimed at children but there is enough 1950s style Science Fiction and Scientific facts involved to keep fans of the genre interested. It has space ships with no seat belts, astronauts wearing woolly jumpers with collars and ties underneath and space walks on the moon with no glass visors in the helmets. The three Pathfinders series were released on a 3 DVD box set on Network in 2011.

The Prisoner

This series of 17 episodes was produced, co-created and co-written by lead actor Patrick McGoohan in 1967 and released by ITC. It has became a cult classic and there are now weekend trips to visit 'The Village' which is in fact the Portmeirion resort in Mid Wales. The resort was designed and built by Sir Clough William-Ellis in 1925 and was still under construction at the time of filming as it was not completed until 1975. The character Number 6's phrase 'I am not a number, I am a free man' has entered modern vocabulary. For those who have never seen the series McGoohan plays Number 6 in 'The Village' which is an inescapable prison and Number 6 has no idea where he is or who are his jailers and who are his friends. The Prisoner: The Complete Series a 6 DVD box set is available on Network, The Prisoner (Original Soundtrack) is 3 CD set also released by Network in 2009.

The Protectors

Not to be confused with the 1970s series staring Robert Vaughn, the show ran for one series in 1964 on ABC Television, it starred Andrew Foulds as Souter, Michael Atkinson as Shoesmith and Ann Moorish as Heather and all three appear in every episode. Between them they run an agency called SIS in London which protects the interests of insurance companies which sounds dull but the episodes were very well written and characters are engaging. The series was released by Network on a four DVD set called The Protectors: The Complete ABC Series in 2014.

Public Eye

This gritty Private Detective series ran from 1965 to 1975 for seven series, The lead role is played by Alfred Burke as Frank Marker and the first four series were made in 1960s so they are all we are concerned with. ABC Television made the first three series and only five episodes exist. The fourth series was produced by Thames Television in 1969 and exists in it entirety but unlike many of it's contemporaries of that time was made in Black & White. Series 4 The 1969 Episodes were released on DVD in 2004 and the first three series were released in a 2012 three DVD set called The ABC Years. A 17 DVD box set called A Box Named Frank containing every episode was in 2012. All released by Network.

Randall & Hopkirk (Deceased)

This ITC light-hearted private eye series ran for 28 episodes between 1969 to 1970. As the title suggests it is a buddy detective series with one of the pair being a ghost who for some reason cannot walk through walls. The team in completed by the ghosts (ex)wife Jean who is the secretary of the detective agency but does not know of the ghosts existence. Randall was played by Mike Pratt, Hopkirk by Kenneth Cope. Annette Andre plays Jean Hopkirk who appears in all but three of the episodes. All the episodes are in colour and in 2000 a re-make was made staring Reeves and Mortimer which ran for two series. The series is available as an 8 DVD set released in 2017 by Network. They also released a 3 CD soundtrack box set in 2010 and in 2013 a vinyl album of selected tracks. The theme tune was released as a single in 1970 by Norrie Paramor & His Orchestra (Polydor-56375)

The Saint

This long running series ran from 1962 to 1968 for 188 episodes and was made by ITC, unlike many other series of this time it remains intact with no missing episodes and 71 of the episodes are in Black and White. The show starred Roger Moore as The Saint and he appeared in every episode, unusually he was also the producer and director of many of the shows and also wore his own clothing most of the episodes. The Saint novels were written originally by Leslie Charteris in the 1950s and most of the early episodes of adaptations of these but in time original material was used. The car used in the series was a white Volvo P1800 which had a number plate of ST1.
There are two main Region 2 DVD Collections which cover all the episodes The Complete Monochrome Series (18 DVD box set) and The Complete Colour Years (14 DVD box set) The soundtrack music by Edwin Astley is available on a four CD box set, all are on Network. The theme tune was released in 1965 as a single (Danger Man on the B Side) RCA 1492.

Strange Report

This 1969 ITC series of 16 episodes stared Anthony Quayle as Adam Strange, he was supported by Kaz Garas and Anneke Wills who also appeared in every episode. Strange is a retired Home Office criminologist who works on unsolved crimes using his home laboratory. The reason the series did not have usual 28-30 usual ITC run was because some episodes were due to be filmed in the USA but this never happened. There is a five DVD box set (one DVD is extras) called Strange Report Special Edition released by Network in 2009 and a CD Strange Report Original Soundtrack released in 2014. The theme song was released as a single recorded by Roger Webb and released in 1971 on Columbia DB 8803.

The Third Man

Of all the shows in this book this was the hardest to catalogue as much of the information in the public domain is just wrong or non-existent. The show ran from 1959 to 1965 for 77 episodes and began production is the USA before switching to the UK in 1960. The show stared Michael Rennie as Harry Lime who is an art dealer who tackles crime in his spare time. The is a 10 Episode Import DVD released by Timeless and I have listed the UK episodes on the DVD, there is also a page on YouTube which lists it has the first 36 episodes but I cannot find anything else so I do not know if more episodes exist.

Undermind

This is little known 1965 science fiction series was made by ABC Television and ran for eleven episodes. Aliens are controlling certain peoples minds with radio beams remotely and the effected people are making preparations for an attack on Earth. Drew Heriot (Dennis Quilley) and his bereaved sister-in-law Anne Heriot (Rosemary Nichols) are the only ones who know of the plot and set out to thwart it. The DVD was released by Network in 2012 in a 3 DVD set.

The Lost & Unreleased Series

The Cheaters (1960-1962)

Apart from a four minute snippet on YouTube nothing seems to be available about this series about an insurance investigator which ran for two series and 39 episodes, the show starred John Ireland. Apparently is still exists and was repeated on television in the 1970's.

The Informer (1966-1967)

Disgraced barrister uses his connections to become a Police informer, two episodes exist but have never been released. The show ran for 21 episodes over two series. The only thing of this show available is the theme song released on a 7'' single by David Lindup and His Orchestra released in 1966 Columbia DB 7979. You can hear it on YouTube.

Mask Of Janus (1965)

Eleven episode Spy series has four existing episodes but I can find no details of any releases.

R3 (1964-1965)

This 26 episode Sci-Fi series is completely lost which is a shame, the only thing remaining is the theme song released by Ken Thorne & His Orchestra, it actually the B side of From Rogues To Riches and was released on HMV POP 1380 in 1965, It is also on YouTube.

The Rat Catchers (1966-1967)

Spy series which ran for two series and had 25 episodes, apparently two episodes exist but I could not find any trace apart from two snippets on YouTube. The theme song by the Johnny Pearson Orchestra was released on Columbia DB 7851 in 1966

The Spies

1966 follow up to The Mask Of Janus and ran for 15 episodes, nothing exists.

The Music of ITC

Network released an excellent 117 track double CD called the Music of ITC in 2009.

CD 1 tracks 01-06 Danger Man (half hour series) 07-13 Danger Man (one hour series) 14-15 Gideon's Way 16-22 The Baron 23-31 The Saint 32-37 Man in a Suitcase 38-44 The Prisoner 45-53 The Champions 54-61 Department S.
CD 2 tracks 01-06 Randall & Hopkirk (deceased) 07-13 Strange Report 14-17 The Persuaders 18-25 Jason King 26-33 The Protectors 34-36 The Adventurer 37-44 The Zoo Gang 45-52 The Return Of The Saint

The Surviving Episodes (First known UK broadcast date in brackets)

A For Andromeda + The Andromeda Breakthrough

1-6. The Face Of The Tiger (07-11-61)
2-1. Cold Front (28-06-62)
2-2. Gale Warning (05-07-62)
2-3. Arazan Forecast (12-07-62)
2-4. Storm Centres (19-07-62)
2-5. Hurricane (26-07-62)
2-6. The Roman Peace (02-08-62)

Adam Adamant Lives!

Series 1
01. A Vintage Year For Scoundrels (20-06-66)
02. Death Has a Thousand Faces (30-06-66)
03. More Deadly Than The Sword (07-07-66)
04. The Sweet Smell Of Disaster (14-07-66)
05. Allah Is Not Always With You (21-07-66)
06. The Terribly Happy Embalmers (04-06-66)
07. To Set a Deadly Fashion (11-08-66)
08. The Last Sacrifice (18-08-66)
09. Sing a Song Of Murder (25-08-66)
10. The Doomsday Plan (01-09-66)
11. Death By Appointment Only (08-09-66)
12. Beauty Is An Ugly Word (15-09-66)
13. The League Of Uncharitable Ladies (12-09-66)
15. The Village Of Evil (06-10-66)
16. D For Destruction (13-06-66)
Series 2
18. Black Echo (07-01-67)
29. A Sinister Sort Of Service (25-03-67)

The Avengers

The Avengers Series 1
1-06. Girl On The Trapeze (11-02-61)
1-15. The Frighteners (27-11-61)
1-20. Tunnel Of Fear (05-08-61)

The Avengers Series 2
2-01. Mr Teddy Bear (29-09-62)
2-02. Propellant 23 (06-10-62)
2-03. The Decapod (13-10-62)
2-04. Bullseye (20-10-62)
2-05. Mission To Montreal (27-10-62)
2-06. The Removal Men (03-11-62)
2-07. The Mauritius Penny (10-11-62)
2-08. Death Of Great Dane (17-11-62)
2-09. The Sell Out (24-11-62)
2-10. Death On The Rocks (01-12-62)

2-11. Traitor In Zebra (08-12-62)
2-12. The Big Thinker (15-12-62)
2-13. Death Dispatch (22-12-62)
2-14. Dead On Course (29-12-62)
2-15. Intercrime (05-01-63)
2-16. Immortal Clay (12-01-63)
2-17. Box Of Tricks (19-01-63)
2-18. Warlock (26-01-63)
2-19. The Golden Egg (02-02-63)
2-20. School For Traitors (09-02-63)
2-21. The White Dwarf (16-02-63)
2-22. Man In The Mirror (23-02-63)
2-23. Conspiracy Of Silence (02-03-63)
2-24. A Chorus Of Frogs (09-03-63)
2-25. Six Hands Across a Table (16-03-63)
2-26. Killer Whale (23-03-63)

The Avengers Series 3
3-01. Brief For Murder (28-09-63)
3-02. The Undertakers (05-10-63)
3-03. Man With Two Shadows (12-10-63)
3-04. The Nutshell (19-10-63)
3-05. Death Of a Batman (26-01-63)
3-06. November Five (02-11-63)
3-07. The Gilded Cage (09-11-63)
3-08. Second Sight (16-11-63)
3-09. The Medicine Men (23-11-63)
3-10. The Grandeur That Was Rome (30-11-63)
3-11. The Golden Fleece (07-12-63)
3-12. Don't Look Behind You (14-12-63)
3-13. Death a La Carte (21-12-63)
3-14. Dressed To Kill (28-12-63)
3-15. The White Elephant (04-01-64)
3-16. The Little Wonders (11-01-64)
3-17. The Wringer (18-01-64)
3-18. Mandrake (25-01-64)
3-19. The Secrets Broker (01-02-64)
3-20. Trojan Horse (08-02-64)
3-21. Build a Better Mousetrap (15-02-64)
3-22. The Outside-In Man (22-02-64)
3-23. The Charmers (29-02-64)
3-24. Concerto (07-03-64)
3-25. Espirit de Corps (14-03-64)
3-26. Lobster Quadrille (21-03-64)

The Avengers Series 4
4-01. The Town Of No Return (02-10-65)
4-02. The Gravediggers (09-01-65)
4-03. The Cybernauts (16-10-65)
4-04. Death At Bargain Prices (23-10-65)
4-05. Castle De'ath (30-10-65)
4-06. The Master Minds (06-11-65)
4-07. The Murder Market (13-11-65)
4-08. A Surfeit Of H2o (20-11-65)
4-09. The Hour That Never Was (27-11-65)
4-10. Dial a Deadly Number (04-12-65)
4-11. Man Eater Of Surrey Green (11-12-65)
4-12. Twos a Crowd (18-12-65)

4-13. Too Many Christmas Trees (25-12-65)
4-14. Silent Dust (01-01-66)
4-15. Room Without a View (08-01-65)
4-16. Small Game For Big Hunters (15-01-65)
4-17. The Girl From AUNTIE (22-01-66)
4-18. The Thirteenth Hole (29-01-66)
4-19. Quick-Quick Slow Death (05-02-66)
4-20. The Danger Makers (12-02-66)
4-21. A Touch Of Brimstone (19-02-66)
4-22. What The Butler Saw (26-02-66)
4-23. The House That Jack Built (05-03-66)
4-24. A Sense Of History (12-03-66)
4-25. How To Succeed.... At Murder (19-03-66)
4-26. Honey For The Prince (26-03-66)

The Avengers Series 5
5-01. From Venus With Love (14-01-67)
5-02. The Fear Merchants (21-01-67)
5-03. Escape In Time (26-01-67)
5-04. The See Through Man (04-02-67)
5-05. The Bird Who Knew Too Much (11-02-67)
5-06. The Winged Avenger (18-02-67)
5-07. The Living Dead (25-02-67)
5-08. The Hidden Tiger (04-03-67)
5-09. The Correct Way To Kill (11-03-67)
5-10. Never, Never Say Die (18-03-67)
5-11. Epic (25-03-67)
5-12. The Superlative Seven (01-04-67)
5-13. A Funny Thing Happened On The Way To The Station (08-04-67)
5-14. Something Nasty In The Nursery (15-04-67)
5-15. The Joker (22-04-67)
5-16. Who's Who (29-04-67)
5-17. Return Of The Cybernauts (30-09-67)
5-18. Death's Door (07-10-67)
5-19. The £50,000 Breakfast (14-10-67)
5-20. Dead Man's Treasure (21-10-67)
5-21. You Have Just Been Murdered (28-10-67)
5-22. The Positive Negative Man (4-11-67)
5-23. Murdersville (11-11-67)
5-24. Mission, Highly Improbable (18-11-67)

The Avengers Series 6
6-01. The Forget Me Knot (25-09-68)
6-02. Game (02-10-68)
6-03. Super Secret Cypher Snatch (09-10-68)
6-04. You'll Catch Your Death (16-10-68)
6-05. Split (23-10-68)
6-06. Whoever Shot George Oblique Stroke XR40? (30-10-68)
6-07. False Witness (06-01-68)
6-08. All Done With Mirrors (13-11-68)
6-09. Legacy Of Death (20-11-68)
6-10. Noon Doomsday (27-11-68)
6-11. Look (Stop Me If You've Heard This One) But There Were These Two Fellers (04-12-68)
6-12. Have Guns - Will Haggle (11-12-68)
6-13. They Keep Killing Steed (18-12-68)
6-14. The Interrogators (01-01-69)
6-15. The Rotters (08-01-69)
6-16. Invasion Of The Earthman (15-01-69)

6-17. Killer (22-01-69)
6-18. The Morning After (29-10-69)
6-19. The Curious Case Of The Countless Clues (05-02-69)
6-20. Wish You Were Here (12-02-69)
6-21. Love All (19-02-69)
6-22. Stay Tuned (26-02-69)
6-23. Take Me To Your Leader (05-03-69)
6-24. Fog (12-03-69)
6-25. Who Was That Man I Saw You With (19-03-69)
6-26. Homicide & Old Lace (26-03-69)
6-27. Thingamajig (16-04-69)
6-28. My Wildest Dream (07-04-69)
6-29. Requiem (16-04-69)
6-30. Take-Over (23-04-69)
6-31. Pandora (30-04-69)
6-32. Get-a-Way (14-05-69)
6-33. Bizarre (21-05-69)

The Baron

01. Diplomatic Immunity (28-09-66)
02. Epitaph For a Hero (05-10-66)
03. Something For a Rainy Day (12-10-66)
04. Red Horse, Red Rider (19-10-66)
05. Enemy Of The State (26-10-66)
06. Masquerade (Part 1) (02-11-66)
07. The Killing (Part 2) (09-11-66)
08. The Persuaders (16-11-66)
09. And Suddenly You're Dead (23-11-66)
10. The Legends of Ammak (30-11-66)
11. Samurai West (07-12-66)
12. The Maze (14-12-67)
13. Portrait Of Louisa (21-12-67)
14. There's Someone Close Behind You (28-12-67)
15. Storm Warning (Part 1) (04-01-67)
16. The Island (Part 2) (11-01-67)
17. Time To Kill (18-01-67)
18. A Memory Of Evil (25-01-67)
19. You Can't Win Them All (01-02-67)
20. The High Terrace (08-02-67)
21. The Seven Eyes Of Night (15-02-67)
22. Night Of The Hunter (22-02-67)
23. The Edge Of Fear (01-03-67)
24. Long Ago & Far Away (08-03-67)
25. So Dark The Night (15-03-67)
26. The Long, Long Day (22-03-67)
27. Roundabout (29-03-67)
28. The Man Outside (05-04-67)
29. Countdown (12-04-67)
30. Farewell To Yesterday (19-04-67)

Callan

Series 1
1-01. The Good Ones Are Dead (08-07-67)
1-06. You Should Have Got Here Sooner (12-08-67)
Series 2
2-01. Red Knight, White Knight (08-01-69)
2-02. The Most Promising Girl Of Her Year (15-01-69)
2-04. The Little Bits & Pieces Of Love (29-01-69)
2-05. Let's Kill Everybody (05-02-69)
2-06. Heir Apparent (12-02-69)
2-09. Death Of a Friend (05-03-69)
2-13. The Worst Soldier I Ever Saw (02-04-69)
2-14. Nice People Die At Home (09-04-69)

The Champions

01. The Beginning (25-09-68)
02. The Invisible Man (02-10-68)
03. Reply Box 666 (09-10-68)
04. The Experiment (16-10-68)
05. Happening (23-10-68)
06. Operation Deep Freeze (30-10-68)
07. The Survivors (06-11-68)
08. To Trap a Rat (13-11-68)
09. The Iron Man (20-11-68)
10. The Ghost Plane (27-11-68)
11. The Dark Island (04-12-68)
12. The Fanatics (11-12-68)
13. Twelve Hours (18-12-68)
14. The Search (01-01-68)
15. The Gilded Cage (08-01-68)
16. Shadow Of The Panther (15-01-68)
17. A Case Of Lemmings (22-01-68)
18. The Interrogation (29-01-69)
19. The Mission (05-02-69)
20. The Silent Enemy (12-02-69)
21. The Body Snatchers (19-02-69)
22. Get Me Out Of Here (26-02-69)
23. The Night People (05-03-69)
24. Project Zero (12-03-69)
25. Desert Journey (19-03-69)
26. Full Circle (26-03-69)
27. Nutcracker (02-04-69)
28. The Final Countdown (16-04-69)
29. The Gun Runners (23-04-69)
30. Autokill (30-04-69)

City Beneath The Sea

01. The Pirates (1711-62)
02. Escape To Algeria (24-11-62)
03. Tide Of Evil (01-12-62)
04. Cellar Of Fear (08-12-62)
05. Power To Destroy (22-12-62)

06. Operation Grand Design (22-12-62)
07. Three Hours To Doomsday (29-12-62)

The Corridor People

01. Victim As Birdwatcher (26-08-66)
02. Victim As Whitebait (02-09-66)
03. Victim As Red (09-09-66)
04. Victim As Black (16-09-66)

Danger Man

Series 1
1-01. View From The Villa (11-09-60)
1-02. Time to Kill (18-11-60)
1-03. Josetta (25-09-60)
1-04. The Blue Veil (02-10-60)
1-05. The Lovers (09-10-60)
1-06. The Girl In Pink Pyjamas (16-10-60)
1-07. Position Of Trust (23-10-60)
1-08. The Lonely Chair (30-10-60)
1-09. The Sanctuary (06-11-60)
1-10. An Affair Of State (13-11-60)
1-11. The Key (20-11-60)
1-12. The Sisters (27-11-60)
1-13. The Prisoner (04-12-60)
1-14. The Traitor (11-12-60)
1-15. Colonel Rodriguez (18-12-60)
1-16. The Island (01-01-61)
1-17. Find & Return (08-01-61)
1-18. The Girl Who Likes G.I.'s (15-01-61)
1-19. Name, Date & Place (22-01-61)
1-20. The Vacation (29-01-61)
1-21. The Conspirators (05-02-61)
1-22. The Honeymooners (02-04-61)
1-23. The Gallows Tree (09-04-61)
1-24. The Relaxed Informer (16-04-61)
1-25. The Brothers (23-04-61)
1-26. The Journey Ends Halfway (30-04-61)
1-27. Bury The Dead (07-05-61)
1-28. Sabotage (14-05-61)
1-29. The Contessa (21-05-61)
1-30. The Leak (28-05-61)
1-31. The Trap (04-06-61)
1-32. The Actor (11-06-61)
1-33. Hired Assassin (18-06-61)
1-34. The Deputy Coyannis Story (16-12-61)
1-35. Find & Destroy (23-12-61)
1-36. Under the Lake (30-12-61)
1-37. The Nurse (06-01-61)
1-38. Dead Man Walks (13-01-62)
1-39. Deadline (20-01-62)

Danger Man Series 2
2-01. Yesterday's Enemies (13-10-64)
2-02. The Professionals (20-10-64)

2-03. Colony Three (27-10-64)
2-04. The Galloping Major (03-11-64)
2-05. Fair Exchange (10-11-64)
2-06. Fish On The Hook (17-11-64)
2-07. The Colonels Daughter (24-11-64)
2-08. The Battle Of The Cameras (01-12-64)
2-09. No Marks For Servility (08-12-64)
2-10. A Man To Be Trusted (15-12-64)
2-11. Don't Nail Him Yet (22-12-64)
2-12. A Date With Doris (29-12-64)
2-13. That's Two Of Us Sorry (05-01-64)
2-14. Such Men Are Dangerous (12-01-65)
2-15. Whatever Happened To George Foster (19-01-65)
2-16. A Room in The Basement (02-02-65)
2-17. The Affair At Castelevara (09-02-65)
2-18. The Ubiquitous Mr Lovegrove (16-02-65)
2-19. It's Up To The Lady (23-02-65)
2-20. Have a Glass of Wine (02-03-65)
2-21. The Mirror's New (09-03-65)
2-22. Parallel Lines Sometimes Meet (16-03-65)

Danger Man Series 3
3-01. The Black Book (30-09-65)
3-02. A Very Dangerous Game (07-10-65)
3-03. Sting In The Tail (14-10-65)
3-04. You're Not In Any Trouble Are You (21-10-65)
3-05. Loyalty Always Pays (28-10-65)
3-06. The Mercenaries (04-11-65)
3-07. Judgement Day (11-11-65)
3-08. The Outcast (18-11-65)
3-09. English Lady Take Lodgers (25-11-65)
3-10. Are You Going To Be More Permanent? (02-12-65)
3-11. To Our Best Friend (09-12-65)
3-12. The Man On The Beach (16-12-65)
3-13. Say It With Flowers (23-12-65)
3-14. The Man Who Wouldn't Talk (30-12-65)
3-15. Somebody Is Liable To Get Hurt (06-01-66)
3-16. Dangerous Secret (13-01-66)
3-17. I Can Only Offer You Sherry (20-01-66)
3-18. The Hunting Party (27-01-66)
3-19. Two Birds With One Bullet (10-03-66)
3-20. I Am Afraid You Have The Wrong Number (17-03-66)
3-21. The Man With The Foot (24-03-66)
3-22. The Paper Chase (31-03-66)
3-23. Not So Jolly Roger (07-04-66)
3-24. Koroshi (12-02-67)
3-25. Shinda Shima (26-02-67)

Department S

01. Six Days (09-03-69)
02. The Trojan Tanker (16-03-69)
03. Cellar Full Of Silence (23-03-69)
04. The Pied Piper Of Hambledown (30-03-69)
05. One Of Aircraft Is Empty (06-4-69)
06. The Man In The Elegant Room (13-04-69)
07. Handicap Dead (20-04-69)
08. A Ticket To Nowhere (27-04-69)
09. Black Out (17-09-69)
10. Double Death Of Charlie Crippen (14-09-69)
11. Who Plays The Dummy (01-10-69)
12. The Treasure Of the Costa Del Sol (08-10-69)
13. The Man Who Got a New Face (15-10-69)
14. Les Fleurs Du Mal (22-10-69)
15. The Shift That Never Was (25-10-69)
16. The Man From X (05-11-69)
17. Dead Men Die Twice (12-11-69)
18. The Perfect Operation (26-12-69)
19. The Duplicated Man (03-12-69)
20. The Mysterious Man In The Flying Machine (10-12-69)
21. Death On Reflection (17-12-69)
22. Last Train to Redbridge (14-01-70)
23. A Small War Of Nerves (21-01-70)
24. The Bones Of Byrom Blain (28-01-70)
25. Spencer Bodily Is 60 Years Old (11-02-70)
26. The Ghost Of Mary Burnham (18-02-70)
27. A Fish Out Of Water (25-02-70)
28. The Soup Of The Day (04-03-70)

Doctor Who

01. An Unearthly Child: 4 Episodes (23-11-63)
02. The Daleks: 6 Episodes (21-12-63)
03. The Edge Of Destruction: 2 Episodes (04-02-64)
05. The Keys Of Marinus: 6 Episodes (11-04-64)
06. The Aztecs: 4 Episodes (23-05-64)
07. The Sensorites: 6 Episodes (20-06-64)
08. The Reign Of Terror: 4 Episodes (08-08-64)
09. Planet Of Giants: 3 Episodes (31-10-64)
10. Dalek Invasion Of Earth (1964)
11. The Rescue: 2 Episodes (02-01-65)
12. The Romans: 4 Episodes (16-01-65)
13. The Web Planet: 6 Episodes (13-02-65)
14. The Crusade: 2 Episodes (27-03-65)
15. The Space Museum: 4 Episodes (24-04-65)
16. The Chase: 6 Episodes (22-05-65)
17. The Time Meddler: 4 Episodes (03-07-65)
18. Galaxy 4: Air Lock (25-09-65)
19. Mission To The Unknown (09-10-65)
21. The Daleks' Master Plan: 3 Episodes (20-11-65)
23. The Ark: 4 Episodes (05-03-66)
24. The Celestial Toymaker: The Final Test (23-04-66)
25. The Gunfighters: 4 Episodes (30-04-66)
27. The War Machines: 4 Episodes (25-06-66)

29. The Tenth Planet: 3 Episodes (08-10-66)
32. The Underwater Menace: 2 Episodes (21-01-67)
33. The Moonbase: 2 Episodes (18-02-67)
35. The Faceless Ones: Episode 1 (08-04-67)
36. The Evil Of The Daleks: Episode 2 (27-05-67)
37. The Tomb Of The Cybermen: 4 Episodes (02-09-67)
38. The Abominable Snowman: Episode 2 (07-10-67)
39. The Ice Warriors: 4 Episodes (11-11-67)
40. The Enemy Of The World: 6 Episodes (23-12-67)
41. The Web Of Fear: 5 Episodes (03-02-68)
43. The Wheel in Space: 2 Episodes (11-05-68)
44. The Dominators: 5 Episodes (10-08-68)
45. The Mind Robber: 5 Episodes (14-09-68)
46. The Invasion: 6 Episodes (09-11-68)
47. The Krotons: 4 Episodes (28-12-68)
48. The Seeds Of Death: 6 Episodes (25-01-69)
49. The Space Pirates: Episode 2 (15-03-69)
50. The War Games: 10 Episodes (19-04-69)

Ghost Squad

Series 1
1-01. Hong Kong Story (23-09-61)
1-02. Bullet With My Name On It (16-09-61)
1-03. Ticket For Blackmail (09-09-61)
1-04. Broken Doll (07-10-61)
1-05. High Wire (30-09-61)
1-06. Eyes Of The Bat (14-10-61)
1-07. Still Waters (21-10-61)
1-08. Assassin (28-10-61)
1-09. Million Dollar Ransom (11-11-61)
1-10. Catspaw (05-01-61)
1-11 The Green Shoes (29-12-61)
1-12. Princess (12-01-61)
1-13. Death From a Distance (04-11-61)

Ghost Squad Series 2
2-01. Interrupted Requiem (02-02-63)
2-02. East Of Mandalay (09-02-63)
2-03. Sentences Of Death (04-05-63)
2-04. The Golden Silence (08-06-63)
2-05. The Retirement Of The Gentle Dove (30-03-63)
2-06. The Missing People (29-06-63)
2-07. Lost in Transit (15-06-63)
2-08. The Man With The Delicate Hands (22-06-63)
2-09. Hot Money (25-05-63)
2-10. The Grand Duchess (11-05-63)
2-11. A First Class Way To Die (13-07-63)
2-12. Quarantine At Kavar (01-06-63)
2-13. The Desperate Diplomat (18-05-63)
2-14. The Big Time (12-01-63)
2-15. The Last Jump (23-02-63)
2-16. Escape Route (16-02-63)
2-17. Mr Five Per Cent (06-04-63)
2-18. The Heir Apparent (09-03-63)
2-19. Death of a Sportsman (26-01-63)
2-20. P.G..7. (06-07-63)

2-21. Polsky (02-03-63)
2-22. The Magic Bullet (16-03-63)
2-23. The Menacing Mazurka (23-03-63)
2-24. Gertrude (13-04-63)
2-25. The Thirteenth Girl (27-04-63)
2-26. Sabotage (20-04-63)

Interpol Calling

01. The Angola Brights (14-09-59)
02. The Thirteen Innocents (21-09-59)
03. The Money Game (28-09-59)
04. The Sleeping Giant (05-10-59)
05. The Two Headed Monster (12-10-59)
06. The Long Weekend (19-10-59)
07. You Can't Die Twice (26-10-59)
08. Diamond S.O.S. (02-11-59)
09. Private View (09-11-59)
10. Dead On Arrival (16-11-59)
11. Air Switch (23-11-59)
12. The Chinese Mask (07-12-59)
13. Slave Ship (14-12-59)
14. The Man's a Clown (21-12-59)
15. Last Man Lucky (28-12-59)
16. No Flowers For Onno (04-01-59)
17. Mr George (11-01-60)
18. The Thousand Mile Alibi (18-01-60)
19. Act Of Piracy (25-01-60)
20. Game For Three Hands (01-02-60)
21. The Collector (08-02-60)
22. The Heiress (15-02-60)
23. Payment in Advance (22-02-60)
24. Finger Of Guilt (07-03-60)
25. The Girl With The Grey Hair (14-03-60)
26. Trail At Cranby's Creek (21-03-60)
27. Ascent To Murder (28-03-60)
28. Slow Boat To Amsterdam (04-04-60)
29. White Blackmail (11-04-60)
30. A Foreign Body (18-04-60)
31. In The Swim (25-04-60)
32. The Three Keys (02-05-60)
33. Eight Days Inclusive (09-05-60)
34. Dressed To Kill (06-05-60)
35. Cargo Of Death (23-05-60)
36. Desert Hijack (30-05-60)
37. Pipeline (06-06-60)
38. The Absent Assassin (13-06-60)
39. Checkmate (20-06-60)

Man In a Suitcase

01. Brainwash (27-09-67)
02. The Sitting Pigeon (04-10-67)
03. Day Of Execution (11-10-67)
04. Variation On a Million Bucks Part 1 (18-10-67)
05. Variation On a Million Bucks Part 2 (25-10-67)
06. Man From The Dead (01-11-67)
07. Sweet Sue (08-11-67)
08. Essay In Evil (15-11-67)
09. The Girl Who Never Was (22-11-67)
10. All That Glitters (29-11-67)
11. Dead Man's Shoes (06-12-67)
12. Find The Lady (13-12-67)
13. The Bridge (20-12-67)
14. The Man Who Stood Still (27-12-67)
15. Burden Of Proof (03-01-67)
16. The Whisper (10-01-67)
17. Why They Killed Nolan (17-01-67)
18. The Boston Square (24-01-67)
19. Somebody Loses, Somebody… Wins? (31-01-67)
20. Blind Spot (07-02-67)
21. No Friend Of Mine (14-02-67)
22. Jigsaw Man (21-02-67)
23. Web With Four Spiders (28-02-67)
24. Which Way Did He Go, McGill (06-03-67)
25. Property Of A Gentleman (13-03-67)
26. The Revolutionaries (20-03-67)
27. Who's Mad Now (27-03-67)
28. Three Blinks Of The Eyes (03-04-67)
29. Castle In The Clouds (10-04-67)
30. Night Flight To Andorra (17-04-67)

Man Of The World

Series 1
1-01. Death Of a Conference (29-09-62)
1-02. Masquerade In Spain (06-10-62)
1-03. Blaze Of Glory (13-10-62)
1-04. The Runaways (20-10-62)
1-05. The Frontier (27-10-62)
1-06. The Sentimental Agent (03-11-62)
1-07. The Highland Story (10-11-62)
1-08. The Nature Of Justice (17-11-62)
1-09. The Mindreader (24-11-62)
1-10. Portrait Of a Girl (01-12-62)
1-11. Specialist For the Kill (08-12-62)
1-12. A Family Affair (15-12-62)
1-13. Shadow Of the Wall (22-12-62)

Man Of The World Series 2
2-01. The Bandit (11-05-63)
2-02. The Enemy (18-05-63)
2-03. Double Exposure (25-05-63)
2-04. Jungle Mission (01-06-63)
2-05. In The Picture (08-06-63)

2-06. The Bullfighter (15-06-63)
2-07. The Prince (22-06-63)

Out Of The Unknown

1-01. No Place Like Earth (04-10-65)
1-02. The Counterfeit Man (11-10-65)
1-03. Stranger In the Family (18-10-65)
1-04. The Dead Past (25-10-65)
1-05. Time In Advance (01-11-65)
1-06. Come Buttercup, Come Daisy, Come…? (08-11-65)
1-07. Sucker Bait (15-11-65)
1-10. Some Lapse In Time (06-12-65)
1-11. Thirteen To Centauraus (13-12-65)
1-12. The Midas Plague (20-12-65)
2-01. The Machine Stops (06-10-66)
2-03. Lambda One (20-10-66)
2-04. Level Seven (27-10-66)
2-08. Tunnel Under The World (01-12-66)
3-03. The Last Lonely Man (21-01-69)
3-08. Little Black Bag (25-02-69)

Out Of This World

02. Little Lost Robot (07-07-1962)

Pathfinders In Space

01. Convoy To The Moon (11-09-60)
02. Spaceship From Nowhere (18-09-60)
03. Luna Bridgehead (25-09-60)
04. The Man In The Moon (02-10-60)
05. The World Of Lost Toys (09-10-60)
06. Disaster On The Moon (16-10-60)
07. Rescue In Space (23-10-60)

Pathfinders To Mars

01. The Impostor (11-12-60)
02. Sabotage In Space (17-12-60)
03. The Hostage (25-12-60)
04. Lichens! (01-01-61)
05. Zero Hour On The Red Planet (08-01-61)
06. Falling Into The Sun (15-01-61)

Pathfinders To Venus

01. S.O.S. From Venus (05-3-61)
02. Into the Poison Cloud (12-03-61)
03. The Living Planet (19-03-61)
04. The Creature (26-03-61)
05. The Venus People (02-04-61)
06. The City (09-04-61)
07. The Valley Of Monsters (16-04-61)
08. Planet On Fire (23-04-61)

The Prisoner

01. Arrival (29-09-6
02. The Chimes Of Big Ben (06-10-67)
03. A.B. & C. (13-10-67)
04. Free For All (20-10-67)
05. The Schizoid Man (27-10-67)
06. The General (03-11-67)
07. Many Happy Returns (10-11-67)
08. Dance Of The Dead (17-11-67)
09. Checkmate (14-11-67)
10. Hammer Into Anvil (01-12-67)
11. It's Your Funeral (08-12-67)
12. A Change Of Mind (15-12-67)
13. Do Not Forsake Me Oh My Darling (22-12-67)
14. Living In Harmony (29-12-67)
15. The Girl Who Was Death (18-01-67)
16. Once Upon a Time (25-01-67)
17. Fall Out (01-02-68)

The Protectors

01. Landscape With Bandits (28-03-64)
02. The Bottle Shop (04-04-64)
03. Happy Is The Loser (11-04-64)
04. No Forwarding Address (18-04-64)
05. The Loop Men (25-04-64)
06. The Stamp Collection (02-05-64)
07. It Could Happen Here (09-05-64)
08. Freedom! (16-05-64)
09. The Pirate (23-05-64)
10. The Deadly Chameleon (30-5-64)
11. Who Killed Lazoryck? (06-06-64)
12. Channel Crossing (13-06-64)
13. Cargo From Corinth (20-06-64)
14. The Reluctant Thief (27-06-64)

Public Eye

1-02. Nobody Kills Santa Claus (30-01-65)
1-12. The Morning Wasn't So Hot (10-04-65)
2-02. Don't Forget You're Mine (09-07-66)
2-07. Works With Chess, Not With Life (13-08-66)
3-09. The Bromsgrove Venus (16-03-68)
4-01. Welcome To Brighton? (30-07-69)
4-02. Divide & Conquer (06-08-69)
4-03. Paid In Full (13-08-69)
4-04. My Life's My Own (20-08-69)
4-05. Case For The Defence (27-08-69)
4-06. The Comedian's Graveyard (03-09-69)
4-07. A Fixed Address (19-06-69)

Randall & Hopkirk (Deceased)

01. My Late Lamented Friend & Partner (21-09-69)
02. A Disturbing Case (28-09-69)
03. All Work & No Pay (05-10-69)
04. Never Trust a Ghost (12-10-69)
05. That's How Murder Snowballs (19-10-69)
06. Just For The Record (26-10-69)
07. Murder Ain't What It Used To Be (02-11-69)
08. Whoever Heard Of a Ghost Dying (09-11-69)
09. The House On Haunted Hill (16-11-69)
10. When Did You Start To Stop Seeing Things? (23-11-69)
11. The Ghost Who Saved The Bank At Monte Carlo (30-11-69)
12. For The Girl Who Has Everything (07-12-69)
13. But What a Sweet Little Room (14-12-69)
14. Who Killed Cock Robin? (21-12-69)
15. The Man From Nowhere (28-12-69)
16. When The Spirit Moves You (02-01-70)
17. Somebody Just Walked Over My Grave (09-01-70)
18. Could You Recognize The Man Again (16-01-70)
19. A Sentimental Journey (23-01-70)
20. Money To Burn (30-01-70)
21. The Ghost Talks (06-02-70)

22. It's Supposed To Be Thicker Than Water (13-02-70)
23. The Trouble With Women (20-02-70)
24. Vendetta For a Dead Man (27-02-70)
25. You Can Always Find a Fall Guy (06-03-70)
26. The Smile Behind The Veil (13-03-70)

The Saint

Series 1
1-01. The Talented Husband (4-10-62)
1-02. The Latin Touch (11-10-62)
1-03. The Careful Terrorist (18-10-62)
1-04. The Covetous Headsman (25-10-62)
1-05. The Loaded Tourist (01-11-62)
1-06. The Pearls Of Peace (08-11-62)
1-07. The Arrow Of God (15-11-62)
1-08. The Element Of Doubt (22-11-62)
1-09. The Effete Angler (29-11-62)
1-10. The Golden Journey (06-12-62)
1-11. The Man Who Was Lucky (13-12-62)
1-12. The Charitable Countess (20-12-62)

The Saint Series 2
2-01. The Fellow Traveller (19-09-63)
2-02. Starring The Saint (26-09-63)
2-03. Judith (03-10-63)
2-04. Teresa (10-10-63)
2-05. The Elusive Elishaw (17-10-63)
2-06. Marcia (24-10-63)
2-07. The Work Of Art (31-10-63)
2-08. Iris (07-11-63)
2-09. The King Of The Beggars (14-11-63)
2-10. The Rough Diamonds (21-11-63)
2-11. The Saint Plays With Fire (28-11-63)
2-12. The Well Meaning Mayor (05-12-63)
2-13. The Sporting Chance (12-12-63)
2-14. The Bunco Artists (19-12-63)
2-15. The Benevolent Burglary (26-12-63)
2-16. The Wonderful War (02-01-64)
2-17. The Noble Sportsman (09-01-64)
2-18. The Romantic Matron (16-01-64)
2-19. Luella (23-01-64)
2-20. The Lawless Lady (30-01-64)
2-21. The Good Medicine (06-02-64)
2-22. The Invisible Millionaire (13-02-64)
2-23. The High Fence (20-02-64)
2-24. Sophia (24-02-64)
2-25. The Gentle Ladies (05-03-64)
2-26. The Ever Loving Spouse (12-03-64)
2-27. The Saint Sees It Through (19-03-64)

The Saint Series 3
3-01. The Miracle Tea Party (8-10-64)
3-02. Lida (15-10-64)
3-03. Jeannine (22-10-64)
3-04. The Scorpion (29-10-64)
3-05. The Revolution Racket (05-11-64)

3-06. The Saint Steps In (12-11-64)
3-07. The Loving Brothers (19-11-64)
3-08. The Man Who Liked Toys (26-11-64)
3-09. The Death Penalty (03-12-64)
3-10. The Imprudent Politician (10-12-64)
3-11. The Hijackers (17-12-64)
3-12. The Unkind Philanthropist (24-12-64)
3-13. The Damsel In Distress (31-12-64)
3-14. The Contact (07-01-65)
3-15. The Set-Up (14-01-65)
3-16. The Rhine Maiden (21-01-65)
3-17. The Inescapable World (28-01-65)
3-18. The Sign Of The Claw (04-02-65)
3-19. The Golden Frog (11-02-65)
3-20. The Frightened Inn-Keeper (18-02-65)
3-21. Sibao (25-02-65)
3-22. The Crime Of The Century (04-03-65)
3-23. The Happy Suicide (11-03-65)

The Saint Series 4
4-01. The Chequered Flag (01-07-65)
4-02. The Abductors (08-07-65)
4-03. The Crooked Ring (15-07-65)
4-04. The Smart Detective (22-07-65)
4-05. The Persistent Parasites (29-07-65)
4-06. The Man Who Could No Die (05-08-65)
4-07. The Saint Bids Diamonds (12-08-65)
4-08. The Spanish Cow (19-08-65)
4-09. The Old Treasure Story (26-08-65)

The Saint Series 5
5-01. The Queens Ransom (30-09-66)
5-02. Interlude In Venice (07-10-66)
5-03. The Russian Prisoner (14-10-66)
5-04. The Reluctant Revolution (21-10-66)
5-05. The Helpful Pirate (28-10-66)
5-06. The Convenient Monster (04-11-66)
5-07. The Angel's Eye (11-11-66)
5-08. The Man Who Liked Lions (18-11-66)
5-09. The Better Mouse Trap (25-11-66)
5-10. Little Girl Lost (02-12-66)
5-11. Paper Chase (09-12-66)
5-12. Locate & Destroy (16-12-66)
5-13. Flight Plan (23-12-66)
5-14. Escape Route (30-12-66)
5-15. The Persistent Patriots (06-01-67)
5-16. The Fast Women (13-01-67)
5-17. The Death Game (20-01-67)
5-18. The Art Collectors (27-01-67)
5-19. To Kill a Saint (24-02-67)
5-20. The Counterfeit Countess (03-03-67)
5-21. Simon & Delilah (24-03-67)
5-22. Island Of Chance (07-04-67)
5-23. The Gadget Lovers (21-04-67)
5-24. A Double In Diamonds (05-05-67)
5-25. The Power Artists (19-05-67)
5-26. When Spring Is Sprung (02-06-67)
5-27. The Gadic Collection (22-06-67)

The Saint Series 6
6-01. The Best Laid Schemes (29-09-68)
6-02. Invitation To Danger (06-10-68)
6-03. Legacy For The Saint (13-10-68)
6-04. The Desperate Diplomat (20-10-68)
6-05. The Organization Man (27-10-67)
6-06. The Double Take (03-11-68)
6-07. The Time To Die (10-11-68)
6-08. The Master Plan (17-11-68)
6-09. The House On Dragons Rock (24-11-68)
6-10. The Scales Of Justice (01-12-68)
6-11. The Fiction Makers Part 1 (08-12-68)
6-12. The Fiction Makers Part 2 (15-12-68)
6-13. The People Importers (22-12-68)
6-14. Where The Money Is (29-12-68)
6-15. Vendetta For The Saint Part 1 (05-01-68)
6-16. Vendetta For The Saint Part 2 (12-01-68)
6-17. The Ex-King Of Diamonds (19-01-68)
6-18. The Man Who Gambled With Life (26-01-68)
6-19. Portrait Of Brenda (02-02-69)
6-20. The World Beater (09-02-69)

Strange Report

01. REPORT 5055 CULT Murder Shrieks Out (21-09-69)
02. REPORT 0649 SKELETON Let Sleeping Heroes Lie (28-09-69)
03. REPORT 2641 HOSTAGE If You Won't Learn Die (05-10-69)
04. REPORT 2641 LONELY HEARTS Who Killed Dan Cupid? (12-10-69)
05. REPORT 8319 GRENADE What Price Change? (19-10-69)
06. REPORT 3906 COVER-GIRLS Last Years Model (26-10-69)
07. REPORT 3424 EPIDEMIC A Most Curious Crime (02-11-69)
08. REPORT 2475 REVENGE When a Man Hates (09-11-69)
09. REPORT 1021 SHRAPNEL The Wish In the Dream (23-11-69)
10. REPORT 8944 HAND A Matter Of Witchcraft (30-11-69)
11. REPORT 1553 RACIST A Most Dangerous Proposal (07-12-69)
12. REPORT 7931 SNIPER When Is Your Cousin Not? (14-12-69)
13. REPORT 4821 X-RAY Who Weeps For The Doctor (21-12-69)
14. REPORT 2493 KIDNAP Whose Pretty Girl Are You? (28-12-69)
15. REPORT 4407 HEART No Choice For The Donor (04-01-70)
16. REPORT 4977 SWINDLE Square Root Of Evil (11-01-70)

The Third Man

2-02. One Kind Word (07-09-59)
2-06. Barcelona Passage (01-10-59)
2-10. Toys Of The Dead (03-11-59)
4-07. Diamond In the Rough (11-05-62)
5-01. A Question In Ice (27-06-64)

Undermind

01. Instance One (08-05-65)
02. Flowers Of Havoc (15-05-65)
03. The New Dimension (22-05-65)
04. Death In England (29-05-65)
05. Too Many Enemies (05-06-65)
06. Intent To Destroy (12-06-65)
07. Song Of Death (19-06-65)
08. Puppets Of Evil (26-06-65)
09. Test For The Future (03-07-65)
10. Waves Of Sound (10-07-65)
11. End Signal (17-07-65)

Episode Directors

Alan Bridges (director)
Out Of The Unknown 1-03. Stranger In the Family (18-10-65)
Alan Cooke (director)
Out Of The Unknown 2-08. Tunnel Under The World (01-12-66)
Alvin Rakoff (director)
The Saint 6-17. The Ex-King Of Diamonds (19-01-68)
Anthea Browne-Wilkinson (director)
Adam Adamant Lives 15. The Village Of Evil (06-10-66)
Anthony Bushell (director)
Danger Man 1-24. The Relaxed Informer (16-04-61) 1-30. The Leak (28-05-61)
Man Of The World 1-05. The Frontier (27-10-62) 1-09. The Mind-reader (24-11-62) 1-12. A Family Affair (15-12-62)
The Saint 1-09. The Effete Angler (29-11-62)
The Third Man 2-10. Toys Of The Dead (03-11-59)
Antony Keary (director)
Ghost Squad 2-06. The Missing People (29-06-63) 2-13. The Desperate Diplomat (18-05-63)
2-16. Escape Route (16-02-63) 2-24. Gertrude (13-04-63)
Anthony Terploff (director)
The Avengers 2-22. Man In The Mirror (23-02-63)
Barry Letts (director)
Doctor Who 40. The Enemy Of The World: 6 Episodes (23-12-67)
Basil Coleman (director)
Public Eye 2-07. Works With Chess, Not With Life (13-08-66)
Bill Bain (director)
The Avengers 3-02. The Undertakers (05-10-63) 3-06. November Five (02-11-63) 3-07. The Gilded Cage (09-11-63) 3-14. Dressed To Kill (28-12-63) 3-18. Mandrake (25-01-64) 3-23. The Charmers (29-02-64)
The Protectors 02. The Bottle Shop (04-04-64) 07. It Could Happen Here (09-05-64)
Undermind 01. Instance One (08-05-65) 03. The New Dimension (22-05-65) 06. Intent To Destroy (12-06-65)
Bill Lethwaite (director)
Interpol Calling 28. Slow Boat To Amsterdam (04-04-60) 39. Checkmate (20-06-60)
Bill Sellars (director)
Doctor Who 24. The Celestial Toymaker: The Final Test (23-04-66)
Brandon Brady (director)
The Avengers 2-09, The Sell Out (24-11-62)
Brian Smedley-Aston (director)
Strange Report 09. REPORT 1021 SHRAPNEL The Wish In the Dream (23-11-69)
16. REPORT 4977 SWINDLE Square Root Of Evil (11-01-70)
Charles Crichton (director)
The Avengers 4-04. Death At Bargain Prices (23-10-65) 4-20. The Danger Makers (12-02-66) 5-09. The Correct Way To Kill (11-3-67) 6-07. False Witness (06-01-68) 6-14. The Interrogators (1-1-69)
Danger Man 2-01. Yesterday's Enemies (13-10-64)
Man In a Suitcase 01. Brainwash (27-09-67) 03. Day Of Execution (11-10-67) 16. The Whisper (10-01-67) 17. Why They Killed Nolan (17-01-67) 21. No Friend Of Mine (14-02-67) 22. Jigsaw Man (21-02-67) 28. Three Blinks Of The Eyes (03-04-67)
Strange Report 01. REPORT 5055 CULT Murder Shrieks Out (21-09-69) 03. REPORT 2641 HOSTAGE If You Won't Learn Die (05-10-69) 05. REPORT 8319 GRENADE What Price Change? (19-10-69) 08. REPORT 2475 REVENGE When a Man Hates (09-11-69) 13. REPORT 4821 X-RAY Who Weeps For The Doctor (21-12-69)
Charles Friend (director)
Danger Man 1-04. The Blue Veil (02-10-60) 1-08. The Lonely Chair (30-10-60) 1-09. The Sanctuary (06-11-60) 1-22. The Honeymooners (02-04-61) 1-25. The Brothers (23-04-61) 1-33. Hired Assassin

(18-06-61) 1-35. Find & Destroy (23-12-61) 1-38. Dead Man Walks (13-01-62)
Interpol Calling 06. The Long Weekend (19-10-59) 08. Diamond S.O.S. (02-11-59) 14. The Man's a Clown (21-12-59) 17. Mr George (11-01-60) 18. The Thousand Mile Alibi (18-01-60) 25. The Girl With The Grey Hair (14-03-60)

Christopher Barry (director)
Doctor Who 02. The Daleks: 4 Episodes (21-12-63) 11. The Rescue: 2 Episodes (02-01-65) 12. The Romans: 4 Episodes (16-01-65)

Christopher Morahan (director)
Ghost Squad 2-10. The Grand Duchess (11-05-63)

Cliff Owen (director)
The Avengers 6-17. Killer (22-01-69)
The Third Man 2-02. One Kind Word (07-09-59) 2-06. Barcelona Passage (01-10-59)

Clive Donner (director)
Danger Man 1-26. The Journey Ends Halfway (30-04-61) 1-27. Bury The Dead (07-05-61)

Cyril Frankel (director)
The Avengers 6-06. Whoever Shot George Oblique Stroke XR40? (30-10-68)
The Baron 03. Something For a Rainy Day (12-10-66) 06. Masquerade (Part 1) (02-11-66) 07. The Killing (Part 2) (09-11-66) 09. And Suddenly You're Dead (23-11-66)
The Champions 01. The Beginning (25-09-68) 02. The Invisible Man (02-10-68) 03. Reply Box 666 (09-10-68) 04. The Experiment (16-10-68) 05. Happening (23-10-68) 07. The Survivors (06-11-68) 11 The Dark Island (4-12-68) 18. The Interrogation (29-1-69) 22. Get Me Out Of Here (26-02-69)
Department S 01. Six Days (09-03-69) 06. The Man In The Elegant Room (13-04-69) 08. A Ticket To Nowhere (27-04-69) 13. The Man Who Got a New Face (15-10-69) 14. Les Fleurs Du Mal (22-10-69) 15. The Shift That Never Was (25-10-69) 18. The Perfect Operation (26-12-69) 20. The Mysterious Man In The Flying Machine (10-12-69) 26. The Ghost Of Mary Burnham (18-02-70) 27. A Fish Out Of Water (25-02-70)
Randall & Hopkirk (Deceased) 01. My Late Lamented Friend & Partner (21-09-69) 12. For The Girl Who Has Everything (07-12-69) 17. Somebody Just Walked Over My Grave (09-01-70) 21. The Ghost Talks (6-2-70) 23. The Trouble With Women (20-2-70) 24. Vendetta For a Dead Man (27-2-70) 25 You Can Always Find a Fall Guy (6-3-70) 26. The Smile Behind The Veil (13-3-70)

Daniel Petrie (director)
Strange Report 07. REPORT 3424 EPIDEMIC A Most Curious Crime (02-11-69) 14. REPORT 2493 KIDNAP Whose Pretty Girl Are You? (28-12-69)

David Boisseau (director)
The Corridor People 01. Victim As Birdwatcher (26-08-66) 02. Victim As Whitebait (02-09-66) 03. Victim As Red (09-09-66) 04. Victim As Black (16-09-66)

David Eady (director)
The Saint 3-11. The Hijackers (17-12-64)

David Greene (director)
Man Of The World 1-01. Death of a Conference (29-9-62) 1-02. Masquerade In Spain (6-10-62)
The Saint 1-06. The Pearls Of Peace (08-11-62)

David Sullivan Proudfoot (director)
Adam Adamant Lives 01. A Vintage Year For Scoundrels (20-06-66)

David Maloney (director)
Doctor Who 45. The Mind Robber: 5 Episodes (14-09-68) 47. The Krotons: 4 Episodes (28-12-68) 50. The War Games: 10 Episodes (19-04-69)

David Tomblin (director)
The Prisoner 14. Living In Harmony (29-12-67) 15. The Girl Who Was Death (18-01-67)

Dennis Vance (director)
Ghost Squad 2-02. East Of Mandalay (9-2-63) 2-05. The Retirement Of The Gentle Dove (30-03-63) 2-15. The Last Jump (23-2-63) 2-18. The Heir Apparent (9-3-63) 2-21. Polsky (02-03-63)

Derek Martinus (director)
Doctor Who 18. Galaxy 4: Air Lock (25-09-65) 19. Mission To The Unknown (09-10-65) 29. The Tenth Planet: 3 Episodes (08-10-66) 36. The Evil Of The Daleks: Episode 2 (27-05-67) 39. The Ice Warriors: 4 Episodes (11-11-67)

Don Chaffey (director)

The Avengers 6-09. Legacy Of Death (20-11-68) 6-20. Wish You Were Here (12-02-69)6-22. Stay Tuned (26-02-69) 6-25. Who Was That Man I Saw You With (19-03-69) 6-29. Requiem (16-04-69)
Danger Man 2-03. Colony Three (27-10-64) 2-08. The Battle Of The Cameras (01-12-64) 2-09. No Marks For Servility (08-12-64) 2-14. Such Men Are Dangerous (12-01-65) 2-15. Whatever Happened To George Foster (19-01-65) 2-16. A Room in The Basement (02-02-65) 2-22. Parallel Lines Sometimes Meet (16-03-65) 3-02. A Very Dangerous Game (7-10-65) 3-04. You're Not In Any Trouble Are You (21-10-65) 3-06. The Mercenaries (4-11-65) 3-07. Judgment Day (11-11-65) 3-10. Are You Going To Be More Permanent? (2-12-65) 3-23. Not So Jolly Roger (7-4-66)
Man In a Suitcase 18. The Boston Square (24-01-67)
The Prisoner 01. Arrival (29-09-67) 08. Dance Of The Dead (17-11-67) 09. Checkmate (14-11-67) 02. The Chimes Of Big Ben (06-10-67)

Don Leaver (director)

The Avengers 1-06, Girl On The Trapeze (11-02-61) 3-03. Man With Two Shadows (12-10-63) 3-17. The Wringer (18-01-64) 3-25. Espirit de Corps (14-3-64) 4-10. Dial a Deadly Number (04-12-65) 4-23. The House That Jack Built (05-03-66) 4-25. How To Succeed At Murder (19-03-66)
Public Eye 1-02. Nobody Kills Santa Claus (30-01-65)

Don Sharp (director)

The Avengers 6-16. Invasion Of The Earthman (15-01-69) 6-19. The Curious Case Of The Countless Clues (05-02-69) 6-32. Get-a-Way (14-05-69)
Ghost Squad 1-02. Bullet With My Name On It (16-09-61) 1-01. Hong Kong Story (23-09-61) 1-04. Broken Doll (07-10-61) 1-06. Eyes Of The Bat (14-10-61) 1-09. Million Dollar Ransom (11-11-61) 1-11 The Green Shoes (29-12-61)

Doreen Montgomery (director)

The Avengers 2-18. Warlock (26-01-63)

Douglas Camfield (director)

Doctor Who 09. Planet Of Giants: 1 Episode (31-10-6) 14. The Crusade: 2 Episodes (27-03-65) 17. The Time Meddler: 4 Episodes (03-07-65) 21. The Daleks' Master Plan: 3 Episodes (20-11-65) 41. The Web Of Fear: 5 Episodes (03-02-68) 46. The Invasion: 6 Episodes (09-11-68)
Out Of The Unknown 3-03. The Last Lonely Man (21-01-69)

Douglas James (director)

Out Of This World 02. Little Lost Robot (07-07-1962)

Edwin Rhodes (director)

The Avengers 2-17, Box Of Tricks (19-01-63)

Eric Hills (director)

Out Of The Unknown 3-08. Little Black Bag (incomplete) (25-02-69)

Eric Palce (director)

The Avengers 2-03, The Decapod (13-10-62) 2-04, Bullseye (20-10-62) 2-10, Death On The Rocks (01-12-62) 2-14, Dead On Course (29-12-62)

Ernest Morris (director)

The Saint 2-26. The Ever Loving Spouse (12-03-64)

Frank Cox (director)

Doctor Who 03. Edge Of Destruction: 1 Episode (04-02-64) 07. The Sensorites: 2 Episodes (20-06-64)

Freddie Francis (director)

The Champions 16. Shadow Of The Panther (15-01-68)
Man In a Suitcase 08. Essay In Evil (15-11-67) 24. Which Way Did He Go, McGill (06-03-67) 27. Who's Mad Now (27-03-67) 30. Night Flight To Andorra (17-04-67)
The Saint 5-27. The Gadic Collection (22-6-67) 6-18. The Man Who Gambled With Life (26-1-68)

Geoffrey Nethercott (director)

Ghost Squad 2-12. Quarantine At Kavar (01-06-63)

Geoffrey Orme (director)

The Avengers 2-22. Man In The Mirror (23-02-63)

George Pollock (director)

Danger Man 3-20. I Am Afraid You Have The Wrong Number (17-03-66) 3-17. I Can Only Offer You Sherry (20-01-66)
Interpol Calling 18. The Thousand Mile Alibi (18-01-60)

George Spenton-Foster (director)
Out Of The Unknown 1-02. The Counterfeit Man (11-10-65) 2-03. Lambda One (20-10-66)
Gerald Blake (director)
Doctor Who 38. The Abominable Snowman: Episode 2 (07-10-67)
Gerry Mill (director)
Doctor Who 35. The Faceless Ones: Episode 1 (08-04-67)
Gerry O'Hara (director)
The Avengers 4-09. The Hour That Never Was (27-11-65) 4-16. Small Game For Big Hunters (15-01-65)
Man In a Suitcase 02. The Sitting Pigeon (04-10-67)
Gil Taylor (director)
Department S 16. The Man From X (05-11-69)
Gordon Flemyng (director)
The Avengers 5-02. The Fear Merchants (21-01-67) 5-06. The Winged Avenger (18-02-67)
The Saint 5-09. The Better Mouse Trap (25-11-66)
Guy Verney (director)
The Avengers 1-20, Tunnel Of Fear (05-08-61)
City Beneath The Sea 01. The Pirates (1711-62)
Pathfinders In Space 01. Convoy To The Moon (11-09-60) 02. Spaceship From Nowhere (18-09-60) 03. Luna Bridgehead (25-09-60) 04. The Man In The Moon (02-10-60) 05. The World Of Lost Toys (09-10-60) 06. Disaster On The Moon (16-10-60) 07. Rescue In Space (23-10-60)
Pathfinders To Mars 01. The Impostor (11-12-60) 02. Sabotage In Space (17-12-60) 03. The Hostage (25-12-60) 04. Lichens! (01-01-61) 05. Zero Hour On The Red Planet (08-01-61) 06. Falling Into The Sun (15-01-61)
Pathfinders To Venus 01. S.O.S. From Venus (05-3-61) 02. Into the Poison Cloud (12-03-61) 03. The Living Planet (19-03-61) 04. The Creature (26-03-61) 05. The Venus People (02-04-61) 07. The Valley Of Monsters (16-04-61)
Public Eye 4-03. Paid In Full (13-08-69) 4-05. Case For The Defence (27-08-69)
Harry Booth (director)
Man Of The World 1-03. Blaze Of Glory (13-10-62) 1-08. The Nature Of Justice (17-11-62) 1-13. Shadow Of the Wall (22-12-62) 2-04. Jungle Mission (01-06-63) 2-06. The Bullfighter (15-06-63)
Henric Hirsch (director)
Doctor Who 08. The Reign Of Terror: 4 Episodes (08-08-64)
Herbert Wise (director)
Man In a Suitcase 10. All That Glitters (29-11-67)
Hugh Rennie (director)
Ghost Squad 2-23. The Menacing Mazurka (23-03-63)
James Ferman (director)
Ghost Squad 2-19. Death of a Sportsman (26-01-63) 2-22. The Magic Bullet (16-03-63)
James Hill (director)
The Avengers 4-05. Castle De'ath (30-10-65) 4-19. Quick-Quick Slow Death (05-02-66) 4-21. A Touch Of Brimstone (19-02-66) 4-26. Honey For The Prince (26-03-66) 6-01. The Forget Me Knot (25-09-68) 6-11. Look (Stop Me If You've Heard This One) But There Were These Two Fellers (04-12-68)
The Saint 2-02. Starring The Saint (26-09-63) 2-23. The High Fence (20-02-64) 3-16. The Rhine Maiden (21-01-65)
James Mitchell (director)
The Avengers 2-16, Immortal Clay (12-01-63) 2-20. School For Traitors (09-02-63)
Jeremy Scott (director)
The Avengers 2-06, The Removal Men (03-11-62) 2-08, Death Of Great Dane (17-11-62)
Jeremy Summers (director)
The Baron 05 Enemy Of The State (26-10-66) 12 The Maze (14-12-67) 17 Time To Kill (18-1-67)
Danger Man 3-21. The Man With The Foot (24-03-66)
Interpol Calling 36. Desert Hijack (30-05-60)
Man In a Suitcase 20. Blind Spot (07-02-67)
Man Of The World 1-11. Specialist For the Kill (08-12-62) 2-03. Double Exposure (25-05-63)
Randall & Hopkirk (Deceased) 03. All Work & No Pay (05-10-69) 06. Just For The Record (26-10-69)

07. Murder Ain't What It Used To Be (02-11-69) 10. When Did You Start To Stop Seeing Things? (23-11-69) 11. The Ghost Who Saved The Bank At Monte Carlo (30-11-69) 18. Could You Recognise The Man Again (16-01-70) 26. The Smile Behind The Veil (13-03-70)

The Saint 1-05. The Loaded Tourist (01-11-62) 1-12. The Charitable Countess (20-12-62) 2-22. The Invisible Millionaire (13-2-64) 2-25. The Gentle Ladies (5-3-64) 2-12. The Well Meaning Mayor (5-12-63) 2-13. The Sporting Chance (12-12-63) 2-15. The Benevolent Burglary (26-12-63) 2-20. The Lawless Lady (30-1-64) 3-09. The Death Penalty (3-12-64) 3-12. The Unkind Philanthropist (24-12-64) 4-02. The Abductors (8-7-65) 5-08. The Man Who Liked Lions (18-11-66)

Jim Goddard (director)

Public Eye 3-09. The Bromsgrove Venus (16-03-68) 4-02. Divide & Conquer (06-08-69)

Jim O'Connolly (director)

The Saint 5-23. The Gadget Lovers (21-04-67) 5-26. When Spring Is Sprung (02-06-67) 6-15. Vendetta For The Saint Part 1 (05-01-68) 6-16. Vendetta For The Saint Part 2 (12-01-68)

John Ainsworth (director)

The Saint 1-03. The Careful Terrorist (18-10-62) 1-08. The Element Of Doubt (22-11-62)

John Crockett (director)

Doctor Who 06. The Aztecs: 4 Episodes (23-05-64)

John Elliot (director)

The Andromeda Breakthrough 2-1. Cold Front (28-06-62) 2-3. Arazan Forecast (12-07-62) 2-5. Hurricane (26-07-62)

John Gilbert (director)

The Avengers 2-11, Traitor In Zebra (08-12-62)

John Gilling (director)

The Champions 10. The Ghost Plane (27-11-68) 12. The Fanatics (11-12-68) 26. Full Circle (26-03-69) 28. The Final Countdown (16-04-69) 29. The Gun Runners (23-04-69)

Department S 03. Cellar Full Of Silence (23-03-69) 07. Handicap Dead (20-04-69) 10. Double Death Of Charlie Crippen (14-09-69) 11. Who Plays The Dummy (01-10-69) 12. The Treasure Of the Costa Del Sol (08-10-69) 15. The Shift That Never Was (25-10-69) 22. Last Train to Redbridge (14-01-70)

The Saint 1-02. The Latin Touch (11-10-62) 1-11. The Man Who Was Lucky (13-12-62) 2-08. Iris (07-11-63) 2-09. The King Of The Beggars (14-11-63) 4-08. The Spanish Cow (19-08-65) 5-24. A Double In Diamonds (05-05-67) 6-19. Portrait Of Brenda (02-02-69) 3-22. The Crime Of The Century (04-03-65)

John Glen (director)

Man In a Suitcase 19. Somebody Loses, Somebody… Wins? (31-01-67)

John Gorrie (director)

Doctor Who 05. The Keys Of Marinus: 6 Episodes (11-04-64)

Out Of The Unknown 1-04. The Dead Past (25-10-65)

John Hough (director)

The Avengers 6-03. Super Secret Cypher Snatch (09-10-68) 6-18. The Morning After (29-10-69) 6-24. Fog (12-03-69) 6-26. Homicide & Old Lace (26-03-69)

John Knight (director)

The Andromeda Breakthrough 2-2. Gale Warning (05-07-62) 2-4. Storm Centres (19-07-62) 2-6. The Roman Peace (02-08-62)

John Krish (director)

The Avengers -03. Escape In Time (26-01-67) 5-07. The Living Dead (25-02-67) 5-13. A Funny Thing Happened On The Way To The Station (08-04-67)

The Saint 2-06. Marcia (24-10-63)

John Lucarotti (director)

The Avengers 2-26. Killer Whale (23-03-63)

John Llewellyn Moxey (director)

The Avengers 5-16. Who's Who (29-04-67*)*

The Baron 02. Epitaph For a Hero (05-10-66) 04. Red Horse, Red Rider (19-10-66) 10. The Legends of Ammak (30-11-66) 11. Samurai West (07-12-66) 13. Portrait Of Louisa (21-12-67)

The Champions 09. The Iron Man (20-11-68)

Man Of The World 2-02. The Enemy (18-05-63) 2-05. In The Picture (08-06-63)

The Saint 2-05. The Elusive Elishaw (17-10-63) 3-03. Jeannine (22-10-64) 3-10. The Imprudent

Politician (10-12-64) 3-19. The Golden Frog (11-02-65) 4-04. The Smart Detective (22-07-65) 5-03. The Russian Prisoner (14-10-66) 6-01. The Best Laid Schemes (29-09-68)

Jon Manchip White (director)
The Avengers 2-02, Propellant 23 (06-10-62)

John Nelson-Burton (director)
Ghost Squad 2-01. Interrupted Requiem (02-02-63) 2-04. The Golden Silence (08-06-63) 2-09. Hot Money (25-05-63)

John Paddy Carstairs (director)
The Saint 1-07. The Arrow Of God (15-11-62) 2-18. The Romantic Matron (16-01-64)

Jonathan Alwyn (director)
The Avengers 3-19. The Secrets Broker (01-02-64) 3-22. The Outside-In Man (22-02-64)
The Protectors 03. Happy Is The Loser (11-04-64) 08. Freedom! (16-05-64) 13. Cargo From Corinth (20-06-64)
Public Eye 4-06. The Comedian's Graveyard (03-09-69)

Julia Smith (director)
Doctor Who 32. The Underwater Menace: 2 Episodes (21-01-67)

Julian Aymes (director)
Danger Man 1-15. Colonel Rodriguez (18-12-60)

Kim Mills (director)
The Avengers 3-05. Death Of a Batman (26-01-63) 3-09. The Medicine Men (23-11-63) 3-10. The Grandeur That Was Rome (30-11-63) 3-13. Death a La Carte (21-12-63) 3-24. Concerto (07-03-64) 3-26. Lobster Quadrille (21-03-64)
City Beneath The Sea 02. Escape To Algeria (24-11-62) 03. Tide Of Evil (01-12-62) 04. Cellar Of Fear (08-12-62)
The Protectors 12. Channel Crossing (13-06-64)
Public Eye 1-02. Nobody Kills Santa Claus (30-01-65) 1-12. The Morning Wasn't So Hot (10-04-65) 2-02. Don't Forget You're Mine (09-07-66) 4-01. Welcome To Brighton? (30-07-69) 4-04. My Lifes My Own (20-08-69) 4-07. A Fixed Address (19-06-69)

Laurence Bourne (director)
Adam Adamant Lives 29. A Sinister Sort Of Service (25-03-67)
The Avengers 3-15. The White Elephant (04-01-64) 3-16. The Little Wonders (11-01-64) 3-20. Trojan Horse (08-02-64)
The Protectors 06. The Stamp Collection (02-05-64) 10. The Deadly Chameleon (30-5-64) 14. The Reluctant Thief (27-06-64)
Undermind 07. Song Of Death (19-06-65) 09. Test For The Future (03-07-65)

Leonard Fincham (director)
The Avengers 2-13. Death Dispatch (22-12-62)

Lester Powell (director)
The Avengers 2-05, Mission To Montreal (27-10-62)

Leonard Lewis (director)
Adam Adamant Lives 03. More Deadly Than The Sword (07-07-66) 07. To Set a Deadly Fashion (11-08-66)

Leslie Norman (director)
The Avengers 6-27. Thingamajig (16-04-69) 6-33. Bizarre (21-05-69)
The Baron 01. Diplomatic Immunity (28-09-66) 08. The Persuaders (16-11-66) 30. Farewell To Yesterday (19-04-67)
The Champions 14. The Search (01-01-68)
Department S 23. A Small War Of Nerves (21-01-70) 25. Spencer Bodily Is 60 Years Old (11-02-70) 28. The Soup Of The Day (04-03-70)
Randall & Hopkirk (Deceased) 04. Never Trust a Ghost (12-10-69) 19. A Sentimental Journey (23-01-70) 22. It's Supposed To Be Thicker Than Water (13-02-70)
The Saint 3-02. Lida (15-10-64) 3-18. The Sign Of The Claw (04-02-65) 3-07. The Loving Brothers (19-11-64) 4-01. The Chequered Flag (01-07-65) 4-03. The Crooked Ring (15-07-65) 5-02. Interlude In Venice (07-10-66) 4-07. The Saint Bids Diamonds (12-08-65) 5-04. The Reluctant Revolution (21-10-66) 5-07. The Angel's Eye (11-11-66) 5-06. The Convenient Monster (04-11-66) 5-11. Paper Chase (09-12-66) 5-12. Locate & Destroy (16-12-66) 5-16. The Fast Women (13-01-67) 5-17. The Death

Game (20-01-67) 5-20. The Counterfeit Countess (03-03-67) 5-22. Island Of Chance (07-04-67) 5-25. The Power Artists (19-05-67) 6-05. The Organization Man (27-10-67) 6-06. The Double Take (03-11-68) 6-08. The Master Plan (17-11-68) 6-20. The World Beater (09-02-69)

Malcolm Hulke (director)
The Avengers 2-07, The Mauritius Penny (10-11-62) 2-15, Intercrime (05-01-63) 2-21. The White Dwarf (16-02-63)

Mark Lawton (director)
The Protectors 11. Who Killed Lazoryck? (06-06-64)

Martin Woodhouse (director)
The Avengers 2-01, Mr Teddy Bear (29-09-62) 2-12, The Big Thinker (15-12-62) 2-19. The Golden Egg (02-02-63) 2-24. A Chorus Of Frogs (09-03-63)

Max Varnel (director)
Interpol Calling 10. Dead On Arrival (16-11-59)

Mervyn Pinfield (director)
Doctor Who 07. The Sensorites: 6 Episodes (20-06-64) 09. Planet Of Giants: 2 Episodes (31-10-64) 15. The Space Museum: 4 Episodes (24-04-65)¹

Michael Ferguson (director)
Doctor Who 27. The War Machines: 4 Episodes (25-06-66) 48. The Seeds Of Death: 6 Episodes (25-01-69)

Michael Hart (director)
Doctor Who 49. The Space Pirates: Episode 2 (15-03-69)

Michael Hayes (director)
A For Andromeda 1-6. The Face Of The Tiger (07-11-61)

Michael Imison (director)
Doctor Who 23. The Ark: 4 Episodes (05-03-66)

Michael Truman (director)
Danger Man 1-03. Josetta (25-09-60) 1-21. The Conspirators (05-02-61) 1-23. The Gallows Tree (09-04-61) 1-32. The Actor (11-06-61) 2-02. The Professionals (20-10-64) 2-19. It's Up To The Lady (23-02-65) 2-11. Don't Nail Him Yet (22-12-64) 2-21. The Mirror's New (09-03-65) 3-01. The Black Book (30-09-65) 3-08. The Outcast (18-11-65) 3-09. English Lady Take Lodgers (25-11-65) 3-14. The Man Who Wouldn't Talk (30-12-65) 3-24. Koroshi (12-02-67)
The Saint 1-01. The Talented Husband (4-10-62) 1-04. The Covetous Headsman (25-10-62)

Moira Armstrong (director)
Adam Adamant Lives 09. Sing a Song Of Murder (25-08-66) 11. Death By Appointment Only (08-09-66) 16. D For Destruction (13-06-66) 18. Black Echo (07-01-67)

Morris Barry (director)
Doctor Who 33. The Moonbase: 2 Episodes (18-02-67) 37. The Tomb Of The Cybermen: 4 Episodes (02-09-67) 44. The Dominators: 5 Episodes (10-08-68)

Naiomi Capon (director)
Out Of The Unknown 1-07. Sucker Bait (15-11-65)

Norman Harrison (director)
Ghost Story 1-03. Ticket For Blackmail (09-09-61) 1-05. High Wire (30-09-61)
Interpol Calling 30. A Foreign Body (18-04-60)

Paddy Russell (director)
Out Of The Unknown 1-06. Come Buttercup, Come Daisy, Come…? (08-11-65)

Pat Jackson (director)
Danger Man 3-18. The Hunting Party (27-01-66)
Man In a Suitcase 04. Variation On a Million Bucks Part 1 (18-10-67) 06. Man From The Dead (01-11-67) 13. The Bridge (20-12-67)
The Prisoner 3. A.B. & C. (13-10-67) 05. The Schizoid Man (27-10-67) 10. Hammer Into Anvil (01-12-67) 13. Do Not Forsake Me Oh My Darling (22-12-67)

Patrick McGoohan (director)
Danger Man 1-20. The Vacation (29-01-61) 3-11. To Our Best Friend (09-12-65)
3-22. The Paper Chase (31-03-66)
The Prisoner 04. Free For All (20-10-67) 07. Many Happy Returns (10-11-67) 12. A Change Of Mind

(15-12-67) 16. Once Upon a Time (25-01-67) 17. Fall Out (01-02-68)

Patrick Dromgoole (director)
Undermind 08. Puppets Of Evil (26-06-65)

Paul Clappessoni (director)
Adam Adamant Lives 05. Allah Is Not Always With You (21-07-66) 06. The Terribly Happy
Embalmers (04-06-66) 10. The Doomsday Plan (01-09-66)

Paul Dickson (director)
The Avengers 6-04. You'll Catch Your Death (16-10-68)
The Champions 06. Operation Deep Freeze (30-10-68) 13. Twelve Hours (18-12-68) 17. A Case Of
Lemmings (22-01-68) 21. The Body Snatchers (19-02-69)
Department S 05. One Of Aircraft Is Empty (06-4-69) 19. The Duplicated Man (03-12-69) 24. The
Bones Of Byrom Blain (28-01-70)
*Randall & Hopkirk (Deceased)*05. That's How Murder Snowballs (19-10-69)

Pennington Richards (director)
Danger Man 1-16. The Island (01-01-61) 1-31. The Trap (04-06-61)
Interpol Calling 01. The Angola Bright's (14-09-59) 02. The Thirteen Innocents (21-09-59) 03. The
Money Game (28-09-59) 04. The Sleeping Giant (05-10-59) 05. The Two Headed Monster (12-10-59)
07. You Can't Die Twice (26-10-59) 09. Private View (09-11-59) 11. Air Switch (23-11-59) 12. The
Chinese Mask (07-12-59) 13. Slave Ship (14-12-59) 15. Last Man Lucky (28-12-59) 16. No Flowers
For Onno (04-01-59) 19. Act Of Piracy (25-01-60) 20. Game For Three Hands (01-02-60) 21. The
Collector (08-02-60) 22. The Heiress (15-02-60) 23. Payment in Advance (22-02-60) 26. Trail At
Cranby's Creek (21-03-60) 33. Eight Days Inclusive (09-05-60) 35. Cargo Of Death (23-05-60)

Peter Dews (director)
Undermind 05. Too Many Enemies (05-06-65)

Peter Duffell (director)
The Avengers 5-06. The Winged Avenger (18-02-67)
Man In a Suitcase 25. Property Of A Gentleman (13-03-67) 26. The Revolutionaries (20-03-67)
29. Castle In The Clouds (10-04-67)
Strange Report 04. REPORT 2641 LONELY HEARTS Who Killed Dan Cupid? (12-10-69) 06.
REPORT 3906 COVER-GIRLS Last Years Model (26-10-69) 10. REPORT 8944 HAND A Matter Of
Witchcraft (30-11-69) 11. REPORT 1553 RACIST A Most Dangerous Proposal (07-12-69)

Peter Duguid (director)
Callan 2-01. Red Knight, White Knight (08-01-69) 2-02. The Most Promising Girl Of Her Year (15-01-
68) 2-06. Heir Apparent (12-02-69) 2-09. Death Of a Friend (05-03-69) 2-14. Nice People Die At Home
(09-04-69)

Peter Graham Scott (director)
The Avengers 4-06. The Master Minds (06-11-65) 4-07. The Murder Market (13-11-65)
4-24. A Sense Of History (12-03-66)
Danger Man 1-05. The Lovers (09-10-60) 1-06. The Girl In Pink Pyjamas (16-10-60) 1-10. An Affair
Of State (13-11-60) 1-11. The Key (20-11-60) 1-28. Sabotage (14-05-61) 1-37. The Nurse (06-01-61) 1-
39. Deadline (20-01-62)
The Prisoner 06. The General (03-11-67)

Peter Hammond (director)
The Avengers 1-15, The Frighteners (27-11-61) 3-01. Brief For Murder (28-09-63) 3-08. Second Sight
(16-11-63) 3-11. The Golden Fleece (07-12-63) 3-12. Don't Look Behind You (14-12-63)
3-21. Build a Better Mousetrap (15-02-64)
The Protectors 01. Landscape With Bandits (28-03-64) 05. The Loop Men (25-04-64) 09. The Pirate
(23-05-64)

Peter Henreid (director)
The Third Man 4-07. Diamond In the Rough (11-05-62)

Peter Ling (director)
The Avengers 2-17, Box Of Tricks (19-01-63)

Peter Maxell (director)
Danger Man 2-04. The Galloping Major (03-11-64) 2-10. A Man To Be Trusted (15-12-64) 2-20. Have
a Glass of Wine (02-03-65)

Peter Medak (director)

Strange Report 02. REPORT 0649 SKELETON Let Sleeping Heroes Lie (28-09-69) 12. REPORT 7931 SNIPER When Is Your Cousin Not? (14-12-69)

Peter Potter (director)
Out Of The Unknown 1-01. No Place Like Earth (4-10-65) 1-11. Thirteen To Centauraus (13-12-65)
Undermind 02. Flowers Of Havoc (15-5-65) 04. Death In England (29-05-65) 11. End Signal (17-07-65)

Peter Sasdy (director)
Callan 2-04. The Little Bits & Pieces Of Love (29-01-69)
Ghost Squad 2-03. Sentences Of Death (04-05-63) 2-08. The Man With The Delicate Hands (22-06-63) 2-11. A First Class Way To Die (13-07-63) 2-14. The Big Time (12-01-63) 2-20. P.G.7. (06-07-63) 2-25. The Thirteenth Girl (27-04-63)
Out Of The Unknown 1-05. Time In Advance (01-11-65) 1-12. The Midas Plague (20-12-65)

Peter Sykes (director)
The Avengers 6-10. Noon Doomsday (27-11-68) 6-21. Love All (19-02-69)

Peter Yates (director)
Danger Man 3-03. Sting In The Tail (14-10-65) 3-12. The Man On The Beach (16-12-65) 3-13. Say It With Flowers (23-12-65) 3-19. Two Birds With One Bullet (10-03-66) 3-25. Shinda Shima (26-02-67) 3-24. Koroshi (12-02-67)
The Saint 2-01. The Fellow Traveler (19-09-63) 2-07. The Work Of Art (31-10-63) 2-10. The Rough Diamonds (21-11-63) 2-14. The Bunco Artists (19-12-63) 2-17. The Noble Sportsman (09-01-64) 3-13. The Damsel In Distress (31-12-64)

Phil Brown (director)
Ghost Squad 2-07. Lost in Transit (15-06-63) 2-17. Mr Five Per Cent (06-04-63)

Philip Dudley (director)
Adam Adamant Lives! 04. The Sweet Smell Of Disaster (14-07-66) 02. Death Has a Thousand Faces (30-06-66) 08. The Last Sacrifice (18-08-66) 12. Beauty Is An Ugly Word (15-09-66)

Philip Leacock (director)
Danger Man 2-07. The Colonels Daughter (24-11-64)

Philip Saville (director)
Out Of The Unknown 2-01. The Machine Stops (06-10-66)

Piers Haggard (director)
Callan 1-06. You Should Have Got Here Sooner (12-08-67)

Quintin Lawrence (director)
The Avengers 4-02. The Gravediggers (09-01-65)
The Baron 23. The Edge Of Fear (01-03-67)
Danger Man 2-12. A Date With Doris (29-12-64)

Ralph Smart (director)
Danger Man 1-02. Time to Kill (18-11-60) 1-07. Position Of Trust (23-10-60)

Ray Austin (director)
The Avengers 6-08. All Done With Mirrors (13-11-68) 6-12. Have Guns Will Haggle (11-12-68)
Department S 02. The Trojan Tanker (16-03-69) 09. Black Out (17-09-69) 17. Dead Men Die Twice (12-11-69) 21. Death On Reflection (17-12-69)
Randall & Hopkirk (Deceased) 02. A Disturbing Case (28-09-69) 08. Whoever Heard Of a Ghost Dying (09-11-69) 09. The House On Haunted Hill (16-11-69) 16. When The Spirit Moves You (02-01-70) 20. Money To Burn (30-01-70) 25. You Can Always Find a Fall Guy (06-03-70)
The Saint 6-04. The Desperate Diplomat (20-10-68) 6-13. The People Importers (22-12-68)

Raymond Menmuir (director)
The Avengers 3-04. The Nutshell (19-10-63)
The Protectors 04. No Forwarding Address (18-04-64)
Undermind 10. Waves Of Sound (10-07-65)

Reed De Rouen (director)
The Avengers 2-25. Six Hands Across a Table (16-03-63)

Reginald Collin (director)
Pathfinders To Venus 06. The City (09-04-61) 08. Planet On Fire (23-04-61)

Rex Tucker (director)

Doctor Who 25. The Gunfighters: 4 Episodes (30-04-66)

Richard Martin (director)

Doctor Who 02. The Daleks: 3 Episodes (21-12-63) 03. The Edge Of Destruction: 1 Episode (04-02-64) 10. Dalek Invasion Of Earth 6 episodes (1964) 13. The Web Planet: 6 Episodes (13-02-65) 16. The Chase: 6 Episodes (22-05-65)

Ridley Scott (director)

Adam Adamant Lives 13. The League Of Uncharitable Ladies (12-09-66)

Robert Asher (director)

The Avengers 5-04. The See Through Man (04-02-67) 5-21. You Have Just Been Murdered (28-10-67) 5-23. Murdersville (11-11-67)

The Baron 20. The High Terrace (08-02-67) 21. The Seven Eyes Of Night (15-02-67) 24. Long Ago & Far Away (08-03-67) 29. Countdown (12-04-67)

The Champions 19. Mission (05-02-69) 20. Silent Enemy (12-02-69) 23. The Night People (05-03-69)

The Prisoner 11. It's Your Funeral (08-12-67)

The Saint 5-19. To Kill a Saint (24-02-67) 6-10. The Scales Of Justice (01-12-68)

Strange Report 15. REPORT 4407 HEART No Choice For The Donor (04-01-70)

Robert S Baker (director)

The Saint 1-10. The Golden Journey (06-12-62) 2-27. The Saint Sees It Through (19-03-64) 2-11. The Saint Plays With Fire (28-11-63) 2-16. The Wonderful War (02-01-64)

Robert Day (director)

The Avengers 5-01. From Venus With Love (14-01-67) 5-10. Never, Never Say Die (18-03-67) 5-17. Return Of The Cybernauts (30-09-67) 5-19. The £50,000 Breakfast (14-10-67) 5-22. The Positive Negative Man (4-11-67) 5-24. Mission, Highly Improbable (18-11-67)

Danger Man 2-06. Fish On The Hook (17-11-64)

Robert Fuest (director)

The Avengers 6-02. Game (02-10-68) 6-13. They Keep Killing Steed (18-12-68) 6-15. The Rotters (08-01-69) 6-23. Take Me To Your Leader (05-03-69) 6-28. My Wildest Dream (07-04-69) 6-30. Take-Over (23-04-69) 6-31. Pandora (30-04-69)

Robert M Leeds (director)

The Third Man 5-01. A Question In Ice (27-06-64)

Robert Lynn (director)

Ghost Squad 1-07. Still Waters (21-10-61) 1-08. Assassin (28-10-61) 1-10. Catspaw (05-01-61) 1-12. Princess (12-01-61) 1-13. Death From a Distance (04-11-61)

Interpol Calling 24. Finger Of Guilt (07-03-60) 27. Ascent To Murder (28-03-60) 29. White Blackmail (11-04-60) 31. In The Swim (25-04-60) 32. The Three Keys (02-05-60) 34. Dressed To Kill (06-05-60) 38. The Absent Assassin (13-06-60)

The Saint 2-03. Judith (03-10-63)

Robert Tronson (director)

The Baron 27. Roundabout (29-03-67)

Callan 2-05. Let's Kill Everybody (05-02-69) 2-13. The Worst Soldier I Ever Saw (02-04-69)

Man In a Suitcase 05. Variation On a Million Bucks Part 2 (25-10-67) 07. Sweet Sue (08-11-67) 09. The Girl Who Never Was (22-11-67) 12. Find The Lady (13-12-67) 23. Web With Four Spiders (28-02-67)

Randall & Hopkirk (Deceased) 15. The Man From Nowhere (28-12-69)

The Saint 3-23. The Happy Suicide (11-03-65) 4-05. The Persistent Parasites (29-07-65)

Roger Jenkins (director)

Out Of The Unknown 1-10. Some Lapse In Time (06-12-65)

Roger Marshall (director)

The Avengers 2-06, The Removal Men (03-11-62) 2-08, Death Of Great Dane (17-11-62) 2-23. Conspiracy Of Silence (02-03-63)

Roger Moore (director)

The Saint 2-24. Sophia (24-02-64) 3-01. The Miracle Tea Party (8-10-64) 3-14. The Contact (07-01-65) 4-09. The Old Treasure Story (26-08-65) 5-14. Escape Route (30-12-66) 6-02. Invitation To Danger (06-10-68) 6-14. Where The Money Is (29-12-68) 6-09. The House On Dragons Rock (24-11-68)

Roy Baker (director)

The Baron 14. There's Someone Close Behind You (28-12-67) 22. Night Of The Hunter (22-02-67) 26.

The Long, Long Day (22-03-67) 27. Roundabout (29-03-67) 28. The Man Outside (05-04-67)

Roy Rossotti (director)

The Avengers 5-05. The Bird Who Knew Too Much (11-02-67)

Roy Ward Baker (director)

The Avengers 4-01. The Town Of No Return (02-10-65) 4-12. Twos a Crowd (18-12-65) 4-13. Too Many Christmas Trees (25-12-65) 4-14. Silent Dust (01-1-66) 4-15. Room Without a View (8-1-65) 4-17. The Girl From AUNTIE (22-1-66) 4-18. The Thirteenth Hole (29-1-66) 6-05. Split (23-10-68)
The Champions 27. Nutcracker (02-04-69) 30. Autokill (30-04-69)
Department S 04. The Pied Piper Of Hambledown (30-03-69)
Randall & Hopkirk (Deceased) 13. But What a Sweet Little Room (14-12-69) 14. Who Killed Cock Robin? (21-12-69)
The Saint 2-04. Teresa (10-10-63) 2-19. Luella (23-01-64) 2-21. The Good Medicine (06-02-64) 3-04. The Scorpion (29-10-64) 3-15. The Set-Up (14-01-65) 3-20. The Frightened Inn-Keeper (18-02-65) 5-01. The Queens Ransom (30-09-66) 5-05. The Helpful Pirate (28-10-66) 5-10. Little Girl Lost (02-12-66) 5-13. Flight Plan (23-12-66) 5-15. The Persistent Patriots (06-01-67) 5-18. The Art Collectors (27-01-67) 5-21. Simon & Delilah (24-03-67) 6-03. Legacy For The Saint (13-10-68) 6-07. The Time To Die (10-11-68) 6-11. The Fiction Makers Part 1 (08-12-68) 6-12. The Fiction Makers Part 2 (15-12-68)

Rudolph Cartier (director)

Out Of The Unknown 2-04. Level Seven (27-10-66)

Sam Wanamaker (director)

The Champions 08. To Trap a Rat (13-11-68)

Seth Holt (director)

Danger Man 1-11. The Key (20-11-60) 1-12. The Sisters (27-11-60) 1-17. Find & Return (08-01-61) 1-36. Under the Lake (30-12-61)

Sidney Hayers (director)

The Avengers 4-03. The Cybernauts (16-10-65) 4-08. A Surfeit Of H2o (20-11-65) 4-11. Man Eater Of Surrey Green (11-12-65) 5-08. The Hidden Tiger (04-03-67) 5-15. The Joker (22-04-67) 5-18. Death's Door (07-10-67) 5-20. Dead Man's Treasure (21-10-67)

Stuart Burge (director)

Danger Man 3-16. Dangerous Secret (13-01-66)

Terry Bishop (director)

Danger Man 1-01. View From The Villa (11-09-60) 1-13. The Prisoner (04-12-60) 1-14. The Traitor (11-12-60) 1-29. The Contessa (21-05-61)

Toby Robertson (director)

Callan 1-01. The Good Ones Are Dead (08-07-67)

Tristan DeVere Cole (director)

Doctor Who 43. The Wheel in Space: 2 Episodes (11-05-68)

Waris Hussein (director)

Doctor Who 01. An Unearthly Child: 4 Episodes (23-11-63)

William Slater (director)

Adam Adamant Lives 01. A Vintage Year For Scoundrels (20-06-66)

Screenplay Writers

A. Sanford Wolf (writer)
The Saint 6-01, The Best Laid Schemes (29-09-68)

Anthony Coburn (writer)
Doctor Who 01. An Unearthly Child: 4 Episodes (23-11-63)

Anthony Marriott (writer)
Public Eye 1-02. Nobody Kill Santa Claus (30-01-65) 1-12. The Morning Wasn't So Hot (10-04-65) 2-02. Don't Forget You're Mine (09-7-66) 2-07. Works With Chess, Not With Life (13-8-66) 3-09. The Bromsgrove Venus (16-03-68) 4-01. Welcome To Brighton? (30-07-69) 4-02. Divide & Conquer (06-08-69) 4-03. Paid In Full (13-08-69) 4-04. My Life's My Own (20-08-69) 4-05. Case For The Defence (27-08-69) 4-06. The Comedian's Graveyard (03-09-69) 4-07. A Fixed Address (19-06-69)

Anthony Skene (writer)
The Prisoner 03, A.B. & C. (13-10-67) 07, Many Happy Returns (10-11-67) 08, Dance Of The Dead (17-11-67)
Public Eye 3-09. The Bromsgrove Venus (16-03-68)

Anthony Terploff (writer)
The Avengers 2-09 The Sell Out (24-11-62) 2-22. Man In The Mirror (23-02-63)

Arthur Berlin (writer)
Man Of The World 2-07. The Prince (22-06-63)

Arthur Dales (writer)
Strange Report 11. REPORT 1553 RACIST A Most Dangerous Proposal (07-12-69)

Barbara Hammer (writer)
Interpol Calling 07, You Can't Die Twice (26-10-59)

Basil Dawson (writer)
Ghost Squad 2-19. Death of a Sportsman (26-01-63) 2-12. Quarantine At Kavar (01-06-63) 2-07. Lost in Transit (15-06-63) 2-20. P.G.7. (06-07-63)

Berkley Mather (writer)
The Avengers 1-15. The Frighteners (27-11-61)

Bernie Cooper (writer)
Man In a Suitcase 01. Brainwash (27-09-67) 24, Which Way Did He Go, McGill (06-03-67)

Bill Craig (writer)
Ghost Squad 1-10. Catspaw (05-01-61) 2-01. Interrupted Requiem (02-02-63) 2-02. East Of Mandalay (09-02-63)

Bill Strutton (writer)
Doctor Who 13. The Web Planet: 6 Episodes (13-02-65)
The Protectors 01, Landscape With Bandits (28-03-64) 08, Freedom! (16-05-64) 14. The Reluctant Thief (27-06-64)
The Saint 2-08, Iris (07-11-63) 2-10, The Rough Diamonds (21-11-63)
Strange Report 05. REPORT 8319 GRENADE What Price Change? (19-10-69)
Undermind 07, Song Of Death (19-06-65)

Brian Clemens (writer)
Adam Adamant Lives! 06, The Happy Embalmers (04-06-66)
The Avengers 3-01, Brief For Murder (28-09-63) 3-12, Don't Look Behind You (14-12-63) 3-14, Dressed To Kill (28-12-63) 4-01, The Town Of No Return (02-10-65) 4-04, Death At Bargain Prices (23-10-65) 4-21, A Touch Of Brimstone (19-02-66) 4-22, What The Butler Saw (26-02-66) 4-23, The House That Jack Built (05-03-66) 4-25, How To Succeed…. At Murder (19-03-66) 4-26, Honey For The Prince (26-03-66) 5-05, The Bird Who Knew Too Much (11-02-67) 5-07, The Living Dead (25-02-67) 5-09, The Correct Way To Kill (11-03-67) 5-11, Epic (25-03-67) 5-12, The Superlative Seven (01-04-67) 5-13, A Funny Thing Happened On The Way To The Station (08-04-67) 5-15, The Joker (22-04-67) 5-23, Murdersville (11-11-67) 6-01, The Forget Me Knot (25-09-68) 6-05, Split (23-10-68) 6-13, They Keep Killing Steed (18-12-68) 6-14, The Interrogators (01-01-69) 6-18, The Morning After (29-10-69) 6-29, Requiem (16-04-69) 6-31, Pandora (30-04-69) 6-33, Bizarre (21-05-69)
The Baron 12, The Maze (14-12-67) 26, The Long, Long Day (22-03-67)
The Champions 05, Happening (23-10-68) 30, Autokill (30-04-69)

Danger Man 1-01, View From The Villa (11-09-60) 1-06, The Girl In Pink Pyjamas (16-10-60) 1-12, The Sisters (27-11-60) 1-16, The Island (01-01-61) 1-27, Bury The Dead (07-05-61) 1-30, The Leak (28-05-61) 1-37, The Nurse (06-01-61) 1-38, Dead Man Walks (13-01-62)
Ghost Squad 1-02. Bullet With My Name On It (16-09-61)
Man Of The World 2-05. In The Picture (08-06-63)
The Protectors 10, The Deadly Chameleon (30-5-64)

Brian Degas (writer)
The Baron 11, Samurai West (07-12-66)
The Saint 3-08, The Man Who Liked Toys (26-11-64) 3-16, The Rhine Maiden (21-1-65) 3-23, The Happy Suicide (11-3-65) 4-02, The Abductors (8-7-65)
Strange Report 02. REPORT 0649 SKELETON Let Sleeping Heroes Lie (28-09-69)

Brian Hayles (writer)
Doctor Who 24. The Celestial Toymaker: The Final Test (23-04-66) 39. The Ice Warriors: 4 Episodes (11-11-67) 48. The Seeds Of Death: 6 Episodes (25-01-69)

Bruce Stewart (writer)
Out Of The Unknown 2-03. Lambda One (20-10-66)

C. Scott Forbes (writer)
The Saint 5-21, Simon & Delilah (24-03-67)

Clive Donner (writer)
Out Of The Unknown 2-01. The Machine Stops (06-10-66)

Colin Finbow (writer)
The Avengers 4-08, A Surfeit Of H2o (20-11-65)

Connery Chappell (writer)
Ghost Squad 1-01. Hong Kong Story (23-09-61)
Interpol Calling 32, The Three Keys (02-05-60)

David Campton (writer)
Out Of The Unknown 1-03. Stranger In the Family (18-10-65) 2-08. Tunnel Under The World (01-12-66)

David Chantler (writer)
Interpol Calling 02, The Thirteen Innocents (21-09-59) 05, The Two Headed Monster (12-10-59) 06, The Long Weekend (19-10-59) 17, Mr George (11-01-60) 21, The Collector (08-02-60) 22, The Heiress (15-02-60) 34, Dressed To Kill (06-05-60)

David Ellis (writer)
Doctor Who 35. The Faceless Ones: Episode 1 (08-04-67)

David Stone (writer)
Danger Man 2-04, The Galloping Major (03-11-64) 2-15, Whatever Happened To George Foster (19-01-65) 2-18, The Ubiquitous Mr Lovegrove (16-02-65) 2-20, Have a Glass of Wine (02-03-65) 3-05, Loyalty Always Pays (28-10-65) 3-08, The Outcast (18-11-65)

David Tombin (writer)
The Prisoner 01, Arrival (29-09-67) 14, Living In Harmony (29-12-67)

David Weir (writer)
Danger Man 2-07, The Colonels Daughter (24-11-64)

David Whitaker (writer)
Doctor Who 03. The Edge Of Destruction: 2 Episodes (04-02-64) 11. The Rescue: 2 Episodes (02-01-65) 14. The Crusade: 2 Episodes (27-03-65) 40. The Enemy Of The World: 6 Episodes (23-12-67) 43. The Wheel in Space: 2 Episodes (11-05-68)
Undermind 03, The New Dimension (22-05-65) 09, Test For The Future (03-07-65)

Dennis Spooner (writer)
The Avengers 1-06, Whoever Shot George Oblique Stroke XR40? (30-10-68) 6-11, Look (Stop Me If You've Heard This One) But There Were These Two Fellers (04-12-68)
The Baron 01, Diplomatic Immunity (28-09-66) 05, Enemy Of The State (26-10-66) 08, The Persuaders (16-11-66) 09, And Suddenly You're Dead (23-11-66) 17, Time To Kill (18-01-67) 18, A Memory Of Evil (25-01-67) 19, You Can't Win Them All (01-02-67) 20, The High Terrace (08-02-67) 23, The Edge Of Fear (01-03-67) 24, Long Ago & Far Away (08-03-67) 25, So Dark The Night (15-03-67)
The Champions 01, The Beginning (25-9-68) 14, The Search (1-1-68) 18, The Interrogation (29-01-69)

Doctor Who 08. The Reign Of Terror: 4 Episodes (08-08-64) 12. The Romans: 4 Episodes (16-01-65) 17. The Time Meddler: 4 Episodes (03-07-65)

Derek & Donald Ford (writers)
Adam Adamant Lives! 18, Black Echo (07-01-67)
The Saint 5-24, A Double In Diamonds (05-05-67)

Derrick Sherwin (writer)
Doctor Who 45. The Mind Robber: 5 Episodes (14-09-68) 46. The Invasion: 6 Episodes (09-11-68)

Dick Sharples (writer)
Ghost Squad 1-08. Assassin (28-10-61) 1-09 Million Dollar Ransom (11-11-61) 1-12 Princess (12-01-61)
The Saint 1-02, The Latin Touch (11-10-62) 1-03, The Careful Terrorist (18-10-62) 1-12, The Charitable Countess (20-12-62)

Don Brinkley (writer)
Strange Report 07. REPORT 3424 EPIDEMIC A Most Curious Crime (02-11-69) 14. REPORT 2493 KIDNAP Whose Pretty Girl Are You? (28-12-69)

Don Inglis (writer)
Danger Man 1-04, The Blue Veil (02-10-60)

Donald Cotton (writer)
Doctor Who 25. The Gunfighters: 4 Episodes (30-04-66)

Donald James (writer)
The Avengers 6-12, Have Guns - Will Haggle (11-12-68)
The Champions 02, The Invisible Man (02-10-68) 07, The Survivors (06-11-68) 10, The Ghost Plane (27-11-68) 13, Twelve Hours (18-12-68) 19, The Mission (05-02-69) 20, The Silent Enemy (12-02-69) 23, The Night People (05-03-69) 28, The Final Countdown (16-04-69)
Department S 04, The Pied Piper Of Hambledown (30-03-69) 15, The Shift That Never Was (25-10-69)
The Saint 6-05, The Organisation Man (27-10-67) 6-13, The World Beater (09-02-69) 6-20, The World Beater (09-02-69)
Randall & Hopkirk (Deceased) 03, All Work & No Pay (05-10-69) 06, Just For The Record (26-10-69) 12, For The Girl Who Has Everything (07-12-69) 15, The Man From Nowhere (28-12-69) 17, Somebody Just Walked Over My Grave (09-01-70) 18, Could You Recognise The Man Again (16-01-70) 19, A Sentimental Journey (23-01-70) 20, Money To Burn (30-01-70) 22, It's Supposed To Be Thicker Than Water (13-02-70) 24, Vendetta For a Dead Man (27-2-70) 25, You Can Always Tell a Fall Guy (06-03-70)

Donald Jonson (writer)
Danger Man 2-01, Yesterday's Enemies (13-10-64) 2-03, Colony Three (27-10-64) 3-07, Judgement Day (11-11-65) 3-08, The Outcast (18-11-65)
Man In a Suitcase 09 Girl Who Never Was (22-11-67) 17 Why They Killed Nolan (17-1-67)

Donald Whittaker (writer)
Doctor Who 36. The Evil Of The Daleks: Episode 2 (27-05-67)

Doreen Montgomery (writer)
Danger Man 1-05, The Lovers (09-10-60)

Edmund Ward (writer)
Man In a Suitcase 02, The Sitting Pigeon (04-10-67) 15, Burden Of Proof (03-01-67) 23, Web With Four Spiders (28-02-67)

Edward Boyd (writer)
The Corridor People All Episodes (26-08-66)

Edward DeBlasio (writer)
Strange Report 10. REPORT 8944 HAND A Matter Of Witchcraft (30-11-69) 15. REPORT 4407 HEART No Choice For The Donor (04-01-70)

Edwin Richfield (writer)
Interpol Calling 13, Slave Ship (14-12-59) 19, Act Of Piracy (25-01-60)

Eric Paice (writer)
The Avengers 3-06, November Five (02-11-63) 3-16, The Little Wonders (11-01-64) 3-25, Espirit de Corps (14-03-64)
Pathfinders In Space All 6 Episodes (1960)
Pathfinders To Venus All Episodes (1960)

Pathfinders To Mars All Episodes (1960)
Fiona McConnell (writer)
The Protectors 04, No Forwarding Address (18-04-64)
Francis Megahy (writer)
Man In a Suitcase 01, Brainwash (27-09-67) 24, Which Way Did He Go, McGill (06-03-67)
Fred Hoyle (writer)
A For Andromeda 1-6. The Face Of The Tiger (07-11-61)
Andromeda Breakhrough All Episodes (1962)
Geoffrey Orme (writer)
Doctor Who 32. The Underwater Menace: 2 Episodes (21-01-67)
Interpol Calling 13, Slave Ship (14-12-59)
George Markstein (writer)
The Prisoner 01, Arrival (29-09-67)
Gerald Kelsey (writer)
The Champions 28, The Final Countdown (16-04-69) 29, The Gun Runners (23-04-69)
Department S 01, Six Days (09-03-69) 22, Last Train to Reflection (14-01-70)
Ghost Squad 1-08. Assassin (28-10-61) 1-09. Million Dollar Ransom (11-11-61) 1-12. Princess (12-01-61)
The Prisoner 09, Checkmate (14-11-67)
Randall & Hopkirk (Deceased) 21, The Ghost Talks (6-0-70) 26, The Smile Behind The Veil (13-03-70)
The Saint 1-02, The Latin Touch (11-10-62) 1-03, The Careful Terrorist (18-10-62) 1-12, The Charitable Countess (20-12-62)
Gerry Davis (writer)
Doctor Who 29. The Tenth Planet: 3 Episodes (08-10-66) 37. The Tomb Of The Cybermen: 4 Episodes (02-09-67)
Gil Winfield (writer)
Interpol Calling 11, Air Switch (23-11-59) 13, Slave Ship (14-12-59)
The Third Man 2-06. Barcelona Passage (01-10-59)
Glyn Jones (writer)
Doctor Who 15. The Space Museum: 4 Episodes (24-04-65)
Harold Orton (writer)
Interpol Calling 36, Desert Hijack (30-05-60
Harry Driver (writer)
Adam Adamant Lives! 12, Beauty Is An Ugly Word (15-09-66) 15, The Village Of Evil (06-10-66)
Harry W. Junkin (writer)
The Baron 30, Farewell To Yesterday (19-04-67)
Department S 19, The Duplicated Man (03-12-69) 23, A Small War Of Nerves (21-01-70) 25, Spencer Bodily Is 60 Years (11-02-70) 26, The Ghost Of Mary Burnham (18-02-70)
The Saint 2-01, The Fellow Traveller (19-09-63) 2-02, Starring The Saint (26-09-63) 2-05, The Elusive Elishaw (17-10-63) 2-06, Marcia (24-10-63) 2-19, Luella (23-01-64) 2-20, The Lawless Lady (30-01-64) 2-23, The High Fence (20-02-64) 5-03, The Russian Prisoner (14-10-66) 5-07, The Angel's Eye (11-11-66) 5-08, The Man Who Liked Lions (18-11-66) 5-11, Paper Chase (09-12-66) 5-17, The Death Game (20-01-67) 5-24, A Double In Diamonds (05-05-67) 5-27, The Gadic Collection (22-06-67) 6-08, The Master Plan (17-11-68) 6-09, The House On Dragons Rock (24-11-68) 6-11, The Fiction Makers Part 1 (08-12-68) 6-12, The Fiction Makers Part 2 (15-12-68) 6-15, Vendetta For The Saint Part 1 (05-01-68) 6-16, Vendetta For The Saint Part 2 (12-1-68) 6-18, The Man Who Gambled With Life (26-1-68) 6-19, Portrait Of Brenda (02-02-69)
Henry Lincoln (writer)
Doctor Who 38. The Abominable Snowman: Episode 2 (07-10-67) 41. The Web Of Fear: 5 Episodes (03-02-68) 44. The Dominators: 5 Episodes (10-08-68)
Hugh Leonard (writer)
Undermind 04, Death In England (29-05-65)
Ian Kennedy Martin (writer)
The Protectors 06, The Stamp Collection (02-05-64)
The Saint 2-27, The Saint Sees It Through (19-03-64)

41

Ian McCormick (writer)
Interpol Calling 02, The Thirteen Innocents (21-09-59) 05, The Two Headed Monster (12-10-59) 06. The Long Weekend (19-10-59) 17. Mr George (11-01-60) 21. The Collector (08-02-60) 22. The Heiress (15-02-60) 34. Dressed To Kill (06-05-60)
The Third Man 2-02. One Kind Word (07-09-59)

Ian Rakoff (writer)
The Prisoner 14. Living In Harmony (29-12-67)

Ian Stuart Black (writer)
Danger Man 1-02. Time to Kill (18-11-60) 1-06. The Girl In Pink Pyjamas (16-10-60) 1-26. The Journey Ends Halfway (30-04-61) 1-28. Sabotage (14-05-61) 1-39. Deadline (20-01-62)
Doctor Who 27. The War Machines: 4 Episodes (25-06-66)
Man Of The World 1-13. Shadow Of the Wall (22-12-62) 2-01. The Bandit (11-05-63)
The Saint 3-09 The Death Penalty (03-12-64)

Ian Wilson (writer)
Randall & Hopkirk (Deceased) 02 A Disturbing Case (28-09-69)

J.B. Priestly (writer)
Out Of The Unknown 2-04. Level Seven (27-10-66)

Jack Davies (writer)
Man Of The World 1-06. The Sentimental Agent (03-11-62) 2-04. Jungle Mission (01-06-63)

Jack Saunders (writer)
The Saint 1-01 The Talented Husband (4-10-62)

Jack Whittingham (writer)
Danger Man 1-11. The Key (20-11-60) 1-36. Under the Lake (30-12-61

James Foster (writer)
Danger Man 2-17. The Affair At Castelevara (09-02-65)

James Mitchell (writer)
The Avengers 3-03 Man With Two Shadows (12-10-63)
Callan 1-01. The Good Ones Are Dead (08-07-67) 1-06. You Should Have Got Here Sooner (12-08-67) 2-01. Red Knight, White Knight (08-1-69) 2-02. The Most Promising Girl Of Her Year (15-1-69) 2-04. The Little Bits & Pieces Of Love (29-1-69) 2-13 The Worst Soldier I Ever Saw (2-4-69)

Jan Read (writer)
Danger Man 2-13 That's Two Of Us Sorry (05-01-64)
Man In a Suitcase 19. Somebody Loses, Somebody… Wins? (31-01-67)26. The Revolutionaries (20-03-67) 29. Castle In The Clouds (10-04-67) 30. Night Flight To Andorra (17-04-67)
Strange Report 09. REPORT 1021 SHRAPNEL The Wish In the Dream (23-11-69)

Jacques Gillies (writer)
Danger Man 3-13 Say It With Flowers (23-12-65)

Jeremy Burnham (writer)
The Avengers 6-04. You'll Catch Your Death (16-10-68) 6-07. False Witness (6-1-68) 6-21. Love All (19-02-69) 6-24. Fog (12-03-69) 6-25. Who Was That Man I Saw You With (19-3-69)

Jeremy Paul (writer)
Out Of The Unknown 1-04. The Dead Past (25-10-65) 3-03. The Last Lonely Man (21-01-69)

Jesse Lasky (writer)
Danger Man 3-19 Two Birds With One Bullet (10-03-66)

Jo Eisinger (writer)
Danger Man 1-05. The Lovers (09-10-60) 1-07. Position Of Trust (23-10-60) 1-17. Find & Return (08-01-61) 1-12. The Sisters (27-11-60) 1-34. The Deputy Coyannis Story (16-12-61)

John Alwyn (writer)
The Avengers 2-02. Propellant 23 (06-10-62) 2-10. Death On The Rocks (01-12-62) 2-13. Death Dispatch (22-12-62) 2-20. School For Traitors (09-02-63)

John Elliot (writer)
A For Andromeda 1-6. The Face Of The Tiger (07-11-61)
Andromeda Breakhrough All Episodes (1962)

John Gilling (writer)
The Saint 1-11. The Man Who Was Lucky (13-12-62) 2-14. The Bunco Artists (19-12-63)

John Greame (writer)

The Saint 2-09. The King Of The Beggars (14-11-63) 2-16. The Wonderful War (02-01-64) 2-17. The Noble Sportsman (09-01-64) 2-18. The Romantic Matron (16-01-64) 2-25. The Gentle Ladies (05-03-64) 3-07. The Loving Brothers (19-11-64)

John Kershaw (writer)

Callan 2-6 Heir Apparent (12-02-69)

John Kruse (writer)

The Avengers 1-20 Tunnel Of Fear (05-08-61)

Interpol Calling 18. The Thousand Mile Alibi (18-01-60) 19. Act Of Piracy (25-01-60)

The Saint 2-04. Teresa (10-10-63) 2-09. The King Of The Beggars (14-11-63) 2-11. The Saint Plays With Fire (28-11-63) 2-16. The Wonderful War (2-1-64) 2-20. The Lawless Lady (30-1-64) 3-06. The Saint Steps In (12-11-64) 5-17. The Death Game (20-1-67) 5-23. The Gadget Lovers (21-04-67) 5-25. The Power Artists (19-5-67) 6-06. The Double Take (3-11-67) 6-11. The Fiction Makers Part 1 (08-12-68) 6-12. The Fiction Makers Part 2 (15-12-68) 6-15. Vendetta For The Saint Part 1 (5-1-68) 6-16. Vendetta For The Saint Part 2 (12-1-68) 6-17. The Ex-King Of Diamonds (19-1-68)

Strange Report 03. REPORT 2641 HOSTAGE If You Won't Learn Die (05-10-69)

The Third Man 2-10. Toys Of The Dead (03-11-59)

Undermind 07. Song Of Death (19-06-65)

John Leaver (writer)

The Avengers 2-03. The Decapod (13-10-62) 2-05. Mission To Montreal (27-10-62) 2-06. The Removal Men (03-11-62) 2-09. The Sell Out (24-11-62)

John Lucarotti (writer)

The Avengers 3-13. Death a La Carte (21-12-63) 3-15. The White Elephant (04-01-64)

Doctor Who 06. The Aztecs: 4 Episodes (23-05-64)

Ghost Squad 2-23. The Menacing Mazurka (23-03-63) 2-04. The Golden Silence (08-06-63) 2-11. A First Class Way To Die (13-07-63)

The Protectors 09. The Pirate (23-05-64) 13. Cargo From Corinth (20-06-64

John Pennington (writer)

Adam Adamant Lives! 09. Sing a Song Of Murder (25-08-66) 13. The League Of Uncharitable Ladies (12-09-66)

John Pudney (writer)

Man Of The World 2-01. The Bandit (11-05-62)

John Roddick (writer)

Danger Man 1-08. The Lonely Chair (30-10-60) 1-09. The Sanctuary (06-11-60) 1-14. The Traitor (11-12-60) 2-06. Fish On The Hook (17-11-64)

Man Of The World 1-03. Blaze Of Glory (13-10-62)

The Saint 1-04 The Covetous Headsman (25-10-62)

John Stanton (writer)

Man In a Suitcase 21 No Friend Of Mine (14-02-67)

The Saint 5-04 The Reluctant Revolution (21-10-66)

John Warwick (writer)

The Third Man 5-01. A Question In Ice (27-06-64)

Joseph Morhaim (writer)

The Saint 6-01 The Best Laid Schemes (29-09-68)

Julian Bond (writer)

Ghost Squad 2-18. The Heir Apparent (09-03-63) 2-10. The Grand Duchess (11-05-63)

Man Of The World 2-02. The Enemy (18-05-63) 3 -08. Little Black Bag (25-02-69)

The Saint 1-08, The Element Of Doubt (22-11-62)

Kenneth Cavander (writer)

Out Of The Unknown 2-01. The Machine Stops (06-10-66)

Kevin B Laffan (writer)

Man In a Suitcase 08, Essay In Evil (15-11-67) 26, The Revolutionaries (20-03-67)

Kim Mills (writer)

The Avengers 2-12. The Big Thinker (15-12-62) 2-17. Box Of Tricks (19-01-63) 2-22. Man In The Mirror (23-02-63) 2-26. Killer Whale (23-03-63)

Kit Peddler (writer)

Doctor Who 29. The Tenth Planet: 3 Episodes (08-10-66) 33. The Moonbase: 2 Episodes (18-02-67) 37. The Tomb Of The Cybermen: 4 Episodes (02-09-67) 43. The Wheel in Space: 2 Episodes (11-05-68) 46. The Invasion: 6 Episodes (09-11-68)

Larry Forrester (writer)
Interpol Calling 01 The Angola Bright's (14-09-59) 04. The Sleeping Giant (05-10-59) 23. Payment in Advance (22-02-60) 26. Trail At Cranby's Creek (21-03-60) 27. Ascent To Murder (28-03-60) 37. Pipeline (06-06-60) 38. The Absent Assassin (13-06-60)
The Protectors 05 The Loop Men (25-04-64) 11. Who Killed Lazoryck? (06-06-64)
The Saint 2-01 The Fellow Traveller (19-09-63) 2-15. The Benevolent Burglary (26-12-63)

Leigh Vance (writer)
The Avengers 6-08 All Done With Mirrors (13-11-68)
The Saint 5-01. The Queens Ransom (30-09-66) 5-09. The Better Mouse Trap (25-11-66) 5-10. Little Girl Lost (02-12-66) 5-16. The Fast Women (13-01-67) 5-22. Island Of Chance (07-04-67)
Strange Report 16. REPORT 4977 SWINDLE Square Root Of Evil (11-01-70)

Leo Lehman (writer)
Out Of This World 02. Little Lost Robot (07-07-1962)

Leon Griffiths (writer)
Ghost Squad The Big Time (12-01-63)
Out Of The Unknown 1-10. Some Lapse In Time (06-12-65)

Leonard Fincham (writer)
Interpol Calling 08. Diamond S.O.S. (02-11-59) 11. Air Switch (23-11-59) 22. The Heiress (15-02-60) 25. The Girl With The Grey Hair (14-03-60) 35. Cargo Of Death (23-05-60)

Leonard Grahame (writer)
The Saint 2-03 Judith (03-10-63)

Lesley Scott (writer)
Doctor Who 23. The Ark: 4 Episodes (05-03-66)

Leslie Darbon (writer)
Department S 10. Double Death Of Charlie Crippen (14-09-69) 18. The Perfect Operation (26-12-69) 28. The Soup Of The Day (04-03-70)

Lewis Davidson *(writer)*
Danger Man 1-22 The Honeymooners (02-04-61)
Ghost Squad 1-05. High Wire (30-09-61)
Interpol Calling 03 The Money Game (28-09-59) 12 The Chinese Mask (07-12-59)
The Protectors 03 Happy Is The Loser (11-04-64)
The Saint 2-14 The Bunco Artists (19-12-63)

Lewis Griefer (writer)
Ghost Squad 2-13. The Desperate Diplomat (18-05-63)
The Prisoner 06 The General (03-11-67)

Lindsay Galloway (writer)
Ghost Squad 1-01. Hong Kong Story (23-09-61) 1-02. Bullet With My Name On It (16-09-61) 1-03. Ticket For Blackmail (09-09-61) 1-13. Death From a Distance (04-11-61)
Interpol Calling 28 Slow Boat To Amsterdam (04-04-60)
Man Of The World 1-05. The Frontier (27-10-62) 1-07. The Highland Story (10-11-62) 2-03. Double Exposure (25-05-63)

Lindsay Hardy (writer)
Man Of The World 1-11. Specialist For the Kill (08-12-62) 1-02. Masquerade In Spain (06-10-62)

Louis Marks (writer)
Danger Man 2-02
Doctor Who 09. Planet Of Giants: 3 Episodes (31-10-64)
Ghost Squad 2-09. Hot Money (25-05-63)

Ludovic Peters (writer)
The Avengers 3-19 The Secrets Broker (01-02-64)

Malcolm Hulke (writer)
The Avengers 3-02. The Undertakers (05-10-63) 3-09. The Medicine Men (23-11-63) 3-20. Trojan Horse (08-02-64) 3-24. Concerto (07-03-64) 4-02. The Gravediggers (09-01-65)

44

Doctor Who 35. Faceless Ones: Episode 1 (08-04-67) 50. War Games: 10 Episodes (19-04-69) *Danger Man* 2-22 Parallel Lines Sometimes Meet (16-03-65)

Pathfinders In Space All 6 Episodes (1960)

Pathfinders To Venus All Episodes (1960)

Pathfinders To Mars All Episodes (1960)

The Protectors 07. It Could Happen Here (09-05-64) 12. Channel Crossing (13-06-64)

Marc Brandel (writer)

Danger Man 1-18. The Girl Who Likes G.I.'s (15-01-61) 1-23. The Gallows Tree (09-04-61) 1-32. The Actor (11-06-61) 2-05. Fair Exchange (10-11-64)

Man Of The World 2-06. The Bullfighter (15-06-63)

Martin Hall (writer)

Strange Report 08. REPORT 2475 REVENGE When a Man Hates (09-11-69)

Martin Woodhouse (writer)

The Avengers 2-01. Mr Teddy Bear (29-09-62) 2-24. A Chorus Of Frogs (09-03-63) 2-12. The Big Thinker (15-12-62) 3-08. Second Sight (16-11-63) 2-19. The Golden Eggs (02-02-63) 3-17. The Wringer (18-01-64) 4-24. A Sense Of History (12-03-66)

The Protectors 02 The Bottle Shop (04-04-64)

Maurice Marlowe (writer)

Ghost Squad 2-22. The Magic Bullet (16-03-63)

Max Marquis (writer)

Ghost Squad 1-07. Still Waters (21-10-61)

Interpol Calling 10 Dead On Arrival (16-11-59)

Max Stirling (writer)

Undermind 08 Puppets Of Evil (26-06-65)

Meade Roberts (writer)

Out Of The Unknown 1-07. Sucker Bait (15-11-65)

Mervyn Haisman (writer)

Doctor Who 38. The Abominable Snowman: Episode 2 (07-10-67) 41. The Web Of Fear: 5 Episodes (03-02-68) 44. The Dominators: 5 Episodes (10-08-68)

Michael Connor (writer)

Interpol Calling 35 Cargo Of Death (23-05-60)

Michael Cramoy (writer)

The Baron 10 The Legends of Ammak (30-11-66)

The Prisoner 11 It's Your Funeral (08-12-67)

The Saint 3-19. The Golden Frog (11-02-65) -04. The Smart Detective (22-07-65) 4-08. The Spanish Cow (19-08-65)

Michael Pertwee (writer)

Danger Man 1-28. Sabotage (14-05-61) 2-06. Fish On The Hook (17-11-64)

Man Of The World 1-04. The Runaways (20-10-62) 1-10. Portrait Of a Girl (01-12-62)

The Saint 5-15. The Persistent Patriots (06-01-67) 5-20. The Counterfeit Countess (03-03-67) 5-26. When Spring Is Sprung (02-06-67) 5-18. The Art Collectors (27-01-67)

Michael Winder (writer)

The Avengers 5-20 Dead Man's Treasure (21-10-67)

The Saint 5-14. Escape Route (30-12-66) 5-19. To Kill a Saint (24-02-67) 6-03. Legacy For The Saint (13-10-68)

Mike Pratt (writer)

Randall & Hopkirk (Deceased) 02 A Disturbing Case (28-09-69)

Mike Watts (writer)

Out Of The Unknown 1-06. Come Buttercup, Come Daisy, Come…? (08-11-65)

Morris Farhi (writer)

Strange Report 01. REPORT 5055 CULT Murder Shrieks Out (21-09-69)

Neville Dasey (writer)

Interpol Calling 15 Last Man Lucky (28-12-59)

Nicholas Palmer (writer)

Strange Report 12. REPORT 7931 SNIPER When Is Your Cousin Not? (14-12-69)

Norman Borisoff (writer)
Man Of The World 1-12. A Family Affair (15-12-62)
The Saint 1-07. The Arrow Of God (15-11-62) 1-09. The Effete Angler (29-11-62) 2-04. Teresa (10-10-63) 2-21. The Good Medicine (06-02-64) 2-26. The Ever Loving Spouse (12-03-64)
Norman Hudis (writer)
Danger Man 3-24. Koroshi (12-02-67) 3-25. Shinda Shima (26-02-67)
The Saint 3-10. The Imprudent Politician (10-12-64) 3-20. The Frightened Inn-Keeper (18-02-65) 4-01. The Chequered Flag (01-07-65) 4-03. The Crooked Ring (15-07-65) 4-05. The Persistent Parasites (29-07-65)
Oscar Brodny (writer)
Danger Man 1-10 An Affair Of State (13-11-60)
Paddy Manning O'Brine (writer)
The Saint 3-01 Miracle Tea Party (8-10-64) 3-15 Set-Up (14-01-65) 5-02 Interlude In Venice (7-10-66)
Pat & Jesse Lasky (writers)
The Saint 4-07. The Saint Bids Diamonds (12-08-65)
Pat Silver (writer)
Danger Man 3-19 Two Birds With One Bullet (10-03-66)
Patrick Campbell (writer)
Ghost Squad 1-04. Broken Doll (07-10-61)
Patrick McGoowan (writer)
The Prisoner 04 Free For All (20-10-67) 16. Once Upon a Time (25-01-67) 17. Fall Out (1-2-68)
Paul Erickson (writer)
Doctor Who 23. The Ark: 4 Episodes (05-03-66)
Out Of The Unknown 1-05. Time In Advance (01-11-65)
Interpol Calling 32 The Three Keys (02-05-60)
The Saint 3-04. The Scorpion (29-10-64) 3-11. The Hi-jackers (17-12-64) 3-13. The Damsel In Distress (31-12-64)
Peter Ling (writer)
Doctor Who 45. The Mind Robber: 5 Episodes (14-09-68)
Peter R Newman (writer)
Doctor Who 07. The Sensorites: 6 Episodes (20-06-64)
Peter Yeldham (writer)
Ghost Squad 2-16. Escape Route (16-02-63) 2-06. The Missing People (29-06-63)
Philip Broadley (writer)
The Champions 03. Reply Box 666 (09-10-68) 04. The Experiment (16-10-68) 09. The Iron Man (20-11-68) 15. The Gilded Cage (08-01-68) 17. A Case Of Lemmings (22-01-68)
Department S 02. The Trojan Tanker (16-03-69) 07. Handicap Dead (20-04-69) 09. Black Out (17-09-69) 12. The Treasure Of the Costa Del Sol (08-10-69) 13. The Man Who Got a New Face (15-10-69) 14. Les Fleurs Du Mal (22-10-69) 17. Dead Men Die Twice (12-11-69) 20. The Mysterious Man In The Flying Machine (10-12-69) 21. Death On Reflection (17-12-69) 27. A Fish Out Of Water (25-02-70)
Danger Man 2-08. The Battle Of The Cameras (01-12-64) 2-11. Don't Nail Him Yet (22-12-64) 2-12. A Date With Doris (29-12-64) 2-19. It's Up To The Lady (23-02-65) 3-22. The Paper Chase (31-03-66)
Man In a Suitcase 03. Day Of Execution (11-10-67) 07. Sweet Sue (08-11-67) 12. Find The Lady (13-12-67)
Out Of The Unknown 1-02. The Counterfeit Man (11-10-65)
Philip Chambers (writer)
The Avengers 3-04. The Nutshell (19-10-63) 6-26. Homicide & Old Lace (26-03-69)
Philip Leverne (writer)
The Avengers 4-03. The Cybernauts (16-10-65) 4-11. Man Eater Of Surrey Green (11-12-65) 4-12. Twos a Crowd (18-12-65) 4-16. Small Game For Big Hunters (15-1-65) 5-01. From Venus With Love (14-1-67) 5-02. The Fear Merchants (21-01-67) 5-03. Escape In Time (26-01-67) 5-04. See Through Man (4-2-67) 5-08. The Hidden Tiger (04-03-67) 5-09. The Correct Way To Kill (11-3-67) 5-14. Something Nasty In The Nursery (15-4-67) 5-16. Who's Who (29-4-67) 5-17. Return Of The Cybernauts (30-9-67) 5-18. Death's Door (7-10-67) 5-21. You Have Just Been Murdered (28-10-67) 5-24. Mission, Highly Improbable (18-11-67) 6-19. The Curious Case Of The Countless Clues (5-2-69) 6-

28. My Wildest Dream (7-4-69) 6-32. Get-a-Way (14-5-69)

Ghost Squad 2-08. The Man With The Delicate Hands (22-06-63) 2-05. The Retirement Of The Gentle Dove (30-03-63)

Phyllis Norman (writer)

The Avengers 3-11 The Golden Fleece (07-12-63)

Ralph Smart (writer)

The Champions 08. To Trap a Rat (13-11-68) 22. Get Me Out Of Here (26-02-69)

Danger Man 1-01. View From The Villa (11-09-60) 1-03. Josetta (25-09-60) 1-04. The Blue Veil (02-10-60) 1-06. The Girl In Pink Pyjamas (16-10-60) 1-08. The Lonely Chair (30-10-60) 1-09. The Sanctuary (06-11-60) 1-11. The Key (20-11-60) 1-13. The Prisoner (04-12-60) 1-15. Colonel Rodriguez (18-12-60) 1-16. The Island (01-01-61) 1-18. The Girl Who Likes G.I.'s (15-01-61) 1-19. Name, Date & Place (22-01-61) 1-20. The Vacation (29-01-61) 1-21. The Conspirators (05-02-61) 1-22. The Honeymooners (02-04-61) 1-23. The Gallows Tree (09-04-61) 1-24. The Relaxed Informer (16-04-61) 1-25. The Brothers (23-04-61) 1-27. Bury The Dead (07-05-61) 1-29. The Contessa (21-05-61) 1-30. The Leak (28-05-61) 1-31. The Trap (04-06-61) 1-33. Hired Assassin (18-06-61) 1-35. Find & Destroy (23-12-61) 1-37. The Nurse (06-01-61) 1-38. Dead Man Walks (13-01-62) 2-09. No Marks For Servility (8-12-64) 2-14. Such Men Are Dangerous (12-01-65) 2-16. A Room in The Basement (02-02-65) 3-02. A Very Dangerous Game (07-10-65) 3-06. The Mercenaries (04-11-65) 3-11. To Our Best Friend (9-12-65) 3-14. The Man Who Wouldn't Talk (30-12-65) 3-16. Dangerous Secret (13-01-66) 3-17. I Can Only Offer You Sherry (20-01-66) 3-20. I Am Afraid You Have The Wrong Number (17-3-66) 3-22. The Paper Chase (31-03-66)

Randall & Hopkirk (Deceased) 01. My Late Lamented Friend & Partner (21-09-69) 13. But What a Sweet Little Room (14-12-69)

Ray Austin (writer)

Randall & Hopkirk (Deceased) 05 That's How Murder Snowballs (19-10-69)

Ray Jenkins (writer)

Callan 2-05. Let's Kill Everybody (05-02-69) 2-09. Death Of a Friend (05-03-69)

Raymond Bowers (writer)

Danger Man 2-10. A Man To Be Trusted (15-12-64) 3-21. The Man With The Foot (24-03-66)

Man In a Suitcase 14 The Man Who Stood Still (27-12-67)

Raymond Menmuir (writer)

The Avengers 2-24 A Chorus Of Frogs (09-03-63)

Reed De Rouen (writer)

Man In a Suitcase 22 Jigsaw Man (21-02-67) 30 Night Flight To Andorra (17-04-67)

Rex Edwards (writer)

The Avengers 3-10 The Grandeur That Was Rome (30-11-63)

Richard Bates (writer)

The Avengers 3-26 Lobster Quadrille (21-03-64)

Richard Harris (writer)

Adam Adamant Lives! 08. The Last Sacrifice (18-08-66) 10. The Doomsday Plan (01-09-66) 13. The League Of Uncharitable Ladies (12-09-66)

The Avengers 5-06. The Winged Avenger (18-02-67) 6-02. Game (02-10-68)

Ghost Squad 2-15. The Last Jump (23-02-63)

The Saint 1-05. The Loaded Tourist (01-11-62) 1-06. The Pearls Of Peace (08-11-62)

Richard Levison (writer)

The Third Man 4-07. Diamond In the Rough (11-05-62)

Richmond Harding (writer)

The Avengers 2-01. Mr Teddy Bear (29-09-62) 2-07. The Mauritius Penny (10-11-62) 2-11. Traitor In Zebra (08-12-62) 2-14. Dead On Course (29-12-62) 2-16. Immortal Clay (12-01-63) 2-21. The White Dwarf (16-02-63) 2-25. Six Hands Across a Table (16-03-63)

Robert Banks Stewart (writer)

Adam Adamant Lives! 4 The Sweet Smell Of Disaster (14-07-66)

The Avengers 4-06 The Master Minds (06-11-65)

Callan 2-14 Nice People Die At Home (09-04-69)

Ghost Squad 1-06. Eyes Of The Bat (14-10-61)

Undermind 01. Instance One (08-05-65) 02. Flowers Of Havoc (15-05-65) 05. Too Many Enemies (05-

06-65)

Robert Holmes (writer)
Doctor Who 47. The Krotons: 4 Episodes (28-12-68) 49. The Space Pirates: Episode 2 (15-3-69)
Ghost Squad 1-11 The Green Shoes (29-12-61)
Undermind 10. Waves Of Sound (10-07-65) 11. End Signal (17-07-65)
The Saint 6-10 The Scales Of Justice (01-12-68)

Robert Muller (writer)
Man In a Suitcase 13 The Bridge (20-12-67)

Robert Stewart (writer)
Danger Man 1-13 The Prisoner (04-12-60)
Interpol Calling 14. The Man's a Clown (21-12-59) 16. No Flowers For Onno (04-01-59) 20. Game For Three Hands (01-02-60) 24. Finger Of Guilt (07-03-60) 25. The Girl With The Grey Hair (14-03-60) 29. White Blackmail (11-04-60) 30. A Foreign Body (18-04-60) 31. In The Swim (25-04-60) 32. The Three Keys (02-05-60) 33. Eight Days Inclusive (09-05-60) 34. Dressed To Kill (06-05-60) 36. Desert Hijack (30-05-60)

Robert Thompson (writer)
Man Of The World 1-01. Death Of a Conference (29-09-62) 1-09. The Mindreader (24-11-62) 1-12. A Family Affair (15-12-62)

Roger Marshall (writer)
The Avengers 3-05. Death Of a Batman (26-01-63) 3-07. The Gilded Cage (09-11-63) 3-18. Mandrake (25-01-64) 4-09. The Hour That Never Was (27-11-65) 4-10. Dial a Deadly Number (04-12-65) 4-14. Silent Dust (01-01-66) 4-15. Room Without a View (08-01-65) 5-19. The £50,000 Breakfast (14-10-67)
Public Eye 1-02. Nobody Kill Santa Claus (30-01-65) 1-12. The Morning Wasn't So Hot (10-04-65) 2-02. Don't Forget You're Mine (09-07-66) 2-07. Works With Chess, Not With Life (13-08-66) 3-09. The Bromsgrove Venus (16-03-68) 4-01. Welcome To Brighton? (30-07-69) 4-02. Divide & Conquer (06-08-69) 4-03. Paid In Full (13-08-69) 4-04. My Life's My Own (20-08-69) 4-05. Case For The Defence (27-08-69) 4-06. The Comedian's Graveyard (03-09-69) 4-07. A Fixed Address (19-06-69)

Roger Parkes (writer)
The Prisoner 12 A Change Of Mind (15-12-67)

Roger Woddis (writer)
The Prisoner 10 Hammer Into Anvil (01-12-67)
Strange Report 04. REPORT 2641 LONELY HEARTS Who Killed Dan Cupid? (12-10-69) 13. REPORT 4821 X-RAY Who Weeps For The Doctor (21-12-69)

Ronald Duncan (writer)
The Saint 4-09. The Old Treasure Story (26-08-65)

Roy Russell (writer)
The Saint 5-05. The Helpful Pirate (28-10-66)

Sam Neuman (writer)
Interpol Calling 39 Checkmate (20-06-60)

Stanley Miller (writer)
Out Of The Unknown 1-01 No Place Like Earth (4-10-65) 1-11 Thirteen To Centauraus (13-12-65)

Stanley R Greenburg (writer)
Man In a Suitcase 04. Variation On a Million Bucks Part 1 (18-10-67) 05. Variation On a Million Bucks Part 2 (25-10-67) 06. Man From The Dead (01-11-67) 10. All That Glitters (29-11-67) 22. Jigsaw Man (21-02-67)

Terence Maples (writer)
Strange Report 06. REPORT 3906 COVER-GIRLS Last Years Model (26-10-69)

Terrance Dicks (writer)
The Avengers 3-24. Concerto (07-03-64) 6-26. Homicide & Old Lace (26-03-69)
Doctor Who 50. The War Games: 10 Episodes (19-04-69)

Terrence Feely (writer)
Callan 2-14 Nice People Die At Home (09-04-69)
The Prisoner 15 The Girl Who Was Death (18-01-67)
The Saint 5-06 The Convenient Monster (04-11-66)

Terrence Frisby (writer)

Adam Adamant Lives! 3. More Deadly Than The Sword (07-07-66)

Terry Nation (writer)

The Avengers 6-09. Legacy Of Death (20-11-68) 6-10. Noon Doomsday (27-11-68) 6-16. Invasion Of The Earthman (15-01-69) 6-23. Take Me To Your Leader (05-03-69) 6-27. Thingamajig (16-04-69) 6-28. My Wildest Dream (07-04-69) 6-29. Requiem (16-04-69) 6-30. Take-Over (23-04-69)

The Baron 01. Diplomatic Immunity (28-09-66) 02. Epitaph For a Hero (05-10-66) 03. Something For a Rainy Day (12-10-66) 04. Red Horse, Red Rider (19-10-66) 06. Masquerade (Part 1) (02-11-66) 07. The Killing (Part 2) (09-11-66) 09. And Suddenly You're Dead (23-11-66) 13. Portrait Of Louisa (21-12-67) 14. There's Someone Close Behind You (28-12-67) 15. Storm Warning (Part 1) (04-01-67) 16. The Island (Part 2) (11-01-67) 17. Time To Kill (18-01-67) 21. The Seven Eyes Of Night (15-02-67) 22. Night Of The Hunter (22-02-67) 25. So Dark The Night (15-03-67) 27. Roundabout (29-03-67) 28. The Man Outside (05-04-67) 29. Countdown (12-04-67)

The Champions 21 The Body Snatchers (19-02-69)

Department S 03. Cellar Full Of Silence (23-3-69) 06 The Man In The Elegant Room (13-04-69)

Doctor Who 02. The Daleks: 6 Episodes (21-12-63) 05. The Keys Of Marinus: 6 Episodes (11-04-64) 10. Dalek Invasion Of Earth (1964) 16. The Chase: 6 Episodes (22-05-65) 19. Mission To The Unknown (09-10-65) 21. The Daleks' Master Plan: 3 Episodes (20-11-65)

The Saint 3-02. Lida (15-10-64) 3-03. Jeannine (22-10-64) 3-05. The Revolution Racket (05-11-64) 3-14. The Contact (07-01-65) 3-17. The Inescapable World (28-01-65) 3-18. The Sign Of The Claw (04-02-65) 3-21. Sibao (25-02-65) 3-22. The Crime Of The Century (04-03-65) 4-06. The Man Who Could No Die (05-08-65) 6-02. Invitation To Danger (06-10-68) 6-04. The Desperate Diplomat (20-10-68) 6-07. The Time To Die (10-11-68) 6-14. Where The Money Is (29-12-68)

Tom O'Grady (writer)

Interpol Calling 08 Diamond S.O.S. (02-11-59)

Troy Kennedy Martin (writer)

Out Of The Unknown 1-12. The Midas Plague (20-12-65)

Tudor Gates (writer)

Ghost Squad 2-21. Polsky (02-03-63)

Man Of The World 1-01. Death Of a Conference (29-9-62) 1-08. The Nature Of Justice (17-11-62)

Strange Report 02. REPORT 0649 SKELETON Let Sleeping Heroes Lie (28-09-69)

Tony Williamson (writer)

Adam Adamant Lives! 01. A Year For Scoundrels (20-06-66) 02. Death Has a Thousand Faces (30-06-66) 05. Allah Is Not Always With You (21-07-66) 07. To Set a Deadly Fashion (11-08-66) 11. Death By Appointment Only (08-9-66) 16. D Is For Destruction (13-6-66) 29. A Sinister Sort Of Service (25-0-67)

The Avengers 5-22. The Positive Negative Man (4-11-67) 6-03. Super Secret Cypher Snatch (09-10-68) 6-06. Whoever Shot George Oblique Stroke XR40? (30-10-68) 6-17. Killer (22-01-69) 6-20. Wish You Were Here (12-02-69) 6-22. Stay Tuned (26-02-69)

The Champions 11. The Dark Island (04-12-68) 16. Shadow Of The Panther (15-01-68) 24. Project Zero (12-03-69)

Danger Man 3-23 Not So Jolly Roger (07-04-66)

Department S 05. One Of Aircraft Is Empty (06-4-69) 08. A Ticket To Nowhere (27-04-69) 11. Who Plays The Dummy (01-10-69) 16. The Man From X (05-11-69) 24. The Bones Of Byrom Blain (28-1-70)

Randall & Hopkirk (Deceased) 04. Never Trust a Ghost (12-10-69) 07. Murder Ain't What It Used To Be (02-11-69) 08. Whoever Heard Of a Ghost Dying (09-11-69) 09. House On Haunted Hill (16-11-69) 10. When Did You Start To Stop Seeing Things? (23-11-69) 11. The Ghost Who Saved The Bank At Monte Carlo (30-11-69) 14. Who Killed Cock Robin? (21-12-69) 16. When The Spirit Moves You (02-01-70)

Victor Canning (writer)

Man In a Suitcase 20 Blind Spot (07-02-67)

Vince Powell (writer)

Adam Adamant Lives! 12. Beauty Is An Ugly Word (15-9-66) 15. The Village Of Evil (6-10-66)

Vincent Tilsley (writer)

The Prisoner 02. The Chimes Of Big Ben (06-10-67) 13. Do Not Forsake Me Oh My Darling (22-12-67)

Wilfred Greatorex (writer)
Danger Man 2-02. The Professionals (20-10-64) 2-05. Fair Exchange (10-11-64)
Man In a Suitcase 18 The Boston Square (24-01-67) 25 Property Of A Gentleman (13-03-67)
William Emms (writer)
Doctor Who 18. Galaxy 4: Air Lock (25-09-65)
William Link (writer)
The Third Man 4-07. Diamond In the Rough (11-05-62)
Wilton Schiller (writer)
Man Of The World 1-09. The Mindreader (24-11-62)

Credited Cast Members

Existing episodes only credited, no actors included who are not in person.

A

A.J. Brown (Cast Member)
The Avengers 4-16. Small Game For Big Hunters (15-01-65) 5-06. The Winged Avenger (18-02-67)
Out Of The Unknown 1-12. The Midas Plague (20-12-65)
Randall & Hopkirk (Deceased) 18. Could You Recognise The Man Again (16-01-70)
Achillies Georgiou (Cast Member)
The Avengers 6-02. Game (02-10-68)
Adrian Drotsky (Cast Member)
Out Of The Unknown 1-07. Sucker Bait (15-11-65)
Adrian Ropes (Cast Member)
The Avengers 4-20. The Danger Makers (12-02-66) 5-01. From Venus With Love (14-01-67) 6-06. Whoever Shot George Oblique Stroke XR40? (30-10-68)
Randall & Hopkirk (Deceased) 02. A Disturbing Case (28-09-69)
Adrienne Corri (Cast Member)
Adam Adamant Lives! 04. The Sweet Smell Of Disaster (14-07-66)
The Champions 23. The Night People (05-03-69)
Danger Man 2-15. Whatever Happened To George Foster (19-01-65) 2-18. The Ubiquitous Mr Lovegrove (16-02-65)
Department S: 13. The Man Who Got a New Face (15-10-69)
Randall & Hopkirk (Deceased) 03. All Work & No Pay (05-10-69)
Adrienne Hill (Cast Member)
Doctor Who 21. The Daleks' Master Plan: 3 Episodes (20-11-65)
Agath Angelos (Cast Member)
Man In A Suitcase 05. Variation On a Million Bucks Part 2 (25-10-67)
The Saint 6-15. Vendetta For The Saint Part 1 (05-01-68)
Aidan Turner (Cast Member)
The Saint 2-19. Luella (23-01-64)
Aileen Lewis (Cast Member)
The Avengers 3-01. Brief For Murder (28-09-63) 4-04. Death At Bargain Prices (23-10-65)
Aimee Delamain (Cast Member)
The Avengers 3-06. November Five (02-11-63) 6-25. Who Was That Man I Saw You With (19-03-69)
Aimi MacDonald (Cast Member)
The Avengers 5-17. Return Of The Cybernauts (30-09-67)
The Saint 6-15. Vendetta For The Saint Part 1 (05-01-68) 6-16. Vendetta For The Saint Part 2 (12-01-68)
Al Mancini (Cast Member)
Department S: 01. Six Days (09-03-69)
The Prisoner 06. The General (03-11-67)
Al Mulock (Cast Member)
Ghost Squad 2-12. Quarantine At Kavar (01-06-63)
The Protectors 07. It Could Happen Here (09-05-64)
Alan Beaton (Cast Member)
The Avengers 4-07. The Murder Market (13-11-65)
Alan Baulch (Cast Member)
Man In A Suitcase 10. All That Glitters (29-11-67)
Alan Bennion (Cast Member)
Doctor Who 48. The Seeds Of Death: 6 Episodes (25-01-69)
Alan Browning (Cast Member)
The Avengers 6-25. Who Was That Man I Saw You With (19-03-69)
The Saint 2-04. Teresa (10-10-63)

Alan Casley (Cast Member)
The Avengers 2-05. Mission To Montreal (27-10-62)
Alan Chuntz (Cast Member)
The Avengers 4-03. The Cybernauts (16-10-65) 4-11. Man Eater Of Surrey Green (11-12-65)
5-10. Never, Never Say Die (18-03-67)
Danger Man 3-17. I Can Only Offer You Sherry (20-01-66)
The Saint 4-07. The Saint Bids Diamonds (12-08-65)
Alan Curtis (Cast Member)
The Avengers 2-05. Mission To Montreal (27-10-62)
The Corridor People All Episodes (1966)
The Saint 3-09. The Death Penalty (03-12-64) 3-19. The Golden Frog (11-02-65)
Alan Downer (Cast Member)
Out Of The Unknown 3 -08. Little Black Bag (25-02-69)
The Saint 5-09. The Better Mouse Trap (25-11-66)
Alan Foss (Cast Member)
Adam Adamant Lives! 07. To Set a Deadly Fashion (11-08-66)
Alan Gerrard (Cast Member)
The Avengers 4-19. Quick-Quick Slow Death (05-02-66)
Strange Report 05. REPORT 8319 GRENADE What Price Change? (19-10-69)
Alan Gifford (Cast Member)
The Champions 11. The Dark Island (04-12-68)
Danger Man 1-29. The Contessa (21-05-61) 2-17. The Affair At Castelevara (09-02-65)
Interpol Calling 20. Game For Three Hands (01-02-60)
Man Of The World 1-12. A Family Affair (15-12-62)
Randall & Hopkirk (Deceased) 07. Murder Ain't What It Used To Be (02-11-69)
The Saint 1-03. The Careful Terrorist (18-10-62) 1-08. The Element Of Doubt (22-11-62)
Alan Haywood (Cast Member)
The Avengers 2-24. A Chorus Of Frogs (09-03-63) 3-07. The Gilded Cage (09-11-63)
The Saint 5-24. A Double In Diamonds (05-05-67) 5-24. A Double In Diamonds (05-05-67) 5-25. The
Power Artists (19-05-67)
Out Of The Unknown 1-06. Come Buttercup, Come Daisy, Come…? (08-11-65)
Alan Hockey (Cast Member)
Department S: 05. One Of Aircraft Is Empty (06-4-69)
Alan Johns (Cast Member)
Doctor Who 37. The Tomb Of The Cybermen: 4 Episodes (02-09-67)
Alan Judd (Cast Member)
Doctor Who 10. Dalek Invasion Of Earth (1964)
Alan Lake (Cast Member)
The Avengers 5-17. Return Of The Cybernauts (30-09-67)
Department S: 17. Dead Men Die Twice (12-11-69)
The Saint 5-12. Locate & Destroy (16-12-66)
Alan Mason (Cast Member)
The Avengers 2-13. Death Dispatch (22-12-62)
Strange Report 12. REPORT 7931 SNIPER When Is Your Cousin Not? (14-12-69)
Alan MacNaughton (Cast Member)
The Avengers 4-01. The Town Of No Return (02-10-65) 6-25. Who Was That Man I Saw You With
(19-03-69) *The Baron* 09. And Suddenly You're Dead (23-11-66) 12. The Maze (14-12-67)
The Champions 28. The Final Countdown (16-04-69)
Department S: 11. Who Plays The Dummy (01-10-69)
Randall & Hopkirk (Deceased) 21. The Ghost Talks (06-02-70)
The Saint 5-17. The Death Game (20-01-67) 6-03. Legacy For The Saint (13-10-68)
Strange Report 12. REPORT 7931 SNIPER When Is Your Cousin Not? (14-12-69)
Alan Meacham (Cast Member)
Department S: 13. The Man Who Got a New Face (15-10-69)
Alan Rolfe (Cast Member)
The Avengers 2-07. The Mauritius Penny (10-11-62)
Alan Rowe (Cast Member)
Doctor Who 33. The Moonbase: 2 Episodes (18-02-67)

Man Of The World 1-01. Death Of a Conference (29-09-62) 2-04. Jungle Mission (01-06-63)
The Saint 6-17. The Ex-King Of Diamonds (19-01-68)
Alan Tilvern (Cast Member)
Danger Man 1-06. The Girl In Pink Pyjamas (16-10-60)
Doctor Who 09. Planet Of Giants: 3 Episodes (31-10-64)
Interpol Calling 05. The Two Headed Monster (12-10-59)
Out Of The Unknown 1-01. No Place Like Earth (04-10-65)
The Saint 3-19. The Golden Frog (11-02-65)
Alan Watts (Cast Member)
Man In A Suitcase 15. Burden Of Proof (03-01-67)
Alan Wheatley (Cast Member)
The Avengers 6-25. Who Was That Man I Saw You With (19-03-69)
The Baron 23. The Edge Of Fear (01-03-67)
Danger Man 1-33. Hired Assassin (18-06-61) 2-14. Such Men Are Dangerous (12-01-65)
Department S: 08. A Ticket To Nowhere (27-04-69)
Doctor Who 02. The Daleks: 6 Episodes (21-12-63)
The Protectors 12. Channel Crossing (13-06-64)
Alan White (Cast Member)
The Champions 06. Operation Deep Freeze (30-10-68)
Danger Man 3-18. The Hunting Party (27-01-66)
Man In A Suitcase 04. Variation On a Million Bucks Part 1 (18-10-67)
Doctor Who 29. The Tenth Planet: 3 Episodes (08-10-66)
The Prisoner 08. Dance Of The Dead (17-11-67)
Alarice Gordon (Cast Member)
Danger Man: 3-22. The Paper Chase (31-03-66)
Alastair Hunter (Cast Member)
Man In A Suitcase 15. Burden Of Proof (03-01-67)
The Saint 5-06. The Convenient Monster (04-11-66)
Allan McClelland (Cast Member)
Strange Report 02. REPORT 0649 SKELETON Let Sleeping Heroes Lie (28-09-69)
Alban Blakelock (Cast Member)
The Avengers 2-18. Warlock (26-01-63)
Albert Lampert (Cast Member)
Out Of The Unknown 3-03. The Last Lonely Man (21-01-69)
Albert Lieven (Cast Member)
The Avengers 4-08. A Surfeit Of H2o (20-11-65)
Man Of The World 2-05. In The Picture (08-06-63)
Albert Shepherd (Cast Member)
Danger Man 3-19. Two Birds With One Bullet (10-03-66)
Department S: 24. The Bones Of Byrom Blain (28-01-70)
Strange Report 06. REPORT 3906 COVER-GIRLS Last Years Model (26-10-69)
Alec Coleman (Cast Member)
Adam Adamant Lives! 16. D Is For Destruction (13-06-66)
Alec Mango (Cast Member)
The Avengers 2-23. Conspiracy Of Silence (02-03-63) 4-12. Twos a Crowd (18-12-65)
Danger Man 1-35. Find & Destroy (23-12-61)
Ghost Squad 1-10. Catspaw (05-01-61)
Interpol Calling 19. Act Of Piracy (25-01-60)
The Saint 1-07. The Arrow Of God (15-11-62) 2-16. The Wonderful War (02-01-64) 3-05. The Revolution Racket (05-11-64)
The Third Man 2-06. Barcelona Passage (01-10-59)
Alec Ross (Cast Member)
The Avengers 3-01. Brief For Murder (28-09-63) 6-03. Super Secret Cypher Snatch (09-10-68)
Ghost Squad 2-21. Polsky (02-03-63)
Man Of The World 1-09. The Mindreader (24-11-62)
The Protectors 13. Cargo From Corinth (20-06-64)
Aleksander Browne (Cast Member)
Ghost Squad 2-19. Death of a Sportsman (26-01-63)

Alethea Charlton (Cast Member)
Doctor Who 01. An Unearthly Child: 2 Episodes (23-11-63)
Alex Gallier (Cast Member)
Department S: 27. A Fish Out Of Water (25-02-70)
Alex McCridle (Cast Member)
The Saint 3-19. The Golden Frog (11-02-65)
Alex McDonald (Cast Member)
The Avengers 3-16. The Little Wonders (11-01-64)
Undermind 03. The New Dimension (22-05-65)
Alex Scott (Cast Member)
Adam Adamant Lives! 09. Sing a Song Of Murder (25-08-66)
The Avengers 4-13. Too Many Christmas Trees (25-12-65) 6-02. Game (02-10-68)
The Baron 24. Long Ago & Far Away (08-03-67)
Danger Man 1-28. Sabotage (14-05-61) 2-02. The Professionals (20-10-64)
Department S: 14. Les Fleurs Du Mal (22-10-69)
Ghost Squad 1-03. Ticket For Blackmail (09-09-61)
Man In A Suitcase 14. The Man Who Stood Still (27-12-67)
Randall & Hopkirk (Deceased) 26. The Smile Behind The Veil (13-03-70)
The Saint 2-07. The Work Of Art (31-10-63) 5-22. Island Of Chance (07-04-67) 6-09. The House On Dragons Rock (24-11-68) 6-16. Vendetta For The Saint Part 2 (12-01-68)
Strange Report 05. REPORT 8319 GRENADE What Price Change? (19-10-69)
Undermind 08. Puppets Of Evil (26-06-65)
Alexander Archdale (Cast Member)
Danger Man The Lonely Chair (30-10-60)
Alexander Davion (Cast Member)
The Avengers 3-14. Dressed To Kill (28-12-63)
Man Of The World 2-04. Jungle Mission (01-06-63)
Out Of The Unknown 1-02. The Counterfeit Man (11-10-65)
The Saint 2-04. Teresa (10-10-63)
Alexanda Knox (Cast Member)
The Saint 1-02. The Latin Touch (11-10-62)
Alexander Stewart (Cast Member)
Danger Man 3-07. Judgement Day (11-11-65)
Alexandra Bastedo (Cast Member)
The Champions All Episodes
Department S: 13. The Man Who Got a New Face (15-10-69)
Randall & Hopkirk (Deceased) 08. Whoever Heard Of a Ghost Dying (09-11-69)
The Saint 3-22. The Crime Of The Century (04-03-65) 5-20. The Counterfeit Countess (03-3-67)
Alexandra Dane (Cast Member)
Ghost Squad 2-17. Mr Five Per Cent (06-04-63)
The Saint 2-21. The Good Medicine (06-02-64)
Alexandra Stevenson (Cast Member)
Man In A Suitcase 18. The Boston Square (24-01-67)
Alexandra Stewart (Cast Member)
The Saint 5-09. The Better Mouse Trap (25-11-66)
Alexis Chesnakov (Cast Member)
Ghost Squad 2-22. The Magic Bullet (16-03-63)
The Saint 5-03. The Russian Prisoner (14-10-66)
Alexis Kanner (Cast Member)
The Prisoner 14. Living In Harmony (29-12-67) 17. Fall Out (01-02-68)
The Saint 2-26. The Ever Loving Spouse (12-03-64)
Alf Joint (Cast Member)
Adam Adamant Lives! 29. A Sinister Sort Of Service (25-03-67)
The Avengers 4-21. A Touch Of Brimstone (19-02-66)
Danger Man 3-16. Dangerous Secret (13-01-66)
The Prisoner 04. Free For All (20-10-67)
Alfred Bell (Cast Member)
Strange Report 08. REPORT 2475 REVENGE When a Man Hates (09-11-69) 10. REPORT 8944

HAND A Matter Of Witchcraft (30-11-69)
Alfred Burke (Cast Member)
The Avengers 2-07. The Mauritius Penny (10-11-62) 4-17. The Girl From AUNTIE (22-01-66)
Danger Man 1-21. The Conspirators (05-02-61)
Ghost Squad 1-02. Bullet With My Name On It (16-09-61)
Interpol Calling 01. The Angola Bright's (14-09-59)
Man Of The World 1-05. The Frontier (27-10-62)
Public Eye: All Episodes
Randall & Hopkirk (Deceased) 03. All Work & No Pay (05-10-69)
The Saint 2-02. Starring The Saint (26-09-63) 2-16. The Wonderful War (02-01-64)
Alfred Maron (Cast Member)
The Avengers 6-10. Noon Doomsday (27-11-68)
Alice Fraser (Cast Member)
The Avengers 3-01. Brief For Murder (28-09-63)
Alister Williamson (Cast Member)
Adam Adamant Lives! 07. To Set a Deadly Fashion (11-08-66) The Avengers 5-07. The Living Dead (25-02-67)
Ghost Squad 2-20. P.G.7. (06-07-63)
The Saint 1-08. The Element Of Doubt (22-11-62)
Aliza Gur (Cast Member)
Ghost Squad 2-26. Sabotage (20-04-63)
Allan Cuthbertson (Cast Member)
The Avengers 4-04. Death At Bargain Prices (23-10-65) 5-18. Death's Door (07-10-67) 6-03. Super Secret Cypher Snatch (09-10-68)
Callan 2-13. The Worst Soldier I Ever Saw (02-04-69)
The Champions 04. The Experiment (16-10-68)
Danger Man 1-16. The Island (01-01-61)
Man In A Suitcase 21. No Friend Of Mine (14-02-67)
The Saint 5-26. When Spring Is Sprung (02-06-67)
The Third Man 2-06. Barcelona Passage (01-10-59)
Allan McClelland (Cast Member)
The Avengers 2-12. The Big Thinker (15-12-62)
The Saint 2-15. The Benevolent Burglary (26-12-63)
Alphonse Martell (Cast Member)
The Third Man 1-25. How To Buy a Country (24-09-59)
Alethea Charlton (Cast Member)
Doctor Who 17. The Time Meddler: 4 Episodes (03-07-65)
Alfred Bell (Cast Member)
Strange Report 09. REPORT 1021 SHRAPNEL The Wish In the Dream (23-11-69)
Alvaro Fontana (Cast Member)
Danger Man 2-10. A Man To Be Trusted (15-12-64) 2-12. A Date With Doris (29-12-64)
The Saint 3-19. The Golden Frog (11-02-65)
Amanda Barrie (Cast Member)
Danger Man 3-24. Koroshi (12-02-67)
Amelia Bayntun (Cast Member)
Adam Adamant Lives! 13. The League Of Uncharitable Ladies (12-09-66)
Amy Dalby (Cast Member)
The Avengers 6-14. The Interrogators (01-01-69)
Annabella Johnston (Cast Member)
Out Of The Unknown 3-03. The Last Lonely Man (21-01-69)
Andre Boulay (Cast Member)
The Saint 1-04. The Covetous Headsman (25-10-62) 2-03. Judith (03-10-63)
Andre Charisse (Cast Member)
The Protectors 12. Channel Crossing (13-06-64)
The Saint 5-01. The Queens Ransom (30-09-66)
Andre Dakar (Cast Member)
Danger Man 1-39. Deadline (20-01-62)
Andre Maranne (Cast Member)

Ghost Squad 1-05. High Wire (30-09-61) 2-07. Lost in Transit (15-06-63)
Interpol Calling 06. The Long Weekend (19-10-59)
Doctor Who 33. The Moonbase: 2 Episodes (18-02-67)
Man Of The World 2-05. In The Picture (08-06-63)
The Protectors 06. The Stamp Collection (02-05-64)
The Saint 2-14. The Bunco Artists (19-12-63) 2-15. The Benevolent Burglary (26-12-63)
Andre Morell (Cast Member)
The Avengers 3-05. Death Of a Batman (26-01-63) 4-04. Death At Bargain Prices (23-10-65)
Danger Man 2-17. The Affair At Castelevara (09-02-65)
The Saint 3-20. The Frightened Inn-Keeper (18-2-65) 3-22. The Crime Of The Century (4-3-65)
Andrea Van Gyseghem (Cast Member)
Danger Man 2-05. Fair Exchange (10-11-64)
The Prisoner 11. It's Your Funeral (08-12-67)
The Saint 5-27. The Gadic Collection (22-06-67)
Andreas Lysandrou (Cast Member)
Danger Man 2-19. It's Up To The Lady (23-02-65)
Man In A Suitcase 05. Variation On a Million Bucks Part 2 (25-10-67)
Andreas Maladrinos (Cast Member)
Danger Man 1-01. View From The Villa (11-09-60) 3-22. The Paper Chase (31-03-66)
Ghost Squad 2-09. Hot Money (25-05-63)
Man Of The World 1-02. Masquerade In Spain (06-10-62)
The Saint 2-24. Sophia (24-02-64) 5-12. Locate & Destroy (16-12-66) 5-27. The Gadic Collection (22-06-67)
Andrew Andreas (Cast Member)
Adam Adamant Lives! 05. Allah Is Not Always With You (21-07-66)
Andrew Crawford (Cast Member)
Danger Man 1-23. The Gallows Tree (09-04-61)
Andrew Downie (Cast Member)
Danger Man 1-36. Under the Lake (30-12-61)
Man Of The World 1-07. The Highland Story (10-11-62)
Andrew Fauds (Cast Member)
Danger Man 1-37. The Nurse (06-01-61) 3-23. Not So Jolly Roger (07-04-66)
The Protectors All Episodes (1964)
Andrew Keir (Cast Member)
The Avengers 5-02. The Fear Merchants (21-01-67) 6-32. Get-a-Way (14-05-69)
The Champions 10. The Ghost Plane (27-11-68)
The Saint 6-10. The Scales Of Justice (01-12-68)
Andrew Laurence (Cast Member)
The Avengers 5-23. Murdersville (11-11-67)
Danger Man 3-03. Sting In The Tail (14-10-65)
Andrew Robertson (Cast Member)
Adam Adamant Lives! 10. The Doomsday Plan (01-09-66)
Andrew Sachs (Cast Member)
Randall & Hopkirk (Deceased) 17. Somebody Just Walked Over My Grave (09-01-70)
The Saint 1-05. The Loaded Tourist (01-11-62)
Andy Alston (Cast Member)
The Avengers 1-06. Girl On The Trapeze (11-02-61)
Andy Brewer (Cast Member)
Public Eye 1-02. Nobody Kill Santa Claus (30-01-65)
Andy Devine (Cast Member)
Callan 2-04. The Little Bits & Pieces Of Love (29-01-69)
Andy Ho (Cast Member)
Adam Adamant Lives! 03. More Deadly Than The Sword (07-07-66)
The Baron 15. Storm Warning (Part 1) (04-01-67)
The Champions 11. The Dark Island (04-12-68)
Danger Man 1-32. The Actor (11-06-61)
Out Of The Unknown 2-03. Lambda One (20-10-66)
Angela Browne (Cast Member)

The Avengers 2-15. Intercrime (05-01-63)
Danger Man 1-06. The Girl In Pink Pyjamas (16-10-60)
Ghost Squad 1-03. Ticket For Blackmail (09-09-61) 1-02. Bullet With My Name On It (16-09-61) 1-01. Hong Kong Story (23-09-61) 1-05. High Wire (30-09-61) 1-04. Broken Doll (07-10-61) 1-06. Eyes Of The Bat (14-10-61) 1-07. Still Waters (21-10-61) 1-08. Assassin (28-10-61) 1-13. Death From a Distance (04-11-61) 1-09. Million Dollar Ransom (11-11-61) 1-11 The Green Shoes (29-12-62) 1-10. Catspaw (05-01-61)
Man In A Suitcase 06. Man From The Dead (01-11-67)
The Prisoner 12. A Change Of Mind (15-12-67)
The Saint 2-05. The Elusive Elishaw (17-10-63)
Angela Douglas (Cast Member)
The Avengers 6-29. Requiem (16-04-69)
The Saint 5-17. The Death Game (20-01-67)
Angela Lovell (Cast Member)
The Baron 10. The Legends of Ammak (30-11-66)
Department S: 13. The Man Who Got a New Face (15-10-69)
Danger Man 3-14. The Man Who Wouldn't Talk (30-12-65)
Department S: 05. One Of Aircraft Is Empty (06-4-69)
Man In A Suitcase 08. Essay In Evil (15-11-67)
Undermind 03. The New Dimension (22-05-65)
Angela Morant (Cast Member)
Callan 2-14. Nice People Die At Home (09-04-69)
Angela Scoular (Cast Member)
The Avengers 6-03. Super Secret Cypher Snatch (09-10-68)
Angela White (Cast Member)
Ghost Squad 1-13. Death From a Distance (04-11-61)
Angelo Muscat (Cast Member)
The Prisoner 01. Arrival (29-09-67) 02. The Chimes Of Big Ben (06-10-67) 03. A.B. & C. (13-10-67) 04. Free For All (20-10-67) 05. The Schizoid Man (27-10-67) 06. The General (03-11-67) 08. Dance Of The Dead (17-11-67) 09. Checkmate (14-11-67) 10. Hammer & Anvil (01-12-67) 11. It's Your Funeral (08-12-67) 12. A Change Of Mind (15-12-67) 16. Once Upon a Time (25-01-67) 17. Fall Out (01-02-68)
Angharad Rees (Cast Member)
The Avengers 6-13. They Keep Killing Steed (18-12-68)
Angus Lennie (Cast Member)
The Saint 2-01. The Fellow Traveller (19-09-63)
Anita Sharp-Bolster (Cast Member)
Danger Man 2-20. Have a Glass of Wine (02-03-65)
The Saint 1-02. The Latin Touch (11-10-62)
Anita West (Cast Member)
Danger Man 3-08. The Outcast (18-11-65)
The Saint 1-08. The Element Of Doubt (22-11-62)
Ann Barrass (Cast Member)
The Baron 11. Samurai West (07-12-66)
The Prisoner 16. Once Upon a Time (25-01-67)
Ann Bell (Cast Member)
The Baron 18. A Memory Of Evil (25-01-67)
Danger Man 3-11. To Our Best Friend (09-12-65)
Department S: 19. The Duplicated Man (03-12-69)
The Saint 3-17. The Inescapable World (28-01-65) 5-18. The Art Collectors (27-01-67)
Ann Castle (Cast Member)
Randall & Hopkirk (Deceased) 24. Vendetta For a Dead Man (27-02-70)
Ann Davis (Cast Member)
Doctor Who 10. Dalek Invasion Of Earth (1964)
Ann Firbank (Cast Member)
Danger Man 1-16. The Island (01-01-61)
Strange Report 13. REPORT 4821 X-RAY Who Weeps For The Doctor (21-12-69)
Ann Gillis (Cast Member)

Man Of The World 2-07. The Prince (22-06-63)
The Saint 2-18. The Romantic Matron (16-01-64) 4-05. The Persistent Parasites (29-07-65)
Ann Hamilton (Cast Member)
The Avengers 5-22. The Positive Negative Man (4-11-67)
Ann Heffernan (Cast Member)
Danger Man 2-20. Have a Glass of Wine (02-03-65)
Ann Holloway (Cast Member)
Department S: 28. The Soup Of The Day (04-03-70)
Ann Jay (Cast Member)
The Avengers 2-12. The Big Thinker (15-12-62)
Ann Lancaster (Cast Member)
Out Of The Unknown 1-06. Come Buttercup, Come Daisy, Come…? (08-11-65)
Ann Lynn (Cast Member)
Callan 2-09. Death Of a Friend (05-03-69)
The Baron 03. Something For a Rainy Day (12-10-66)
The Champions 21. The Body Snatchers (19-02-69)
Danger Man 2-20. Have a Glass of Wine (02-03-65)
Ghost Squad 2-03. Sentences Of Death (04-05-63)
Public Eye 2-07. Works With Chess, Not With Life (13-08-66)
The Saint 5-26. When Spring Is Sprung (02-06-67)
Ann Mitchell (Cast Member)
The Protectors 14. The Reluctant Thief (27-06-64)
Ann Moorish (Cast Member)
The Protectors All Episodes (1964)
Ann Rye (Cast Member)
The Avengers 6-21. Love All (19-02-69)
Ann Sidney (Cast Member)
The Avengers 5-06. The Winged Avenger (18-02-67)
Ann Taylor (Cast Member)
The Avengers 1-15. The Frighteners (27-11-61)
Ann Tirard (Cast Member)
Doctor Who 12. The Romans: 4 Episodes (16-01-65)
The Saint 5-27. The Gadic Collection (22-06-67)
Anna Carteret (Cast Member)
The Saint 6-19. Portrait Of Brenda (02-02-69)
Anna Gaylor (Cast Member)
Danger Man 1-18. The Girl Who Likes GI's (15-01-61)
Anna Mai (Cast Member)
Adam Adamant Lives! 03. More Deadly Than The Sword (07-07-66)
Danger Man 3-25. Shinda Shima (26-02-67)
Anna Matisse (Cast Member)
Department S: 17. Dead Men Die Twice (12-11-69)
Anna May Wong (Cast Member)
Danger Man 1-26. The Journey Ends Halfway (30-04-61)
Anna Quayle (Cast Member)
The Avengers 5-09. The Correct Way To Kill (11-03-67)
Anna Sharkey (Cast Member)
The Avengers 2-18. Warlock (26-01-63)
Anna Wing (Cast Member)
Public Eye 4-05. Case For The Defence (27-08-69)
Annabelle Lee (Cast Member)
Strange Report 13. REPORT 4821 X-RAY Who Weeps For The Doctor (21-12-69)
Annabel Maule (Cast Member)
Interpol Calling 15. Last Man Lucky (28-12-59)
Anne Blake (Cast Member)
Danger Man 3-19. Two Birds With One Bullet (10-03-66)
Department S: 06. The Man In The Elegant Room (13-04-69)
Ghost Squad 2-08. The Man With The Delicate Hands (22-06-63)

The Saint 5-06. The Convenient Monster (04-11-66)
The Third Man 2-02. One Kind Word (07-09-59)
Anne Carroll (Cast Member)
Ghost Squad 2-13. The Desperate Diplomat (18-05-63)
Anne Chapman (Cast Member)
Man In A Suitcase 28. Three Blinks Of The Eyes (03-04-67)
Anne Cropper (Cast Member)
The Protectors 05. The Loop Men (25-04-64)
Anne Cunningham (Cast Member)
The Avengers 4-25. How To Succeed…. At Murder (19-03-66)
Anne De Vigier (Cast Member)
Randall & Hopkirk (Deceased) 13. But What a Sweet Little Room (14-12-69)
The Saint 6-19. Portrait Of Brenda (02-02-69)
Anne Godfrey (Cast Member)
The Avengers 2-09. The Sell Out (24-11-62)
The Protectors 11. Who Killed Lazoryck? (06-06-64)
The Saint 6-06. The Double Take (03-11-68)
Undermind 08. Puppets Of Evil (26-06-65)
Anne Jay (Cast Member)
The Avengers 2-13. Death Dispatch (22-12-62)
Anne Kristen (Cast Member)
Adam Adamant Lives! 09. Sing a Song Of Murder (25-08-66)
Anne Lawson (Cast Member)
The Saint 4-04. The Smart Detective (22-07-65)
Out Of The Unknown 1-12. The Midas Plague (20-12-65)
Anne Ridler (Cast Member)
Doctor Who 43. The Wheel in Space: 2 Episodes (11-05-68)
Public Eye 4-01. Welcome To Brighton? (30-07-69)
Anne Rutter (Cast Member)
The Avengers 6-03. Super Secret Cypher Snatch (09-10-68) 6-26. Homicide & Old Lace (26-03-69)
Anne Sharp (Cast Member)
The Champions 23. The Night People (05-03-69)
The Baron 28. The Man Outside (05-04-67)
Randall & Hopkirk (Deceased) 01. My Late Lamented Friend & Partner (21-09-69)
The Saint 1-07. The Arrow Of God (15-11-62) 2-07. The Work Of Art (31-10-63) 2-20. The Lawless Lady (30-01-64)
Anne Wakefield (Cast Member)
Ghost Squad 1-05. High Wire (30-09-61)
Anneke Wills (Cast Member)
The Avengers 5-19. The £50,000 Breakfast (14-10-67)
Doctor Who 29. The Tenth Planet: 3 Episodes (08-10-66) 32. The Underwater Menace: 2 Episodes (21-01-67) 33. The Moonbase: 2 Episodes (18-02-67) 35. The Faceless Ones Episode 1 (08-04-67)
The Saint 5-05. The Helpful Pirate (28-10-66) 3-14. Dressed To Kill (28-12-63)
Strange Report all episodes (1969)
Annette Andre (Cast Member)
Adam Adamant Lives! 12. Beauty Is An Ugly Word (15-09-66)
The Avengers 3-18. Mandrake (25-01-64)
The Baron 27. Roundabout (29-03-67)
The Prisoner 11. It's Your Funeral (08-12-67)
Randall & Hopkirk (Deceased) 25 episodes (1969)
The Saint 3-06. The Saint Steps In (12-11-64) 3-07. The Loving Brothers (19-11-64) 4-02. The Abductors (8-7-65) 5-19. To Kill a Saint (24-02-67) 6-09. House On Dragons Rock (24-11-68)
Annette Carell (Cast Member)
The Avengers 5-02. The Fear Merchants (21-01-67)
The Baron 24. Long Ago & Far Away (08-03-67)
Man In A Suitcase 09. The Girl Who Never Was (22-11-67)
The Prisoner 03. A.B. & C. (13-10-67)

The Saint 4-05. The Persistent Parasites (29-07-65)
Annette Kerr (Cast Member)
The Avengers 2-10. Death On The Rocks (01-12-62)
Annie Ross (Cast Member)
The Saint 3-23. The Happy Suicide (11-03-65)
Anouska Hempel (Cast Member)
The Avengers 3-04. The Nutshell (19-10-63)
Anthea Wyndham (Cast Member)
The Avengers 3-14. Dressed To Kill (28-12-63)
The Saint 2-20. The Lawless Lady (30-01-64)
Anthony Ainley (Cast Member)
The Avengers 6-10. Noon Doomsday (27-11-68)
Department S: 08. A Ticket To Nowhere (27-04-69)
Anthony Baird (Cast Member)
The Avengers 2-08. Death Of Great Dane (17-11-62) 3-01. Brief For Murder (28-09-63)
Danger Man 2-19. It's Up To The Lady (23-02-65)
Randall & Hopkirk (Deceased) 19. A Sentimental Journey (23-01-70)
Anthony Bate (Cast Member)
The Avengers 1-20. Tunnel Of Fear (5-8-61) 6-19 Curious Case Of The Countless Clues (5-2-69)
The Champions 19. The Mission (05-02-69)
Out Of The Unknown 2-04. Level Seven (27-10-66)
The Saint 2-05. The Elusive Elishaw (17-10-63) 3-10. The Imprudent Politician (10-12-64) 6-09. The House On Dragons Rock (24-11-68)
Anthony Blackshaw (Cast Member)
Adam Adamant Lives! 16. D Is For Destruction (13-06-66)
The Avengers 3-25. Espirit de Corps (14-3-64) 2-07. The Mauritius Penny (10-11-62) 6-03. Super Secret Cypher Snatch (09-10-68)
The Baron 07. The Killing (Part 2) (09-11-66)
The Protectors 06. The Stamp Collection (02-05-64)
The Saint 6-09. The House On Dragons Rock (24-11-68) 6-12. The Fiction Makers Part 2 (15-12-68)
Anthony Booth (Cast Member)
The Avengers 2-12. The Big Thinker (15-12-62)
The Saint 3-16. The Rhine Maiden (21-01-65) 5-03. The Russian Prisoner (14-10-66)
Anthony Bushell (Cast Member)
Danger Man 1-18. The Girl Who Likes GI's (15-01-61)
Anthony Chinn (Cast Member)
Danger Man 1-22. The Honeymooners (02-04-61) 1-26. The Journey Ends Halfway (30-04-61)
3-02. A Very Dangerous Game (07-10-65)
Anthony Dawes
The Avengers 3-22. The Outside-In Man (22-02-64) 5-11. Epic (25-03-67)
The Saint 5-25. The Power Artists (19-05-67)
Out Of The Unknown 1-12. The Midas Plague (20-12-65)
Anthony Dawson (Cast Member)
Danger Man 1-12. The Sisters (27-11-60) 1-29. The Contessa (21-05-61) 2-11. Don't Nail Him Yet (22-12-64) 3-02. A Very Dangerous Game (07-10-65)
The Saint 1-07. The Arrow Of God (15-11-62)
Anthony Dutton (Cast Member)
The Avengers 6-08 All Done With Mirrors (13-11-68) 5-17. Return Of The Cybernauts (30-9-67)
Department S: 15. The Shift That Never Was (25-10-69)
Anthony Higgins (Cast Member)
Strange Report 05. REPORT 8319 GRENADE What Price Change? (19-10-69)
Anthony Hopkins (Cast Member)
Department S: 23. A Small War Of Nerves (21-01-70)
Anthony Jacobs (Cast Member)
Danger Man 1-02. Time to Kill (18-11-60)
Doctor Who 25. The Gunfighters: 4 Episodes (30-04-66)
Ghost Squad 2-07. Lost in Transit (15-06-63) Interpol Calling 32. The Three Keys (02-05-60)
The Saint 1-12. The Charitable Countess (20-12-62)

Anthony Lang (Cast Member)
The Avengers 4-07. The Murder Market (13-11-65)
Anthony Marlowe (Cast Member)
Ghost Squad 2-01. Interrupted Requiem (2-2-63) 2-02. East Of Mandalay (09-02-63) 2-06. The Missing People (29-06-63) 2-15. The Last Jump (23-2-63) 2-19. Death of a Sportsman (26-01-63) 2-21. Polsky (02-03-63) 2-18. The Heir Apparent (09-03-63) 2-22. The Magic Bullet (16-03-63) 2-05. The Retirement Of The Gentle Dove (30-3-63) 2-26. Sabotage (20-4-63) 2-25. The Thirteenth Girl (27-4-63) 2-03. Sentences Of Death (04-5-63) 2-10. The Grand Duchess (11-5-63) 2-13. The Desperate Diplomat (18-5-63) 2-09. Hot Money (25-5-63) 2-07. Lost in Transit (15-6-63)
Randall & Hopkirk (Deceased) 16. When The Spirit Moves You (02-01-70)
Anthony Morton (Cast Member)
 Ghost Squad 2-06. The Missing People (29-06-63)
The Saint 3-12. The Unkind Philanthropist (24-12-64)
Anthony Newlands (Cast Member)
The Avengers 4-10. Dial a Deadly Number (04-12-65) 6-02. Game (02-10-68)
The Champions 22. Get Me Out Of Here (26-02-69)
Danger Man 3-17. I Can Only Offer You Sherry (20-01-66)
The Protectors 08. Freedom! (16-05-64)
The Saint 1-12. The Charitable Countess (20-12-62) 2-21. The Good Medicine (06-02-64) 6-16. Vendetta For The Saint Part 2 (12-01-68)
Anthony Nicholls (Cast Member)
The Avengers 2-20. School For Traitors (09-02-63) 6-06. Whoever Shot George Oblique Stroke XR40? (30-10-68)
The Champions 01-30 All Episodes
Department S: 26. The Ghost Of Mary Burnham (18-02-70)
Man In A Suitcase 13. The Bridge (20-12-67)
The Saint 2-25. The Gentle Ladies (05-03-64) 5-07. The Angel's Eye (11-11-66)
Anthony Quayle (Cast Member)
Man Of The World 2-02. The Enemy (18-05-63)
The Saint 2-17. The Noble Sportsman (09-01-64)
Strange Report all episodes (1969)
Anthony Roye (Cast Member)
The Avengers 6-31. Pandora (30-04-69)
Anthony Ruth (Cast Member)
Adam Adamant Lives! 01 A Year For Scoundrels (20-06-66)
The Avengers 2-09. The Sell Out (24-11-62)
Anthony Sagar (Cast Member)
The Avengers 6-30. Take-Over (23-04-69)
Ghost Squad 2-11. A First Class Way To Die (13-07-63)
Randall & Hopkirk (Deceased) 01. My Late Lamented Friend & Partner (21-09-69)
Anthony Sheppard (Cast Member)
The Andromeda Breakthrough 2-1. Cold Front (28-06-62)
The Avengers 6-13. They Keep Killing Steed (18-12-68)
The Saint 6-20. The World Beater (09-02-69)
Anthony Stambouleih (Cast Member)
The Saint 6-17. The Ex-King Of Diamonds (19-01-68)
Anthony Sweeney (Cast Member)
Out Of The Unknown 2-04. Level Seven (27-10-66)
Anthony Valentine (Cast Member)
The Avengers 5-05. The Bird Who Knew Too Much (11-02-67) 6-17. Killer (22-01-69)
Callan 1-01. The Good Ones Are Dead (08-07-67) 1-06. You Should Have Got Here Sooner (12-08-67) 2-01. Red Knight, White Knight (08-01-69) 2-02. The Most Promising Girl Of Her Year (15-01-69) 2-04. The Little Bits & Pieces Of Love (29-01-69) 2-05. Let's Kill Everybody (05-02-69) 2-06. Heir Apparent (12-02-69) 2-09. Death Of a Friend (05-03-69) 2-13. The Worst Soldier I Ever Saw (02-04-69) 2-14. Nice People Die At Home (09-04-69)
Department S: 28. The Soup Of The Day (04-03-70)
Anthony Viccars (Cast Member)
Danger Man 1-03. Josetta (25-09-60) 1-10. An Affair Of State (13-11-60)

Anton Diffring (Cast Member)
The Barron 05. Enemy Of The State (26-10-66)
Ghost Squad 1-13. Death From a Distance (04-11-61)
Strange Report 16. REPORT 4977 Square Root Of Evil (11-01-70)
Anton Rodgers (Cast Member)
The Champions 03. Reply Box 666 (09-10-68)
Danger Man: 2-01. Yesterday's Enemies (13-10-64)
Department S: 05. One Of Aircraft Is Empty (06-4-69)
Man In A Suitcase 04. Variation On a Million Bucks Part 1 (18-10-67) 05. Variation On a Million Bucks Part 2 (25-10-67)
The Prisoner 05. The Schizoid Man (27-10-67)
Randall & Hopkirk (Deceased) 16. When The Spirit Moves You (02-01-70)
The Saint 5-24. A Double In Diamonds (05-05-67)
Anthony Jochim (Cast Member)
The Third Man 1-24. A Pocketful Of Sin (01-04-60)
Anthony Woodruff (Cast Member)
Out Of The Unknown 3-03. The Last Lonely Man (21-01-69)
Antony Scott (Cast Member)
Department S: 20. The Mysterious Man In The Flying Machine (10-12-69)
April Olrich (Cast Member)
The Avengers 2-17. Box Of Tricks (19-01-63)
April Wilding (Cast Member)
Danger Man: 2-01. Yesterday's Enemies (13-10-64)
Araby Lockhart (Cast Member)
The Saint 6-17. The Ex-King Of Diamonds (19-01-68)
Archie Duncan (Cast Member)
Ghost Squad 2-24. Gertrude (13-04-63)
The Protectors 05. The Loop Men (25-04-64)
Arne Gordon (Cast Member)
Doctor Who 13. The Web Planet: 6 Episodes (13-02-65)
Out Of The Unknown 1-12. The Midas Plague (20-12-65)
Arnold Bell (Cast Member)
Interpol Calling 39. Checkmate (20-06-60)
Arnold Chazen (Cast Member)
Doctor Who 33. The Moonbase: 2 Episodes (18-02-67)
Arnold Diamond (Cast Member)
The Avengers 5-16. Who's Who (29-04-67) 6-24. Fog (12-03-69)
The Baron 21. The Seven Eyes Of Night (15-02-67) 30. Farewell To Yesterday (19-04-67)
Danger Man 2-04. The Galloping Major (03-11-64)
Department S: 13. The Man Who Got a New Face (15-10-69)
Ghost Squad 2-18. The Heir Apparent (09-03-63) 2-07. Lost in Transit (15-06-63)
Interpol Calling 07. You Can't Die Twice (26-10-59) 32. The Three Keys (02-05-60)
Randall & Hopkirk (Deceased) 23. The Trouble With Women (20-02-70)
The Saint 2-15. The Benevolent Burglary (26-12-63) 3-09. The Death Penalty (03-12-64) 4-05. The Persistent Parasites (29-7-65) 4-08. The Spanish Cow (19-08-65) 5-09. The Better Mouse Trap (25-11-66)
Arnold Marle (Cast Member)
Ghost Squad 2-10. The Grand Duchess (11-05-63)
Arnold Ridley (Cast Member)
The Avengers 5-10. Never, Never Say Die (18-03-67)
Arnold Yarrow (Cast Member)
Ghost Squad 2-19. Death of a Sportsman (26-01-63)
The Andromeda Breakthrough 3 Episodes (1962)
Art Thomas (Cast Member)
The Avengers 4-21. A Touch Of Brimstone (19-02-66)
Arthur Blake (Cast Member)
Doctor Who 13. The Web Planet: 6 Episodes (13-02-65)
Arthur Brough (Cast Member)

Adam Adamant Lives! 06. The Happy Embalmers (04-06-66)
Arthur Cox (Cast Member)
The Avengers 5-01. From Venus With Love (14-01-67) 6-06. Whoever Shot George Oblique Stroke XR40? (30-10-68)
Department S: 25. Spencer Bodily Is 60 Years Old (11-02-70)
Doctor Who 44. The Dominators: 5 Episodes (10-08-68)
Arthur Gomez (Cast Member)
Interpol Calling 01. The Angola Bright's (14-09-59)
The Saint 3-09. The Death Penalty (03-12-64)
Arthur Griffiths (Cast Member)
The Avengers 2-13. Death Dispatch (22-12-62)
Man In A Suitcase 29. Castle In The Clouds (10-04-67)
Arthur Gross (Cast Member)
The Avengers 4-04. Death At Bargain Prices (23-10-65)
The Prisoner 10. Hammer & Anvil (01-12-67)
The Saint 5-07. The Angel's Eye (11-11-66)
Arthur Hewlett (Cast Member)
The Avengers 2-09. The Sell Out (24-11-62)
The Baron 10. The Legends of Ammak (30-11-66)
The Saint 2-05. The Elusive Elishaw (17-10-63)
Arthur Howard (Cast Member)
Strange Report 16. REPORT 4977 Square Root Of Evil (11-01-70)
Arthur Howell (Cast Member)
Man In A Suitcase 04. Variation On a Million Bucks Part 1 (18-10-67) 05. Variation On a Million Bucks Part 2 (25-10-67) 06. Man From The Dead (01-11-67)
Arthur Lawrence (Cast Member)
Interpol Calling 31. In The Swim (25-04-60)
Arthur Lovegrove (Cast Member)
The Avengers 3-22. The Outside-In Man (22-02-64)
Strange Report 16. REPORT 4977 Square Root Of Evil (11-01-70)
Arthur Lowe (Cast Member)
The Avengers 5-20. Dead Man's Treasure (21-10-67)
Arthur Pentelow (Cast Member)
The Avengers 3-21. Build a Better Mousetrap (15-02-64) 6-07. False Witness (06-01-68)
The Baron 12. The Maze (14-12-67)
Arthur White (Cast Member)
The Prisoner 11. It's Your Funeral (08-12-67)
Assad Obeid (Cast Member)
The Andromeda Breakthrough 4 Episodes (1962)
Astor Sklair (Cast Member)
Pathfinders In Space 7 Episodes (1960)
Pathfinders To Venus 3 Episodes (1961)
Pathfinders To Mars 4 Episodes (1961)
Astro Morris (Cast Member)
The Avengers 2-23. Conspiracy Of Silence (2-3-63) 4-25. How To Succeed At Murder (19-3-66)
The Baron 02. Epitaph For a Hero (05-10-66)
Athene Seyler (Cast Member)
The Avengers 4-11. Man Eater Of Surrey Green (11-12-65)
Aubrey Morris (Cast Member)
The Avengers 4-14. Silent Desire (01-01-66)
The Champions 02. The Invisible Man (02-10-68)
City Beneath The Sea 2 episodes (1962)
Danger Man: 2-01. Yesterday's Enemies (13-10-64) 2-17. The Affair At Castelevara (09-02-65)   3-22. The Paper Chase (31-03-66)
Man In A Suitcase 04. Variation On a Million Bucks Part 1 (18-10-67) 05. Variation On a Million Bucks Part 2 (25-10-67)
The Prisoner 08. Dance Of The Dead (17-11-67)
The Saint 3-02. Lida (15-10-64)

Aubrey Richards (Cast Member)
The Avengers 4-02. The Gravediggers (09-01-65) 6-02. Game (02-10-68)
Doctor Who 37. The Tomb Of The Cybermen: 4 Episodes (02-09-67)
Audine Leith (Cast Member)
Man In A Suitcase 27. Who's Mad Now (27-03-67)
Audrey Bayley (Cast Member)
Ghost Squad 2-23. The Menacing Mazurka (23-03-63)
Audrey Noble (Cast Member)
Adam Adamant Lives! 07. To Set a Deadly Fashion (11-08-66)
Public Eye 2-02. Don't Forget You're Mine (09-07-66)
Aubrey Richards (Cast Member)
Undermind 04. Death In England (29-05-65) 05. Too Many Enemies (05-06-65)
Austin Trevor (Cast Member)
Interpol Calling 22. The Heiress (15-02-60)
Avice Landone (Cast Member)
The Avengers 3-19. The Secrets Broker (01-02-64)
The Saint 2-25. The Gentle Ladies (05-03-64)

64

B

Bakshi Prem (Cast Member)
Danger Man 2-06. Fish On The Hook (17-11-64) 3-07. Judgement Day (11-11-65)
The Saint 5-27. The Gadic Collection (22-06-67)
Balbina (Cast Member)
Interpol Calling 06. The Long Weekend (19-10-59) 30. A Foreign Body (18-04-60)
Ballard Berkley (Cast Member)
Ghost Squad 2-05. The Retirement Of The Gentle Dove (30-03-63)
Balu Patel (Cast Member)
Danger Man 2-07. The Colonels Daughter (24-11-64)
Barbara Bates (Cast Member)
The Saint 1-05. The Loaded Tourist (01-11-62)
Barbara Chilcott (Cast Member)
Danger Man 1-39. Deadline (20-01-62)
Barbara Evans (Cast Member)
Ghost Squad 1-12. Princess (12-01-61)
Barbara Graley (Cast Member)
Danger Man 3-18. The Hunting Party (27-01-66)
Barbara Grimes (Cast Member)
Callan 2-06. Heir Apparent (12-02-69)
Barbara Joss (Cast Member)
Doctor Who 13. The Web Planet: 6 Episodes (13-02-65)
Barbara Keogh (Cast Member)
Ghost Squad 2-04. The Golden Silence (08-06-63)
Barbara Leake (Cast Member)
Danger Man 2-15. Whatever Happened To George Foster (19-01-65)
Barbara Lott (Cast Member)
Danger Man 2-13. That's Two Of Us Sorry (05-01-64)
Barbara Mullen (Cast Member)
The Saint 2-25. The Gentle Ladies (05-03-64)
Barbara Murray (Cast Member)
Danger Man 1-12. The Sisters (27-11-60)
Department S: 17. Dead Men Die Twice (12-11-69)
The Saint 2-08. Iris (07-11-63) 2-21. The Good Medicine (06-02-64)
Strange Report 15. REPORT 4407 No Choice For The Donor (04-01-70)
Barbara New (Cast Member)
Public Eye 4-01. Welcome To Brighton? (30-07-69)
Barbara Ogivie (Cast Member)
The Saint 2-14. The Bunco Artists (19-12-63)
Barbara Roscoe (Cast Member)
The Avengers 4-07. The Murder Market (13-11-65)
The Saint 1-04. The Covetous Headsman (25-10-62)
Barbara Shelley (Cast Member)
The Avengers 5-01. From Venus With Love (14-01-67)
Danger Man 1-01. View From The Villa (11-09-60) 1-14. The Traitor (11-12-60)
Ghost Squad 2-13. The Desperate Diplomat (18-05-63)
Interpol Calling 39. Checkmate (20-06-60)
Man In A Suitcase 10. All That Glitters (29-11-67)
The Saint 1-04. The Covetous Headsman (25-10-62)
Barbara Steele (Cast Member)
Danger Man 3-12. The Man On The Beach (16-12-65)
Barbara Yu Ling (Cast Member)
The Avengers 3-11. The Golden Fleece (07-12-63)
Danger Man 1-22. The Honeymooners (02-04-61) 3-25. Shinda Shima (26-02-67)
The Prisoner 01. Arrival (29-09-67)
Bari Jonson (Cast Member)

The Avengers 6-26. Homicide & Old Lace (26-03-69)
Danger Man 3-05. Loyalty Always Pays (28-10-65)
Barrie Ingham (Cast Member)
The Avengers 5-21. You Have Just Been Murdered (28-10-67)
The Baron 24. Long Ago & Far Away (08-03-67)
Danger Man 1-20. The Vacation (29-01-61)
Randall & Hopkirk (Deceased) 24. Vendetta For a Dead Man (27-02-70)
Undermind 09. Test For The Future (03-07-65)
Barrie Rutter (Cast Member)
Public Eye 4-07. A Fixed Address (19-06-69)
Barry Andrews (Cast Member)
Department S: 25. Spencer Bodily Is 60 Years Old (11-02-70)
The Saint 6-18. The Man Who Gambled With Life (26-01-68)
Barry Ashton (Cast Member)
Doctor Who 33. The Moonbase: 2 Episodes (18-02-67)
Barry Evans (Cast Member)
Undermind 02. Flowers Of Havoc (15-05-65)
Barry Fletcher (Cast Member)
Out Of The Unknown 3-03. The Last Lonely Man (21-01-69)
Barry Jackson (Cast Member)
A For Andromeda 1-6. The Face Of The Tiger (07-11-61)
Adam Adamant Lives! 12. Beauty Is An Ugly Word (15-09-66)
Doctor Who 12. The Romans: 4 Episodes (16-01-65) 19. Mission To The Unknown (09-10-65)
Barry Jones (Cast Member)
The Saint 2-26. The Ever Loving Spouse (12-03-64)
Barry Justice (Cast Member)
The Protectors 01. Landscape With Bandits (28-03-64)
Barry Keegan (Cast Member)
Danger Man 1-09. The Sanctuary (06-11-60)
Ghost Squad 1-09. Million Dollar Ransom (11-11-61)
The Saint 2-15. The Benevolent Burglary (26-12-63) 3-02. Lida (15-10-64)
Barry Letts (Cast Member)
The Avengers 3-17. The Wringer (18-01-64)
City Beneath The Sea 2 episodes (1962)
Barry Lineham (Cast Member)
Adam Adamant Lives! 03. More Deadly Than The Sword (07-07-66)
The Andromeda Breakthrough 4 Episodes (1962)
The Avengers 3-11. The Golden Fleece (07-12-63) 6-32. Get-a-Way (14-05-69)
The Baron 24. Long Ago & Far Away (08-03-67)
Danger Man 2-05. Fair Exchange (14-03. The Crooked Ring (15-07-65)
Public Eye 1-12. The Morning Wasn't So Hot (10-04-65)
Barry Morse (Cast Member)
The Saint 5-04. The Reluctant Revolution (21-10-66)
Barry Shawzin (Cast Member)
The Baron 30. Farewell To Yesterday (19-04-67)
Ghost Squad 2-02. East Of Mandalay (09-02-63)
Man In A Suitcase 26. The Revolutionaries (20-03-67)
The Saint 3-19. The Golden Frog (11-02-65) 4-04. The Smart Detective (22-07-65)
Barry Stanton (Cast Member)
Callan 2-09. Death Of a Friend (05-03-69)
The Saint 6-18. The Man Who Gambled With Life (26-01-68)
Barry Warren (Cast Member)
The Avengers 4-13. Too Many Christmas Trees (25-12-65) 6-07. False Witness (06-01-68)
Undermind 11. End Signal (17-07-65)
Barry Wilsher (Cast Member)
The Avengers 2-02. Propellant 23 (06-10-62)
The Saint 2-25. The Gentle Ladies (05-03-64)
Bart Allison (Cast Member)

Doctor Who 12. The Romans: 4 Episodes (16-01-65)
Bart Collins (Cast Member)
Man Of The World 2-05. In The Picture (08-06-63)
Bartlett Mullins (Cast Member)
Adam Adamant Lives! 01 A Year For Scoundrels (20-06-66)
Danger Man 1-34. The Deputy Coyannis Story (16-12-61)
The Prisoner 12. A Change Of Mind (15-12-67)
The Saint 2-26. The Ever Loving Spouse (12-03-64)
Basil Clarke (Cast Member)
Man In A Suitcase 24. Which Way Did He Go, McGill (06-03-67)
Randall & Hopkirk (Deceased) 12. For The Girl Who Has Everything (07-12-69)
Basil Dignam (Cast Member)
The Avengers 3-21. Build a Better Mousetrap (15-02-64)
The Champions 02. The Invisible Man (02-10-68)
Department S: 05. One Of Aircraft Is Empty (06-4-69) 18. The Perfect Operation (26-12-69) 19. The Duplicated Man (03-12-69)
Ghost Squad 2-08. The Man With The Delicate Hands (22-06-63)
Interpol Calling 32. The Three Keys (02-05-60)
Man In A Suitcase 09. The Girl Who Never Was (22-11-67) 18. The Boston Square (24-01-67)
The Prisoner 09. Checkmate (14-11-67)
The Protectors 10. The Deadly Chameleon (30-5-64)
Randall & Hopkirk (Deceased) 10. When Did You Start To Stop Seeing Things? (23-11-69)
The Saint 2-22. The Invisible Millionaire (13-02-64) 3-01. The Miracle Tea Party (8-10-64)
Strange Report 05. REPORT 8319 GRENADE What Price Change? (19-10-69)
Basil Henson (Cast Member)
The Champions 28. The Final Countdown (16-04-69)
Basil Hoskins (Cast Member)
The Avengers 3-22. The Outside-In Man (22-02-64)
The Prisoner 10. Hammer & Anvil (01-12-67)
Basil Howes (Cast Member)
The Saint 1-08. The Element Of Doubt (22-11-62)
Bay White (Cast Member)
Out Of The Unknown 1-03. Stranger In the Family (18-10-65)
Bee Duffell (Cast Member)
The Prisoner 08. Dance Of The Dead (17-11-67) 09. Checkmate (14-11-67)
Bek Nelson (Cast Member)
The Third Man 1-25. How To Buy a Country (24-09-59)
Bella Emberg (Cast Member)
Undermind 10. Waves Of Sound (10-07-65)
Ben Carruthers (Cast Member)
The Champions 11. The Dark Island (04-12-68)
Ben Howard (Cast Member)
The Avengers 3-04. The Nutshell (19-10-63)
Benedicta Leigh (Cast Member)
Man Of The World 1-13. Shadow Of the Wall (22-12-62)
Benn Simmons (Cast Member)
The Avengers 1-15. The Frighteners (27-11-61) 2-08. Death Of Great Dane (17-11-62)
Benny Nightingale (Cast Member)
The Avengers 1-15. The Frighteners (27-11-61)
Danger Man 3-05. Loyalty Always Pays (28-10-65)
Beresford Williams (Cast Member)
Danger Man 3-01. The Black Book (30-09-65)
Bernard Archard (Cast Member)
The Avengers 4-06. The Master Minds (06-11-65) 6-05. Split (23-10-68)
Danger Man 1-29. The Contessa (21-05-61) 3-17. I Can Only Offer You Sherry (20-01-66)
Man Of The World 1-08. The Nature Of Justice (17-11-62)
Bernard Barnsley (Cast Member)
The Avengers 3-07. The Gilded Cage (09-11-63)

Bernard Bresslaw (Cast Member)
Danger Man 3-08. The Outcast (18-11-65)
Bernard Brown (Cast Member)
The Avengers 3-24. Concerto (07-03-64)
Bernard Cribbins (Cast Member)
The Avengers 4-17. The Girl From AUNTIE (22-01-66) 6-11. Look (Stop Me If You've Heard This One) But There Were These Two Fellers (04-12-68)
Interpol Calling 28. Slow Boat To Amsterdam (04-04-60)
Bernard Davies (Cast Member)
Danger Man 2-05. Fair Exchange (10-11-64)
Bernard Goldman (Cast Member)
The Avengers 2-01. Mr Teddy Bear (29-09-62)
The Protectors 06. The Stamp Collection (02-05-64)
Bernard G High (Cast Member)
Doctor Who 41. The Web Of Fear: 5 Episodes (03-02-68)
The Saint 6-20. The World Beater (09-02-69)
Bernard Holley (Cast Member)
Doctor Who 37. The Tomb Of The Cybermen: 4 Episodes (02-09-67)
Bernard Horsfall (Cast Member)
The Avengers 4-03. The Cybernauts (16-10-65) 5-02. The Fear Merchants (21-01-67) 6-13. They Keep Killing Steed (18-12-68)
Department S: 01. Six Days (09-03-69)
Pathfinders To Mars 2 Episodes (1961)
The Saint 5-17. The Death Game (20-01-67)
Bernard Kay (Cast Member)
The Avengers 2-04. Bullseye (20-10-62)
The Champions 07. The Survivors (06-11-68)
The Baron 09. And Suddenly You're Dead (23-11-66)
Doctor Who 10. Dalek Invasion Of Earth (1964) 14. The Crusade: 2 Episodes (27-03-65)
Out Of The Unknown 1-06. Come Buttercup, Come Daisy, Come…? (08-11-65)
Randall & Hopkirk (Deceased) 17. Somebody Just Walked Over My Grave (09-01-70)
Bernard Hunter (Cast Member)
Ghost Squad 1-11 The Green Shoes (29-12-62)
Bernard Lee (Cast Member)
The Baron 06. Masquerade (Part 1) (02-11-66) 07. The Killing (Part 2) (09-11-66)
The Champions 21. The Body Snatchers (19-02-69)
Danger Man 2-15 Whatever Happened To George Foster (19-1-65) 3-21 The Man With The Foot (24-03-66)
Man In A Suitcase 09. The Girl Who Never Was (22-11-67)
Strange Report 05. REPORT 8319 GRENADE What Price Change? (19-10-69)
Bernard Severn (Cast Member)
The Avengers 6-24. Fog (12-03-69)
Bernard Spear (Cast Member)
Ghost Squad 2-03. Sentences Of Death (04-05-63)
Bernard Stone (Cast Member)
Callan 1-06. You Should Have Got Here Sooner (12-08-67)
Bernice Rassin (Cast Member)
The Avengers 2-13. Death Dispatch (22-12-62)
Bert Palmer (Cast Member)
The Avengers 2-16. Immortal Clay (12-01-63)
Beryl Baxter (Cast Member)
The Avengers 3-22. The Outside-In Man (22-02-64)
The Protectors 06. The Stamp Collection (02-05-64)
Undermind 11. End Signal (17-07-65)
Beryl Nesbitt (Cast Member)
Adam Adamant Lives!: 02. Death Has a Thousand Faces (30-06-66)
Bessie Love (Cast Member)
Man Of The World 1-10. Portrait Of a Girl (01-12-62)

Randall & Hopkirk (Deceased) 10. When Did You Start To Stop Seeing Things? (23-11-69)
Beth Owen (Cast Member)
The Avengers 5-17. Return Of The Cybernauts (30-09-67)
Bette Bourne (Cast Member)
The Avengers 4-24. A Sense Of History (12-03-66) 6-04. You'll Catch Your Death (16-10-68)
The Baron 22. Night Of The Hunter (22-02-67)
The Prisoner 06. The General (03-11-67)
The Saint 5-25. The Power Artists (19-05-67)
Bettina Jonic (Cast Member)
Man In A Suitcase 19. Somebody Loses, Somebody… Wins? (31-01-67)
Bettine Le Beau (Cast Member)
Danger Man 1-18. The Girl Who Likes GI's (15-01-61)
The Prisoner 03. A. B. & C. (13-10-67)
Bettine Milne (Cast Member)
The Avengers 2-15. Intercrime (05-01-63)
Betty Cardno (Cast Member)
Adam Adamant Lives! 13. The League Of Uncharitable Ladies (12-09-66)
The Saint 5-10. Little Girl Lost (02-12-66)
Betty Henderson (Cast Member)
Ghost Squad 2-04. The Golden Silence (08-06-63)
Betty McDowall (Cast Member)
The Corridor People Victim as Red (1966)
Interpol Calling 22. The Heiress (15-02-60)
The Prisoner 06. The General (03-11-67)
The Saint 3-07. The Loving Brothers (19-11-64)
Betty Woolfe (Cast Member)
Randall & Hopkirk (Deceased) 13. But What a Sweet Little Room (14-12-69)
Beverly Garland (Cast Member)
Danger Man 1-27. Bury The Dead (07-05-61)
Beverly Winn (Cast Member)
Randall & Hopkirk (Deceased) 17. Somebody Just Walked Over My Grave (09-01-70)
Bill Brandon (Cast Member)
Man In A Suitcase 01. Brainwash (27-09-67)
Bill Burns (Cast Member)
Adam Adamant Lives! 16. D Is For Destruction (13-06-66)
The Avengers 6-18. The Morning After (29-10-69)
Bill Cartwright (Cast Member)
The Protectors 11. Who Killed Lazoryck? (06-06-64)
The Saint 2-18. The Romantic Matron (16-01-64)
Bill Cummings (Cast Member)
The Avengers 6-18. The Morning After (29-10-69)
The Champions 05. Happening (23-10-68)
The Prisoner 03. A.B. & C. (13-10-67) 14. Living In Harmony (29-12-67)
Bill Dean (Cast Member)
Man In A Suitcase 09. The Girl Who Never Was (22-11-67)
Bill Edwards (Cast Member)
Danger Man 1-18. The Girl Who Likes G.I.'s (15-01-61)
Man Of The World 2-07. The Prince (22-06-63)
Bill Fraser (Cast Member)
The Avengers 4-16. Small Game For Big Hunters (15-01-65)
Bill Haydn (Cast Member)
The Avengers 2-18. Warlock (26-01-63)
Bill Horsley (Cast Member)
Ghost Squad 2-18. The Heir Apparent (09-03-63)
Bill Kerr (Cast Member)
Doctor Who 40. The Enemy Of The World: 6 Episodes (23-12-67)
Ghost Squad 1-01. Hong Kong Story (23-09-61)
Bill Lyons (Cast Member)

Adam Adamant Lives! 29. A Sinister Sort Of Service (25-03-67)
Out Of The Unknown 3 -08. Little Black Bag (25-02-69)
Bill MacIlwrath (Cast Member)
Ghost Squad 2-24. Gertrude (13-04-63)
Bill Maxam (Cast Member)
The Avengers 1-20. Tunnel Of Fear (05-08-61)
Bill Nagy (Cast Member)
The Avengers 2-21. The White Dwarf (16-02-63)
The Champions 11. The Dark Island (04-12-68)
Danger Man 1-29. The Contessa (21-05-61) 1-33. Hired Assassin (18-06-61) 2-21. The Mirror's New (09-03-65)
Department S: 02. The Trojan Tanker (16-03-69)
Ghost Squad 1-10. Catspaw (05-01-61)
Interpol Calling 12. The Chinese Mask (07-12-59) 24. Finger Of Guilt (07-03-60)
Out Of The Unknown 1-07. Sucker Bait (15-11-65)
The Saint 1-02. The Latin Touch (11-10-62) 1-08. The Element Of Doubt (22-11-62) 2-21. The Good Medicine (06-02-64)
Bill Nick (Cast Member)
The Prisoner 14. Living In Harmony (29-12-67)
Bill Owen (Cast Member)
Man In A Suitcase 13. The Bridge (20-12-67)
Bill Reed (Cast Member)
The Avengers 4-21. A Touch Of Brimstone (19-02-66)
Randall & Hopkirk (Deceased) 16. When The Spirit Moves You (02-01-70)
Bill Risley (Cast Member)
The Avengers 4-03. The Cybernauts (16-10-65)
Bill Shine (Cast Member)
The Avengers 6-11. Look (Stop Me If You've Heard This One) But There Were These Two Fellers (04-12-68)
Bill Starkey (Cast Member)
Doctor Who 15. The Space Museum: 4 Episodes (24-04-65)
Bill Treacher (Cast Member)
Undermind 02. Flowers Of Havoc (15-05-65)
Out Of The Unknown 1-01. No Place Like Earth (04-10-65)
Bill Wallis (Cast Member)
The Avengers 4-21. A Touch Of Brimstone (19-02-66) 5-22. Positive Negative Man (4-11-67)
Billy Cornelius (Cast Member)
The Protectors 06. The Stamp Collection (02-05-64)
Randall & Hopkirk (Deceased) 19. A Sentimental Journey (23-01-70)
Billy Dean (Cast Member)
Out Of The Unknown 1-07. Sucker Bait (15-11-65)
Billy Hamon (Cast Member)
Public Eye 4-03. Paid In Full (13-08-69) 4-04. My Lifes My Own (20-08-69) 4-05. Case For The Defence (27-08-69)
Billy John (Cast Member)
The Avengers 2-12. The Big Thinker (15-12-62) 3-01. Brief For Murder (28-09-63) 3-06. November Five (02-11-63) 3-10. The Grandeur That Was Rome (30-11-63) 3-19. The Secrets Broker (01-02-64)
Billy Milton (Cast Member)
The Avengers 2-08. Death Of Great Dane (17-11-62)
The Baron 03. Something For a Rainy Day (12-10-66)
The Protectors 01. Landscape With Bandits (28-03-64)
Randall & Hopkirk (Deceased) 18. Could You Recognise The Man Again (16-01-70)
Billy Russell (Cast Member)
Strange Report 02. REPORT 0649 SKELETON Let Sleeping Heroes Lie (28-09-69)
Blake Butler (Cast Member)
Out Of The Unknown 1-10. Some Lapse In Time (06-12-65)
The Saint 6-06. The Double Take (03-11-68)
Bob Anderson (Cast Member)

Danger Man 3-17. I Can Only Offer You Sherry (20-01-66)
Bob Bryan (Cast Member)
Pathfinders To Venus 3 Episodes (1961)
Bob Kanter (Cast Member)
The Saint 1-06. The Pearls Of Peace (08-11-62)
Bob Raymond (Cast Member)
The Avengers 3-04. The Nutshell (19-10-63) 3-10. The Grandeur That Was Rome (30-11-63)
Bob Sessions (Cast Member)
Department S: 25. Spencer Bodily Is 60 Years Old (11-02-70)
Bobbie Oswald (Cast Member)
Strange Report 06. REPORT 3906 COVER-GIRLS Last Years Model (26-10-69)
Bobby R Naidoo (Cast Member)
Danger Man 1-26. The Journey Ends Halfway (30-04-61) 1-28. Sabotage (14-05-61)
Man Of The World 1-05. The Frontier (27-10-62)
Boris Karloff (Cast Member)
Out Of This World 02. Little Lost Robot (07-07-1962)
Boscoe Holder (Cast Member)
Danger Man 2-22. Parallel Lines Sometimes Meet (16-03-65)
The Saint 3-21. Sibao (25-02-65)
Brandon Brady (Cast Member)
The Champions 11. The Dark Island (04-12-68)
Department S: 03. Cellar Full Of Silence (23-03-69)
The Saint 2-13. The Sporting Chance (12-12-63)
Brenda Cowling (Cast Member)
The Avengers 3-09. The Medicine Men (23-11-63)
Brenda Dunrich (Cast Member)
Danger Man 2-02. The Professionals (20-10-64)
Brenda Kempner (Cast Member)
The Saint 6-08. The Master Plan (17-11-68)
Brenda Lawrence (Cast Member)
Danger Man 2-16. A Room in The Basement (02-02-65)
Man In A Suitcase 03. Day Of Execution (11-10-67) 22. Jigsaw Man (21-02-67)
Brenda Saunders (Cast Member)
Public Eye 4-04. My Life's My Own (20-08-69) 4-05. Case For The Defence (27-08-69)
Brewster Mason (Cast Member)
The Saint 3-09. The Death Penalty (03-12-64)
Brian Badcoe (Cast Member)
The Avengers 6-02. Game (02-10-68)
Department S: 16. The Man From X (05-11-69)
The Saint 6-10. The Scales Of Justice (01-12-68)
Brian Blessed (Cast Member)
The Avengers 5-12. The Superlative Seven (01-04-67) 6-18. The Morning After (29-10-69)
Ghost Squad 1-10. Catspaw (05-01-61)
Randall & Hopkirk (Deceased) 11. The Ghost Who Saved The Bank At Monte Carlo (30-11-69)
Brian Coburn (Cast Member)
The Saint 6-03. Legacy For The Saint (13-10-68)
Brian Croucher (Cast Member)
Public Eye 4-03. Paid In Full (13-08-69)
Brian Dent (Cast Member)
Ghost Squad 2-08. The Man With The Delicate Hands (22-06-63)
Brian Forster (Cast Member)
Doctor Who 50. The War Games: 10 Episodes (19-04-69)
Brian Gilmer (Cast Member)
Adam Adamant Lives! 18. Black Echo (07-01-67)
Danger Man 3-10. Are You Going To Be More Permanent? (02-12-65)
Brian Haines (Cast Member)
The Avengers 5-08. The Hidden Tiger (04-03-67)
Ghost Squad 2-02. East Of Mandalay (09-02-63)

Brian Hankins (Cast Member)
The Avengers 3-19. The Secrets Broker (01-02-64)
The Protectors 04. No Forwarding Address (18-04-64)
Brian Harrison (Cast Member)
Department S: 08. A Ticket To Nowhere (27-04-69)
The Saint 5-24. A Double In Diamonds (05-05-67) 6-04. The Desperate Diplomat (20-10-68)
Brian Hawksley (Cast Member)
Man In A Suitcase 16. The Whisper (10-01-67)
Brian Hayes (Cast Member)
Adam Adamant Lives! 11. Death By Appointment Only (08-09-66)
Brian Jackson (Cast Member)
Danger Man 1-15. Colonel Rodriguez (18-12-60)
Ghost Squad 2-01. Interrupted Requiem (02-02-63)
Brian Mason (Cast Member)
The Avengers 2-26. Killer Whale (23-03-63) 3-10. The Grandeur That Was Rome (30-11-63)
Brian McDermott (Cast Member)
Department S: 07. Handicap Dead (20-04-69)
Public Eye 1-12. The Morning Wasn't So Hot (10-04-65)
The Saint 4-05. The Persistent Parasites (29-07-65)
Brian McNeil (Cast Member)
The Avengers 3-23. The Charmers (29-02-64)
Brian Nash (Cast Member)
Interpol Calling 17. Mr George (11-01-60)
Brian Nissen (Cast Member)
Ghost Squad 2-08. The Man With The Delicate Hands (22-06-63)
Brian Oulton (Cast Member)
The Avengers 3-23. The Charmers (29-02-64) 6-21. Love All (19-02-69)
Department S: 03. Cellar Full Of Silence (23-03-69)
Randall & Hopkirk (Deceased) 04. Never Trust a Ghost (12-10-69)
The Saint 2-01. The Fellow Traveller (19-09-63)
Brian Peck (Cast Member)
Man In A Suitcase 03. Day Of Execution (11-10-67)
Brian Phelan (Cast Member)
The Baron 05. Enemy Of The State (26-10-66)
Danger Man 2-13. That's Two Of Us Sorry (05-01-64)
Brian Proudfoot (Cast Member)
Doctor Who 12. The Romans: 4 Episodes (16-01-65)
Brian Rawlinson (Cast Member)
The Baron 26. The Long, Long Day (22-03-67)
Danger Man 1-24. The Relaxed Informer (16-04-61)
The Protectors 07. It Could Happen Here (09-05-64)
Brian Tully (Cast Member)
The Saint 6-18. The Man Who Gambled With Life (26-01-68)
Brian Vaughan (Cast Member)
The Avengers 2-18. Warlock (26-01-63)
Ghost Squad 2-07. Lost in Transit (15-06-63)
Brian Weske (Cast Member)
Danger Man 2-20. Have a Glass of Wine (02-03-65) 3-11. To Our Best Friend (09-12-65)
The Saint 2-02. Starring The Saint (26-09-63)
Brian Wilde (Cast Member)
The Avengers 5-02. The Fear Merchants (21-01-67)
The Baron 13. Portrait Of Louisa (21-12-67)
The Protectors 03. Happy Is The Loser (11-04-64)
Brian Worth (Cast Member)
The Champions 03. Reply Box 666 (09-10-68)
Danger Man 2-17. The Affair At Castelevara (09-02-65) 3-08. The Outcast (18-11-65) 3-14. The Man Who Wouldn't Talk (30-12-65)
Department S: 23. A Small War Of Nerves (21-01-70)

Interpol Calling 18. The Thousand Mile Alibi (18-01-60)
The Prisoner 07. Many Happy Returns (10-11-67)
The Saint 4-04. The Smart Detective (22-07-65)
Brian Wright (Cast Member)
Man Of The World 2-03. Double Exposure (25-05-63)
Bridget Armstrong (Cast Member)
Man In A Suitcase 22. Jigsaw Man (21-02-67)
Bridget Brice (Cast Member)
Department S: 08. A Ticket To Nowhere (27-04-69)
Public Eye 2-07. Works With Chess, Not With Life (13-08-66)
Bridget McConnell (Cast Member)
Ghost Squad 1-02. Bullet With My Name On It (16-09-61)
Out Of The Unknown 1-10. Some Lapse In Time (06-12-65)
Brigit Forsyth (Cast Member)
Doctor Who 36. The Evil Of The Daleks: Episode 2 (27-05-67)
Briget Skemp (Cast Member)
Pathfinders To Venus 4 Episodes (1961)
Bronson Shaw (Cast Member)
Doctor Who 47. The Krotons: 4 Episodes (28-12-68)
Brook Williams (Cast Member)
The Avengers 6-20. Wish You Were Here (12-02-69)
Brown Derby (Cast Member)
The Baron 25. So Dark The Night (15-03-67)
Interpol Calling 12. The Chinese Mask (07-12-59)
The Saint 5-06. The Convenient Monster (04-11-66)
Bruce Barnabe (Cast Member)
The Avengers 3-15. The White Elephant (04-01-64)
Bruce Beeby (Cast Member)
The Champions 24. Project Zero (12-03-69)
Ghost Squad 1-09. Million Dollar Ransom (11-11-61)
Randall & Hopkirk (Deceased) 18. Could You Recognise The Man Again (16-01-70)
Bruce Boa (Cast Member)
The Avengers 2-14. Dead On Course (29-12-62)
The Champions 30. Autokill (30-04-69)
Man In A Suitcase 26. The Revolutionaries (20-03-67)
The Saint 2-13. The Sporting Chance (12-12-63) 3-21. Sibao (25-02-65) 6-03. Legacy For The Saint (13-10-68)
Bruce Montague (Cast Member)
The Baron 04. Red Horse, Red Rider (19-10-66)
Public Eye 1-02. Nobody Kill Santa Claus (30-01-65)
The Saint 2-21. The Good Medicine (06-02-64)
Undermind 06. Intent To Destroy (12-06-65)
Bruce Wightman (Cast Member)
Danger Man 2-05. Fair Exchange (10-11-64)
Doctor Who 14. The Crusade: 2 Episodes (27-03-65)
Bruno Barnabe (Cast Member)
The Avengers 4-26. Honey For The Prince (26-03-66) 6-04. You'll Catch Your Death (16-10-68)
Interpol Calling 16. No Flowers For Onno (04-01-59)
Bryan Coleman (Cast Member)
Adam Adamant Lives! 07. To Set a Deadly Fashion (11-08-66)
Danger Man 1-38. Dead Man Walks (13-01-62)
Bryan Hunt (Cast Member)
Out Of The Unknown 2-08. Tunnel Under The World (01-12-66)
Bryan Kendrick (Cast Member)
Adam Adamant Lives! 04. The Sweet Smell Of Disaster (14-07-07)
The Avengers: 6-23. Take Me To Your Leader (05-03-69)
The Saint 5-18. The Art Collectors (27-01-67)
Bryan Marshall (Cast Member)

The Avengers 6-25. Who Was That Man I Saw You With (19-03-69)
The Saint 2-02. Starring The Saint (26-09-63) 6-02. Invitation To Danger (06-10-68)
Bryan Mosley (Cast Member)
The Avengers 4-02. The Gravediggers (09-01-65) 6-26. Homicide & Old Lace (26-03-69)
Out Of The Unknown 3-03. The Last Lonely Man (21-01-69)
The Protectors 05. The Loop Men (25-04-64)
The Saint 5-26. When Spring Is Sprung (02-06-67)
Burt Kwouk (Cast Member)
The Avengers 3-26. Lobster Quadrille (21-03-64) 4-03. The Cybernauts (16-10-65)
The Champions 01. The Beginning (25-09-68)
Danger Man 1-26. The Journey Ends Halfway (30-04-61) 1-32. The Actor (11-06-61) 3-02. A Very Dangerous Game (07-10-65) 3-24. Koroshi (12-02-67)
Man Of The World 1-05. The Frontier (27-10-62)
Out Of The Unknown 1-07. Sucker Bait (15-11-65)
The Saint 3-18. The Sign Of The Claw (04-02-65) 5-23. The Gadget Lovers (21-04-67) 6-08. The Master Plan (17-11-68)
Budd Knapp (Cast Member)
The Third Man 2-02. One Kind Word (07-09-59)

C

Carl Bernard (Cast Member)
Danger Man 1-05. The Lovers (09-10-60)
Ghost Squad 2-05. The Retirement Of The Gentle Dove (30-03-63)
Carl Duering (Cast Member)
Interpol Calling 23. Payment in Advance (22-02-60)
Man In A Suitcase 19. Somebody Loses, Somebody… Wins? (31-01-67)
The Saint 2-27. The Saint Sees It Through (19-03-64)
Cameron Hall (Cast Member)
Ghost Squad 2-10. The Grand Duchess (11-05-63)
The Saint 2-12. The Well Meaning Mayor (05-12-63)
Cameron Miller (Cast Member)
Danger Man 3-10. Are You Going To Be More Permanent? (02-12-65)
Camilla Hasse (Cast Member)
The Prisoner 08. Dance Of The Dead (17-11-67)
Campbell Singer (Cast Member)
The Avengers 2-25. Six Hands Across a Table (16-03-63) 5-16. Who's Who (29-04-67)
Danger Man 1-03. Josetta (25-09-60) 1-15. Colonel Rodriguez (18-12-60)
The Saint 1-11. The Man Who Was Lucky (13-12-62) 5-23. The Gadget Lovers (21-04-67)
Cardew Robinson (Cast Member)
The Avengers 5-19. The £50,000 Breakfast (14-10-67) 6-14. The Interrogators (01-01-69)
Carl Bernard (Cast Member)
Man In A Suitcase 19. Somebody Loses, Somebody… Wins? (31-01-67)
Carl Conway (Cast Member)
The Saint 5-11. Paper Chase (09-12-66)
Carl Duering (Cast Member)
Interpol Calling 30. A Foreign Body (18-04-60)
Carl Jaffe (Cast Member)
Danger Man 1-02. Time to Kill (18-11-60)
Man Of The World 1-01. Death Of a Conference (29-09-62)
The Third Man 2-06. Barcelona Passage (01-10-59)
Carla Challoner (Cast Member)
Out Of The Unknown 1-11. Thirteen To Centauraus
Carleton Hobbs (Cast Member)
The Avengers 2-09. The Sell Out (24-11-62)
Strange Report 10. REPORT 8944 HAND A Matter Of Witchcraft (30-11-69)
Carlos Douglas (Cast Member)
Danger Man 2-12. A Date With Doris (29-12-64)
Man In A Suitcase 12. Find The Lady (13-12-67)
Carlos Pierre (Cast Member)
Man In A Suitcase 30. Night Flight To Andorra (17-04-67)
Carlos Thompson (Cast Member)
Man Of The World 1-06. The Sentimental Agent (03-11-62)
Calvin Lockhart (Cast Member)
The Corridor People Victim as Black (1966)
Carmen Dene (Cast Member)
The Avengers 4-26. Honey For The Prince (26-03-66)
Carol Cleveland (Cast Member)
The Avengers 4-21. A Touch Of Brimstone (19-02-66)
Man In A Suitcase 02. The Sitting Pigeon (04-10-67)
Randall & Hopkirk (Deceased) 12. For The Girl Who Has Everything (07-12-69)
The Saint 2-13. The Sporting Chance (12-12-63) 3-22. The Crime Of The Century (04-03-65)
Carol Dilworth (Cast Member)
Randall & Hopkirk (Deceased) 12. For The Girl Who Has Everything (07-12-69)
Carol Friday (Cast Member)
The Saint 6-17. The Ex-King Of Diamonds (19-01-68)

Carol Gray (Cast Member)
The Avengers 4-19. Quick-Quick Slow Death (05-02-66)
Carol Rachell (Cast Member)
Department S: 16. The Man From X (05-11-69)
Carol Ward (Cast Member)
The Avengers 3-24. Concerto (07-03-64)
Carole Ann Ford (Cast Member)
Doctor Who 01. An Unearthly Child: 4 Episodes (23-11-63) 02. The Daleks: 6 Episodes (21-12-63) 03. The Edge Of Destruction: 2 Episodes (04-02-64) 05. The Keys Of Marinus: 6 Episodes (11-04-64) 07. The Sensorites: 6 Episodes (20-06-64) 08. The Reign Of Terror: 4 Episodes (08-08-64) 06. The Aztecs: 4 Episodes (23-05-64) 09. Planet Of Giants: 3 Episodes (31-10-64) 10. Dalek Invasion Of Earth: 6 Episodes (21-11-64)
Public Eye 1-12. The Morning Wasn't So Hot (10-04-65)
Carole Gray (Cast Member)
The Saint 1-04. The Covetous Headsman (25-10-62)
Carole Lorimer (Cast Member)
Man Of The World 1-10. Portrait Of a Girl (01-12-62)
Carole Simpson (Cast Member)
The Saint 1-02. The Latin Touch (11-10-62)
Carole Shelley (Cast Member)
The Protectors 10. The Deadly Chameleon (30-5-64)
Caroline Blakiston (Cast Member)
The Avengers 4-02. The Gravediggers (09-01-65) 5-22. The Positive Negative Man (4-11-67)
The Baron 25. So Dark The Night (15-03-67)
The Champions 04. The Experiment (16-10-68)
City Beneath The Sea All episodes (1962)
Department S: 15. The Shift That Never Was (25-10-69)
Public Eye 1-02. Nobody Kill Santa Claus (30-01-65)
Randall & Hopkirk (Deceased) 04. Never Trust a Ghost (12-10-69)
The Saint 5-06. The Convenient Monster (04-11-66)
Strange Report 14. REPORT 2493 Whose Pretty Girl Are You? (28-12-69)
Caroline Hunt (Cast Member)
Doctor Who 08. The Reign Of Terror: 4 Episodes (08-08-64)
Caroline Lancaster (Cast Member)
Adam Adamant Lives! 07. To Set a Deadly Fashion (11-08-66)
Caroline Leigh (Cast Member)
Interpol Calling 34. Dressed To Kill (06-05-60)
Carolyn Methven (Cast Member)
Man Of The World 1-09. The Mindreader (24-11-62)
Caroline Mortimer (Cast Member)
The Saint 6-05. The Organisation Man (27-10-67)
Carolyn Pertwee (Cast Member)
Ghost Squad 2-18. The Heir Apparent (09-03-63)
Caron Gardner (Cast Member)
The Avengers 2-13. Death Dispatch (22-12-62)
Danger Man 3-08. The Outcast (18-11-65)
Department S: 09. Black Out (17-09-69)
The Saint 2-27. The Saint Sees It Through (19-03-64) 5-25. The Power Artists (19-05-67)
Cate Bauer (Cast Member)
The Third Man 1-25. How To Buy a Country (24-09-59)
Catherine Feller (Cast Member)
Ghost Squad 1-02. Bullet With My Name On It (16-09-61)
The Saint 5-01. The Queens Ransom (30-09-66)
Catherine Howe (Cast Member)
Doctor Who 32. The Underwater Menace: 2 Episodes (21-01-67)
Undermind 08. Puppets Of Evil (26-06-65)
Catherine Woodville (Cast Member)
The Avengers Propellant 23 (1962)

Danger Man Colony Three (1964)
The Saint The Damsel In Distress (1964) The Scorpion (1964)
Cathy Graham (Cast Member)
Department S: 21. Death On Reflection (17-12-69)
Cec Linder (Cast Member)
Interpol Calling 07. You Can't Die Twice (26-10-59)
The Saint 4-05. The Persistent Parasites (29-07-65)
Cecil Brock (Cast Member)
Danger Man 1-03. Josetta (25-09-60)
Cecil Cheng (Cast Member)
Adam Adamant Lives! 03. More Deadly Than The Sword (07-07-66)
The Avengers 6-14. The Interrogators (01-01-69)
Danger Man 3-02. A Very Dangerous Game (07-10-65)
Department S: 28. The Soup Of The Day (04-03-70)
Cecil Montgomery (Cast Member)
Ghost Squad 2-20. P.G.7. (06-07-63)
Cecil Parker (Cast Member)
The Avengers 5-19. The £50,000 Breakfast (14-10-67)
The Saint 5-24. A Double In Diamonds (05-05-67)
Cecilia Darby (Cast Member)
Strange Report 10. REPORT 8944 HAND A Matter Of Witchcraft (30-11-69)
Cecilia May (Cast Member)
The Avengers 3-21. Build a Better Mousetrap (15-02-64)
Celia Lovsky (Cast Member)
The Third Man 1-25. How To Buy a Country (24-09-59)
Charles Carson (Cast Member)
The Avengers 2-04. Bullseye (20-10-62)
Danger Man 1-11. The Key (20-11-60) 3-02. A Very Dangerous Game (07-10-65)
Undermind 09. Test For The Future (03-07-65)
Charles Farrell (Cast Member)
Danger Man 1-09. The Sanctuary (06-11-60) 1-18. The Girl Who Likes G.I.'s (15-01-61)
Ghost Squad 2-04. The Golden Silence (08-06-63)
The Saint 3-12. The Unkind Philanthropist (24-12-64)
Charles Gray (Cast Member)
Danger Man 1-11. The Key (20-11-60) 1-34. The Deputy Coyannis Story (16-12-61)
Charles Haggith (Cast Member)
Adam Adamant Lives! 10. The Doomsday Plan (01-09-66)
Charles Heslop (Cast Member)
Man Of The World 1-09. The Mindreader (24-11-62)
Charles Hill (Cast Member)
Danger Man 1-33. Hired Assassin (18-06-61) 2-12. A Date With Doris (29-12-64)
Ghost Squad 2-07. Lost in Transit (15-06-63)
Public Eye 1-12. The Morning Wasn't So Hot (10-04-65)
Charles Hodgson (Cast Member)
The Avengers 4-19. Quick-Quick Slow Death (05-02-66)
Man In A Suitcase 25. Property Of A Gentleman (13-03-67)
Charles Houston (Cast Member)
The Avengers 6-17. Killer (22-01-69)
The Baron 08. The Persuaders (16-11-66)
Danger Man 1-01. View From The Villa (11-09-60) 3-21. The Man With The Foot (24-03-66)
Department S: 01. Six Days (09-03-69)
Interpol Calling 26. Trial At Cranby's Creek (21-03-60)
The Saint 1-11. The Man Who Was Lucky (13-12-62) 3-01. The Miracle Tea Party (8-10-64) 6-02.
Invitation To Danger (06-10-68) 6-15. Vendetta For The Saint Part 1 (05-01-68)
Charles Hyatt (Cast Member)
The Saint 5-22. Island Of Chance (07-04-67)
Charles Irwin (Cast Member)
Danger Man 1-16. The Island (01-01-61)

The Saint 1-02. The Latin Touch (11-10-62)
Charles Korvin (Cast Member)
Interpol Calling All Episodes
Charles Lamb (Cast Member)
The Avengers 4-02. The Gravediggers (09-01-65)
Department S: 23. A Small War Of Nerves (21-01-70)
Randall & Hopkirk (Deceased) 07. Murder Ain't What It Used To Be (02-11-69)
Charles Laszlo (Cast Member)
Danger Man 2-02. The Professionals (20-10-64) 2-03. Colony Three (27-10-64)
Charles Laurence (Cast Member)
Man In A Suitcase 09. Girl Who Never Was (22-11-67) 30. Night Flight To Andorra (17-04-67)
Charles Lloyd Pack (Cast Member)
The Avengers 4-14. Silent Dust (01-01-66) 6-04. You'll Catch Your Death (16-10-68)
Danger Man 1-11. The Key (20-11-60) 1-20. The Vacation (29-01-61)
Man In A Suitcase 15. Burden Of Proof (03-01-67) 28. Three Blinks Of The Eyes (03-04-67)
Man Of The World 1-13. Shadow Of the Wall (22-12-62)
The Prisoner 11. It's Your Funeral (08-12-67)
Randall & Hopkirk (Deceased) 08. Whoever Heard Of a Ghost Dying (09-11-69)
Strange Report 02. REPORT 0649 SKELETON Let Sleeping Heroes Lie (28-09-69) 04. REPORT 2641 LONELY HEARTS Who Killed Dan Cupid? (12-10-69) 09. REPORT 1021 SHRAPNEL The Wish In the Dream (23-11-69) 10. REPORT 8944 HAND A Matter Of Witchcraft (30-11-69) 13. REPORT 4821 X-RAY Who Weeps For The Doctor (21-12-69) 15. REPORT 4407 HEART No Choice For The Donor (04-01-70) 07. REPORT 3424 EPIDEMIC A Most Curious Crime (02-11-69)
Charles Morgan (Cast Member)
The Avengers 6-14. The Interrogators (01-01-69)
Doctor Who 39. The Ice Warriors: 4 Episodes (11-11-67)
Ghost Squad 2-11. A First Class Way To Die (13-07-63)
Randall & Hopkirk (Deceased) 02. A Disturbing Case (28-09-69)
The Saint 2-22. The Invisible Millionaire (13-02-64)
Charles Rayford (Cast Member)
The Avengers 4-08. A Surfeit Of H2o (20-11-65)
Charles Rea (Cast Member)
The Saint 5-25. The Power Artists (19-05-67)
Charles Richardson (Cast Member)
Interpol Calling 20. Game For Three Hands (01-02-60)
Charles Simon (Cast Member)
The Saint 2-01. The Fellow Traveller (19-09-63)
Charles Thomas (Cast Member)
The Baron 27. Roundabout (29-03-67)
Charles Tingwell (Cast Member)
Adam Adamant Lives! 04. The Sweet Smell Of Disaster (14-07-07)
The Avengers 3-04. The Nutshell (19-10-63) 5-17. Return Of The Cybernauts (30-09-67)
Danger Man 2-17. The Affair At Castelevara (09-02-65)
Out Of The Unknown 1-02. The Counterfeit Man (11-10-65) 2-03. Lambda One (20-10-66)
Charles Vance (Cast Member)
Danger Man 1-24. The Relaxed Informer (16-04-61)
Charlie Bird (Cast Member)
The Avengers 2-19. The Golden Egg (02-02-63)
Charlotte Rampling (Cast Member)
The Avengers 5-12. The Superlative Seven (01-04-67)
Charlotte Selwyn (Cast Member)
The Avengers 2-15. Intercrime (05-01-63)
The Saint 5-25. The Power Artists (19-05-67) 6-04. The Desperate Diplomat (20-10-68)
Undermind 10. Waves Of Sound (10-07-65)
Cheryl St Clair (Cast Member)
Man In A Suitcase 28. Three Blinks Of The Eyes (03-04-67)
Chin Yu (Cast Member)
Danger Man 1-32. The Actor (11-06-61)

Chris Adcock (Cast Member)
The Avengers 4-11. Man Eater Of Surrey Green (11-12-65)
Interpol Calling 21. The Collector (08-02-60)
The Saint 4-06. The Man Who Could No Die (05-08-65)
Chris Gannon (Cast Member)
Randall & Hopkirk (Deceased) 13. But What a Sweet Little Room (14-12-69)
Chris Tranchell (Cast Member)
Doctor Who 35. The Faceless Ones: Episode 1 (08-04-6
Christian Chittell (Cast Member)
The Avengers 6-15. The Rotters (08-01-69)
Christian Holder (Cast Member)
Ghost Squad 2-08. The Man With The Delicate Hands (22-06-63)
Christian Roberts (Cast Member)
The Avengers 6-16. Invasion Of The Earthman (15-01-69)
Christina Ferdinando (Cast Member)
The Avengers 2-18. Warlock (26-01-63)
Christina Gregg (Cast Member)
Man Of The World 1-02. Masquerade In Spain (06-10-62)
The Saint 2-25. The Gentle Ladies (05-03-64)
Christine Lander (Cast Member)
Out Of The Unknown 1-11. Thirteen To Centauraus (13-12-63)
Christina Taylor (Cast Member)
The Champions 21. The Body Snatchers (19-02-69)
Christine Child (Cast Member)
The Baron 30. Farewell To Yesterday (19-04-67)
Danger Man 3-03. Sting In The Tail (14-10-65)
Christine Finn (Cast Member)
Adam Adamant Lives! 11. Death By Appointment Only (08-09-66)
The Protectors 03. Happy Is The Loser (11-04-64)
Christine Hargreaves (Cast Member)
Out Of The Unknown 1-06. Come Buttercup, Come Daisy, Come…? (08-11-65)
Christine Pryor (Cast Member)
Department S: 26. The Ghost Of Mary Burnham (18-02-70)
Christine Shaw (Cast Member)
The Avengers 3-04. The Nutshell (19-10-63)
Christopher Benjamin (Cast Member)
The Avengers 4-25. How To Succeed…. At Murder (19-03-66) 5-10. Never, Never Say Die (18-03-67) 6-05. Split (23-10-68)
The Baron 21. The Seven Eyes Of Night (15-02-67)
Danger Man 3-24. Koroshi (12-02-67)
The Prisoner 01. Arrival (29-09-67) 02. The Chimes Of Big Ben (06-10-67) 15. The Girl Who Was Death (18-01-67)
The Saint 6-08. The Master Plan (17-11-68)
Christopher Carlos (Cast Member)
The Champions 16. Shadow Of The Panther (15-01-68)
Danger Man 1-39. Deadline (20-01-62) 2-10. A Man To Be Trusted (15-12-64) 2-22. Parallel Lines Sometimes Meet (16-03-65) 3-06. The Mercenaries (04-11-65)
The Saint 3-21. Sibao (25-02-65) 5-22. Island Of Chance (07-04-67)
The Third Man 2-10. Toys Of The Dead (03-11-59)
Christopher Chittell (Cast Member)
The Avengers 6-16. Invasion Of The Earthman (15-01-69)
Christopher Coll (Cast Member)
Adam Adamant Lives! 15. The Village Of Evil (06-10-66)
The Avengers 2-26. Killer Whale (23-03-63)
Doctor Who 48. The Seeds Of Death: 6 Episodes (25-01-69)
Man In A Suitcase 13. The Bridge (20-12-67)
Christopher Greatorex (Cast Member)
The Avengers 5-19. The £50,000 Breakfast (14-10-67)

Christopher Hodge (Cast Member)
The Protectors 05. The Loop Men (25-04-64)
Christopher Lee (Cast Member)
The Avengers 5-10. Never, Never Say Die (18-03-67) 6-14. The Interrogators (01-01-69)
Christopher Malcolm (Cast Member)
Strange Report 06. REPORT 3906 COVER-GIRLS Last Years Model (26-10-69)
Christopher Matthews (Cast Member)
Doctor Who 29. The Tenth Planet: 3 Episodes (08-10-66)
Christopher Mitchell (Cast Member)
Strange Report 01. REPORT 5055 CULT Murder Shrieks Out (21-09-69)
Christopher Rhodes (Cast Member)
Danger Man 1-36. Under the Lake (30-12-61)
Interpol Calling 22. The Heiress (15-02-60)
The Saint 2-18. The Romantic Matron (16-01-64)
Christopher Robbie (Cast Member)
The Avengers 3-16. The Little Wonders (11-01-64)
Christopher Sandford (Cast Member)
Danger Man 3-11. To Our Best Friend (09-12-65) 3-23. Not So Jolly Roger (07-04-66)
Christopher Witty (Cast Member)
Ghost Squad 1-08. Assassin (28-10-61)
Cicely Courtneidge (Cast Member)
Man Of The World 2-03. Double Exposure (25-05-63)
Cicely Paget-Bowman (Cast Member)
Danger Man 2-03. Colony Three (27-10-64)
Claire Davenport (Cast Member)
The Baron 01. Diplomatic Immunity (28-09-66)
Claire Gordon (Cast Member)
Danger Man 1-03. Josetta (25-09-60)
Claire Nielson (Cast Member)
Ghost Squad 2-06. The Missing People (29-06-63) 2-15. The Last Jump (23-02-63) 2-21. Polsky (02-03-63) 2-18. The Heir Apparent (09-03-63) 2-24. Gertrude (13-04-63) 2-03. Sentences Of Death (04-05-63) 2-10. The Grand Duchess (11-05-63) 2-09. Hot Money (25-05-63) 2-12. Quarantine At Kavar (01-06-63) 2-04. The Golden Silence (08-06-63) 2-11. A First Class Way To Die (13-07-63) 2-20. P.G.7. (06-07-63) 2-01. Interrupted Requiem (02-02-63) 2-02. East Of Mandalay (09-02-63) 2-22. The Magic Bullet (16-03-63) 2-23. The Menacing Mazurka (23-03-63) 2-13. The Desperate Diplomat (18-05-63) 2-07. Lost in Transit (15-06-63) 2-08. The Man With The Delicate Hands (22-06-63)
Clare Jenkins (Cast Member)
Adam Adamant Lives! 29. A Sinister Sort Of Service (25-03-67)
Doctor Who 43. The Wheel in Space: 2 Episodes (11-05-68)
Randall & Hopkirk (Deceased) 26. The Smile Behind The Veil (13-03-70)
Clare Kelly (Cast Member)
The Avengers 2-08. Death Of Great Dane (17-11-62)
Ghost Squad 2-22. The Magic Bullet (16-03-63)
The Saint 2-22. The Invisible Millionaire (13-02-64)
Claude Farell (Cast Member)
The Andromeda Breakthrough 6 Episodes (1962)
Clay Johns (Cast Member)
The Saint 1-03. The Careful Terrorist (18-10-62)
Clemence Bettany (Cast Member)
Man Of The World 1-12. A Family Affair (15-12-62)
Clement McCallin (Cast Member)
Ghost Squad 2-23. The Menacing Mazurka (23-03-63)
Cleo Sylvestre (Cast Member)
Strange Report 11. REPORT 1553 RACIST A Most Dangerous Proposal (07-12-69)
Cliff Diggins (Cast Member)
The Avengers 4-02. The Gravediggers (09-01-65) 4-09. The Hour That Never Was (27-11-65) 5-12. The Superlative Seven (01-04-67) 6-23. Take Me To Your Leader (05-03-69)
The Saint 5-20. The Counterfeit Countess (03-03-67)

Clifford Cox (Cast Member)
The Avengers 5-21. You Have Just Been Murdered (28-10-67)
Ghost Squad 2-10. The Grand Duchess (11-05-63)
Randall & Hopkirk (Deceased) 06. Just For The Record (26-10-69)
Clifford Earl (Cast Member)
The Avengers 5-03. Escape In Time (26-01-67) 6-03. Super Secret Cypher Snatch (09-10-68)
The Baron 11. Samurai West (07-12-66)
Danger Man 1-08 The Lonely Chair (30-10-60)
Department S: 13. The Man Who Got a New Face (15-10-69)
Man In A Suitcase 06. Man From The Dead (01-11-67)
Randall & Hopkirk (Deceased) 25. You Can Always Find a Fall Guy (06-03-70)
The Saint 6-20. The World Beater (09-02-69)
Clifford Evans (Cast Member)
The Avengers 4-10. Dial a Deadly Number (04-12-65) 5-18. Death's Door (07-10-67) 6-06. Whoever Shot George Oblique Stroke XR40? (30-10-68)
The Champions 07. The Survivors (06-11-68)
Man Of The World 1-02. Masquerade In Spain (06-10-62)
Out Of This World 02. Little Lost Robot (07-07-1962)
The Prisoner 13. Do Not Forsake Me Oh My Darling (22-12-67)
The Saint 6-18. The Man Who Gambled With Life (26-01-68)
Clifford Parrish (Cast Member)
The Saint 6-10. The Scales Of Justice (01-12-68)
Clifford Rose (Cast Member)
Callan 2-02. The Most Promising Girl Of Her Year (15-01-69)
Clifton Jones (Cast Member)
Danger Man 2-22. Parallel Lines Sometimes Meet (16-03-65) 3-12. The Man On The Beach (16-12-65)
Man In A Suitcase 16. The Whisper (10-01-67)
Clinton Greyn (Cast Member)
Department S: 20. The Mysterious Man In The Flying Machine (10-12-69)
Clive Baxter (Cast Member)
The Avengers 2-12. The Big Thinker (15-12-62)
Clive Blakely (Cast Member)
The Avengers 5-23. Murdersville (11-11-67)
Clive Cazes (Cast Member)
The Baron 22. Night Of The Hunter (22-02-67) 30. Farewell To Yesterday (19-04-67)
Danger Man 2-17. The Affair At Castelevara (09-02-65) 3-09. English Lady Take Lodgers (25-11-65) 3-19. Two Birds With One Bullet (10-03-66)
Man In A Suitcase 12. Find The Lady (13-12-67)
Randall & Hopkirk (Deceased) 11. The Ghost Who Saved The Bank At Monte Carlo (30-11-69)
The Saint 3-05. The Revolution Racket (05-11-64) 5-04. The Reluctant Revolution (21-10-66)
Clive Colin Bowler (Cast Member)
The Avengers 5-05. The Bird Who Knew Too Much (11-02-67)
Department S: 06. The Man In The Elegant Room (13-04-69)
Clive Dunn (Cast Member)
The Avengers 5-14. Something Nasty In The Nursery (15-04-67)
Clive Endersby (Cast Member)
Out Of The Unknown 1-06. Come Buttercup, Come Daisy, Come...? (08-11-65)
Clive Francis (Cast Member)
Strange Report 11. REPORT 1553 RACIST A Most Dangerous Proposal (07-12-69)
Clive Graham (Cast Member)
The Avengers 6-17. Killer (22-01-69)
Out Of The Unknown 1-03. Stranger In the Family (18-10-65)
Clive Marshall (Cast Member)
Danger Man 3-24. Koroshi (12-02-67)
Clive Merrison (Cast Member)
Doctor Who 37. The Tomb Of The Cybermen: 4 Episodes (02-09-67)
Clive Morton (Cast Member)

Man In A Suitcase 21. No Friend Of Mine (14-02-67)
Clive Russell (Cast Member)
Danger Man 2-06. Fish On The Hook (17-11-64)
Colette Dunne (Cast Member)
The Saint 5-10. Little Girl Lost (02-12-66)
Colette O'Neil (Cast Member)
Adam Adamant Lives! 15. The Village Of Evil (06-10-66)
Colette Wilde (Cast Member)
The Avengers 2-24. A Chorus Of Frogs (9-3-63) 3-10. The Grandeur That Was Rome (30-11-63)
Danger Man 1-06. The Girl In Pink Pyjamas (16-10-60)
Ghost Squad 1-05. High Wire (30-09-61)
Interpol Calling 07. You Can't Die Twice (26-10-59) 36. Desert Hijack (30-05-60)
The Protectors 07. It Could Happen Here (09-05-64)
Colin Blakely (Cast Member)
The Champions 18. The Interrogation (29-01-69)
Man In A Suitcase 01. Brainwash (27-09-67) 16. The Whisper (10-01-67)
Colin Cresswell (Cast Member)
Ghost Squad 2-23. The Menacing Mazurka (23-03-63)
Colin Croft (Cast Member)
Interpol Calling 11. Air Switch (23-11-59)
Colin Douglas (Cast Member)
Danger Man 1-01. View From The Villa (11-9-60) 2-15 Whatever Happened To George Foster (19-1-65)
Doctor Who 40. The Enemy Of The World: 6 Episodes (23-12-67)
Ghost Squad 2-10. The Grand Duchess (11-05-63)
Colin Ellis (Cast Member)
The Avengers 4-19. Quick-Quick Slow Death (05-02-66)
Colin Fry (Cast Member)
The Avengers 2-09. The Sell Out (24-11-62) 2-24. A Chorus Of Frogs (09-03-63)
The Protectors 03. Happy Is The Loser (11-04-64)
Colin Gordon (Cast Member)
The Baron 01. Diplomatic Immunity (28-09-66) 02. Epitaph For a Hero (05-10-66) 05. Enemy Of The State (26-10-66) 08. The Persuaders (16-11-66) 18. A Memory Of Evil (25-01-67) 30. Farewell To Yesterday (19-04-67)
Department S: 23. A Small War Of Nerves (21-01-70)
Doctor Who 35. The Faceless Ones: Episode 1 (08-04-67)
Man Of The World 1-10. Portrait Of a Girl (01-12-62)
The Prisoner 03. A.B. & C. (13-10-67) 06. The General (03-11-67)
Colin Jeavons (Cast Member)
Adam Adamant Lives! 07. To Set a Deadly Fashion (11-08-66)
The Avengers 4-21. A Touch Of Brimstone (19-02-66) 5-06. The Winged Avenger (18-02-67)
The Baron 11. Samurai West (07-12-66)
Doctor Who 32. The Underwater Menace: 2 Episodes (21-01-67)
Man In A Suitcase 28. Three Blinks Of The Eyes (03-04-67)
Colin Rix (Cast Member)
The Avengers 3-10. The Grandeur That Was Rome (30-11-63)
The Baron 25. So Dark The Night (15-03-67)
The Protectors 07. It Could Happen Here (09-05-64)
Randall & Hopkirk (Deceased) 24. Vendetta For a Dead Man (27-02-70)
The Saint 5-26. When Spring Is Sprung (02-06-67)
Colin Vancao (Cast Member)
Adam Adamant Lives! 11. Death By Appointment Only (08-09-66)
Randall & Hopkirk (Deceased) 11. The Ghost Who Saved The Bank At Monte Carlo (30-11-69)
Colin Warman (Cast Member)
Doctor Who 41. The Web Of Fear: 5 Episodes (03-02-68)
Conrad Monk (Cast Member)
The Baron 09. And Suddenly You're Dead (23-11-66) 24. Long Ago & Far Away (08-03-67)
The Champions 30. Autokill (30-04-69)

Conrad Phillips (Cast Member)
The Avengers 4-14. Silent Dust (01-01-66)
The Prisoner 06. The General (03-11-67)
The Saint 3-01. The Miracle Tea Party (8-10-64)
Constance Chapman (Cast Member)
The Avengers 2-21. The White Dwarf (16-02-63)
Constantine Gregory (Cast Member)
Department S: 19. The Duplicated Man (03-12-69)
Man In A Suitcase 20. Blind Spot (07-02-67)
Coral Atkins (Cast Member)
The Avengers 3-13. Death a La Carte (21-12-63)
Corrine Burford (Cast Member)
The Avengers 3-24. Concerto (07-03-64)
Court Benson (Cast Member)
Danger Man 1-01. View From The Villa (11-09-60)
Craig Stevens (Cast Member)
Man Of The World all episodes
Cynthia Bizeray (Cast Member)
The Avengers 5-24. Mission, Highly Improbable (18-11-67)
Cyril Chamberlain (Cast Member)
Danger Man 3-02. A Very Dangerous Game (07-10-65)
The Saint 3-22. The Crime Of The Century (04-03-65)
Cyril Cross (Cast Member)
Ghost Squad 2-17. Mr Five Per Cent (06-04-63)
Cyril Delevanti (Cast Member)
The Third Man 4-07. Diamond In the Rough (11-05-62)
Cyril Luckham (Cast Member)
Department S: 18. The Perfect Operation (26-12-69)
Randall & Hopkirk (Deceased) 14. Who Killed Cock Robin? (21-12-69)
The Saint 2-08. Iris (07-11-63) 2-08. Iris (07-11-63)
Cyril Raymond (Cast Member)
Danger Man 1-19. Name, Date & Place (22-01-61)
Cyril Renison (Cast Member)
The Avengers 2-09. The Sell Out (24-11-62)
Randall & Hopkirk (Deceased) 13. But What a Sweet Little Room (14-12-69)
Cyril Shaps (Cast Member)
Danger Man 1-15. Colonel Rodriguez (18-12-60) 1-33. Hired Assassin (18-06-61)
Department S: 27. A Fish Out Of Water (25-02-70)
Doctor Who 37. The Tomb Of The Cybermen: 4 Episodes (02-09-67)
Interpol Calling 13. Slave Ship (14-12-59) 32. The Three Keys (02-05-60)
Man In A Suitcase 14. The Man Who Stood Still (27-12-67)
Man Of The World 1-06. The Sentimental Agent (03-11-62)
Randall & Hopkirk (Deceased) 17. Somebody Just Walked Over My Grave (09-01-70)
The Saint 5-07. The Angel's Eye (11-11-66)

D

D. Geoff Tomlinson (Cast Member)
The Corridor People 2 Episodes (1966)
Dafna Dan (Cast Member)
The Baron 23. The Edge Of Fear (01-03-67)
Dafydd Havard (Cast Member)
Danger Man 2-15. Whatever Happened To George Foster (19-01-65)
The Saint 6-09. The House On Dragons Rock (24-11-68)
Dalia Penn (Cast Member)
The Baron 26. The Long, Long Day (22-03-67)
Dallas Adams (Cast Member)
Strange Report 07. REPORT 3424 EPIDEMIC A Most Curious Crime (02-11-69)
Dallas Cavell (Cast Member)
The Avengers 2-17. Box Of Tricks (19-01-63)
The Champions 06. Operation Deep Freeze (30-10-68)
Doctor Who 08. The Reign Of Terror: 4 Episodes (08-08-64)
Ghost Squad 2-12. Quarantine At Kavar (01-06-63)
Dan Darnelli (Cast Member)
The Avengers 4-09. The Hour That Never Was (27-11-65)
Danger Man 2-08. The Battle Of The Cameras (01-12-64)
Dan Jackson (Cast Member)
Danger Man 3-05. Loyalty Always Pays (28-10-65)
Ghost Squad 2-22. The Magic Bullet (16-03-63)
Dan Meadon (Cast Member)
The Avengers 6-07. False Witness (06-01-68)
Dandy Nichols (Cast Member)
Man In A Suitcase 06. Man From The Dead (01-11-67)
Daniel Moynihan (Cast Member)
The Avengers 3-03 Man With Two Shadows (12-10-63) 4-09 Hour That Never Was (27-11-65)
Strange Report 06. REPORT 3906 COVER-GIRLS Last Years Model (26-10-69)
Daniel Nicolades (Cast Member)
Danger Man 3-24. Koroshi (12-02-67)
Daniel Thorndike (Cast Member)
The Avengers 2-21. The White Dwarf (16-02-63)
Danny Daniels (Cast Member)
Danger Man 2-04. The Galloping Major (03-11-64)
Man In A Suitcase 21. No Friend Of Mine (14-02-67)
The Saint 5-22. Island Of Chance (07-04-67)
Danny Green (Cast Member)
Randall & Hopkirk (Deceased) 06. Just For The Record (26-10-69)
Daphne Anderson (Cast Member)
The Avengers 2-22. Man In The Mirror (23-02-63)
Daphne Davey (Cast Member)
The Avengers 3-24. Concerto (07-03-64)
Daphne Heard (Cast Member)
Undermind 03. The New Dimension (22-05-65)
Daphne Slater (Cast Member)
Out Of The Unknown 1-03. Stranger In the Family (18-10-65)
Darryl Kavann (Cast Member)
Man In A Suitcase 08. Essay In Evil (15-11-67)
Dave Blake Kelly (Cast Member)
The Champions 20. The Silent Enemy (12-02-69)
Ghost Squad 2-18. The Heir Apparent (09-03-63)
Dave Carter (Cast Member)
Adam Adamant Lives!: 02. Death Has a Thousand Faces (30-06-66)
Callen: 2-15. Death Of a Hunter (16-04-69)

Randall & Hopkirk (deceased): 01. My Late Lamented Friend & Partner (21-09-69)
David Andrews (Cast Member)
The Avengers 1-15. The Frighteners (27-11-61)
David Arlen (Cast Member)
The Prisoner 02. The Chimes Of Big Ben (06-10-67)
David Ashford (Cast Member)
Strange Report 03. REPORT 2641 HOSTAGE If You Won't Learn Die (05-10-69)
David Baron (Cast Member)
The Avengers 6-21. Love All (19-02-69)
Doctor Who 39. The Ice Warriors: 4 Episodes (11-11-67)
David Battley (Cast Member)
The Protectors 14. The Reluctant Thief (27-06-64)
David Bauer (Cast Member)
The Avengers 3-16. The Little Wonders (11-01-64) 4-17. The Girl From AUNTIE (22-01-66)
The Baron 28. The Man Outside (05-04-67)
The Champions 04. The Experiment (16-10-68)
Department S: 17. Dead Men Die Twice (12-11-69)
The Prisoner 14. Living In Harmony (29-12-67)
Randall & Hopkirk (Deceased) 02. A Disturbing Case (28-09-69)
The Saint 1-08. The Element Of Doubt (22-11-62) 2-03. Judith (03-10-63) 2-08. Iris (07-11-63) 2-26.
The Ever Loving Spouse (12-03-64) 5-22. Island Of Chance (07-04-67)
Strange Report 14. REPORT 2493 Whose Pretty Girl Are You? (28-12-69)
The Third Man 3-01. A Question In Ice (27-06-64)
Undermind 07. Song Of Death (19-06-65)
David Baxter (Cast Member)
Man In A Suitcase 04. Variation On a Million Bucks Part 1 (18-10-67)
David Beale (Cast Member)
The Baron 23. The Edge Of Fear (01-03-67)
Department S: 09. Black Out (17-09-69)
David Bird (Cast Member)
The Avengers 6-24. Fog (12-03-69)
David Blake Kelly (Cast Member)
Out Of The Unknown 1-12. The Midas Plague (20-12-65)
David Burke (Cast Member)
The Avengers 3-05. Death Of a Batman (26-01-63)
The Baron 19. You Can't Win Them All (01-02-67)
David Calderisi (Cast Member)
The Baron 17. Time To Kill (18-01-67)
The Saint 1-02. The Latin Touch (11-10-62)
David Cameron (Cast Member)
Interpol Calling 04. The Sleeping Giant (05-10-59)
David Cargill (Cast Member)
The Avengers 2-13. Death Dispatch (22-12-62)
The Baron 23. The Edge Of Fear (01-03-67)
Danger Man 2-12. A Date With Doris (29-12-64) 2-14. Such Men Are Dangerous (12-01-65)
Man In A Suitcase 23. Web With Four Spiders (28-02-67) 26. The Revolutionaries (20-03-67)
Out Of The Unknown 2-04. Level Seven (27-10-66)
The Saint 1-05. The Loaded Tourist (01-11-62) 6-04. The Desperate Diplomat (20-10-68)
David Charlesworth (Cast Member)
Danger Man 2-12. A Date With Doris (29-12-64)
David Cole (Cast Member)
Doctor Who 25. The Gunfighters: 4 Episodes (30-04-66)
Man In A Suitcase 07. Sweet Sue (08-11-67**)**
David Collings (Cast Member)
Danger Man 3-03. Sting In The Tail (14-10-65)
Out Of The Unknown 2-04. Level Seven (27-10-66)
Strange Report 13. REPORT 4821 X-RAY Who Weeps For The Doctor (21-12-69)
David Conville (Cast Member)

Undermind 06. Intent To Destroy (12-06-65)
David Craig (Cast Member)
Public Eye 2-02. Don't Forget You're Mine (09-07-66)
David Davenport (Cast Member)
Ghost Squad 2-15. The Last Jump (23-02-63) 2-09. Hot Money (25-05-63)
David Davies (Cast Member)
The Avengers 3-06. November Five (02-11-63)
Interpol Calling 13. Slave Ship (14-12-59)
David Dodimead (Cast Member)
Doctor Who 29. The Tenth Planet: 3 Episodes (08-10-66)
David Downer (Cast Member)
Randall & Hopkirk (Deceased) 10. When Did You Start To Stop Seeing Things? (23-11-69)
David Forbes (Cast Member)
Randall & Hopkirk (Deceased) 26. The Smile Behind The Veil (13-03-70)
David Garfield (Cast Member)
The Baron 22. Night Of The Hunter (22-02-67)
Callan 2-04. The Little Bits & Pieces Of Love (29-01-69)
Man In A Suitcase 02. The Sitting Pigeon (04-10-67) 09. The Girl Who Never Was (22-11-67)
The Prisoner 01. Arrival (29-09-67)
The Saint 4-02. The Abductors (08-07-65) 6-09. The House On Dragons Rock (24-11-68)
David Gargill (Cast Member)
Randall & Hopkirk (Deceased) 18. Could You Recognise The Man Again (16-01-70)
David Garth (Cast Member)
Adam Adamant Lives Death By Appointment Only (8-9-66) A Sinister Sort Of Service (25-3-67)
The Avengers 2-12. The Big Thinker (15-12-62) 4-25. How To Succeed…. At Murder (19-03-66) 6-20. Wish You Were Here (12-02-69)
The Baron 17. Time To Kill (18-01-67)
Ghost Squad 2-04. The Golden Silence (08-06-63)
The Saint 4-05. The Persistent Parasites (29-07-65)
David Glover (Cast Member)
The Avengers 5-04. The See Through Man (04-02-67) 6-10. Noon Doomsday (27-11-68)
David Graham (Cast Member)
The Avengers 2-22. Man In The Mirror (23-02-63)
Doctor Who 25. The Gunfighters: 4 Episodes (30-04-66)
Man Of The World 1-01. Death Of a Conference (29-09-62)
The Protectors 02. The Bottle Shop (04-04-64)
The Saint 2-16. The Wonderful War (02-01-64) 3-12. The Unkind Philanthropist (24-12-64)
David Gregory (Cast Member)
The Avengers 5-10. Never, Never Say Die (18-03-67)
David Grey (Cast Member)
The Avengers 1-06. Girl On The Trapeze (11-02-61) 6-08. All Done With Mirrors (13-11-68)
Doctor Who 39. The Ice Warriors: 4 Episodes (11-11-67)
David Hargreaves (Cast Member)
Callan 2-02. The Most Promising Girl Of Her Year (15-01-69)
David Healy (Cast Member)
The Baron 16. The Island (Part 2) (11-01-67)
Department S: 28. The Soup Of The Day (04-03-70)
Randall & Hopkirk (Deceased) 07. Murder Ain't What It Used To Be (02-11-69)
The Saint 5-21. Simon & Delilah (24-03-67)
Strange Report 06. REPORT 3906 COVER-GIRLS Last Years Model (26-10-69)
David Hedison (Cast Member)
The Saint 2-19. Luella (23-01-64)
David Hemmings (Cast Member)
Out Of The Unknown 1-02. The Counterfeit Man (11-10-65)
David Hutcheson (Cast Member)
The Avengers 4-11. Man Eater Of Surrey Green (11-12-65)
Danger Man 2-21. The Mirror's New (09-03-65) 3-12. The Man On The Beach (16-12-65)
David Jackson (Cast Member)

The Saint 3-06. The Saint Steps In (12-11-64) 4-08. The Spanish Cow (19-08-65)
David Jason (Cast Member)
Randall & Hopkirk (Deceased) 05. That's How Murder Snowballs (19-10-69)
David Kelly (Cast Member)
Adam Adamant Lives! 29. A Sinister Sort Of Service (25-03-67)
Undermind 03. The New Dimension (22-05-65)
David Kelsey (Cast Member)
The Champions 27. Nutcracker (02-04-69)
Department S: 13. The Man Who Got a New Face (15-10-69)
The Protectors 12. Channel Crossing (13-06-64)
The Saint 5-20. The Counterfeit Countess (03-03-67) 6-18. The Man Who Gambled With Life (26-1-68)
David Kernan (Cast Member)
The Avengers 4-19. Quick-Quick Slow Death (05-02-66) 5-10. Never, Never Say Die (18-03-67)
David King (Cast Member)
A For Andromeda 1-6. The Face Of The Tiger (07-11-61)
The Andromeda Breakthrough 4 Episodes (1962)
The Baron 29. Countdown (12-04-67)
Ghost Squad 2-22. The Magic Bullet (16-03-63) 2-12. Quarantine At Kavar (01-06-63)
Undermind 04. Death In England (29-05-65) 05. Too Many Enemies (05-06-65)
David Knight (Cast Member)
Interpol Calling 34. Dressed To Kill (06-05-60)
Out Of The Unknown 1-07. Sucker Bait (15-11-65)
David Kossoff (Cast Member)
Interpol Calling 06. The Long Weekend (19-10-59)
The Saint 1-03. The Careful Terrorist (18-10-62)
David Lander (Cast Member)
Adam Adamant Lives! 04. The Sweet Smell Of Disaster (14-07-07)
The Baron 17. Time To Kill (18-01-67)
Callan 1-01. The Good Ones Are Dead (08-07-67)
Danger Man 2-12. A Date With Doris (29-12-64) 3-06. The Mercenaries (04-11-65)
Department S: 11. Who Plays The Dummy (01-10-69) 23. A Small War Of Nerves (21-01-70)
Interpol Calling 39. Checkmate (20-06-60)
David Langton (Cast Member)
The Avengers 2-07. The Mauritius Penny (10-11-62) 3-06. November Five (02-11-63) 5-19. The £50,000 Breakfast (14-10-67)
The Champions 27. Nutcracker (02-04-69)
Out Of The Unknown 1-04. The Dead Past (25-10-65)
David Lawton (Cast Member)
Ghost Squad 1-05. High Wire (30-09-61)
The Saint 1-10. The Golden Journey (06-12-62)
David Leland (Cast Member)
Callan 2-09. Death Of a Friend (05-03-69)
David Lodge (Cast Member)
The Avengers 5-11. Epic (25-03-67)
The Champions 23. The Night People (05-03-69) 29. The Gun Runners (23-04-69)
Ghost Squad 2-04. The Golden Silence (08-06-63)
Randall & Hopkirk (Deceased) 14. Who Killed Cock Robin? (21-12-69)
The Saint 3-08. The Man Who Liked Toys (26-11-64)
David Markham (Cast Member)
Ghost Squad 2-22. The Magic Bullet (16-03-63)
David Morrell (Cast Member)
The Avengers 4-09. The Hour That Never Was (27-11-65)
The Baron 12. The Maze (14-12-67)
The Saint 2-12. The Well Meaning Mayor (05-12-63)
David Munro (Cast Member)
Out Of The Unknown 1-02. The Counterfeit Man (11-10-65)
David Nettheim (Cast Member)

The Avengers 3-13. Death a La Carte (21-12-63)
The Baron 22. Night Of The Hunter (22-02-67)
Man In A Suitcase 06. Man From The Dead (01-11-67)
Out Of The Unknown 1-12. The Midas Plague (20-12-65)
The Prisoner 05. The Schizoid Man (27-10-67)
The Saint 5-21. Simon & Delilah (24-03-67)
David Orchard (Cast Member)
Danger Man 3-14. The Man Who Wouldn't Talk (30-12-65)
David Oxley (Cast Member)
Danger Man 1-37. The Nurse (06-01-61)
David Phethean (Cast Member)
Undermind 10. Waves Of Sound (10-07-65) 11. End Signal (17-07-65)
David Prowse (Cast Member)
Department S: 12. The Treasure Of the Costa Del Sol (08-10-69)
The Saint 6-19. Portrait Of Brenda (02-02-69)
David Quilter (Cast Member)
The Avengers 6-03. Super Secret Cypher Snatch (09-10-68)
David Rendall (Cast Member)
The Saint 6-11. The Fiction Makers Part 1 (08-12-68)
David Ritch (Cast Member)
Danger Man 2-17. The Affair At Castelevara (09-02-65)
David Richards (Cast Member)
The Avengers 6-14. The Interrogators (01-01-69)
David Rose (Cast Member)
Callan 2-04. The Little Bits & Pieces Of Love (29-01-69)
David Saire (Cast Member)
The Andromeda Breakthrough 5 Episodes (1962)
Danger Man 2-17. The Affair At Castelevara (09-02-65) 3-07. Judgement Day (11-11-65)
Ghost Squad 1-02. Bullet With My Name On It (16-09-61)
Man In A Suitcase 11. Dead Man's Shoes (06-12-67)
The Saint 3-22. The Crime Of The Century (04-03-65)
David Savile (Cast Member)
Out Of The Unknown 1-02. The Counterfeit Man (11-10-65)
David Scheuer (Cast Member)
Man In A Suitcase 04. Variation On a Million Bucks Part 1 (18-10-67) 19. Somebody Loses, Somebody… Wins? (31-01-67)
David Sinclair (Cast Member)
Randall & Hopkirk (Deceased) 09. The House On Haunted Hill (16-11-69)
David Spenser (Cast Member)
Adam Adamant Lives! 05. Allah Is Not Always With You (21-07-66)
Doctor Who 39. The Ice Warriors: 4 Episodes (11-11-67)
The Saint 5-13. Flight Plan (23-12-66)
David Stoll (Cast Member)
Randall & Hopkirk (Deceased) 10. When Did You Start To Stop Seeing Things? (23-11-69)
David Sumner (Cast Member)
The Avengers 2-10. Death On The Rocks (01-12-62) 6-14. The Interrogators (01-01-69)
Department S: 09. Black Out (17-09-69)
Man In A Suitcase 26. The Revolutionaries (20-03-67)
Man Of The World 1-09. The Mindreader (24-11-62)
Out Of The Unknown 1-07. Sucker Bait (15-11-65)
The Saint 2-20. The Lawless Lady (30-01-64)
David Swift (Cast Member)
The Avengers 4-22. What The Butler Saw (26-02-66)
The Baron 24. Long Ago & Far Away (08-03-67)
Undermind 01. Instance One (08-05-65)
David Webb (Cast Member)
Randall & Hopkirk (Deceased) 14. Who Killed Cock Robin? (21-12-69)
David Toguri (Cast Member)

Danger Man 3-25. Shinda Shima (26-02-67)
Dawn Addams (Cast Member)
Danger Man 2-06. Fish On The Hook (17-11-64) 2-08. The Battle Of The Cameras (01-12-64)
Department S: 07. Handicap Dead (20-04-69)
The Saint 2-01. The Fellow Traveller (19-09-63) 2-20. The Lawless Lady (30-01-64) 5-01. The Queens Ransom (30-09-66)
The Third Man 2-06. Barcelona Passage (01-10-59)
Dawn Beret (Cast Member)
The Avengers 1-15. The Frighteners (27-11-61)
Department S: 07. Handicap Dead (20-04-69)
Dawn Davis (Cast Member)
The Saint 3-12. The Unkind Philanthropist (24-12-64)
Dayvd Harries (Cast Member)
Department S: 24. The Bones Of Byrom Blain (28-01-70)
Dean Francis (Cast Member)
Danger Man 2-07. The Colonels Daughter (24-11-64)
Deborah Grant (Cast Member)
Public Eye 4-07. A Fixed Address (19-06-69)
Deborah Watling (Cast Member)
Doctor Who 37. The Tomb Of The Cybermen: 4 Episodes (02-09-67) 39. The Ice Warriors: 4 Episodes (11-11-67) 40. The Enemy Of The World: 6 Episodes (23-12-67) 41. The Web Of Fear: 5 Episodes (03-02-68)
Declan Mulholland (Cast Member)
The Avengers 5-02. The Fear Merchants (21-01-67)
Dee Shenderey (Cast Member)
The Avengers 2-02. Propellant 23 (06-10-62)
Del Baker (Cast Member)
The Avengers 4-08. A Surfeit Of H2o (20-11-65)
The Baron 20. The High Terrace (08-02-67)
Danger Man 3-16. Dangerous Secret (13-01-66)
Out Of The Unknown 1-07. Sucker Bait (15-11-65)
Delena Kidd (Cast Member)
The Avengers 1-06. Girl On The Trapeze (11-02-61)
Danger Man 1-19. Name, Date & Place (22-01-61)
Out Of The Unknown 1-10. Some Lapse In Time (06-12-65)
Undermind 08. Puppets Of Evil (26-06-65)
Delia Corrie (Cast Member)
The Avengers 2-07. The Mauritius Penny (10-11-62)
Delphi Lawrence (Cast Member)
Danger Man 1-01. View From The Villa (11-09-60)
Ghost Squad 2-07. Lost in Transit (15-06-63)
Interpol Calling 03. The Money Game (28-09-59)
The Saint 1-11. The Man Who Was Lucky (13-12-62)
Dene Cooper (Cast Member)
The Prisoner 04. Free For All (20-10-67)
Denholm Elliott (Cast Member)
Danger Man 3-18. The Hunting Party (27-01-66)
Denis Cleary (Cast Member)
Adam Adamant Lives! 09. Sing a Song Of Murder (25-08-66)
The Avengers 2-14. Dead On Course (29-12-62)
Denis Goacher (Cast Member)
City Beneath The Sea All episodes (1962)
Denis Holmes (Cast Member)
Ghost Squad 2-21. Polsky (02-03-63)
Denis Quilley (Cast Member)
The Avengers 4-22. What The Butler Saw (26-02-66)
Undermind 02. Flowers Of Havoc (15-05-65) 03. The New Dimension (22-05-65) 04. Death In England (29-05-65) 05. Too Many Enemies (05-06-65)

Denis Shaw (Cast Member)
The Avengers 6-29. Requiem (16-04-69)
Danger Man 3-10. Are You Going To Be More Permanent? (02-12-65)
The Prisoner 01. Arrival (29-09-67) 09. Checkmate (14-11-67)
Denise Buckley (Cast Member)
The Avengers 6-22. Stay Tuned (26-02-69)
Department S: 03. Cellar Full Of Silence (23-03-69)
Man In A Suitcase 17. Why They Killed Nolan (17-01-67)
The Prisoner 08. Dance Of The Dead (17-11-67)
Randall & Hopkirk (Deceased) 23. The Trouble With Women (20-02-70)
The Saint 6-06. The Double Take (03-11-68)
Dennis Alaba Peters (Cast Member)
Department S: 01-28 All Episodes
Dennis Blake (Cast Member)
The Saint 4-04. The Smart Detective (22-07-65)
Dennis Bowen (Cast Member)
Out Of The Unknown 3 -08. Little Black Bag (25-02-69)
Dennis Chin (Cast Member)
Adam Adamant Lives! 03. More Deadly Than The Sword (07-07-66)
The Baron 15. Storm Warning (Part 1) (04-01-67)
Dennis Chinnery (Cast Member)
The Avengers 5-14. Something Nasty In The Nursery (15-04-67)
The Champions 10. The Ghost Plane (27-11-68)
The Prisoner 07. Many Happy Returns (10-11-67)
The Saint 6-02. Invitation To Danger (06-10-68)
Strange Report 03. REPORT 2641 HOSTAGE If You Won't Learn Die (05-10-69)
Dennis Cleary (Cast Member)
Doctor Who 08. The Reign Of Terror: 4 Episodes (08-08-64)
Dennis Edwards (Cast Member)
The Avengers 2-08. Death Of Great Dane (17-11-62)
Doctor Who 12. The Romans: 4 Episodes (16-01-65)
Ghost Squad 2-04. The Golden Silence (08-06-63)
Dennis Plenty (Cast Member)
Adam Adamant Lives! 18. Black Echo (07-01-67)
Dennis Price (Cast Member)
The Avengers 6-06. Whoever Shot George Oblique Stroke XR40? (30-10-68)
Dennis Ramsden (Cast Member)
Danger Man 3-02. A Very Dangerous Game (07-10-65)
Dennis Thorne (Cast Member)
Ghost Squad 2-15. The Last Jump (23-02-63)
Derek Aylward (Cast Member)
The Prisoner 10. Hammer & Anvil (01-12-67)
Derek Benfield (Cast Member)
The Baron 08. The Persuaders (16-11-66)
The Protectors 11. Who Killed Lazoryck? (06-06-64)
Derek Bond (Cast Member)
Callan 2-06. Heir Apparent (12-02-69) 2-09. Death Of a Friend (05-03-69) 2-13. The Worst Soldier I Ever Saw (02-04-69)
The Saint 5-19. To Kill a Saint (24-02-67)
Derek Calder (Cast Member)
Doctor Who 33. The Moonbase: 2 Episodes (18-02-67)
Derek Farr (Cast Member)
The Avengers 4-11. Man Eater Of Surrey Green (11-12-65)
The Saint 1-01. The Talented Husband (4-10-62)
Derek Fowlds (Cast Member)
The Protectors 14. The Reluctant Thief (27-06-64)
Derek Francis (Cast Member)
Danger Man 3-16. Dangerous Secret (13-01-66)

Doctor Who 12. The Romans: 4 Episodes (16-01-65)
Ghost Squad 2-08. The Man With The Delicate Hands (22-06-63)
Man In A Suitcase 25. Property Of A Gentleman (13-03-67)
Undermind 03. The New Dimension (22-05-65)
Derek Gilbert (Cast Member)
Doctor Who 43. The Wheel in Space: 2 Episodes (11-05-68)
Derek Godfrey (Cast Member)
The Avengers 6-28. My Wildest Dream (07-04-69)
The Baron 22. Night Of The Hunter (22-02-67)
Danger Man 1-07. Position Of Trust (23-10-60)
Derek Guyler (Cast Member)
Adam Adamant Lives! 06. The Happy Embalmers (04-06-66)
Derek Hunt (Cast Member)
The Avengers 3-23. The Charmers (29-02-64)
Derek Martin (Cast Member)
Out Of The Unknown 1-02. The Counterfeit Man (11-10-65)
Derek Murcott (Cast Member)
The Champions 10. The Ghost Plane (27-11-68)
Derek Newark (Cast Member)
The Avengers 3-21. Build a Better Mousetrap (15-2-64) 5-01. From Venus With Love (14-01-67)
 6-20. Wish You Were Here (12-02-69)
The Baron 03. Something For a Rainy Day (12-10-66) 15. Storm Warning (Part 1) (04-01-67) 16. The
Island (Part 2) (11-01-67)
Callan 1-06. You Should Have Got Here Sooner (12-08-67)
The Champions 28. The Final Countdown (16-04-69)
Department S: 22. Last Train to Redbridge (14-01-70)
Doctor Who 01. An Unearthly Child: 3 Episodes (23-11-63)
Man In A Suitcase 10. All That Glitters (29-11-67) 20. Blind Spot (07-02-67)
The Saint 5-20. The Counterfeit Countess (03-03-67) 6-14. Where The Money Is (29-12-68)
Derek Nimmo (Cast Member)
Ghost Squad 2-01. Interrupted Requiem (02-02-63)
Undermind 08. Puppets Of Evil (26-06-65)
Derek Prentice (Cast Member)
Man In A Suitcase 19. Somebody Loses, Somebody… Wins? (31-01-67)
Derek Smee (Cast Member)
Man In A Suitcase 09. The Girl Who Never Was (22-11-67)
The Saint 6-17. The Ex-King Of Diamonds (19-01-68)
Derek Sydney (Cast Member)
The Champions 06. Operation Deep Freeze (30-10-68)
Danger Man 1-14. The Traitor (11-12-60)
Doctor Who 12. The Romans: 4 Episodes (16-01-65)
Ghost Squad 2-20. P.G.7. (06-07-63)
The Saint 5-02. Interlude In Venice (07-10-66) 6-15. Vendetta For The Saint Part 1 (05-01-68)
Derek Tansley (Cast Member)
Interpol Calling 12. The Chinese Mask (07-12-59)
Derek Ware (Cast Member)
Doctor Who 14. The Crusade: 2 Episodes (27-03-65)
Derek Waring (Cast Member)
Ghost Squad 2-04. The Golden Silence (08-06-63)
Public Eye 2-07. Works With Chess, Not With Life (13-08-66)
Dermot Kelly (Cast Member)
The Champions 19. The Mission (05-02-69)
Man Of The World 1-03. Blaze Of Glory (13-10-62)
Randall & Hopkirk (Deceased) 09. The House On Haunted Hill (16-11-69)
Dermot Tuohy (Cast Member)
Undermind 03. The New Dimension (22-05-65)
Dermot Walsh (Cast Member)
Danger Man 1-27. Bury The Dead (07-05-61)

Derren Nesbitt (Cast Member)
Danger Man 1-02 Time to Kill (18-11-60) 1-25 The Brothers (23-4-61) 3-03 Sting In The Tail (14-10-65)
Man In A Suitcase 11. Dead Man's Shoes (06-12-67)
Man Of The World 1-11. Specialist For the Kill (08-12-62)
The Prisoner 11. It's Your Funeral (08-12-67)
The Protectors 05. The Loop Men (25-04-64)
The Saint 2-13. The Sporting Chance (12-12-63)
Strange Report 16. REPORT 4977 Square Root Of Evil (11-01-70)
Derrick De Marney (Cast Member)
Danger Man 3-06. The Mercenaries (04-11-65)
Ghost Squad 2-13. The Desperate Diplomat (18-05-63)
Derrick Sherwin (Cast Member)
The Baron 26. The Long, Long Day (22-03-67)
Danger Man 1-07. Position Of Trust (23-10-60)
Dervis Ward (Cast Member)
The Avengers 6-14. The Interrogators (01-01-69)
The Champions 27. Nutcracker (02-04-69)
Interpol Calling 37. Pipeline (06-06-60)
Desmond Cullum-Jones (Cast Member)
Danger Man 3-10. Are You Going To Be More Permanent? (02-12-65)
Desmond Davies (Cast Member)
Ghost Squad 2-23. The Menacing Mazurka (23-03-63)
Desmond Jordan (Cast Member)
The Avengers 6-08. All Done With Mirrors (13-11-68)
Out Of The Unknown 1-06. Come Buttercup, Come Daisy, Come…? (08-11-65)
Desmond Llewelyn (Cast Member)
Danger Man 2-18. The Ubiquitous Mr Lovegrove (16-02-65)
Desmond Newling (Cast Member)
The Protectors 12. Channel Crossing (13-06-64)
Desmond Walter-Ellis (Cast Member)
The Avengers 6-02. Game (02-10-68)
Diana Beevers (Cast Member)
Public Eye 2-02. Don't Forget You're Mine (09-07-66)
Diana Rigg (Cast Member)
The Avengers 51 Episodes
Diane Bester (Cast Member)
The Avengers 2-09. The Sell Out (24-11-62)
Diane Clare (Cast Member)
The Avengers 4-04. Death At Bargain Prices (23-10-65)
Diane Keys (Cast Member)
The Avengers 2-26. Killer Whale (23-03-63)
Dick Bentley (Cast Member)
Randall & Hopkirk (Deceased) 22. It's Supposed To Be Thicker Than Water (13-02-70)
The Saint 3-07. The Loving Brothers (19-11-64)
Dick Haymes (Cast Member)
The Saint 3-14. The Contact (07-01-65)
Dick Offord (Cast Member)
Man In A Suitcase 16. The Whisper (10-01-67)
Dick Pickford (Cast Member)
Adam Adamant Lives! 29. A Sinister Sort Of Service (25-03-67)
Dickie Owen (Cast Member)
Man In A Suitcase 10. All That Glitters (29-11-67)
The Saint 1-11. The Man Who Was Lucky (13-12-62)
Dicky Luck (Cast Member)
The Avengers 4-09. The Hour That Never Was (27-11-65)
Didi Perego (Cast Member)
Man In A Suitcase 16. The Whisper (10-01-67)

Didi Sullivan (Cast Member)
The Avengers 2-16. Immortal Clay (12-01-63)
Man Of The World 1-11. Specialist For the Kill (08-12-62)
Dilys Lane (Cast Member)
Ghost Squad 3-01. An Eye For An Eye (22-02-64)
The Protectors 13. Cargo From Corinth (20-06-64)
Dina Paisner (Cast Member)
The Saint 1-06. The Pearls Of Peace (08-11-62)
Dinny Powell (Cast Member)
Adam Adamant Lives! 15. The Village Of Evil (06-10-66)
The Avengers 5-24. Mission, Highly Improbable (18-11-67)
The Prisoner 05. The Schizoid Man (27-10-67)
Dino Shafeek (Cast Member)
Ghost Squad 2-19. Death of a Sportsman (26-01-63)
Dinsdale Landen (Cast Member)
The Avengers 6-08. All Done With Mirrors (13-11-68)
Dixon Adams (Cast Member)
Ghost Squad 2-23. The Menacing Mazurka (23-03-63)
Doel Luscombe (Cast Member)
Ghost Squad 2-04. The Golden Silence (08-06-63)
The Protectors 11. Who Killed Lazoryck? (06-06-64)
The Saint 5-26. When Spring Is Sprung (02-06-67)
Dolores Dicen (Cast Member)
Man Of The World 2-02. The Enemy (18-05-63)
Dolores Mantez (Cast Member)
Danger Man 3-05. Loyalty Always Pays (28-10-65) 3-12. The Man On The Beach (16-12-65)
Randall & Hopkirk (Deceased) 01. My Late Lamented Friend & Partner (21-09-69)
Don Archell (Cast Member)
The Avengers 5-12. The Superlative Seven (01-04-67)
Don Borisenko (Cast Member)
The Baron 12. The Maze (14-12-67)
Don Vernon (Cast Member)
Randall & Hopkirk (Deceased) 20. Money To Burn (30-01-70)
Donal Donnelly (Cast Member)
The Avengers 2-14. Dead On Course (29-12-62)
Department S: 14. Les Fleurs Du Mal (22-10-69)
Donald Bisset (Cast Member)
The Saint 3-17. The Inescapable World (28-01-65)
Donald Chinn (Cast Member)
Ghost Squad 2-02. East Of Mandalay (09-02-63)
Man Of The World 1-05. The Frontier (27-10-62)
Donald Churchill (Cast Member)
Ghost Squad 1-06. Eyes Of The Bat (14-10-61)
The Saint 1-01. The Talented Husband (4-10-62)
Donald Douglas (Cast Member)
The Avengers 6-18. The Morning After (29-10-69)
The Baron 28. The Man Outside (05-04-67)
Strange Report 03. REPORT 2641 HOSTAGE If You Won't Learn Die (05-10-69)
Donald Eccles (Cast Member)
Adam Adamant Lives! 18. Black Echo (07-01-67)
The Avengers 2-19. The Golden Egg (02-02-63)
Donald Gee (Cast Member)
The Avengers 6-03. Super Secret Cypher Snatch (09-10-68)
Doctor Who 49. The Space Pirates: Episode 2 (15-03-69)
Donald Hewlett (Cast Member)
The Avengers 4-18. The Thirteenth Hole (29-01-66)
The Saint 4-05. The Persistent Parasites (29-07-65)
Donald Houston (Cast Member)

The Champions 07. The Survivors (06-11-68)
Danger Man 2-21. The Mirror's New (09-03-65) 3-11. To Our Best Friend (09-12-65)
Department S: 26. The Ghost Of Mary Burnham (18-02-70)
Man In A Suitcase 08. Essay In Evil (15-11-67)
Out Of The Unknown 1-11. Thirteen To Centauraus
Donald Morley (Cast Member)
The Champions 24. Project Zero (12-03-69)
Ghost Squad 1-03. Ticket For Blackmail (09-09-61)
Interpol Calling 22. The Heiress (15-02-60)
Randall & Hopkirk (Deceased) 04. Never Trust a Ghost (12-10-69)
The Saint 5-16. The Fast Women (13-01-67)
Donald Oliver (Cast Member)
The Avengers 4-11. Man Eater Of Surrey Green (11-12-65)
Ghost Squad 2-18. The Heir Apparent (09-03-63)
The Saint 5-13. Flight Plan (23-12-66)
Donald Pickering (Cast Member)
The Avengers 5-06. The Winged Avenger (18-02-67) 6-26. Homicide & Old Lace (26-03-69)
The Champions 12. The Fanatics (11-12-68)
Doctor Who 35. The Faceless Ones: Episode 1 (08-04-67)
The Saint 5-07. The Angel's Eye (11-11-66)
Donald Pleasence (Cast Member)
Danger Man 1-07. Position Of Trust (23-10-60) 1-17. Find & Return (08-01-61)
Interpol Calling 38. The Absent Assassin (13-06-60)
Donald Sampler (Cast Member)
Doctor Who 43. The Wheel in Space: 2 Episodes (11-05-68)
Donald Scott (Cast Member)
Strange Report 03. REPORT 2641 HOSTAGE If You Won't Learn Die (05-10-69)
Donald Sinden (Cast Member)
The Prisoner 07. Many Happy Returns (10-11-67)
Donald Stewart (Cast Member)
A For Andromeda 1-6. The Face Of The Tiger (07-11-61)
Interpol Calling 15. Last Man Lucky (28-12-59)
Man Of The World 1-04. The Runaways (20-10-62) 1-10. Portrait Of a Girl (01-12-62)
Donald Sutherland (Cast Member)
The Avengers 5-12. The Superlative Seven (01-04-67)
The Champions 16. Shadow Of The Panther (15-01-68)
Man In A Suitcase 03 Day Of Execution (11-10-67) 24 Which Way Did He Go, McGill (6-3-67)
The Saint 3-23. The Happy Suicide (11-03-65) 5-14. Escape Route (30-12-66)
Donald Tandy (Cast Member)
The Avengers 2-06. The Removal Men (03-11-62)
Danger Man 2-12. A Date With Doris (29-12-64)
The Saint 2-25. The Gentle Ladies (05-03-64)
Donald Webster (Cast Member)
The Avengers 2-15. Intercrime (05-01-63)
The Baron 20. The High Terrace (08-02-67)
Donald Wolfit (Cast Member)
Ghost Squad 01-13 All Episodes Series 1
Dora Graham (Cast Member)
The Saint 5-24. A Double In Diamonds (05-05-67)
Dora Reisser (Cast Member)
The Avengers 6-27. Thingamajig (16-04-69)
The Baron 01. Diplomatic Immunity (28-09-66)
Man In A Suitcase 28. Three Blinks Of The Eyes (03-04-67)
Doreen Mantle (Cast Member)
Strange Report 06. REPORT 3906 COVER-GIRLS Last Years Model (26-10-69)
Dorinda Stevens (Cast Member)
The Avengers 3-24. Concerto (07-03-64)
Danger Man 2-14. Such Men Are Dangerous (12-01-65)

Interpol Calling 11. Air Switch (23-11-59) 31. In The Swim (25-04-60)
The Saint 1-03. The Careful Terrorist (18-10-62)
Doris Forsyth (Cast Member)
The Avengers 3-02. The Undertakers (05-10-63)
Doris Hare (Cast Member)
The Avengers 1-15. The Frighteners (27-11-61)
Randall & Hopkirk (Deceased) 13. But What a Sweet Little Room (14-12-69)
The Saint 4-03. The Crooked Ring (15-07-65)
Doris Nolan (Cast Member)
The Saint 1-02. The Latin Touch (11-10-62)
Strange Report 06. REPORT 3906 COVER-GIRLS Last Years Model (26-10-69)
Doris Rogers (Cast Member)
The Avengers 1-20. Tunnel Of Fear (05-08-61)
Dorothea Phillips (Cast Member)
Danger Man 2-15. Whatever Happened To George Foster (19-01-65)
Man Of The World 2-03. Double Exposure (25-05-63)
The Saint 6-10. The Scales Of Justice (01-12-68)
Dorothy Black (Cast Member)
The Saint 2-20. The Lawless Lady (30-01-64)
Dorothy Blythe (Cast Member)
The Avengers 1-06. Girl On The Trapeze (11-02-61)
Dorothy Edwards (Cast Member)
Man In A Suitcase 10. All That Glitters (29-11-67)
Dorothy Frere (Cast Member)
The Saint 4-01. The Chequered Flag (01-07-65)
Dorothy Hersee (Cast Member)
Danger Man 1-08 The Lonely Chair (30-10-60)
Dorothy-Rose Gribble (Cast Member)
Doctor Who 12. The Romans: 4 Episodes (16-01-65)
Dorothy White (Cast Member)
Danger Man 1-10. An Affair Of State (13-11-60)
Doug Robinson (Cast Member)
The Avengers 2-03. The Decapod (13-10-62) 2-10. Death On The Rocks (01-12-62) 3-03. Man With Two Shadows (12-10-63) 3-25. Espirit de Corps (14-03-64)
Douglas Cummings (Cast Member)
The Avengers 3-07. The Gilded Cage (09-11-63) 3-17. The Wringer (18-01-64)
Douglas Ditta (Cast Member)
The Saint 6-05. The Organisation Man (27-10-67)
Douglas Fielding (Cast Member)
Callan 2-01. Red Knight, White Knight (08-01-69)
Douglas Jones (Cast Member)
The Prisoner 14. Living In Harmony (29-12-67)
Douglas Livingstone (Cast Member)
The Baron 19. You Can't Win Them All (01-02-67)
The Saint 5-26. When Spring Is Sprung (02-06-67)
Douglas Muir (Cast Member)
The Avengers 1-20. Tunnel Of Fear (05-08-61) 2-01. Mr Teddy Bear (29-09-62) 2-06. The Removal Men (03-11-62) 2-13. Death Dispatch (22-12-62) 2-16. Immortal Clay (12-01-63) 2-18. Warlock (26-01-63)
Douglas Rye (Cast Member)
The Avengers 1-20. Tunnel Of Fear (05-08-61)
Douglas Sheldon (Cast Member)
The Avengers 5-17. Return Of The Cybernauts (30-09-67)
Douglas Wilmer (Cast Member)
The Avengers 4-20. The Danger Makers (12-02-66)
The Baron 24. Long Ago & Far Away (08-03-67)
Ghost Squad 1-13. Death From a Distance (04-11-61) 2-24. Gertrude (13-04-63)
Interpol Calling 29. White Blackmail (11-04-60)

The Saint 2-09. The King Of The Beggars (14-11-63)
Drewe Henley (Cast Member)
The Avengers 5-13. A Funny Thing Happened On The Way To The Station (08-04-67)
Man In A Suitcase 28. Three Blinks Of The Eyes (03-04-67)
Randall & Hopkirk (Deceased) 19. A Sentimental Journey (23-01-70)
Dudley Foster (Cast Member)
The Avengers 5-14 Something Nasty In The Nursery (15-4-67) 6-20 Wish You Were Here (12-2-69)
Danger Man 1-29. The Contessa (21-05-61)
Ghost Squad 1-06. Eyes Of The Bat (14-10-61)
Randall & Hopkirk (Deceased) 03. All Work & No Pay (05-10-69)
The Saint 4-02. The Abductors (08-07-65)
Dudley Jones (Cast Member)
Doctor Who 29. The Tenth Planet: 3 Episodes (08-10-66)
Randall & Hopkirk (Deceased) 18. Could You Recognise The Man Again (16-01-70)
Undermind 09. Test For The Future (03-07-65)
Dudley Sutton (Cast Member)
The Avengers 6-04. You'll Catch Your Death (16-10-68)
The Baron 15. Storm Warning (Part 1) (04-01-67) 16. The Island (Part 2) (11-01-67)
Department S: 07. Handicap Dead (20-04-69)
Randall & Hopkirk (Deceased) 18. Could You Recognise The Man Again (16-01-70)
The Saint 3-04. The Scorpion (29-10-64)
Duncan Lamont (Cast Member)
The Avengers 6-22. Stay Tuned (26-02-69)
Callan 2-01. Red Knight, White Knight (08-01-69)
Danger Man 1-24. The Relaxed Informer (16-04-61) 2-13. That's Two Of Us Sorry (05-01-64)
Department S: 16. The Man From X (05-11-69)
Man In A Suitcase 10. All That Glitters (29-11-67) 17. Why They Killed Nolan (17-01-67)
Randall & Hopkirk (Deceased) 09. The House On Haunted Hill (16-11-69)
Duncan Macrae (Cast Member)
The Avengers 3-25. Espirit de Corps (14-03-64)
The Prisoner 08. Dance Of The Dead (17-11-67)
Dyson Lovell (Cast Member)
The Avengers 5-13. A Funny Thing Happened On The Way To The Station (08-04-67)
The Saint 2-22. The Invisible Millionaire (13-02-64)
Out Of The Unknown 1-05. Time In Advance (01-11-65)

E

Eamonn Andrews (Cast Member)
Undermind 06. Intent To Destroy (12-06-65)
Earl Cameron (Cast Member)
Danger Man 1-39. Deadline (20-01-62) 2-04. The Galloping Major (03-11-64) 2-22. Parallel Lines Sometimes Meet (16-03-65) 3-05. Loyalty Always Pays (28-10-65) 3-15. Somebody Is Liable To Get Hurt (06-01-66)
Doctor Who 29. The Tenth Planet: 3 Episodes (08-10-66)
The Prisoner 05. The Schizoid Man (27-10-67)
Earl Green (Cast Member)
Department S: 10. Double Death Of Charlie Crippen (14-09-69)
Ghost Squad 2-20. P.G.7. (06-07-63)
Randall & Hopkirk (Deceased) 22. It's Supposed To Be Thicker Than Water (13-02-70)
The Saint 5-02. Interlude In Venice (07-10-66)
Ed Bishop (Cast Member)
Man In A Suitcase 18. The Boston Square (24-01-67)
The Saint 3-05. The Revolution Racket (05-11-64) 3-06. The Saint Steps In (12-11-64) 4-07. The Saint Bids Diamonds (12-08-65) 5-08. The Man Who Liked Lions (18-11-66)
Strange Report 01. REPORT 5055 CULT Murder Shrieks Out (21-09-69)
Ed Devereaux (Cast Member)
The Saint 3-07. The Loving Brothers (19-11-64)
Eddie Byrne (Cast Member)
The Baron 26. The Long, Long Day (22-03-67)
Department S: 15. The Shift That Never Was (25-10-69)
The Saint 1-11. The Man Who Was Lucky (13-12-62) 4-01. The Chequered Flag (01-07-65) 5-09. The Better Mouse Trap (25-11-66) 6-20. The World Beater (09-02-69)
Eddie Eddon (Cast Member)
The Prisoner 14. Living In Harmony (29-12-67)
Eddie Powell (Cast Member)
The Avengers 3-22. The Outside-In Man (22-02-64)
Danger Man 3-17. I Can Only Offer You Sherry (20-01-66)
The Prisoner 10. Hammer & Anvil (01-12-67)
Eddie Stacey (Cast Member)
Adam Adamant Lives! 12. Beauty Is An Ugly Word (15-09-66)
Edgar K Bruce (Cast Member)
Ghost Squad 2-13. The Desperate Diplomat (18-05-63)
Edgar Wreford (Cast Member)
The Avengers 2-17. Box Of Tricks (19-01-63)
Edina Ronay (Cast Member)
The Avengers 2-06. The Removal Men (03-11-62) 3-04. The Nutshell (19-10-63)
The Champions 08. To Trap a Rat (13-11-68)
Department S: 05. One Of Aircraft Is Empty (06-4-69) 14. Les Fleurs Du Mal (22-10-69)
Ghost Squad 2-25. The Thirteenth Girl (27-04-63)
Randall & Hopkirk (Deceased) 04. Never Trust a Ghost (12-10-69)
Edith Saville (Cast Member)
The Saint 2-20. The Lawless Lady (30-01-64)
Edmund Coulter (Cast Member)
Doctor Who 23. The Ark: 4 Episodes (05-03-66)
dric Connor (Cast Member)
The Avengers 3-07. The Gilded Cage (09-11-63)
Danger Man 1-39. Deadline (20-01-62) 2-04. The Galloping Major (03-11-64)
Man In A Suitcase 01. Brainwash (27-09-67)
Eduardo Ciannelli (Cast Member)
The Third Man 1-30. As The Twig Is Bent (03-06-60)
Edward Brayshaw (Cast Member)
The Avengers 6-26. Homicide & Old Lace (26-03-69) 6-27. Thingamajig (16-04-69)

The Baron 04. Red Horse, Red Rider (19-10-66) 17. Time To Kill (18-01-67)
The Champions 17. A Case Of Lemmings (22-01-68)
Danger Man 2-22. Parallel Lines Sometimes Meet (16-03-65)
Department S: 03. Cellar Full Of Silence (23-03-69)
Doctor Who 08. The Reign Of Terror: 4 Episodes (08-08-64)
Randall & Hopkirk (Deceased) 23. The Trouble With Women (20-02-70)
The Saint 6-03. Legacy For The Saint (13-10-68)
Edward Burnham (Cast Member)
The Avengers 5-02. The Fear Merchants (21-01-67)
The Saint 5-10. Little Girl Lost (02-12-66)
Edward Caddick (Cast Member)
The Avengers 5-03. Escape In Time (26-01-67)
Department S: 17. Dead Men Die Twice (12-11-69)
Randall & Hopkirk (Deceased) 25. You Can Always Find a Fall Guy (06-03-70)
Edward Cast (Cast Member)
The Avengers 4-10. Dial a Deadly Number (04-12-65)
The Champions 13. Twelve Hours (18-12-68)
Danger Man 2-11. Don't Nail Him Yet (22-12-64) 2-16. A Room in The Basement (02-02-65)
Department S: 19. The Duplicated Man (03-12-69)
Ghost Squad 1-06. Eyes Of The Bat (14-10-61) 1-11 The Green Shoes (29-12-62)
Man Of The World 2-05. In The Picture (08-06-63)
Strange Report 02. REPORT 0649 SKELETON Let Sleeping Heroes Lie (28-09-69)
The Saint 3-20. The Frightened Inn-Keeper (18-02-65)
Edward Chapman (Cast Member)
Danger Man 2-11. Don't Nail Him Yet (22-12-64)
Edward de Sousa (Cast Member)
The Avengers 2-25. Six Hands Across a Table (16-03-63) 6-19. The Curious Case Of The Countless Clues (05-02-69)
Department S: 10. Double Death Of Charlie Crippen (14-09-69)
Doctor Who 19. Mission To The Unknown (09-10-65)
The Saint 4-01. The Chequered Flag (01-07-65)
Edward Evans (Cast Member)
Man In A Suitcase 23. Web With Four Spiders (28-02-67)
The Saint 1-05. The Loaded Tourist (01-11-62) 6-15. Vendetta For The Saint Part 1 (05-01-68)
Edward Fox (Cast Member)
The Avengers 6-28. My Wildest Dream (07-04-69)
Man In A Suitcase 29. Castle In The Clouds (10-04-67)
Edward Hardwicks (Cast Member)
Danger Man 1-02. Time to Kill (18-11-60)
Edward Harvey (Cast Member)
The Saint 6-10. The Scales Of Justice (01-12-68)
Edward Higgins (Cast Member)
The Avengers 2-07. The Mauritius Penny (10-11-62) 5-17. Return Of The Cybernauts (30-09-67)
The Saint 5-25. The Power Artists (19-05-67)
Edward Jewesbury (Cast Member)
The Avengers 2-07. The Mauritius Penny (10-11-62)
Danger Man 3-05. Loyalty Always Pays (28-10-65)
Interpol Calling 16. No Flowers For Onno (04-01-59)
Edward Judd (Cast Member)
Out Of The Unknown 1-05. Time In Advance (01-11-65)
Edward Kelsey (Cast Member)
The Avengers 2-14. Dead On Course (29-12-62)
Doctor Who 12. The Romans: 4 Episodes (16-01-65)
The Saint 6-03. Legacy For The Saint (13-10-68)
Edward Ogden (Cast Member)
Danger Man 3-25. Shinda Shima (26-02-67)
Edward Palmer (Cast Member)
Adam Adamant Lives! 11. Death By Appointment Only (08-09-66)

Ghost Squad 1-05. High Wire (30-09-61)
Edward Phillips (Cast Member)
Doctor Who 33. The Moonbase: 2 Episodes (18-02-67)
Edward Sinclair (Cast Member)
Danger Man 3-01. The Black Book (30-09-65)
Edward Underdown (Cast Member)
The Avengers 4-07. The Murder Market (13-11-65) 5-07. The Living Dead (25-02-67)
Danger Man 2-03. Colony Three (27-10-64) 2-18. The Ubiquitous Mr Lovegrove (16-02-65)
3-18. The Hunting Party (27-01-66)
Man In A Suitcase 10. All That Glitters (29-11-67) 30. Night Flight To Andorra (17-04-67)
The Saint 3-15. The Set-Up (14-01-65)
Edward Woodward (Cast Member)
The Baron 29. Countdown (12-04-67)
Callen all episodes
The Saint 5-15. The Persistent Patriots (06-01-67)
Edwin Apps (Cast Member)
The Avengers 5-09. The Correct Way To Kill (11-03-67)
Danger Man 2-05. Fair Exchange (10-11-64) 2-11. Don't Nail Him Yet (22-12-64)
Edwin Brown (Cast Member)
The Avengers 2-07. The Mauritius Penny (10-11-62) 3-04. The Nutshell (19-10-63)
The Baron 19. You Can't Win Them All (01-02-67)
Ghost Squad 2-04. The Golden Silence (08-06-63)
The Saint 5-14. Escape Route (30-12-66) 6-08. The Master Plan (17-11-68)
Strange Report 06. REPORT 3906 COVER-GIRLS Last Years Model (26-10-69)
Edwin Finn (Cast Member)
The Avengers 4-11. Man Eater Of Surrey Green (11-12-65)
Undermind 02. Flowers Of Havoc (15-05-65)
Edwin Richfield (Cast Member)
The Avengers 2-06. The Removal Men (03-11-62) 3-15. The White Elephant (4-01-64) 4-13 Too Many
Christmas Trees (25-12-65) 5-20. Dead Man's Treasure (21-10-67) 6-08. All Done With Mirrors (
13-11-68)
The Baron 18. A Memory Of Evil (25-01-67) 27. Roundabout (29-03-67)
Danger Man 3-23. Not So Jolly Roger (07-04-66)
Ghost Squad 1-03. Ticket For Blackmail (09-09-61) 2-17. Mr Five Per Cent (06-04-63)
Interpol Calling All Episodes
The Protectors 06. The Stamp Collection (02-05-64)
Edwin Richminster (Cast Member)
The Avengers 1-06. Girl On The Trapeze (11-02-61)
Edwina Carroll (Cast Member)
Department S: 10. Double Death Of Charlie Crippen (14-09-69)
Eileen Moore (Cast Member)
Danger Man 1-37. The Nurse (06-01-61)
Eileen Way (Cast Member)
Doctor Who 01. An Unearthly Child: 2 Episodes (23-11-63)
Man Of The World 2-06. The Bullfighter (15-06-63)
The Saint 6-16. Vendetta For The Saint Part 2 (12-01-68)
Elaine Little (Cast Member)
The Avengers 2-26. Killer Whale (23-03-63)
Elaine Taylor (Cast Member)
Strange Report 06. REPORT 3906 COVER-GIRLS Last Years Model (26-10-69)
Eleanor Darling (Cast Member)
The Avengers 1-15. The Frighteners (27-11-61)
Eleanor Summerfield (Cast Member)
Department S: 23. A Small War Of Nerves (21-01-70)
Ellis Dale (Cast Member)
Department S: 26. The Ghost Of Mary Burnham (18-02-70)
Eliza Buckingham (Cast Member)
The Saint 4-01. The Chequered Flag (01-07-65)

Elizabeth Ashley (Cast Member)
Danger Man 2-09. No Marks For Servility (08-12-64)
Elizabeth Bell (Cast Member)
Callan 2-02. The Most Promising Girl Of Her Year (15-01-69)
Elizabeth Murray (Cast Member)
The Avengers 2-14. Dead On Course (29-12-62)
Elizabeth Robilard (Cast Member)
The Avengers: 6-23. Take Me To Your Leader (05-03-69)
Elizabeth Sellars (Cast Member)
The Avengers 6-30. Take-Over (23-04-69)
Elizabeth Shepherd (Cast Member)
Danger Man 3-16. Dangerous Secret (13-01-66)
The Corridor People All 4 Episodes (1966)
The Protectors 01. Landscape With Bandits (28-03-64)
Elizabeth Weaver (Cast Member)
Out Of The Unknown 3 -08. Little Black Bag (25-02-69)
The Saint 3-14. The Contact (07-01-65)
Elizabeth Wilson (Cast Member)
Interpol Calling 25. The Girl With The Grey Hair (14-03-60) 37. Pipeline (06-06-60)
Elizabeth Zinn (Cast Member)
Ghost Squad 2-26. Sabotage (20-04-63)
Ellen McIntosh (Cast Member)
The Avengers 2-10. Death On The Rocks (01-12-62)
Ghost Squad 2-01. Interrupted Requiem (02-02-63)
The Saint 2-05. The Elusive Elishaw (17-10-63)
Elma Soiron (Cast Member)
Department S: 27. A Fish Out Of Water (25-02-70)
Elspeth March (Cast Member)
The Saint 1-07. The Arrow Of God (15-11-62) 2-27. The Saint Sees It Through (19-03-64)
Elvi Hale (Cast Member)
Ghost Squad 2-12. Quarantine At Kavar (01-06-63)
Emma Cochrane (Cast Member)
The Avengers 6-04. You'll Catch Your Death (16-10-68)
Emmett Hennessey (Cast Member)
Adam Adamant Lives! 09. Sing a Song Of Murder (25-08-66)
Emrys Jones (Cast Member)
Doctor Who 45. The Mind Robber: 5 Episodes (14-09-68)
Out Of The Unknown 3 -08. Little Black Bag (25-02-69)
Enid Lorimer (Cast Member)
The Avengers 5-14. Something Nasty In The Nursery (15-04-67)
Man Of The World 2-07. The Prince (22-06-63)
Endre Muller (Cast Member)
Danger Man 1-02. Time to Kill (18-11-60)
Ghost Squad 2-08. The Man With The Delicate Hands (22-06-63)
Eric Barker (Cast Member)
The Avengers 6-14. The Interrogators (01-01-69)
Danger Man 2-18. The Ubiquitous Mr Lovegrove (16-02-65)
Eric Chitty (Cast Member)
Strange Report 02. REPORT 0649 SKELETON Let Sleeping Heroes Lie (28-09-69)
Eric Dodson (Cast Member)
The Protectors 04. No Forwarding Address (18-04-64)
Randall & Hopkirk (Deceased) 12. For The Girl Who Has Everything (07-12-69)
The Saint 5-26. When Spring Is Sprung (02-06-67)
Credited Cast Members cont
Eric Elliott (Cast Member)
The Avengers 1-15. The Frighteners (27-11-61) 2-08. Death Of Great Dane (17-11-62)
Doctor Who 23. The Ark: 4 Episodes (05-03-66)
Eric Flynn (Cast Member)

The Avengers 5-23. Murdersville (11-11-67)
Doctor Who 43. The Wheel in Space: 2 Episodes (11-05-68)
Eric Francis (Cast Member)
The Protectors 05. The Loop Men (25-04-64)
Eric Lander (Cast Member)
The Avengers 4-12. Twos a Crowd (18-12-65)
The Champions 24. Project Zero (12-03-69)
Department S: 15. The Shift That Never Was (25-10-69)
Out Of The Unknown 1-03. Stranger In the Family (18-10-65)
Eric Longworth (Cast Member)
The Saint 5-15. The Persistent Patriots (06-01-67)
Eric Mason (Cast Member)
The Baron 22. Night Of The Hunter (22-02-67)
The Saint 5-14. Escape Route (30-12-66) 6-01. The Best Laid Plans (29-09-68)
Eric McCaine (Cast Member)
The Avengers 2-05. Mission To Montreal (27-10-62)
Eric Pohlmann (Cast Member)
The Avengers 2-24. A Chorus Of Frogs (09-03-63)
The Baron 24. Long Ago & Far Away (08-03-67)
The Champions 22. Get Me Out Of Here (26-02-69) 30. Autokill (30-04-69)
Danger Man 1-29. The Contessa (21-05-61) 1-37. The Nurse (06-01-61) 2-12. A Date With Doris (29-12-64) 2-17. The Affair At Castelevara (09-02-65)
Department S: 13. The Man Who Got a New Face (15-10-69)
Ghost Squad 2-26. Sabotage (20-04-63)
Man Of The World 1-03. Blaze Of Glory (13-10-62)
The Saint 2-04. Teresa (10-10-63) 3-05. The Revolution Racket (05-11-64)
The Third Man 2-02. One Kind Word (07-09-59)
The Prisoner 04. Free For All (20-10-67)
Strange Report 02. REPORT 0649 SKELETON Let Sleeping Heroes Lie (28-09-69)
Eric Thompson (Cast Member)
Man In A Suitcase 10. All That Glitters (29-11-67)
Out Of The Unknown 1-06. Come Buttercup, Come Daisy, Come…? (08-11-65)
Eric Woofe (Cast Member)
The Avengers 5-19. The £50,000 Breakfast (14-10-67)
Erica Houen (Cast Member)
Ghost Squad 2-01. Interrupted Requiem (02-02-63)
Erica Rogers (Cast Member)
Man Of The World 1-04. The Runaways (20-10-62) 1-10. Portrait Of a Girl (01-12-62)
The Saint 1-10. Golden Journey (6-12-62) 3-02. Lida (15-10-64) 4-09 Old Treasure Story (26-8-65)
Erik Chitty (Cast Member)
Danger Man 2-14. Such Men Are Dangerous (12-01-65)
Ghost Squad 2-08. The Man With The Delicate Hands (22-06-63)
Erika Remberg (Cast Member)
Man Of The World 2-03. Double Exposure (25-05-63)
The Saint 5-05. The Helpful Pirate (28-10-66)
Ernest Blyth (Cast Member)
Adam Adamant Lives! 06. The Happy Embalmers (04-06-66)
The Avengers 4-10. Dial a Deadly Number (04-12-65)
The Champions 13. Twelve Hours (18-12-68)
Department S: 21. Death On Reflection (17-12-69)
Ernest Clark (Cast Member)
Interpol Calling 09. Private View (09-11-59)
Ernest Hare (Cast Member)
A For Andromeda 1-6. The Face Of The Tiger (07-11-61)
Undermind 01. Instance One (08-05-65)
Ernest Lindsay (Cast Member)
Danger Man 2-05. Fair Exchange (10-11-64)

Ernst Ulman (Cast Member)
Danger Man 3-03. Sting In The Tail (14-10-65)
The Saint 5-01. The Queens Ransom (30-09-66)
Ernst Walder (Cast Member)
The Baron 09. And Suddenly You're Dead (23-11-66)
The Champions 14. The Search (01-01-68)
Danger Man 2-21. The Mirror's New (09-03-65)
Errol John (Cast Member)
Danger Man 2-04. The Galloping Major (03-11-64) 2-22. Parallel Lines Sometimes Meet (16-03-65) 3-05. Loyalty Always Pays (28-10-65)
Interpol Calling 13. Slave Ship (14-12-59)
Man In A Suitcase 21. No Friend Of Mine (14-02-67)
Esmond Knight (Cast Member)
A For Andromeda 1-6. The Face Of The Tiger (07-11-61)
The Champions 20. The Silent Enemy (12-02-69)
Danger Man 1-20. The Vacation (29-01-61)
Interpol Calling 04. The Sleeping Giant (05-10-59)
The Protectors 11. Who Killed Lazoryck? (06-06-64)
The Saint 1-04. The Covetous Headsman (25-10-62)
Esmond Webb (Cast Member)
Adam Adamant Lives! 12. Beauty Is An Ugly Word (15-09-66)
Ester Anderson (Cast Member)
The Avengers 4-16. Small Game For Big Hunters (15-01-65)
Eugene Deckers (Cast Member)
Man Of The World 1-12. A Family Affair (15-12-62)
The Saint 1-04. The Covetous Headsman (25-10-62)
Eunice Gayson (Cast Member)
The Avengers 4-19. Quick-Quick Slow Death (05-02-66)
Danger Man 2-10. A Man To Be Trusted (15-12-64)
The Saint 2-22. The Invisible Millionaire (13-02-64) 4-07. The Saint Bids Diamonds (12-08-65)
Eva Enger (Cast Member)
Randall & Hopkirk (Deceased) 11. The Ghost Who Saved The Bank At Monte Carlo (30-11-69)
Eva Wilshaw (Cast Member)
Adam Adamant Lives! 03. More Deadly Than The Sword (07-07-66)
Evan Thomas (Cast Member)
Ghost Squad 2-20. P.G.7. (06-07-63)
The Saint 2-13. The Sporting Chance (12-12-63)
Eve Bellton (Cast Member)
The Saint 5-10. Little Girl Lost (02-12-66)
Eve Gross (Cast Member)
Adam Adamant Lives! 13. The League Of Uncharitable Ladies (12-09-66)
Eve Lister (Cast Member)
The Saint 3-04. The Scorpion (29-10-64)
Eve Lucette (Cast Member)
Man Of The World 1-09. The Mindreader (24-11-62)
Eve Ross (Cast Member)
Out Of The Unknown 3-03. The Last Lonely Man (21-01-69)
Evelyn Lund (Cast Member)
Undermind 03. The New Dimension (22-05-65)
Ewan Hooper (Cast Member)
The Avengers 4-22. What The Butler Saw (26-02-66)
Man In A Suitcase 30. Night Flight To Andorra (17-04-67)
Strange Report 13. REPORT 4821 X-RAY Who Weeps For The Doctor (21-12-69)
Undermind 06. Intent To Destroy (12-06-65)
Ewan MacDuff (Cast Member)
Danger Man 1-09. The Sanctuary (06-11-60)
Ewan Roberts (Cast Member)
The Avengers 6-22. Stay Tuned (26-02-69)

The Baron 27. Roundabout (29-03-67)
Danger Man 1-23. The Gallows Tree (09-04-61)
The Saint 5-06. The Convenient Monster (04-11-66)
Strange Report 03. REPORT 2641 HOSTAGE If You Won't Learn Die (05-10-69)
Ewen Solon (Cast Member)
Danger Man 1-05. The Lovers (09-10-60)
Ghost Squad 1-11 The Green Shoes (29-12-62)
Man Of The World 1-08. The Nature Of Justice (17-11-62)
Eynon Evans (Cast Member)
Danger Man 2-15. Whatever Happened To George Foster (19-01-65)

F

Fabia Drake (Cast Member)
The Avengers 4-20. The Danger Makers (12-02-66)
Callan 2-04. The Little Bits & Pieces Of Love (29-01-69)
Man In A Suitcase 06. Man From The Dead (01-11-67)
The Prisoner 01. Arrival (29-09-67)
The Saint 4-04. The Smart Detective (22-07-65)
Faith Brook (Cast Member)
Man In A Suitcase 28. Three Blinks Of The Eyes (03-04-67)
The Protectors 02. The Bottle Shop (04-04-64)
Faith Kent (Cast Member)
Man In A Suitcase 29. Castle In The Clouds (10-04-67)
The Saint 3-15. The Set-Up (14-01-65)
Fanny Carby (Cast Member)
Out Of The Unknown 2-08. Tunnel Under The World (01-12-66)
Felicity Gibson (Cast Member)
Doctor Who 44. The Dominators: 5 Episodes (10-08-68)
Felicity Kendal (Cast Member)
Man In A Suitcase 20. Blind Spot (07-02-67)
Felicity Young (Cast Member)
Interpol Calling 26. Trial At Cranby's Creek (21-03-60)
Felix Aylmer (Cast Member)
The Champions 01. The Beginning (25-09-68)
Randall & Hopkirk (Deceased) 22. It's Supposed To Be Thicker Than Water (13-02-70)
Felix Deebank (Cast Member)
The Avengers 2-04. Bullseye (20-10-62)
Fenella Fielding (Cast Member)
The Avengers 3-23. The Charmers (29-02-64)
Danger Man 1-10. An Affair Of State (13-11-60)
The Prisoner 04. Free For All (20-10-67)
Ferdy Mayne (Cast Member)
The Avengers 6-09. Legacy Of Death (20-11-68)
Danger Man 1-04. The Blue Veil (02-10-60) 3-22. The Paper Chase (31-03-66)
Interpol Calling 03. The Money Game (28-09-59)
Man In A Suitcase 26. The Revolutionaries (20-03-67)
The Saint 2-16. The Wonderful War (02-01-64) 5-13. Flight Plan (23-12-66)
The Third Man 2-06. Barcelona Passage (01-10-59)
Fernando Marlowe (Cast Member)
Ghost Squad 2-21. Polsky (02-03-63)
Ferdy Mayne (Cast Member)
Ghost Squad 2-13. The Desperate Diplomat (18-05-63)
Man Of The World 2-06. The Bullfighter (15-06-63)
The Saint 2-08. Iris (07-11-63) 5-24. A Double In Diamonds (05-05-67)
Finlay Currie (Cast Member)
Danger Man 1-23. The Gallows Tree (09-04-61) 2-13. That's Two Of Us Sorry (05-01-64)
Man Of The World 1-07. The Highland Story (10-11-62)
The Prisoner 02. The Chimes Of Big Ben (06-10-67)
The Saint 6-16. Vendetta For The Saint Part 2 (12-01-68)
Fiona Hartford (Cast Member)
The Avengers 6-04. You'll Catch Your Death (16-10-68)
Fiona Lewis (Cast Member)
Department S: 08. A Ticket To Nowhere (27-04-69)
The Saint 5-13. Flight Plan (23-12-66)
Forster Norris (Cast Member)
A For Andromeda 1-6. The Face Of The Tiger (07-11-61)
Fran Brown (Cast Member)

The Avengers 2-06. The Removal Men (03-11-62)
Frances Alger (Cast Member)
Out Of The Unknown 1-04. The Dead Past (25-10-65)
Frances Baker (Cast Member)
Department S: 21. Death On Reflection (17-12-69)
Frances Bennett (Cast Member)
Randall & Hopkirk (Deceased) 13. But What a Sweet Little Room (14-12-69)
Francesca Annis (Cast Member)
Danger Man 2-09. No Marks For Servility (08-12-64) 2-13. That's Two Of Us Sorry (05-01-64)
Ghost Squad 1-05. High Wire (30-09-61)
The Saint 5-12. Locate & Destroy (16-12-66)
Francesca Tu (Cast Member)
Danger Man 3-02. A Very Dangerous Game (07-10-65)
Department S: 18. The Perfect Operation (26-12-69)
Francis Cuka (Cast Member)
Adam Adamant Lives! 29. A Sinister Sort Of Service (25-03-67)
The Champions 22. Get Me Out Of Here (26-02-69)
Francis De Wolff (Cast Member)
Danger Man 2-18. The Ubiquitous Mr Lovegrove (16-02-65)
Interpol Calling 06. The Long Weekend (19-10-59) 28. Slow Boat To Amsterdam (04-04-60)
The Saint 6-01. The Best Laid Plans (29-09-68)
Francis Matthews (Cast Member)
The Avengers 4-18. Thirteenth Hole (29-01-66) 5-24. Mission, Highly Improbable (18-11-67)
Interpol Calling 29. White Blackmail (11-04-60)
The Saint 2-17. The Noble Sportsman (09-01-64) 5-19. To Kill a Saint (24-02-67)
Frank Atkinson (Cast Member)
The Saint 2-22. The Invisible Millionaire (13-02-64)
Frank Barringer (Cast Member)
The Avengers 6-18. The Morning After (29-10-69)
Frank Crenshaw (Cast Member)
Doctor Who 09. Planet Of Giants: 3 Episodes (31-10-64)
Frank Forsyth (Cast Member)
Department S: 03. Cellar Full Of Silence (23-03-69) 22. Last Train to Redbridge (14-01-70)
Man In A Suitcase 08. Essay In Evil (15-11-67) 23. Web With Four Spiders (28-02-67)
Frank Gatliff (Cast Member)
The Avengers 2-09 The Sell Out (24-11-62) 2-24. A Chorus Of Frogs (09-3-63) 6-21. Love All (19-2-69)
The Baron 01. Diplomatic Immunity (28-09-66)
Danger Man 3-14. The Man Who Wouldn't Talk (30-12-65)
Department S: 06. The Man In The Elegant Room (13-04-69)
Ghost Squad 2-20. P.G.7. (06-07-63)
Man In A Suitcase 24. Which Way Did He Go, McGill (6-3-67) 25. Property Of A Gentleman (13-03-67)
Frank George (Cast Member)
Doctor Who 23. The Ark: 4 Episodes (05-03-66)
Frank Jarvis (Cast Member)
Adam Adamant Lives! 01 A Year For Scoundrels (20-06-66)
The Saint 2-09. The King Of The Beggars (14-11-63)
Frank Lieberman (Cast Member)
Ghost Squad 2-11. A First Class Way To Die (13-07-63)
Frank Maher (Cast Member)
The Avengers 3-06. November Five (02-11-63) 3-14. Dressed To Kill (28-12-63) 3-16. The Little Wonders (11-01-64) 5-21. You Have Just Been Murdered (28-10-67)
Danger Man 2-21 The Mirror's New (9-3-65) 3-10 Are You Going To Be More Permanent? (2-12-65)
Man In A Suitcase 20. Blind Spot (07-02-67)
The Prisoner 14. Living In Harmony (29-12-67)
The Saint 5-11. Paper Chase (09-12-66) 6-11. The Fiction Makers Part 1 (08-12-68)

Frank Middlemass (Cast Member)
Ghost Squad 2-18. The Heir Apparent (09-03-63)
Frank Middleton (Cast Member)
The Avengers 6-14. The Interrogators (01-01-69)
Frank Mills (Cast Member)
The Avengers 3-23. The Charmers (29-02-64)
Undermind 01. Instance One (08-05-65)
Frank Olegario (Cast Member)
The Avengers 2-16. Immortal Clay (12-01-63)
Danger Man 2-07. The Colonels Daughter (24-11-64)
Ghost Squad 1-01. Hong Kong Story (23-09-61) 2-19. Death of a Sportsman (26-01-63)
Man Of The World 1-11. Specialist For the Kill (08-12-62)
The Saint 1-06. The Pearls Of Peace (08-11-62) 2-04. Teresa (10-10-63)
Frank Peters (Cast Member)
The Avengers 2-08. Death Of Great Dane (17-11-62)
Frank Seton (Cast Member)
Ghost Squad 2-04. The Golden Silence (08-06-63)
Frank Shelley (Cast Member)
The Avengers 2-20. School For Traitors (09-02-63)
Frank Sieman (Cast Member)
The Avengers 2-25. Six Hands Across a Table (16-03-63) 6-24. Fog (12-03-69)
Ghost Squad 1-02. Bullet With My Name On It (16-09-61)
The Saint 2-25. The Gentle Ladies (05-03-64)
Frank Singuineau (Cast Member)
Man Of The World 2-04. Jungle Mission (01-06-63)
Frank Thornton (Cast Member)
The Champions 23. The Night People (05-03-69)
Danger Man 1-17. Find & Return (08-01-61) 1-33. Hired Assassin (18-06-61)
Frank Tregear (Cast Member)
Ghost Squad 2-17. Mr Five Per Cent (06-04-63)
Frank Windsor (Cast Member)
The Avengers 6-06. Whoever Shot George Oblique Stroke XR40? (30-10-68)
Randall & Hopkirk (Deceased) 01. My Late Lamented Friend & Partner (21-09-69)
Frank Wolff (Cast Member)
The Baron 04. Red Horse, Red Rider (19-10-66)
The Saint 4-09. The Old Treasure Story (26-08-65)
Franz Van Norde (Cast Member)
Callan 2-06. Heir Apparent (12-02-69**)**
Frazer Hines (Cast Member)
Doctor Who 32. The Underwater Menace: 2 Episodes (21-01-67) 33. The Moonbase: 2 Episodes (18-02-67) 35. The Faceless Ones: Episode 1 (08-04-67) 36. The Evil Of The Daleks: Episode 2 (27-05-67) 37. The Tomb Of The Cybermen: 4 Episodes (02-09-67) 38. The Abominable Snowman: Episode 2 (07-10-67) 40. The Enemy Of The World: 6 Episodes (23-12-67) 41. The Web Of Fear: 5 Episodes (03-02-68) 43. The Wheel in Space: 2 Episodes (11-05-68) 44. The Dominators: 5 Episodes (10-08-68) 45. The Mind Robber: 5 Episodes (14-09-68) 46. The Invasion: 6 Episodes (09-11-68) 47. The Krotons: 4 Episodes (28-12-68) 48. The Seeds Of Death: 6 Episodes (25-01-69) 49. The Space Pirates: Episode 2 (15-03-69) 50. The War Games: 10 Episodes (19-04-69)
Fred Beauman (Cast Member)
Man In A Suitcase 30. Night Flight To Andorra (17-04-67)
Fred Davis (Cast Member)
Callan 2-01. Red Knight, White Knight (08-01-69)
Undermind 06. Intent To Destroy (12-06-65)
Fred Ferris (Cast Member)
The Avengers 2-04. Bullseye (20-10-62) 3-01. Brief For Murder (28-09-63)
Doctor Who 09. Planet Of Giants: 3 Episodes (31-10-64)
The Saint 2-01. The Fellow Traveller (19-09-63)
Fred Heggerty (Cast Member)
The Avengers 4-09. The Hour That Never Was (27-11-65)

Man In A Suitcase 06. Man From The Dead (01-11-67)
Out Of The Unknown 1-07. Sucker Bait (15-11-65)
The Prisoner 10. Hammer & Anvil (01-12-67)
Fred Johnson (Cast Member)
The Third Man 2-10. Toys Of The Dead (03-11-59)
Fred McNaughton (Cast Member)
Undermind 03. The New Dimension (22-05-65)
Fred Sadoff (Cast Member)
The Saint 3-23. The Happy Suicide (11-03-65)
Fred Windrush (Cast Member)
Adam Adamant Lives! 07. To Set a Deadly Fashion (11-08-66)
Fred Wood (Cast Member)
The Baron 09. And Suddenly You're Dead (23-11-66)
Freddie Jones (Cast Member)
The Avengers 5-16. Who's Who (29-04-67)
The Baron 25. So Dark The Night (15-03-67)
Fredric Abbott (Cast Member)
The Avengers 2-26. Killer Whale (23-03-63)
Danger Man 3-01. The Black Book (30-09-65) 3-08. The Outcast (18-11-65) 3-12. The Man On The
Beach (16-12-65) 3-20. I Am Afraid You Have The Wrong Number (17-03-66)
The Saint 5-07. The Angel's Eye (11-11-66) 6-01. The Best Laid Plans (29-09-68)
Freda Bamford (Cast Member)
The Avengers 2-25. Six Hands Across a Table (16-03-63)
Freda Knorr (Cast Member)
The Avengers 2-22. Man In The Mirror (23-02-63)
Freda Jackson (Cast Member)
Adam Adamant Lives! 01 A Year For Scoundrels (20-06-66)
Randall & Hopkirk (Deceased) 26. The Smile Behind The Veil (13-03-70)
Freddie Jones (Cast Member)
Randall & Hopkirk (Deceased) 12. For The Girl Who Has Everything (07-12-69)
The Saint 6-07. The Time To Die (10-11-68)
Frederick Abbott (Cast Member)
The Avengers 3-07. The Gilded Cage (09-11-63)
The Baron 01. Diplomatic Immunity (28-09-66)
Department S: 02. The Trojan Tanker (16-03-69)
Man In A Suitcase 25. Property Of A Gentleman (13-03-67)
The Protectors 04. No Forwarding Address (18-04-64)
Frederick Bartman (Cast Member)
The Baron 18. A Memory Of Evil (25-01-67)
Danger Man 2-08. Battle Of The Cameras (1-12-64) 3-9. English Lady Take Lodgers (25-11-65)
Frederick Farley (Cast Member)
The Avengers 2-20. School For Traitors (09-02-63)
Danger Man 3-11. To Our Best Friend (09-12-65)
Ghost Squad 2-09. Hot Money (25-05-63)
Frederick Jaeger (Cast Member)
The Avengers 2-08. Death Of Great Dane (17-11-62) 4-03. The Cybernauts (16-10-65) 5-17. Return Of
The Cybernauts (30-09-67)
Callan 2-14. Nice People Die At Home (09-04-69)
Department S: 23. A Small War Of Nerves (21-01-70)
Interpol Calling 34. Dressed To Kill (06-05-60)
Frederick Peisley (Cast Member)
The Avengers 6-24. Fog (12-03-69)
Danger Man 3-06. The Mercenaries (04-11-65)
Ghost Squad 2-01. Interrupted Requiem (02-02-63)
Frederick Piper (Cast Member)
Danger Man 1-19. Name, Date & Place (22-01-61) 2-09. No Marks For Servility (08-12-64)
Interpol Calling 38. The Absent Assassin (13-06-60)
The Prisoner 01. Arrival (29-09-67)

Frederick Schiller (Cast Member)
The Avengers 2-02. Propellant 23 (06-10-62)
The Champions 07. The Survivors (06-11-68)
Danger Man 1-06. The Girl In Pink Pyjamas (16-10-60)
Ghost Squad 2-21. Polsky (02-03-63)
Frederick Schrecker (Cast Member)
Doctor Who 41. The Web Of Fear: 5 Episodes (03-02-68)
Frederick Treves (Cast Member)
The Andromeda Breakthrough 2-1. Cold Front (28-06-62)
The Avengers 5-08. The Hidden Tiger (04-03-67)
The Baron 27. Roundabout (29-03-67)
Randall & Hopkirk (Deceased) 23. The Trouble With Women (20-02-70)
Fredric Abbott (Cast Member)
The Avengers 2-26. Killer Whale (23-03-63)
Danger Man 3-01. The Black Book (30-09-65) 3-08. The Outcast (18-11-65) 3-12. The Man On The Beach (16-12-65) 3-20. I Am Afraid You Have The Wrong Number (17-03-66)
Strange Report 15. REPORT 4407 No Choice For The Donor (04-01-70)
Frieda Knorr (Cast Member)
The Baron 17. Time To Kill (18-01-67)
Fulton Mackay (Cast Member)
The Avengers 5-17. Return Of The Cybernauts (30-09-67) 6-04. You'll Catch Your Death (16-10-68) 6-33. Bizarre (21-05-69)
The Saint 5-06. The Convenient Monster (04-11-66) 6-01. The Best Laid Plans (29-09-68) 6-15. Vendetta For The Saint Part 1 (05-01-68)

G

Gabor Baraker (Cast Member)
The Champions 14. The Search (01-01-68)
Man Of The World 1-11. Specialist For the Kill (08-12-62)
The Saint 6-15. Vendetta For The Saint Part 1 (05-01-68)
Gabriel Toyne (Cast Member)
Ghost Squad 1-02. Bullet With My Name On It (16-09-61) 1-05. High Wire (30-09-61) 1-07. Still Waters (21-10-61) 2-21. Polsky (02-03-63)
Gabriella Licudi (Cast Member)
Danger Man 3-09. English Lady Take Lodgers (25-11-65)
Ghost Squad 1-04. Broken Doll (07-10-61)
Gabrielle Brune (Cast Member)
Randall & Hopkirk (Deceased) 14. Who Killed Cock Robin? (21-12-69)
Gabrielle Drake (Cast Member)
The Avengers 5-08. The Hidden Tiger (04-03-67)
The Champions 26. Full Circle (26-03-69)
The Saint 6-01. The Best Laid Plans (29-09-68)
Gabrielle Hamilton (Cast Member)
Strange Report 08. REPORT 2475 REVENGE When a Man Hates (09-11-69)
Gaby Vargas (Cast Member)
The Avengers 6-11. Look (Stop Me If You've Heard This One) But There Were These Two Fellers (04-12-68)
Gail Starforth (Cast Member)
The Avengers 2-17. Box Of Tricks (19-01-63)
Gamel Faris (Cast Member)
Interpol Calling 10. Dead On Arrival (16-11-59)
Garard Green (Cast Member)
Ghost Squad 1-08. Assassin (28-10-61)
Gareth Tandy (Cast Member)
Danger Man 1-23. The Gallows Tree (09-04-61)
Garfield Morgan (Cast Member)
The Avengers 5-02 Fear Merchants (21-1-67) 6-02. Game (2-10-68) 6-30. Take-Over (23-4-69)
The Baron 22. Night Of The Hunter (22-02-67)
Department S: 25. Spencer Bodily Is 60 Years Old (11-02-70)
Ghost Squad 2-10. The Grand Duchess (11-05-63)
Man In A Suitcase 02. The Sitting Pigeon (04-10-67)
Randall & Hopkirk (Deceased) 09. The House On Haunted Hill (16-11-69) 25. You Can Always Find a Fall Guy (06-03-70)
The Saint 5-18. The Art Collectors (27-01-67)
Undermind 03. The New Dimension (22-05-65)
Garry Fulsham (Cast Member)
The Saint 3-12. The Unkind Philanthropist (24-12-64)
Garth Adams (Cast Member)
The Protectors 07. It Could Happen Here (09-05-64)
Gary Bond (Cast Member)
The Avengers 6-22. Stay Tuned (26-02-69)
Gary Cockrell (Cast Member)
Danger Man 1-32. The Actor (11-06-61)
The Corridor People All Episodes (1966)
The Saint 1-03. The Careful Terrorist (18-10-62) 2-15. The Benevolent Burglary (26-12-63)
Gary Hope (Cast Member)
The Avengers 3-06. November Five (02-11-63) 5-12. The Superlative Seven (01-04-67)
Danger Man 3-09 English Lady Take Lodgers (25-11-65) 3-12. Man On The Beach (16-12-65)
The Saint 5-01. The Queens Ransom (30-09-66)
Gary Miller (Cast Member)
The Saint 6-13. The People Importers (22-12-68) 6-13. The People Importers (22-12-68)

Gary Raymond (Cast Member)
Man Of The World 1-05. The Frontier (27-10-62)
The Saint 4-08. The Spanish Cow (19-08-65)
Gary Smith (Cast Member)
Doctor Who 44. The Dominators: 5 Episodes (10-08-68)
Gary Watson (Cast Member)
The Avengers 2-16. Immortal Clay (12-01-63) 3-26. Lobster Quadrille (21-03-64) 6-20. Wish You
Were Here (12-02-69)
The Baron 05. Enemy Of The State (26-10-66)
Public Eye 4-04. My Lifes My Own (20-08-69)
Randall & Hopkirk (Deceased) 26. The Smile Behind The Veil (13-03-70)
The Saint 5-26. When Spring Is Sprung (02-06-67)
Garry Marsh (Cast Member)
Man Of The World 1-04. The Runaways (20-10-62)
Gavin Campbell (Cast Member)
Department S: 25. Spencer Bodily Is 60 Years Old (11-02-70)
Gay Hamilton (Cast Member)
Man In A Suitcase 05. Variation On a Million Bucks Part 2 (25-10-67) 29. Castle In The Clouds
(10-04-67)
Out Of The Unknown 2-08. Tunnel Under The World (01-12-66)
Gaylord Cavallaro (Cast Member)
Interpol Calling 39. Checkmate (20-06-60)
Gaynor Steward (Cast Member)
The Prisoner 15. The Girl Who Was Death (18-01-67)
Gene Garvey (Cast Member)
Undermind 05. Too Many Enemies (05-06-65)
Geoff L'Cise (Cast Member)
The Avengers 2-13. Death Dispatch (22-12-62) 3-07. The Gilded Cage (09-11-63)
Geoffrey Alexander (Cast Member)
Adam Adamant Lives! 03. More Deadly Than The Sword (07-07-66)
The Avengers 3-05. Death Of a Batman (26-01-63)
Out Of The Unknown 1-12. The Midas Plague (20-12-65)
Geoffrey Bayldon (Cast Member)
The Avengers 5-03. Escape In Time (26-01-67)
Danger Man 3-02. A Very Dangerous Game (07-10-65)
The Saint 5-18. The Art Collectors (27-01-67) 3-04. The Scorpion (29-10-64)
Geoffrey Bellman (Cast Member)
Ghost Squad 2-03. Sentences Of Death (04-05-63)
Geoffrey Chater (Cast Member)
The Avengers 5-21 You Have Just Been Murdered (28-10-67) 6-04 You'll Catch Your Death
(16-10-68)
The Champions 24. Project Zero (12-03-69)
Department S: 01. Six Days (09-03-69)
Ghost Squad 2-04. The Golden Silence (08-06-63)
The Saint 6-10. The Scales Of Justice (01-12-68)
Geoffrey Cheshire (Cast Member)
Callan 2-09. Death Of a Friend (05-03-69)
Doctor Who 46. The Invasion: 6 Episodes (09-11-68)
The Saint 5-27. The Gadic Collection (22-06-67)
Geoffrey Colville (Cast Member)
The Avengers 5-23. Murdersville (11-11-67) 3-24. Concerto (07-03-64)
Doctor Who 36. The Evil Of The Daleks: Episode 2 (27-05-67)
Strange Report 03. REPORT 2641 HOSTAGE If You Won't Learn Die (05-10-69)
Geoffrey Denton (Cast Member)
The Saint 2-11. The Saint Plays With Fire (28-11-63)
Geoffrey Dunn (Cast Member)
The Andromeda Breakthrough 6 Episodes (1962)
Geoffrey Frederick (Cast Member)

Out Of The Unknown 2-03. Lambda One (20-10-66)
The Saint 3-18. The Sign Of The Claw (04-02-65)
Geoffrey Hinsliff (Cast Member)
Adam Adamant Lives!: 02. Death Has a Thousand Faces (30-06-66)
Geoffrey Hughes (Cast Member)
Randall & Hopkirk (Deceased) 17. Somebody Just Walked Over My Grave (09-01-70)
Geoffrey Keen (Cast Member)
Danger Man 3-19. Two Birds With One Bullet (10-03-66)
Man Of The World 2-07. The Prince (22-06-63)
The Saint 3-06. The Saint Steps In (12-11-64)
Geoffrey Kenion (Cast Member)
Out Of The Unknown 1-02. The Counterfeit Man (11-10-65) 2-03. Lambda One (20-10-66)
Geoffrey King (Cast Member)
Randall & Hopkirk (Deceased) 21. The Ghost Talks (06-02-70)
Geoffrey Lewis (Cast Member)
A For Andromeda 1-6. The Face Of The Tiger (07-11-61)
The Andromeda Breakthrough 2 Episodes (1962)
Geoffrey Lumsden (Cast Member)
Adam Adamant Lives! 10. The Doomsday Plan (01-09-66)
Danger Man 2-04. The Galloping Major (03-11-64)
The Saint 6-01. Best Laid Plans (29-09-68) 6-18. The Man Who Gambled With Life (26-01-68)
Geoffrey Morris (Cast Member)
The Saint 6-06. The Double Take (03-11-68)
Geoffrey Palmer (Cast Member)
The Avengers 2-02. Propellant 23 (06-10-62) 4-08. A Surfeit Of H2o (20-11-65)
The Baron 06. Masquerade (Part 1) (02-11-66) 07. The Killing (Part 2) (09-11-66)
Out Of The Unknown 1-01. No Place Like Earth (04-10-65)
The Saint 2-09. The King Of The Beggars (14-11-63)
Geoffrey Quigley (Cast Member)
The Saint 2-13. The Sporting Chance (12-12-63)
Geoffrey Reed (Cast Member)
The Avengers 5-10. Never, Never Say Die (18-03-67)
The Prisoner 09. Checkmate (14-11-67)
Man In A Suitcase 23. Web With Four Spiders (28-02-67)
Randall & Hopkirk (Deceased) 02. A Disturbing Case (28-09-69)
Geoffrey Russell (Cast Member)
The Avengers 6-02. Game (02-10-68)
Geoffrey Sumner (Cast Member)
The Avengers 5-14. Something Nasty In The Nursery (15-04-67)
Geoffrey Whitehead (Cast Member)
The Avengers 3-21. Build a Better Mousetrap (15-02-64) 6-31. Pandora (30-04-69)
George Alexander (Cast Member)
The Avengers 3-25. Espirit de Corps (14-03-64)
George Baizley (Cast Member)
Danger Man 3-15. Somebody Is Liable To Get Hurt (06-01-66)
George Baker (Cast Member)
The Baron 25. So Dark The Night (15-03-67)
The Prisoner 01. Arrival (29-09-67)
Undermind 11. End Signal (17-07-65)
George Benson (Cast Member)
The Avengers 3-18. Mandrake (25-01-64)
Danger Man 2-20. Have a Glass of Wine (02-03-65)
The Prisoner 04. Free For All (20-10-67)
Out Of The Unknown 1-04. The Dead Past (25-10-65)
George Cole (Cast Member)
Out Of The Unknown 3-03. The Last Lonely Man (21-01-69)
George Cooper (Cast Member)
The Avengers 2-21. The White Dwarf (16-02-63) 6-19. The Curious Case Of The Countless Clues

(05-02-69)
Danger Man 1-14. The Traitor (11-12-60)
Man In A Suitcase 07. Sweet Sue (08-11-67)
Randall & Hopkirk (Deceased) 09. The House On Haunted Hill (16-11-69)
The Saint 2-09. The King Of The Beggars (14-11-63) 6-20. The World Beater (09-02-69)
George Cormack (Cast Member)
Danger Man 3-10. Are You Going To Be More Permanent? (02-12-65)
George Coulouris (Cast Member)
Danger Man 1-25. The Brothers (23-04-61) 3-25. Shinda Shima (26-02-67)
Ghost Squad 1-08. Assassin (28-10-61)
Man Of The World 1-02. Masquerade In Spain (06-10-62)
Pathfinders To Venus 8 Episodes (1961)
Pathfinders To Mars 6 Episodes (1961)
The Prisoner 09. Checkmate (14-11-67)
George Day (Cast Member)
Public Eye 4-04. My Lifes My Own (20-08-69) 4-05. Case For The Defence (27-08-69)
George Eugeniou (Cast Member)
Danger Man: 1-27. Bury The Dead (07-05-61) 2-01. Yesterday's Enemies (13-10-64)
Ghost Squad 2-12. Quarantine At Kavar (01-06-63) 2-22. The Magic Bullet (16-03-63)
Man Of The World 2-04. Jungle Mission (01-06-63) 1-06. The Sentimental Agent (03-11-62)
George Fisher (Cast Member)
The Avengers 4-09. The Hour That Never Was (27-11-65) 3-25. Espirit de Corps (14-03-64) 4-03. The Cybernauts (16-10-65) 4-10. Dial a Deadly Number (04-12-65)
George Ghent (Cast Member)
The Avengers 6-13. They Keep Killing Steed (18-12-68)
Callan 2-01. Red Knight, White Knight (08-01-69)
George Gibson (Cast Member)
Adam Adamant Lives! 07. To Set a Deadly Fashion (11-08-66)
George Hilsdon (Cast Member)
The Avengers 4-07. The Murder Market (13-11-65)
George Holdcroft (Cast Member)
The Avengers 4-06. The Master Minds (06-11-65) 4-09. The Hour That Never Was (27-11-65)
George Howe (Cast Member)
Randall & Hopkirk (Deceased) 26. The Smile Behind The Veil (13-03-70)
George Innes (Cast Member)
The Avengers 6-33. Bizarre (21-05-69)
George Layton (Cast Member)
Doctor Who 49. The Space Pirates: Episode 2 (15-03-69)
George Lee (Cast Member)
Randall & Hopkirk (Deceased) 12. For The Girl Who Has Everything (07-12-69)
George Leech (Cast Member)
Man In A Suitcase 01. Brainwash (27-09-67)
The Prisoner 10. Hammer Into Anvil (01-12-67) 06. The General (03-11-67)
George Little (Cast Member)
The Avengers 2-06. The Removal Men (03-11-62) 3-03. Man With Two Shadows (12-10-63)
Man Of The World 1-05. The Frontier (27-10-62)
The Protectors 13. Cargo From Corinth (20-06-64)
The Saint 2-04. Teresa (10-10-63) 2-18. The Romantic Matron (16-01-64)
George Lowdell (Cast Member)
The Saint 4-09. The Old Treasure Story (26-08-65)
George Macrae (Cast Member)
The Avengers 3-25. Espirit de Corps (14-03-64)
George Madden (Cast Member)
Danger Man 2-03. Colony Three (27-10-64)
George Margo (Cast Member)
Interpol Calling 07. You Can't Die Twice (26-10-59)
George Markstein (Cast Member)
The Prisoner 04. Free For All (20-10-67)

George Merritt (Cast Member)
The Avengers 5-14. Something Nasty In The Nursery (15-04-67)
The Prisoner 08. Dance Of The Dead (17-11-67)
George Mikell (Cast Member)
Danger Man 2-05. Fair Exchange (10-11-64)
Strange Report 01. REPORT 5055 CULT Murder Shrieks Out (21-09-69)
George Moon (Cast Member)
Undermind 10. Waves Of Sound (10-07-65)
George Murcell (Cast Member)
The Avengers 5-21. You Have Just Been Murdered (28-10-67)
The Baron 10. The Legends of Ammak (30-11-66) 17. Time To Kill (18-01-67)
The Champions 03. Reply Box 666 (09-10-68) 09. The Iron Man (20-11-68)
Danger Man 1-27. Bury The Dead (07-05-61)
Ghost Squad 2-04. The Golden Silence (08-06-63)
Randall & Hopkirk (Deceased) 17. Somebody Just Walked Over My Grave (09-01-70)
The Saint 4-07. The Saint Bids Diamonds (12-08-65) 5-17. The Death Game (20-01-67) 5-25. The Power Artists (19-05-67)
George Pastell (Cast Member)
The Avengers 4-26. Honey For The Prince (26-03-66)
The Champions 06. Operation Deep Freeze (30-10-68)
Danger Man 2-07. The Colonels Daughter (24-11-64)
Department S 11 Who Plays The Dummy (1-10-69) 12 Treasure Of the Costa Del Sol (8-10-69)
Doctor Who 37. The Tomb Of The Cybermen: 4 Episodes (02-09-67)
Ghost Squad 1-01. Hong Kong Story (23-9-61) 1-10. Catspaw (05-1-61) 2-20. P.G.7. (06-07-63)
Interpol Calling 05. The Two Headed Monster (12-10-59) 14. The Man's a Clown (21-12-59) 18. The Thousand Mile Alibi (18-01-60) 25. The Girl With The Grey Hair (14-03-60)
Man Of The World 1-02. Masquerade In Spain (06-10-62)
Out Of The Unknown 1-01. No Place Like Earth (04-10-65)
The Saint 5-01. The Queens Ransom (30-09-66) 5-26. When Spring Is Sprung (02-06-67) 1-04. The Covetous Headsman (25-10-62) 6-15. Vendetta For The Saint Part 1 (05-01-68) 6-16. Vendetta For The Saint Part 2 (12-01-68)
The Third Man 2-02. One Kind Word (07-09-59)
George Pravda (Cast Member)
The Baron 09. And Suddenly You're Dead (23-11-66)
Department S: 10. Double Death Of Charlie Crippen (14-09-69)
Ghost Squad 2-23. The Menacing Mazurka (23-03-63)
Man Of The World 1-11. Specialist For the Kill (08-12-62)
The Prisoner 12. A Change Of Mind (15-12-67)
The Protectors 13. Cargo From Corinth (20-06-64)
The Saint 1-09. The Effete Angler (29-11-62) 5-05. The Helpful Pirate (28-10-66) 3-16. The Rhine Maiden (21-01-65)
George Roderick (Cast Member)
The Avengers 2-06. The Removal Men (03-11-62)
Ghost Squad 2-17. Mr Five Per Cent (06-04-63)
The Saint 1-01. The Talented Husband (4-10-62)
George Roubicek (Cast Member)
The Avengers 2-21. The White Dwarf (16-02-63) 6-16. Invasion Of The Earthman (15-01-69)
The Champions 03. Reply Box 666 (09-10-68)
Department S: 18. The Perfect Operation (26-12-69)
The Saint 5-25. The Power Artists (19-05-67)
George Selway (Cast Member)
The Avengers 4-04. Death At Bargain Prices (23-10-65)
Doctor Who 35. The Faceless Ones: Episode 1 (08-04-67)
George Sewell (Cast Member)
Man In A Suitcase 02. The Sitting Pigeon (04-10-67)
Public Eye 4-01. Welcome To Brighton? (30-07-69)
Randall & Hopkirk (Deceased) 24. Vendetta For a Dead Man (27-02-70)
George Sperdakos (Cast Member)

The Saint 1-03. The Careful Terrorist (18-10-62)
George Street (Cast Member)
Man Of The World 2-06. The Bullfighter (15-06-63)
George Tovey (Cast Member)
Adam Adamant Lives! 05. Allah Is Not Always With You (21-07-66)
George Woodbridge (Cast Member)
Out Of The Unknown 1-10. Some Lapse In Time (06-12-65)
George Zenios (Cast Member)
The Baron 24. Long Ago & Far Away (08-03-67)
Danger Man 2-19. It's Up To The Lady (23-02-65)
Man In A Suitcase 05. Variation On a Million Bucks Part 2 (25-10-67)
The Saint 5-14. Escape Route (30-12-66)
Georges Robin (Cast Member)
The Saint 2-03. Judith (03-10-63)
Georgia Brown (Cast Member)
The Saint 5-27. The Gadic Collection (22-06-67)
Georgina Cookson (Cast Member)
Danger Man 1-29. The Contessa (21-05-61)
The Prisoner 03. A.B. & C. (13-10-67) 07. Many Happy Returns (10-11-67)
Georgina Ward (Cast Member)
The Avengers 4-06. The Master Minds (06-11-65)
The Baron 08. The Persuaders (16-11-66)
Danger Man 2-14. Such Men Are Dangerous (12-01-65) 3-01. The Black Book (30-09-65)
Georgine Anderson (Cast Member)
Undermind 01. Instance One (08-05-65)
Gerald Campion (Cast Member)
Department S: 24. The Bones Of Byrom Blain (28-01-70)
Gerald Cross (Cast Member)
The Avengers 2-10. Death On The Rocks (01-12-62)
Ghost Squad 2-21. Polsky (02-03-63)
Gerald Curtis (Cast Member)
Doctor Who 02. The Daleks: 3 Episodes (21-12-63)
Gerald Flood (Cast Member)
City Beneath The Sea All episodes (1962)
Man In A Suitcase 29. Castle In The Clouds (10-04-67)
Man Of The World 1-01. Death Of a Conference (29-09-62)
Out Of This World 02. Little Lost Robot (07-07-1962)
Pathfinders In Space 7 Episodes (1960)
Pathfinders To Mars 6 Episodes (1961)
Pathfinders To Venus 8 Episodes (1961)
Randall & Hopkirk (Deceased) 02. A Disturbing Case (28-09-69)
Gerald Harper (Cast Member)
Adam Adamant Lives! 15 Episodes
The Avengers 2-13. Death Dispatch (22-12-62) 2-12. The Big Thinker (15-12-62) 4-09. The Hour That Never Was (27-11-65) 6-26. Homicide & Old Lace (26-03-69)
The Champions 12. The Fanatics (11-12-68)
The Protectors 03. Happy Is The Loser (11-04-64)
Gerald Heinz (Cast Member)
Danger Man 2-16. A Room in The Basement (02-02-65)
Interpol Calling 07. You Can't Die Twice (26-10-59)
The Saint 2-13. The Sporting Chance (12-12-63) 5-04. The Reluctant Revolution (21-10-66) 4-07. The Saint Bids Diamonds (12-08-65)
The Third Man 2-06. Barcelona Passage (01-10-59)
Gerald Lawson (Cast Member)
Ghost Squad 2-12. Quarantine At Kavar (01-06-63)
Gerald Sim (Cast Member)
Adam Adamant Lives! 13. The League Of Uncharitable Ladies (12-09-66)
The Avengers 2-05. Mission To Montreal (27-10-62) 4-09. Hour That Never Was(27-11-65) 3-17. The

Wringer (18-1-64) 4-10. Dial a Deadly Number (4-12-65) 6-14. Interrogators (1-1-69)
The Baron 23. The Edge Of Fear (01-03-67)
Man In A Suitcase 11. Dead Man's Shoes (06-12-67) 15. Burden Of Proof (03-01-67)
The Protectors 08. Freedom! (16-05-64)
Strange Report 03. REPORT 2641 HOSTAGE If You Won't Learn Die (05-10-69) 03. REPORT 2641
HOSTAGE If You Won't Learn Die (05-10-69)
Gerald Taylor (Cast Member)
Doctor Who 32. The Underwater Menace: 2 Episodes (21-01-67)
Gerald Young (Cast Member)
Out Of The Unknown 3-03. The Last Lonely Man (21-01-69)
The Saint 2-20. The Lawless Lady (30-01-64)
Geraldine Gwyther (Cast Member)
Adam Adamant Lives! 03. More Deadly Than The Sword (07-07-66)
Geraldine Moffat (Cast Member)
Adam Adamant Lives! 13. The League Of Uncharitable Ladies (12-09-66)
The Baron 17. Time To Kill (18-01-67)
Danger Man 3-15. Somebody Is Liable To Get Hurt (06-01-66)
Department S: 01. Six Days (09-03-69)
Out Of The Unknown 3 -08. Little Black Bag (25-02-69)
Strange Report 03. REPORT 2641 HOSTAGE If You Won't Learn Die (05-10-69)
Geraldine Sherman (Cast Member)
Strange Report 08. REPORT 2475 REVENGE When a Man Hates (09-11-69)
Gerard Green (Cast Member)
Ghost Squad 1-01. Hong Kong Story (23-09-61)
Gerda Koeppler (Cast Member)
Man In A Suitcase 19. Somebody Loses, Somebody… Wins? (31-01-67)
Gerry Crampton (Cast Member)
The Avengers 5-20. Dead Man's Treasure (21-10-67) 6-18. The Morning After (29-10-69)
The Prisoner 05. The Schizoid Man (27-10-67) 11. It's Your Funeral (08-12-67)
Gerry Duggan (Cast Member)
The Saint 5-10. Little Girl Lost (02-12-66)
Gerry Lee (Cast Member)
Danger Man 1-26. The Journey Ends Halfway (30-04-61)
Gerry Marsh (Cast Member)
The Avengers 6-11. Look (Stop Me If You've Heard This One) But There Were These Two Fellers
(04-12-68)
Gerry Wain (Cast Member)
Man In A Suitcase 06. Man From The Dead (01-11-67)
Gertan Klauber (Cast Member)
The Avengers 6-26. Homicide & Old Lace (26-03-69)
Danger Man 3-21. The Man With The Foot (24-03-66)
Department S: 10. Double Death Of Charlie Crippen (14-09-69)
Doctor Who 12. The Romans: 4 Episodes (16-01-65)
The Saint 5-20. Counterfeit Countess (03-03-67) 6-16. Vendetta For The Saint Part 2 (12-01-68)
Gil Sutherland (Cast Member)
The Saint 5-15. The Persistent Patriots (06-01-67)
Undermind 02. Flowers Of Havoc (15-05-65)
Gil Winfield (Cast Member)
Danger Man 1-07. Position Of Trust (23-10-60)
Gilbert France (Cast Member)
Danger Man 2-08. The Battle Of The Cameras (01-12-64)
Gilbert Wynne (Cast Member)
Doctor Who 47. The Krotons: 4 Episodes (28-12-68)
Public Eye 1-12. The Morning Wasn't So Hot (10-04-65)
Giles Block (Cast Member)
Doctor Who 44. The Dominators: 5 Episodes (10-08-68)
Gillian Barclay (Cast Member)
The Avengers 2-25. Six Hands Across a Table (16-03-63)

Gillian Ferguson (Cast Member)
Pathfinders In Space 7 Episodes (1960)
Gillian Lewis (Cast Member)
The Avengers 4-11. Man Eater Of Surrey Green (11-12-65)
The Baron 25. So Dark The Night (15-03-67)
Department S: 05. One Of Aircraft Is Empty (06-4-69)
Gillian Lind (Cast Member)
The Saint 6-10. The Scales Of Justice (01-12-68)
Gillian Muir (Cast Member)
The Avengers 2-05. Mission To Montreal (27-10-62) 2-09. The Sell Out (24-11-62)
Gillian Shed (Cast Member)
Out Of The Unknown 3-03. The Last Lonely Man (21-01-69)
Gilly McIver (Cast Member)
Public Eye 4-01. Welcome To Brighton? (30-07-69)
Gina Warwick (Cast Member)
Department S: 04. The Pied Piper Of Hambledown (30-03-69)
Gino Cola (Cast Member)
The Protectors 08. Freedom! (16-05-64)
Gino Melvazzi (Cast Member)
Danger Man 1-25. The Brothers (23-04-61)
The Saint 5-21. Simon & Delilah (24-03-67)
Gita Denise (Cast Member)
Danger Man 3-11. To Our Best Friend (09-12-65)
Gladys Cooper (Cast Member)
Adam Adamant Lives! 18. Black Echo (07-01-67)
Glen Holloway (Cast Member)
The Avengers 3-21. Build a Better Mousetrap (15-02-64)
Glenn Beck (Cast Member)
Danger Man 1-03. Josetta (25-09-60) 1-29. The Contessa (21-05-61)
Man Of The World 1-08. The Nature Of Justice (17-11-62)
Glenn Williams (Cast Member)
Out Of The Unknown 2-04. Level Seven (27-10-66)
Gloria Connell (Cast Member)
The Avengers 6-13. They Keep Killing Steed (18-12-68)
Glyn Dearman (Cast Member)
Adam Adamant Lives! 08. The Last Sacrifice (18-08-66)
Ghost Squad 2-06. The Missing People (29-06-63)
Glyn Houston (Cast Member)
Danger Man 3-12. The Man On The Beach (16-12-65)
Ghost Squad 1-11 The Green Shoes (29-12-62)
The Saint 6-09. The House On Dragons Rock (24-11-68)
Glyn Jones (Cast Member)
Strange Report 03. REPORT 2641 HOSTAGE If You Won't Learn Die (05-10-69)
Glyn Owen (Cast Member)
Danger Man 2-03. Colony Three (27-10-64)
Interpol Calling 33. Eight Days Inclusive (09-05-60)
The Saint 2-01. The Fellow Traveller (19-09-63)
Glynn Edwards (Cast Member)
The Avengers 6-14. The Interrogators (01-01-69)
The Baron 12. The Maze (14-12-67)
The Protectors 06. The Stamp Collection (02-05-64)
The Saint 5-23. The Gadget Lovers (21-04-67) 6-05. The Organisation Man (27-10-67)
Undermind 02. Flowers Of Havoc (15-05-65)
Godfrey James (Cast Member)
The Avengers 1-15. The Frighteners (27-11-61)
Department S: 16. The Man From X (05-11-69)
Strange Report 01. REPORT 5055 CULT Murder Shrieks Out (21-09-69)
Godfey Quigley (Cast Member)

The Avengers 3-15. The White Elephant (04-01-64)
The Champions 22. Get Me Out Of Here (26-02-69)
Man In A Suitcase 19. Somebody Loses, Somebody… Wins? (31-01-67)
The Saint 3-18 Sign Of The Claw (4-2-65) 5-03 Russian Prisoner (14-10-66) 6-01 Best Laid Plans (29-09-68)
Undermind 09. Test For The Future (03-07-65)
Gordon Faith (Cast Member)
Adam Adamant Lives! 01 A Year For Scoundrels (20-06-66)
Strange Report 15. REPORT 4407 No Choice For The Donor (04-01-70)
Gordon Gardner (Cast Member)
The Avengers 2-18. Warlock (26-01-63)
Gordon Gostelow (Cast Member)
Doctor Who 49. The Space Pirates: Episode 2 (15-03-69)
Man In A Suitcase 25. Property Of A Gentleman (13-03-67)
The Protectors 01. Landscape With Bandits (28-03-64)
The Saint 5-11. Paper Chase (09-12-66)
Gordon Jackson (Cast Member)
The Avengers 4-05. Castle De'ath (30-10-65)
Ghost Squad 2-04. The Golden Silence (08-06-63)
Gordon Rollings (Cast Member)
The Avengers 3-13. Death a La Carte (21-12-63)
Gordon Sterne (Cast Member)
Man In A Suitcase 19. Somebody Loses, Somebody… Wins? (31-01-67)
The Prisoner 14. Living In Harmony (29-12-67)
The Saint 2-27. The Saint Sees It Through (19-03-64) 5-11. Paper Chase (09-12-66)
Gordon Stothard (Cast Member)
Doctor Who 43. The Wheel in Space: 2 Episodes (11-05-68)
Gordon Tanner (Cast Member)
Ghost Squad 2-20. P.G.7. (06-07-63)
Interpol Calling 27. Ascent To Murder (28-03-60)
Man Of The World 1-11. Specialist For the Kill (08-12-62)
The Prisoner 14. Living In Harmony (29-12-67)
The Saint 1-07. The Arrow Of God (15-11-62)
Gordon Whiting (Cast Member)
The Avengers 2-19. The Golden Egg (02-02-63) 4-03. The Cybernauts (16-10-65)
Danger Man 3-16. Dangerous Secret (13-01-66)
The Saint 5-12. Locate & Destroy (16-12-66)
Grace Arnold (Cast Member)
The Avengers 2-07. The Mauritius Penny (10-11-62)
Man In A Suitcase 02. The Sitting Pigeon (04-10-67)
The Prisoner 07. Many Happy Returns (10-11-67) 11. It's Your Funeral (08-12-67)
Graeme Bruce (Cast Member)
The Avengers 2-04. Bullseye (20-10-62)
The Saint 2-27. The Saint Sees It Through (19-03-64)
Graham Armitage (Cast Member)
The Avengers 4-19. Quick-Quick Slow Death (5-2-66) 5-09. The Correct Way To Kill (11-03-67)
Randall & Hopkirk (Deceased) 22. It's Supposed To Be Thicker Than Water (13-02-70)
The Saint 6-11. The Fiction Makers Part 1 (8-12-68) 6-12. The Fiction Makers Part 2 (15-12-68)
Graham Ashley (Cast Member)
The Avengers 2-02. Propellant 23 (06-10-62) 6-08. All Done With Mirrors (13-11-68)
Danger Man 3-20. I Am Afraid You Have The Wrong Number (17-03-66)
Doctor Who 32. The Underwater Menace: 2 Episodes (21-01-67)
Strange Report 11. REPORT 1553 RACIST A Most Dangerous Proposal (07-12-69)
Graham Crowden (Cast Member)
Danger Man 2-13. That's Two Of Us Sorry (05-01-64)
Graham Cruikshank (Cast Member)
The Avengers 2-09. The Sell Out (24-11-62)
Graham Haberfield (Cast Member)

Strange Report 07. REPORT 3424 EPIDEMIC A Most Curious Crime (02-11-69)
Graham Lines (Cast Member)
Out Of The Unknown 1-12. The Midas Plague (20-12-65)
Graham Payn (Cast Member)
Danger Man 3-24. Koroshi (12-02-67)
Graham Rigby (Cast Member)
Doctor Who 10. Dalek Invasion Of Earth (1964)
Graham Stark (Cast Member)
Man Of The World 1-02. Masquerade In Spain (06-10-62) 1-04. The Runaways (20-10-62) 2-01. The Bandit (11-05-63)
Out Of The Unknown 1-12. The Midas Plague (20-12-65)
Graham Steward (Cast Member)
The Prisoner 15. The Girl Who Was Death (18-01-67)
Graham Stewart (Cast Member)
Danger Man 1-29. The Contessa (21-05-61)
Grania Hayes (Cast Member)
Adam Adamant Lives! 01 A Year For Scoundrels (20-06-66)
Grant Taylor (Cast Member)
The Avengers 6-17. Killer (22-01-69)
The Champions 05. Happening (23-10-68)
Graydon Gould (Cast Member)
Danger Man 1-18. The Girl Who Likes GI's (15-01-61)
Pathfinders To Venus 8 Episodes (1961)
The Saint 1-08. The Element Of Doubt (22-11-62)
Grazina Frame (Cast Member)
Randall & Hopkirk (Deceased) 05. That's How Murder Snowballs (19-10-69)
Gregory Phillips (Cast Member)
The Champions 21. The Body Snatchers (19-02-69)
Gregory Scott (Cast Member)
The Avengers 2-17. Box Of Tricks (19-01-63)
Gregore Asian (Cast Member)
The Saint 6-06. The Double Take (03-11-68)
Grenville Eves (Cast Member)
Ghost Squad 2-08. The Man With The Delicate Hands (22-06-63)
Gretchen Franklin (Cast Member)
Danger Man 3-13. Say It With Flowers (23-12-65)
The Protectors 10. The Deadly Chameleon (30-5-64)
Gretchen Thomas (Cast Member)
The Third Man 1-25. How To Buy a Country (24-09-59)
Griffith Davies (Cast Member)
The Avengers 4-23. The House That Jack Built (05-03-66)
Department S: 08. A Ticket To Nowhere (27-04-69)
Doctor Who 36. The Evil Of The Daleks: Episode 2 (27-05-67)
Griffith Jones (Cast Member)
The Avengers 6-10. Noon Doomsday (27-11-68)
Danger Man 3-01. The Black Book (30-09-65)
Man In A Suitcase 17. Why They Killed Nolan (17-01-67)
Strange Report 11. REPORT 1553 RACIST A Most Dangerous Proposal (07-12-69)
Guido Adorni (Cast Member)
Danger Man 2-12. A Date With Doris (29-12-64) 3-19. Two Birds With One Bullet (10-03-66) 3-22. The Paper Chase (31-03-66)
Man In A Suitcase 12. Find The Lady (13-12-67)
Gundel Sargent (Cast Member)
Man In A Suitcase 04. Variation On a Million Bucks Part 1 (18-10-67)
Gustav Henry (Cast Member)
Department S: 26. The Ghost Of Mary Burnham (18-02-70)
Guy Cameron (Cast Member)
The Prisoner 05. The Schizoid Man (27-10-67)

Guy Deghy (Cast Member)
The Champions 29. The Gun Runners (23-04-69)
Danger Man 1-14. The Traitor (11-12-60) 1-19. Name, Date & Place (22-01-61) 3-07. Judgement Day (11-11-65) 3-20. I Am Afraid You Have The Wrong Number (17-03-66)
Department S: 19. The Duplicated Man (03-12-69)
Ghost Squad 1-02. Bullet With My Name On It (16-09-61) 1-10. Catspaw (05-01-61) 2-17. Mr Five Per Cent (06-04-63)
Interpol Calling 02. The Thirteen Innocents (21-09-59)
The Saint 1-05. The Loaded Tourist (01-11-62) 2-27. The Saint Sees It Through (19-03-64) 5-03. The Russian Prisoner (14-10-66) 6-15. Vendetta For The Saint Part 1 (05-01-68)
Guy Doleman (Cast Member)
The Avengers 2-25. Six Hands Across a Table (16-03-63)
The Prisoner 01. Arrival (29-09-67)
Strange Report 11. REPORT 1553 RACIST A Most Dangerous Proposal (07-12-69)
Guy Kingsley Porter (Cast Member)
Ghost Squad 1-02. Bullet With My Name On It (16-09-61)
Man Of The World 1-02. Masquerade In Spain (06-10-62
Guy Rolfe (Cast Member)
The Avengers 6-24. Fog (12-03-69)
The Champions 08. To Trap a Rat (13-11-68)
Department S: 21. Death On Reflection (17-12-69)
Interpol Calling 17. Mr George (11-01-60)
The Saint 5-21. Simon & Delilah (24-03-67)
Guy Standeven (Cast Member)
Adam Adamant Lives! 01 A Year For Scoundrels (20-06-66)
Out Of The Unknown 3-03. The Last Lonely Man (21-01-69)
Gwen Nelson (Cast Member)
Randall & Hopkirk (Deceased) 23. The Trouble With Women (20-02-70)
Gwenda Ewen (Cast Member)
The Saint 2-25. The Gentle Ladies (05-03-64)
Gwendolyn Watts (Cast Member)
Adam Adamant Lives! 07. To Set a Deadly Fashion (11-08-66)
The Avengers 3-03. Man With Two Shadows (12-10-63)
Gwynneth Tighe (Cast Member)
The Saint 3-13. The Damsel In Distress (31-12-64)

H

Hal Dyer (Cast Member)
The Baron 11. Samurai West (07-12-66)
Hal Galili (Cast Member)
The Avengers 6-13. They Keep Killing Steed (18-12-68)
Department S: 20. The Mysterious Man In The Flying Machine (10-12-69)
The Saint 2-24. Sophia (24-02-64) 3-05. The Revolution Racket (05-11-64) 5-02. Interlude In Venice (07-10-66) 6-16. Vendetta For The Saint Part 2 (12-01-68)
Hal Hamilton (Cast Member)
Man In A Suitcase 26. The Revolutionaries (20-03-67
Hana Maria Pravda (Cast Member)
Danger Man 2-02. The Professionals (20-10-64)
Department S: 10. Double Death Of Charlie Crippen (14-09-69)
Ghost Squad 2-06. The Missing People (29-06-63)
Hamilton Dyce (Cast Member)
Adam Adamant Lives! 06. The Happy Embalmers (04-06-66)
The Avengers 2-10. Death On The Rocks (01-12-62) 6-04. You'll Catch Your Death (16-10-68)
The Baron 17. Time To Kill (18-01-67)
The Protectors 11. Who Killed Lazoryck? (06-06-64)
The Saint 2-07. The Work Of Art (31-10-63)
Hanjah Kochansky (Cast Member)
Danger Man: 3-22. The Paper Chase (31-03-66)
Hannah Gordon (Cast Member)
The Champions 28. The Final Countdown (16-04-69)
Hannah Hall (Cast Member)
Out Of The Unknown 1-01. No Place Like Earth (04-10-65)
Hans De Vries (Cast Member)
Man In A Suitcase 28. Three Blinks Of The Eyes (03-04-67)
Randall & Hopkirk (Deceased) 11. The Ghost Who Saved The Bank At Monte Carlo (30-11-69)
The Saint 5-11. Paper Chase (09-12-66)
Hans Meyer (Cast Member)
Department S: 20. The Mysterious Man In The Flying Machine (10-12-69)
Harcourt Curacao (Cast Member)
Danger Man 1-39. Deadline (20-01-62)
Harold Berens (Cast Member)
The Avengers 2-05. Mission To Montreal (27-10-62)
The Prisoner 04. Free For All (20-10-67) 15. The Girl Who Was Death (18-01-67)
Randall & Hopkirk (Deceased) 05. That's How Murder Snowballs (19-10-69)
Harold Coyne (Cast Member)
The Avengers 4-09. The Hour That Never Was (27-11-65)
Harold Goldblatt (Cast Member)
The Baron 04. Red Horse, Red Rider (19-10-66)
Danger Man 2-17. The Affair At Castelevara (09-02-65)
Pathfinders In Space 7 Episodes (1960)
Harold Goodwin (Cast Member)
Man In A Suitcase 09 The Girl Who Never Was (22-11-67) 17 Why They Killed Nolan(17-1-67)
Harold Innocent (Cast Member)
The Avengers 3-09. The Medicine Men (23-11-63) 6-14. The Interrogators (01-01-69)
The Champions 30. Autokill (30-04-69)
Randall & Hopkirk (Deceased) 01. My Late Lamented Friend & Partner (21-09-69)
Harold Kasket (Cast Member)
The Avengers 6-22. Stay Tuned (26-02-69)
Danger Man 1-37. The Nurse (06-01-61) 3-13. Say It With Flowers (23-12-65)
Department S: 18. The Perfect Operation (26-12-69)
Ghost Squad 1-13. Death From a Distance (04-11-61)
Interpol Calling 13. Slave Ship (14-12-59) 28. Slow Boat To Amsterdam (04-04-60)

The Saint 3-13. The Damsel In Distress (31-12-64)
Harold Lang (Cast Member)
The Baron 29. Countdown (12-04-67)
Harold Scott (Cast Member)
The Avengers 3-01. Brief For Murder (28-09-63)
Harold Siddons (Cast Member)
Danger Man 1-37. The Nurse (06-01-61)
Harriette Johns (Cast Member)
Man In A Suitcase 27. Who's Mad Now (27-03-67)
Harry Baird (Cast Member)
Danger Man 2-10. A Man To Be Trusted (15-12-64) 3-05. Loyalty Always Pays (28-10-65)
 3-12. The Man On The Beach (16-12-65)
Harry Brooks Jr (Cast Member)
Danger Man 3-02. A Very Dangerous Game (07-10-65)
Harry Brunning (Cast Member)
The Saint 5-16. The Fast Women (13-01-67)
Harry Hutchinson (Cast Member)
The Avengers 4-06. The Master Minds (06-11-65) 6-14. The Interrogators (01-01-69)
Randall & Hopkirk (Deceased) 23. The Trouble With Women (20-02-70)
Harry Knowles (Cast Member)
Callan 2-05. Let's Kill Everybody (05-02-69)
Harry Landis (Cast Member)
The Avengers 3-16. The Little Wonders (11-01-64)
Interpol Calling 10. Dead On Arrival (16-11-59)
Man In A Suitcase 05. Variation On a Million Bucks Part 2 (25-10-67)
The Saint 5-12. Locate & Destroy (16-12-66)
Harry Littlewood (Cast Member)
The Baron 28. The Man Outside (05-04-67)
The Saint 5-06. The Convenient Monster (04-11-66) 6-19. Portrait Of Brenda (02-02-69)
Harry Lockart (Cast Member)
Danger Man 1-33. Hired Assassin (18-06-61) 1-37. The Nurse (06-01-61)
Harry Locke (Cast Member)
Ghost Squad 1-04. Broken Doll (07-10-61)
Randall & Hopkirk (Deceased) 01. My Late Lamented Friend & Partner (21-09-69)
Harry Ross (Cast Member)
Ghost Squad 2-15. The Last Jump (23-02-63)
The Protectors 05. The Loop Men (25-04-64)
Harry Shacklock (Cast Member)
The Avengers 2-07. The Mauritius Penny (10-11-62) 6-27. Thingamajig (16-04-69)
Harry Stamper (Cast Member)
The Avengers 6-23. Take Me To Your Leader (05-03-69)
Harry Tardios (Cast Member)
Danger Man 2-19. It's Up To The Lady (23-02-65)
Man In A Suitcase 05. Variation On a Million Bucks Part 2 (25-10-67)
Harry Towb (Cast Member)
The Avengers 6-17. Killer (22-01-69)
Callan 2-14. Nice People Die At Home (09-04-69)
The Champions 19. The Mission (05-02-69)
Doctor Who 48. The Seeds Of Death: 6 Episodes (25-01-69)
Ghost Squad 2-23. The Menacing Mazurka (23-03-63)
The Saint 1-11. The Man Who Was Lucky (13-12-62) *2*-22. The Invisible Millionaire (13-02-64)
Harry Webster (Cast Member)
Adam Adamant Lives! 05. Allah Is Not Always With You (21-07-66)
The Saint 2-13. The Sporting Chance (12-12-63)
Harvey Ashby (Cast Member)
The Avengers 2-03. The Decapod (13-10-62) 4-04. Death At Bargain Prices (23-10-65) 6-29. Requiem (16-04-69)
Danger Man 2-10. A Man To Be Trusted (15-12-64)

The Saint 5-26. When Spring Is Sprung (02-06-67)
Harvey Hall (Cast Member)
The Avengers 4-06. The Master Minds (06-11-65) 5-04. The See Through Man (04-02-67)
Danger Man 1-02. Time to Kill (18-11-60) 1-06. The Girl In Pink Pyjamas (16-10-60) 2-06. Fish On The Hook (17-11-64)
Department S: 22. Last Train to Redbridge (14-01-70)
Man In A Suitcase 21. No Friend Of Mine (14-02-67)
Man Of The World 1-04. The Runaways (20-10-62)
Out Of The Unknown 3 -08. Little Black Bag (25-02-69)
The Saint 5-12. Locate & Destroy (16-12-66)
Harvey Sokoloff (Cast Member)
Department S: 21. Death On Reflection (17-12-69)
Haydn Jones (Cast Member)
The Avengers 2-22. Man In The Mirror (23-02-63)
City Beneath The Sea 6 episodes (1962)
Out Of This World 02. Little Lost Robot (07-07-1962)
Public Eye 4-04. My Lifes My Own (20-08-69) 4-05. Case For The Defence (27-08-69)
Haydn Ward (Cast Member)
The Avengers 2-10. Death On The Rocks (01-12-62)
Hazel Coppen (Cast Member)
The Saint 6-19. Portrait Of Brenda (02-02-69)
Hazel Court (Cast Member)
Danger Man The Lonely Chair (30-10-60) 1-29. The Contessa (21-05-61)
Ghost Squad 1-13. Death From a Distance (04-11-61)
Interpol Calling 34. Dressed To Kill (06-05-60)
Hazel Futa (Cast Member)
The Saint 1-07. The Arrow Of God (15-11-62)
Hazel Hughes (Cast Member)
The Saint 2-07. The Work Of Art (31-10-63) 2-22. The Invisible Millionaire (13-02-64)
Strange Report 15. REPORT 4407 No Choice For The Donor (04-01-70)
Heather Canning (Cast Member)
Callan 2-05. Let's Kill Everybody (05-02-69)
Public Eye 4-01. Welcome To Brighton? (30-07-69)
Heather Chasen (Cast Member)
Danger Man 1-34. The Deputy Coyannis Story (16-12-61) 1-37. The Nurse (06-01-61)
Heather Downham (Cast Member)
Adam Adamant Lives! 07. To Set a Deadly Fashion (11-08-66)
Heather Emmanuel (Cast Member)
The Andromeda Breakthrough 4 Episodes (1962)
Danger Man 2-04. The Galloping Major (03-11-64)
Heather Seymour (Cast Member)
The Saint 6-09. The House On Dragons Rock (24-11-68)
Hedgar Wallace (Cast Member)
The Avengers 2-13. Death Dispatch (22-12-62)
The Champions 16. Shadow Of The Panther (15-01-68)
Danger Man 1-12. The Sisters (27-11-60)
Man In A Suitcase 24. Which Way Did He Go, McGill (6-3-67) 27. Who's Mad Now (27-03-67)
Out Of The Unknown 1-02. The Counterfeit Man (11-10-65)
The Saint 5-27 The Gadic Collection (22-6-67) 6-18 Man Who Gambled With Life (26-1-68)
Helen Cherry (Cast Member)
Danger Man 2-02. The Professionals (20-10-64)
Helen Christie (Cast Member)
The Protectors 09. The Pirate (23-05-64)
Helen Cotterill (Cast Member)
Strange Report 05. REPORT 8319 GRENADE What Price Change? (19-10-69)
Helen Ford (Cast Member)
Undermind 01. Instance One (08-05-65)
Helen Goss (Cast Member)

Ghost Squad 2-05. The Retirement Of The Gentle Dove (30-03-63)
Helen Horton (Cast Member)
Danger Man 1-35. Find & Destroy (23-12-61)
Helen Lindsay (Cast Member)
The Avengers 3-01. Brief For Murder (28-09-63)
Strange Report 10. REPORT 8944 HAND A Matter Of Witchcraft (30-11-69)
Helen McCarthy (Cast Member)
The Avengers 3-02. The Undertakers (05-10-63)
Helen Sessions (Cast Member)
Ghost Squad 2-19. Death of a Sportsman (26-01-63)
Henri Vidon (Cast Member)
Danger Man 1-24. The Relaxed Informer (16-04-61)
The Saint 2-15. The Benevolent Burglary (26-12-63)
Henry Davies (Cast Member)
Randall & Hopkirk (Deceased) 24. Vendetta For a Dead Man (27-02-70)
Henry De Bray (Cast Member)
Danger Man 2-08. The Battle Of The Cameras (01-12-64)
Henry Gilbert (Cast Member)
The Champions 13. Twelve Hours (18-12-68)
Danger Man 3-17. I Can Only Offer You Sherry (20-01-66)
The Saint 3-15. The Set-Up (14-01-65)
Henry Kay (Cast Member)
Ghost Squad 2-21. Polsky (02-03-63)
Henry Lincoln (Cast Member)
The Avengers 3-13. Death a La Carte (21-12-63)
Ghost Squad 2-24. Gertrude (13-04-63)
Man In A Suitcase 24. Which Way Did He Go, McGill (06-03-67)
The Saint 5-20. The Counterfeit Countess (03-03-67) 5-27. The Gadic Collection (22-06-67)
Henry B Longhurst (Cast Member)
Ghost Squad 2-01. Interrupted Requiem (02-02-63)
Henry McCarthy (Cast Member)
The Saint 3-02. Lida (15-10-64)
Henry McGee (Cast Member)
The Avengers 6-04. You'll Catch Your Death (16-10-68)
Ghost Squad 2-04. The Golden Silence (08-06-63)
The Saint 5-13. Flight Plan (23-12-66)
Henry Oscar (Cast Member)
Ghost Squad 2-18. The Heir Apparent (09-03-63)
Interpol Calling 36. Desert Hijack (30-05-60)
Henry Rayner (Cast Member)
The Avengers 2-04. Bullseye (20-10-62)
Henry Stamper (Cast Member)
The Avengers 6-22. Stay Tuned (26-02-69) 6-23. Take Me To Your Leader (05-03-69)
Doctor Who 40. The Enemy Of The World: 6 Episodes (23-12-67)
Herbert Nelson (Cast Member)
The Avengers 2-18. Warlock (26-01-63) 2-08. Death Of Great Dane (17-11-62)
Hermoine Baddeley (Cast Member)
Danger Man 1-36. Under the Lake (30-12-61)
Hermione Gregory (Cast Member)
Danger Man 1-05. The Lovers (09-10-60)
Hester Cameron (Cast Member)
Pathfinders To Venus 8 Episodes (1961)
Pathfinders To Mars 6 Episodes (1961)
Hilary Heath (Cast Member)
Callan 2-05. Let's Kill Everybody (05-02-69)
The Prisoner 10. Hammer & Anvil (01-12-67)
Hilary Pritchard (Cast Member)
The Avengers 6-30. Take-Over (23-04-69)

Hilary Tindall (Cast Member)
The Baron 21. The Seven Eyes Of Night (15-02-67)
The Champions 10. The Ghost Plane (27-11-68)
Randall & Hopkirk (Deceased) 26. The Smile Behind The Veil (13-03-70)
Hilary Wontner (Cast Member)
The Avengers 4-14. Silent Dust (01-01-66) 5-06. The Winged Avenger (18-02-67)
Randall & Hopkirk (Deceased) 21. The Ghost Talks (06-02-70)
Hilda Barry (Cast Member)
The Prisoner 02. The Chimes Of Big Ben (06-10-67)
Hira Talfrey (Cast Member)
The Avengers 2-06. The Removal Men (03-11-62)
Man In A Suitcase 14. The Man Who Stood Still (27-12-67)
Man Of The World 1-12. A Family Affair (15-12-62)
Holly Doone (Cast Member)
The Prisoner 04. Free For All (20-10-67)
Honor Blackman (Cast Member)
The Avengers 43 Episodes
Danger Man 1-15. Colonel Rodriguez (18-12-60)
Ghost Squad 1-12. Princess (12-01-61)
The Saint 1-07. The Arrow Of God (15-11-62)
Honora Burke (Cast Member)
Man Of The World 2-03. Double Exposure (25-05-63)
Out Of The Unknown 3 -08. Little Black Bag (25-02-69)
Harold Berens (Cast Member)
Danger Man 3-07. Judgment Day (11-11-65)
Horace James (Cast Member)
Man In A Suitcase 21. No Friend Of Mine (14-02-67)
Howard Charlton (Cast Member)
Doctor Who 08. The Reign Of Terror: 4 Episodes (08-08-64)
Howard Douglas (Cast Member)
The Saint 1-01. The Talented Husband (4-10-62) 2-17. The Noble Sportsman (09-01-64)
Howard Greene (Cast Member)
Ghost Squad 1-05. High Wire (30-09-61)
Howard Goorney (Cast Member)
The Avengers 1-06. Girl On The Trapeze (11-02-61) 3-02. The Undertakers (05-10-63)
Danger Man 3-10. Are You Going To Be More Permanent? (02-12-65)
Man In A Suitcase 18. The Boston Square (24-01-67)
Randall & Hopkirk (Deceased) 23. The Trouble With Women (20-02-70)
The Saint 5-24. A Double In Diamonds (05-05-67)
Howard Kingsley (Cast Member)
The Avengers 3-23. The Charmers (29-02-64)
Howard Lang (Cast Member)
Doctor Who 01. An Unearthly Child: 3 Episodes (23-11-63)
Interpol Calling 13. Slave Ship (14-12-59)
Howard Marlon-Crawford (Cast Member)
The Avengers 4-22. What The Butler Saw (26-02-66) 5-07. The Living Dead (25-02-67) 6-22. Stay Tuned (26-02-69)
Danger Man: 2-01. Yesterday's Enemies (13-10-64) 2-09. No Marks For Servility (08-12-64) 3-09. English Lady Take Lodgers (25-11-65)
Interpol Calling 12. The Chinese Mask (07-12-59) 27. Ascent To Murder (28-03-60)
Man In A Suitcase 01. Brainwash (27-09-67)
The Saint 3-20. The Frightened Inn-Keeper (18-02-65)
Howard Pays (Cast Member)
Danger Man The Lonely Chair (30-10-60)
Interpol Calling 15. Last Man Lucky (28-12-59)
Hubert Rees (Cast Member)
Doctor Who 50. The War Games: 10 Episodes (19-04-69)
Hugh Burden (Cast Member)

The Avengers 3-10. The Grandeur That Was Rome (30-11-63)
Man In A Suitcase 26. The Revolutionaries (20-03-67)
Strange Report 02. REPORT 0649 SKELETON Let Sleeping Heroes Lie (28-09-69)
Hugh Cross (Cast Member)
The Avengers: 6-23. Take Me To Your Leader (05-03-69)
Hugh Dickson (Cast Member)
Adam Adamant Lives! 08. The Last Sacrifice (18-08-66)
Hugh Evans (Cast Member)
Pathfinders In Space 7 Episodes (1960)
Pathfinders To Venus 3 Episodes (1961)
Pathfinders To Mars 4 Episodes (1961)
Hugh Futcher (Cast Member)
The Protectors 14. The Reluctant Thief (27-06-64)
The Saint 1-06. The Pearls Of Peace (08-11-62)
Hugh Latimer (Cast Member)
Undermind 01. Instance One (08-05-65)
Hugh Manning (Cast Member)
The Avengers 4-18. The Thirteenth Hole (29-01-66) 5-12. The Superlative Seven (01-04-67)
6-27. Thingamajig (16-04-69)
Hugh McDermott (Cast Member)
Danger Man 1-20. The Vacation (29-01-61) 3-21. The Man With The Foot (24-03-66)
Man In A Suitcase 24. Which Way Did He Go, McGill (06-03-67)
The Saint 3-19. The Golden Frog (11-02-65)
Hugh Morton (Cast Member)
The Avengers 3-25. Espirit de Corps (14-03-64)
Interpol Calling 08. Diamond S.O.S. (02-11-59)
The Saint 5-15. The Persistent Patriots (06-01-67) 6-17. The Ex-King Of Diamonds (19-01-68)
Hugh Moxey (Cast Member)
The Avengers 6-28. My Wildest Dream (07-04-69)
Danger Man 1-21. The Conspirators (05-02-61)
Hugh Walters (Cast Member)
Doctor Who 16. The Chase: 6 Episodes (22-05-65)
Hugo De Vernier (Cast Member)
The Avengers 2-06. The Removal Men (03-11-62)
Danger Man 2-05. Fair Exchange (10-11-64) 2-08. The Battle Of The Cameras (01-12-64)
The Saint 1-12. The Charitable Countess (20-12-62)
Hugo Panczak (Cast Member)
The Champions 07. The Survivors (06-11-68)
Humphery Heathcote (Cast Member)
Man In A Suitcase 02. The Sitting Pigeon (04-10-67)
Humphrey Lestocq (Cast Member)
The Avengers 4-22. What The Butler Saw (26-02-66)
Hyma Beckley (Cast Member)
Department S: 21. Death On Reflection (17-12-69)

I

Iain Anders (Cast Member)
The Avengers 6-05. Split (23-10-68)
Iain Blair (Cast Member)
The Saint 6-06. The Double Take (03-11-68) 6-18. The Man Who Gambled With Life (26-1-68)
Iain Cuthbertson (Cast Member)
Adam Adamant Lives! 16. D Is For Destruction (13-06-66)
The Avengers 6-27. Thingamajig (16-04-69)
Department S: 25. Spencer Bodily Is 60 Years Old (11-02-70)
Ian Ainsley (Cast Member)
The Saint 2-22. The Invisible Millionaire (13-02-64)
Ian Kingly (Cast Member)
The Saint 6-11. The Fiction Makers Part 1 (08-12-68)
Ian Butler (Cast Member)
Randall & Hopkirk (Deceased) 21. The Ghost Talks (06-02-70)
Ian Clark (Cast Member)
Ghost Squad 2-06. The Missing People (29-06-63)
Ian Collin (Cast Member)
Danger Man 2-11. Don't Nail Him Yet (22-12-64)
Ian Cullen (Cast Member)
Department S: 24. The Bones Of Byrom Blain (28-01-70)
The Protectors 05. The Loop Men (25-04-64)
Ian Cunningham (Cast Member)
The Avengers 2-25. Six Hands Across a Table (16-03-63)
Ian Curry (Cast Member)
The Avengers 2-17. Box Of Tricks (19-01-63) 3-04. The Nutshell (19-10-63)
Ian Ellis (Cast Member)
Danger Man 1-21. The Conspirators (05-02-61)
Ian Fairbain (Cast Member)
Adam Adamant Lives! 08. The Last Sacrifice (18-08-66)
Doctor Who 46. The Invasion: 6 Episodes (09-11-68)
Ian Fleming (Cast Member)
Ghost Squad 2-02. East Of Mandalay (09-02-63)
The Prisoner 06. The General (03-11-67)
Ian Flintoff (Cast Member)
Danger Man 2-13. That's Two Of Us Sorry (05-01-64)
Ian Frost (Cast Member)
Out Of The Unknown 3 -08. Little Black Bag (25-02-69)
Ian Gardiner (Cast Member)
The Avengers 1-06. Girl On The Trapeze (11-02-61) 1-15. The Frightener's (27-11-61) 1-20. Tunnel Of Fear (05-08-61)
Ian Hendy (Cast Member)
The Avengers 1-06. Girl On The Trapeze (11-02-61)3-13. Say It With Flowers (23-12-65)
The Saint 6-15. Vendetta For The Saint Part 1 (05-01-68) 6-16. Vendetta For The Saint Part 2 (12-01-68)
Ian MacNaughton (Cast Member)
The Avengers 4-06. The Master Minds (06-11-65)
Ian MacCulloch (Cast Member)
Man In A Suitcase 07. Sweet Sue (08-11-67
Ian Ogilvy (Cast Member)
The Avengers 6-13. They Keep Killing Steed (18-12-68)
Strange Report 14. REPORT 2493 Whose Pretty Girl Are You? (28-12-69)
Ian Parsons (Cast Member)
City Beneath The Sea 1 episode (1962)
The Saint 2-15. The Benevolent Burglary (26-12-63)
Ian Shand (Cast Member)

The Avengers 2-11. Traitor In Zebra (08-12-62) 3-10. The Grandeur That Was Rome (30-11-63)
Ian Thompson (Cast Member)
Doctor Who 13. The Web Planet: 6 Episodes (13-02-65)
Ian Wilson (Cast Member)
The Avengers 2-23. Conspiracy Of Silence (02-03-63)
Ilona Ference (Cast Member)
Ghost Squad 2-05. The Retirement Of The Gentle Dove (30-03-63)
Ilona Rodgers (Cast Member)
Adam Adamant Lives! 06. The Happy Embalmers (04-06-66)
The Avengers 2-25. Six Hands Across a Table (16-3-63) 5-05. The Bird Who Knew Too Much (11-2-67)
Doctor Who 07. The Sensorites: 6 Episodes (20-06-64)
The Saint 5-24. A Double In Diamonds (05-05-67)
Strange Report 16. REPORT 4977 Square Root Of Evil (11-01-70)
Imogen Hassall (Cast Member)
The Avengers 5-03. Escape In Time (26-01-67)
The Champions 03. Reply Box 666 (09-10-68)
The Saint 2-24. Sophia (24-2-64) 5-13 Flight Plan (23-12-66) 6-13. People Importers (22-12-68)
Ingrid Benning (Cast Member)
Ghost Squad 2-25. The Thirteenth Girl (27-04-63)
Ingrid Hafner (Cast Member)
The Avengers 1-06. Girl On The Trapeze (11-02-61) 1-15. The Frighteners (27-11-61) 1-20. Tunnel Of Fear (05-08-61)
The Corridor People Victim as Whitebait (1966)
Ingrid Schoeller (Cast Member)
The Saint 3-11. The Hijackers (17-12-64)
Inia Te Wiata (Cast Member)
The Saint 3-19. The Golden Frog (11-02-65)
Inigo Jackson (Cast Member)
Department S: 22. Last Train to Redbridge (14-01-70)
Doctor Who 23. The Ark: 4 Episodes (05-03-66)
Man In A Suitcase 20. Blind Spot (07-02-67)
The Saint 3-08. The Man Who Liked Toys (26-11-64)
Irene Bradshaw (Cast Member)
The Avengers 2-19. The Golden Egg (02-02-63) 5-23. Murdersville (11-11-67)
Irene Prador (Cast Member)
Danger Man 1-07. Position Of Trust (23-10-60) 1-29. The Contessa (21-05-61)
Irene Sutcliffe (Cast Member)
Pathfinders In Space 7 Episodes (1960)
Iris Russell (Cast Member)
The Avengers 2-05. Mission To Montreal (27-10-62) 3-06. November Five (02-11-63) 6-22. Stay Tuned (26-02-69)
Ghost Squad 1-06. Eyes Of The Bat (14-10-61)
Irvin Allen (Cast Member)
The Saint 4-03. The Crooked Ring (15-07-65)
Isa Miranda (Cast Member)
The Avengers 5-11. Epic (25-03-67)
The Baron 10. The Legends of Ammak (30-11-66)
Isabel Jeans (Cast Member)
The Third Man 2-10. Toys Of The Dead (03-11-59)
Isabel Metliss (Cast Member)
Strange Report 13. REPORT 4821 X-RAY Who Weeps For The Doctor (21-12-69)
Isla Blair (Cast Member)
The Avengers 5-13. A Funny Thing Happened On The Way To The Station (08-04-67)
Department S: 12. The Treasure Of the Costa Del Sol (08-10-69)
The Saint 6-17. The Ex-King Of Diamonds (19-01-68)
Isobel Black (Cast Member)
Adam Adamant Lives! 10. The Doomsday Plan (01-09-66)

The Avengers 4-14. Silent Dust (01-01-66)
Danger Man 3-21. The Man With The Foot (24-03-66)
Department S: 28. The Soup Of The Day (04-03-70)
Man Of The World 2-04. Jungle Mission (01-06-63)

Ivor Dean (Cast Member)

The Avengers 2-06. The Removal Men (03-11-62) 5-20. Dead Man's Treasure (21-10-67) 6-03. Super Secret Cypher Snatch (09-10-68)

Randall & Hopkirk (Deceased) 08. Whoever Heard Of a Ghost Dying (09-11-69) 14. Who Killed Cock Robin? (21-12-69) 18. Could You Recognise The Man Again (16-01-70) 20. Money To Burn (30-01-70)

The Saint 2-02. Starring The Saint (26-09-63) 2-08. Iris (07-11-63) 2-09. The King Of The Beggars (14-11-63) 2-11. The Saint Plays With Fire (28-11-63) 2-20. The Lawless Lady (30-01-64) 2-22. The Invisible Millionaire (13-02-64) 3-08. The Man Who Liked Toys (26-11-64) 3-13. The Damsel In Distress (31-12-64) 3-14. The Contact (07-01-65) 3-15. The Set-Up (14-01-65) 3-22. The Crime Of The Century (04-03-65) 4-04. The Smart Detective (22-07-65) 4-06. The Man Who Could No Die (05-08-65) 5-14. Escape Route (30-12-66) 5-15. The Persistent Patriots (06-01-67) 5-17. The Death Game (20-01-67) 5-20. The Counterfeit Countess (03-03-67) 5-24. A Double In Diamonds (05-05-67) 5-25. The Power Artists (19-05-67) 5-26. When Spring Is Sprung (02-06-67) 6-03. Legacy For The Saint (13-10-68) 6-19. Portrait Of Brenda (02-02-69)

Ivor Salter (Cast Member)

Adam Adamant Lives! 01 A Year For Scoundrels (20-06-66)
The Avengers 1-06. Girl On The Trapeze (11-02-61)
Danger Man: 2-01. Yesterday's Enemies (13-10-64) 2-14. Such Men Are Dangerous (12-01-65)
Ghost Squad 2-13. The Desperate Diplomat (18-5-63) 2-15 The Benevolent Burglary (26-12-63)

J

J.G. Devlin (Cast Member)
The Champions 21. The Body Snatchers (19-02-69)
Man In A Suitcase 24. Which Way Did He Go, McGill (06-03-67)
J. Leslie Frith (Cast Member)
Danger Man 1-33. Hired Assassin (18-06-61)
Jack Allen (Cast Member)
Danger Man 3-11. To Our Best Friend (09-12-65)
The Prisoner 01. Arrival (29-09-67)
Jack Armstrong (Cast Member)
The Avengers 4-09. The Hour That Never Was (27-11-65)
Jack Arrow (Cast Member)
The Saint 2-11. The Saint Plays With Fire (28-11-63)
Jack Barry (Cast Member)
Adam Adamant Lives! 03. More Deadly Than The Sword (07-07-66)
Jack Bligh (Cast Member)
Danger Man 2-15. Whatever Happened To George Foster (19-01-65)
Man In A Suitcase 09. The Girl Who Never Was (22-11-67)
Jack Cooper (Cast Member)
The Avengers 3-21. Build a Better Mousetrap (15-02-64) 4-06. The Master Minds (06-11-65)
Man Of The World 2-02. The Enemy (18-05-63)
The Prisoner 06. The General (03-11-67) 10. Hammer & Anvil (01-12-67)
Jack Cunningham (Cast Member)
Danger Man 1-36. Under the Lake (30-12-61)
Doctor Who 08. The Reign Of Terror: 4 Episodes (08-08-64)
Jack Grossman (Cast Member)
The Avengers 2-10. Death On The Rocks (01-12-62)
Jack Gwillim (Cast Member)
The Avengers 5-08. The Hidden Tiger (04-03-67)
The Champions 26. Full Circle (26-03-69)
Danger Man 2-14. Such Men Are Dangerous (12-01-65) 3-01. The Black Book (30-9-65)
3-06. The Mercenaries (04-11-65)
The Saint 1-09. The Effete Angler (29-11-62) 5-05. The Helpful Pirate (28-10-66)
Jack Hedley (Cast Member)
The Saint 4-09. The Old Treasure Story (26-08-65)
The Third Man 2-06. Barcelona Passage (01-10-59)
Jack Howlett (Cast Member)
Adam Adamant Lives! 04. The Sweet Smell Of Disaster (14-07-07)
Jack Lambert (Cast Member)
The Avengers 4-05. Castle De'ath (30-10-65)
Interpol Calling 31. In The Swim (25-04-60)
Randall & Hopkirk (Deceased) 21. The Ghost Talks (06-02-70)
The Saint 2-16. The Wonderful War (02-01-64)
Jack Le White (Cast Member)
The Avengers 1-06. Girl On The Trapeze (11-02-61)
The Prisoner 02. The Chimes Of Big Ben (06-10-67)
Jack MacGowran (Cast Member)
The Avengers 5-06. The Winged Avenger (18-02-67)
The Champions 05. Happening (23-10-68)
Danger Man 1-37. The Nurse (06-01-61) 2-14. Such Men Are Dangerous (12-01-65)
Randall & Hopkirk (Deceased) 21. The Ghost Talks (06-02-70)
Jack Mandeville (Cast Member)
The Avengers 4-06. The Master Minds (06-11-65) 4-07. The Murder Market (13-11-65)
Jack May (Cast Member)
Adam Adamant Lives! 17 Episodes
The Avengers 3-19. The Secrets Broker (01-02-64)

Danger Man 2-16. A Room in The Basement (02-02-65)
Doctor Who 49. The Space Pirates: Episode 2 (15-03-69)
Out Of The Unknown 1-03. Stranger In the Family (18-10-65)
The Protectors 06. The Stamp Collection (02-05-64)
Jack Melford (Cast Member)
Danger Man The Lonely Chair (30-10-60)
Jack Sharp (Cast Member)
Department S: 13. The Man Who Got a New Face (15-10-69)
Jack Stewart (Cast Member)
The Avengers 2-11. Traitor In Zebra (08-12-62)
Interpol Calling 04. The Sleeping Giant (05-10-59)
Jack Taylor (Cast Member)
Ghost Squad 1-02. Bullet With My Name On It (16-09-61)
Jack Watling (Cast Member)
Danger Man 1-14. The Traitor (11-12-60)
Doctor Who 39. The Ice Warriors: 4 Episodes (11-11-67) 41. Web Of Fear: 5 Episodes (3-2-68)
Ghost Squad 2-15. The Last Jump (23-02-63)
Jack Watson (Cast Member)
The Avengers 4-14. Silent Dust (01-01-66) 5-07. The Living Dead (25-02-67)
Man Of The World 1-09. The Mind-reader (24-11-62)
Jack Wild (Cast Member)
Out Of The Unknown 1-06. Come Buttercup, Come Daisy, Come…? (08-11-65)
Jack Woolgar (Cast Member)
The Avengers 5-07. The Living Dead (25-02-67)
Doctor Who 41. The Web Of Fear: 5 Episodes (03-02-68)
Randall & Hopkirk (Deceased) 06. Just For The Record (26-10-69)
The Saint 5-24. A Double In Diamonds (05-05-67)
Jackie Collins (Cast Member)
Danger Man 1-29. The Contessa (21-05-61)
The Saint 2-02. Starring The Saint (26-09-63)
Jackie Lane (Cast Member)
Doctor Who 23 The Ark:4 Episodes (5-3-66) 24. Celestial Toymaker The Final Test (23-4-66)
25. The Gunfighters: 4 Episodes (30-04-66)
The Protectors 10. The Deadly Chameleon (30-5-64)
Jackie Pallo (Cast Member)
The Avengers 3-18. Mandrake (25-01-64)
Jacky Allouis (Cast Member)
The Avengers 6-06. Whoever Shot George Oblique Stroke XR40? (30-10-68)
The Saint 6-17. The Ex-King Of Diamonds (19-01-68)
Jacqueline Chan (Cast Member)
Ghost Squad 2-02. East Of Mandalay (09-02-63)
The Saint 3-03. Jeannine (22-10-64)
Jacqueline Ellis (Cast Member)
Danger Man 1-20. The Vacation (29-01-61)
Ghost Squad 2-23. The Menacing Mazurka (23-03-63)
Man In A Suitcase 23. Web With Four Spiders (28-02-67)
Man Of The World 1-08. The Nature Of Justice (17-11-62)
The Saint 2-26. The Ever Loving Spouse (12-03-64) 3-19. The Golden Frog (11-02-65)
Jacqueline Hall (Cast Member)
Danger Man 3-16. Dangerous Secret (13-01-66)
Jacqueline Hill (Cast Member)
Doctor Who 01. An Unearthly Child: 4 Episodes (23-11-63) 02. The Daleks: 6 Episodes (21-12-63) 03.
The Edge Of Destruction: 2 Episodes (04-02-64) 05. The Keys Of Marinus: 6 Episodes (11-04-64) 06.
The Aztecs: 4 Episodes (23-05-64) 07. The Sensorites: 6 Episodes (20-06-64) 08. The Reign Of Terror:
4 Episodes (08-08-64) 09. Planet Of Giants: 3 Episodes (31-10-64) 10. Dalek Invasion Of Earth: 6
Episodes (21-11-64) 11. The Rescue: 2 Episodes (02-01-65) 12. The Romans: 4 Episodes (16-01-65)
13. The Web Planet: 6 Episodes (13-02-65) 15. The Space Museum: 4 Episodes (24-04-65) 16. The
Chase: 6 Episodes (22-05-65)

Jacqueline Jones (Cast Member)
The Avengers 2-17. Box Of Tricks (19-01-63)
Jacqueline Pearce (Cast Member)
The Avengers 4-24. A Sense Of History (12-03-66)
Danger Man 2-11. Don't Nail Him Yet (22-12-64)
Man In A Suitcase 07. Sweet Sue (8-11-67) 19. Somebody Loses, Somebody… Wins? (31-1-67)
Jacqueline Ryan (Cast Member)
Undermind 09. Test For The Future (03-07-65)
Jacques Cey (Cast Member)
The Champions 17. A Case Of Lemmings (22-01-68)
Department S: 17. Dead Men Die Twice (12-11-69)
Ghost Squad 1-05. High Wire (30-09-61)
James Appleby (Cast Member)
Adam Adamant Lives! 18. Black Echo (07-01-67)
Doctor Who 35. The Faceless Ones: Episode 1 (08-04-67)
James Belchamber (Cast Member)
The Avengers 4-19. Quick-Quick Slow Death (05-02-66) 6-32. Get-a-Way (14-05-69)
Randall & Hopkirk (Deceased) 05. That's How Murder Snowballs (19-10-69)
The Saint 2-20. The Lawless Lady (30-01-64)
James Blake (Cast Member)
Adam Adamant Lives! 09. Sing a Song Of Murder (25-08-66)
James Bree (Cast Member)
The Avengers 2-16. Immortal Clay (12-01-63) 6-17. Killer (22-01-69)
Randall & Hopkirk (Deceased) 15. The Man From Nowhere (28-12-69)
James Bulmer (Cast Member)
Adam Adamant Lives! 29. A Sinister Sort Of Service (25-03-67)
James Cairncross (Cast Member)
Adam Adamant Lives! 11. Death By Appointment Only (08-09-66)
Doctor Who 08. The Reign Of Terror: 4 Episodes (08-08-64) 47. The Krotons: 4 Episodes (28-12-68)
James Chase (Cast Member)
Out Of The Unknown 3 -08. Little Black Bag (25-02-69)
James Copeland (Cast Member)
Doctor Who 47. The Krotons: 4 Episodes (28-12-68)
The Saint 3-17. The Inescapable World (28-01-65)
James Cossins (Cast Member)
The Avengers 6-31. Pandora (30-04-69)
Strange Report 08. REPORT 2475 REVENGE When a Man Hates (09-11-69)
James Culliford (Cast Member)
The Champions 02. The Invisible Man (02-10-68)
Randall & Hopkirk (Deceased) 21. The Ghost Talks (06-02-70)
James Darwin (Cast Member)
The Avengers 2-09. The Sell Out (24-11-62) 3-23. The Charmers (29-02-64)
James Donnelly (Cast Member)
The Avengers 3-21. Build a Better Mousetrap (15-02-64)
The Champions 26. Full Circle (26-03-69)
Department S: 19. The Duplicated Man (03-12-69)
Randall & Hopkirk (Deceased) 01. My Late Lamented Friend & Partner (21-09-69)
James Drake (Cast Member)
Department S: 07. Handicap Dead (20-04-69)
James Dyrenforth (Cast Member)
Man Of The World 1-10. Portrait Of a Girl (01-12-62)
James Falkland (Cast Member)
The Avengers 3-25. Espirit de Corps (14-03-64)
James Gill (Cast Member)
Ghost Squad 2-18. The Heir Apparent (09-03-63) 2-24. Gertrude (13-04-63)
James Grout (Cast Member)
Man In A Suitcase 02. The Sitting Pigeon (04-10-67)
James Hall (Cast Member)

Doctor Who 08. The Reign Of Terror: 4 Episodes (08-08-64)
James Hayter (Cast Member)
The Avengers 5-13. A Funny Thing Happened On The Way To The Station (08-04-67)
James Hunter (Cast Member)
Undermind 02. Flowers Of Havoc (15-05-65)
Out Of The Unknown 1-11. Thirteen To Centauraus
James Kerry (Cast Member)
The Avengers 6-33. Bizarre (21-05-69)
Department S: 15. The Shift That Never Was (25-10-69)
The Saint 6-20. The World Beater (09-02-69)
James Locker (Cast Member)
The Saint 6-08. The Master Plan (17-11-68)
James Maitland (Cast Member)
Danger Man 2-12. A Date With Doris (29-12-64)
James Maxwell (Cast Member)
The Avengers 3-22. The Outside-In Man (22-02-64) 5-12. The Superlative Seven (01-04-67)
The Champions 20. The Silent Enemy (12-02-69)
Danger Man 2-05. Fair Exchange (10-11-64) 2-12. A Date With Doris (29-12-64)
Out Of The Unknown 1-04. The Dead Past (25-10-65)
The Saint 3-17. The Inescapable World (28-01-65) 5-18. The Art Collectors (27-01-67)
James Mellor (Cast Member)
Doctor Who 43. The Wheel in Space: 2 Episodes (11-05-68)
James Metropole (Cast Member)
Out Of The Unknown 3 -08. Little Black Bag (25-02-69)
James Ottaway (Cast Member)
The Saint 2-05. The Elusive Elishaw (17-10-63)
James Thornhill (Cast Member)
Doctor Who 46. The Invasion: 6 Episodes (09-11-68)
James Vallon (Cast Member)
The Saint 6-18. The Man Who Gambled With Life (26-01-68)
James Villiers (Cast Member)
The Avengers 4-16. Small Game For Big Hunters (15-01-65)
The Baron 08. The Persuaders (16-11-66)
Man In A Suitcase 11. Dead Man's Shoes (06-12-67)
The Saint 2-22. The Invisible Millionaire (13-02-64)
Jan Butlin (Cast Member)
The Avengers 2-20. School For Traitors (09-02-63)
Jan Conrad (Cast Member)
The Avengers 3-04. The Nutshell (19-10-63)
Danger Man 2-02. The Professionals (20-10-64)
Out Of The Unknown 2-03. Lambda One (20-10-66)
Jan Holden (Cast Member)
The Avengers 3-02. The Undertakers (05-10-63) 4-10. Dial a Deadly Number (04-12-65)
The Baron 20. The High Terrace (08-02-67)
The Champions 24. Project Zero (12-03-69)
Interpol Calling 12. The Chinese Mask (07-12-59)
The Saint 4-05. The Persistent Parasites (29-07-65) 5-16. The Fast Women (13-01-67)
Undermind 06. Intent To Destroy (12-06-65)
Jan Rossini (Cast Member)
Randall & Hopkirk (Deceased) 06. Just For The Record (26-10-69)
Jan Waters (Cast Member)
The Saint 5-15. The Persistent Patriots (06-01-67)
Jan Williams (Cast Member)
Man In A Suitcase 29. Castle In The Clouds (10-04-67)
Jane Asher (Cast Member)
The Saint 2-22. The Invisible Millionaire (13-02-64) 2-17. The Noble Sportsman (09-01-64)
Jane Barrett (Cast Member)
The Avengers 2-17. Box Of Tricks (19-01-63)

Jane Blackburn (Cast Member)
The Baron 04. Red Horse, Red Rider (19-10-66)
Jane Bates (Cast Member)
The Saint 6-14. Where The Money Is (29-12-68)
Jane Bolton (Cast Member)
Out Of The Unknown 1-10. Some Lapse In Time (06-12-65)
Jane Bond (Cast Member)
Public Eye 2-02. Don't Forget You're Mine (09-07-66)
Jane Downs (Cast Member)
Out Of The Unknown 1-10. Some Lapse In Time (06-12-65)
Jane Hylton (Cast Member)
Interpol Calling 10. Dead On Arrival (16-11-59)
Jane Jordan Rogers (Cast Member)
Out Of The Unknown 2-04. Level Seven (27-10-66)
Jane Muir (Cast Member)
The Protectors 07. It Could Happen Here (09-05-64)
Jane Merrow (Cast Member)
The Avengers 5-24. Mission, Highly Improbable (18-11-67)
The Baron 04. Red Horse, Red Rider (19-10-66)
Danger Man 2-12. A Date With Doris (29-12-64) 2-16. A Room in The Basement (02-02-65) 3-14.
The Man Who Wouldn't Talk (30-12-65)
Man In A Suitcase 13. The Bridge (20-12-67)
Man Of The World 1-03. Blaze Of Glory (13-10-62)
The Prisoner 05. The Schizoid Man (27-10-67)
Randall & Hopkirk (Deceased) 14. Who Killed Cock Robin? (21-12-69)
The Saint 3-23. The Happy Suicide (11-03-65) 5-07. The Angel's Eye (11-11-66)
Strange Report 11. REPORT 1553 RACIST A Most Dangerous Proposal (07-12-69)
Jane Sherwin (Cast Member)
Doctor Who 50. The War Games: 10 Episodes (19-04-69)
Janet Davies (Cast Member)
The Saint 2-06. Marcia (24-10-63)
Janet Fairhead (Cast Member)
Out Of The Unknown 1-11. Thirteen To Centauraus (13-12-63)
Janet Gallagher (Cast Member)
Out Of The Unknown 1-11. Thirteen To Centauraus (13-12-63)
Janet Hargreaves (Cast Member)
The Avengers 2-14. Dead On Course (29-12-62)
Danger Man 2-22. Parallel Lines Sometimes Meet (16-03-65)
Janet Key (Cast Member)
Department S: 05. One Of Aircraft Is Empty (06-4-69)
Janet Rowsell (Cast Member)
The Protectors 06. The Stamp Collection (02-05-64)
Janet Whiteside (Cast Member)
Public Eye 2-02. Don't Forget You're Mine (09-07-66)
Janine Gray (Cast Member)
The Avengers 3-12. Don't Look Behind You (14-12-63)
Danger Man 1-06. The Girl In Pink Pyjamas (16-10-60)
The Saint 2-01. The Fellow Traveller (19-09-63)
Janna Hill (Cast Member)
The Baron 24. Long Ago & Far Away (08-03-67)
Jared Allen (Cast Member)
The Saint 1-03. The Careful Terrorist (18-10-62)
Jaron Yaltan (Cast Member)
Danger Man 2-07. The Colonels Daughter (24-11-64)
Ghost Squad 1-01. Hong Kong Story (23-09-61)
Jay Denyer (Cast Member)
The Avengers 6-11. Look (Stop Me If You've Heard This One) But There Were These Two Fellers
(04-12-68)

Jayne Sofiano (Cast Member)
The Avengers 6-05. Split (23-10-68)
Man In A Suitcase 11. Dead Man's Shoes (06-12-67)
The Saint 6-18. The Man Who Gambled With Life (26-01-68)
Jean Anderson (Cast Member)
Ghost Squad 1-04. Broken Doll (07-10-61)
Interpol Calling 14. The Man's a Clown (21-12-59)
Jean Aubrey (Cast Member)
The Protectors 05. The Loop Men (25-04-64)
The Saint 4-03. The Crooked Ring (15-07-65)
Jean Benedetti (Cast Member)
The Saint 5-07. The Angel's Eye (11-11-66)
Jean Clarke (Cast Member)
Ghost Squad 1-06. Eyes Of The Bat (14-10-61)
Jean Gregory (Cast Member)
Adam Adamant Lives! 13. The League Of Uncharitable Ladies (12-09-66)
The Avengers 2-15. Intercrime (05-01-63)
Jean Marsh (Cast Member)
Danger Man 1-19. Name, Date & Place (22-01-61)
Department S: 18. The Perfect Operation (26-12-69)
The Saint 2-21. The Good Medicine (06-02-64) 3-10. The Imprudent Politician (10-12-64) 5-14.
Escape Route (30-12-66) 6-10. The Scales Of Justice (01-12-68)
Jean Robinson (Cast Member)
The Andromeda Breakthrough 3 Episodes (1962)
Jean Shaw (Cast Member)
Danger Man 3-18. The Hunting Party (27-01-66)
Jean St Clair (Cast Member)
The Saint 2-19. Luella (23-01-64) 4-07. The Saint Bids Diamonds (12-08-65)
Jean Trend (Cast Member)
Undermind 10. Waves Of Sound (10-07-65)
Jeanna L'Estey (Cast Member)
Man In A Suitcase 14. The Man Who Stood Still (27-12-67) 18. The Boston Square (24-01-67)
Jeanne Moody
Danger Man 1-29 The Contessa (21-5-61) 3-20 I Am Afraid You Have The Wrong Number
(17-3-66) (Cast Member)
The Saint 2-26. The Ever Loving Spouse (12-03-64) 3-02. Lida (15-10-64) 3-08. The Man Who Liked
Toys (26-11-64)
Jeanne Roland (Cast Member)
The Baron 11. Samurai West (07-12-66)
The Champions 17. A Case Of Lemmings (22-01-68)
Danger Man 3-03. Sting In The Tail (14-10-65)
Man In A Suitcase 12. Find The Lady (13-12-67)
The Saint 3-21. Sibao (25-02-65)
Jeanne Watts (Cast Member)
The Saint 2-01. The Fellow Traveller (19-09-63)
Jeanette Sterke (Cast Member)
The Avengers 4-13. Too Many Christmas Trees (25-12-65)
Jeffrey Gardiner (Cast Member)
Strange Report 03. REPORT 2641 HOSTAGE If You Won't Learn Die (05-10-69)
Jeffrey Wickham (Cast Member)
The Baron 16. The Island (Part 2) (11-01-67)
Doctor Who 08. The Reign Of Terror: 4 Episodes (08-08-64)
Jemma Hyde (Cast Member)
Danger Man 3-13. Say It With Flowers (23-12-65)
The Saint 2-09. The King Of The Beggars (14-11-63)
Jennie Linden (Cast Member)
The Saint 4-6 The Man Who Could Not Die (5-8-65) 5-04. The Reluctant Revolution (21-10-66)
Jennifer Clulow (Cast Member)

The Avengers 6-04. You'll Catch Your Death (16-10-68)
The Baron 08. The Persuaders (16-11-66)
Jennifer Croxton (Cast Member)
The Avengers 6-17. Killer (22-01-69)
Jennifer Daniel (Cast Member)
Adam Adamant Lives! 08. The Last Sacrifice (18-08-66)
Ghost Squad 2-11. A First Class Way To Die (13-07-63)
Jennifer Hilary (Cast Member)
Department S: 21. Death On Reflection (17-12-69)
Jennifer Jayne (Cast Member)
Adam Adamant Lives! 05. Allah Is Not Always With You (21-07-66)
Danger Man 1-29. The Contessa (21-05-61)
Ghost Squad 1-09. Million Dollar Ransom (11-11-61)
Man In A Suitcase 24. Which Way Did He Go, McGill (06-03-67)
The Saint 4-02. The Abductors (08-07-65)
Jennifer Wood (Cast Member)
The Avengers 3-19. The Secrets Broker (01-02-64)
Jennifer Wright (Cast Member)
The Saint 3-10. The Imprudent Politician (10-12-64)
Jenny Laird (Cast Member)
Ghost Squad 1-09. Million Dollar Ransom (11-11-61)
Jeremy Anthony (Cast Member)
The Saint 6-13. The People Importers (22-12-68)
Jeremy Brett (Cast Member)
The Baron 21. The Seven Eyes Of Night (15-02-67)
The Champions 25. Desert Journey (19-03-69)
Jeremy Bulloch (Cast Member)
Strange Report 05. REPORT 8319 GRENADE What Price Change? (19-10-69)
Jeremy Burnham (Cast Member)
The Avengers 5-02. The Fear Merchants (21-01-67) 5-17. Return Of The Cybernauts (30-09-67)
The Baron 28. The Man Outside (05-04-67)
Randall & Hopkirk (Deceased) 09. The House On Haunted Hill (16-11-69)
The Saint 3-10. The Imprudent Politician (10-12-64) 5-13. Flight Plan (23-12-66) 5-14. Escape Route (30-12-66)
Undermind 07. Song Of Death (19-06-65)
Jeremy Kemp (Cast Member)
The Protectors 05. The Loop Men (25-04-64)
Undermind 01. Instance One (08-05-65)
Jeremy Lloyd (Cast Member)
The Avengers 5-01. From Venus With Love (14-01-67) 6-27. Thingamajig (16-04-69)
Jeremy Longhurst (Cast Member)
Danger Man 3-24. Koroshi (12-02-67)
The Saint 4-05. The Persistent Parasites (29-07-65)
Jeremy Ranchev (Cast Member)
Danger Man 2-15. Whatever Happened To George Foster (19-01-65)
Jeremy Spenser (Cast Member)
Danger Man 3-03. Sting In The Tail (14-10-65)
Man In A Suitcase 03. Day Of Execution (11-10-67)
Jeremy Tunnicliffe (Cast Member)
Danger Man 2-05. Fair Exchange (10-11-64)
Jeremy Ure (Cast Member)
The Protectors 05. The Loop Men (25-04-64)
Jeremy Wilkin (Cast Member)
Man In A Suitcase 05. Variation On a Million Bucks Part 2 (25-10-67)
Jeremy Young (Cast Member)
Adam Adamant Lives! 06. The Happy Embalmers (04-06-66)
The Avengers 4-21. A Touch Of Brimstone (19-02-66) 5-10. Never, Never Say Die (18-03-67) 5-17. Return Of The Cybernauts (30-09-67)

Department S: 04. The Pied Piper Of Hambledown (30-03-69)

Doctor Who 01 An Unearthly Child 3 Episodes (23-11-63) 19 Mission To The Unknown (9-10-65)

Ghost Squad 2-07. Lost in Transit (15-06-63)

Randall & Hopkirk (Deceased) 25. You Can Always Find a Fall Guy (06-03-70)

The Saint 5-08. The Man Who Liked Lions (18-11-66) 6-17. Ex-King Of Diamonds (19-1-68)

Jerold Wells (Cast Member)

The Champions 23. The Night People (05-03-69)

Man In A Suitcase 16. The Whisper (10-01-67)

Jerome Willis (Cast Member)

Adam Adamant Lives! 09. Sing a Song Of Murder (25-08-66)

The Avengers 2-15. Intercrime (05-01-63) 4-25. How To Succeed…. At Murder (19-03-66) 6-14. The Interrogators (01-01-69)

The Baron 14. There's Someone Close Behind You (28-12-67)

Callan 2-09. Death Of a Friend (05-03-69)

Danger Man 2-21. The Mirror's New (09-03-65) 3-09. English Lady Take Lodgers (25-11-65) 3-15. Somebody Is Liable To Get Hurt (06-01-66)

Out Of The Unknown 1-05. Time In Advance (01-11-65)

Jerry Elboz (Cast Member)

Ghost Squad 2-24. Gertrude (13-04-63)

Jerry Holmes (Cast Member)

Doctor Who 43. The Wheel in Space: 2 Episodes (11-05-68)

Jerry Jardin (Cast Member)

The Avengers 2-13. Death Dispatch (22-12-62)

Jerry Stovin (Cast Member)

The Baron 09. And Suddenly You're Dead (23-11-66)

Danger Man 2-02. The Professionals (20-10-64)

Ghost Squad 2-11. A First Class Way To Die (13-07-63)

Out Of The Unknown 1-01. No Place Like Earth (04-10-65)

The Saint 2-02. Starring The Saint (26-09-63) 3-21. Sibao (25-2-65) 3-23. The Happy Suicide (11-03-65)

Jessica Dunning (Cast Member)

Out Of The Unknown 1-01. No Place Like Earth (04-10-65) 2-03. Lambda One (20-10-66)

Jessie Barclay (Cast Member)

Undermind 11. End Signal (17-07-65)

Jill Cary (Cast Member)

Undermind 01. Instance One (08-05-65)

Jill Curzon (Cast Member)

The Champions 24. Project Zero (12-03-69)

The Saint 4-09. The Old Treasure Story (26-08-65)

Jill Ireland (Cast Member)

Ghost Squad 1-08. Assassin (28-10-61)

Jill Melford (Cast Member)

Danger Man 2-04 The Galloping Major (03-11-64) 2-15 Whatever Happened To George Foster (19-1-65)

Ghost Squad 2-26. Sabotage (20-04-63)

The Saint 2-06. Marcia (24-10-63)

Jim O'Brady (Cast Member)

Man In A Suitcase 02. The Sitting Pigeon (04-10-67)

Jimmy Falana (Cast Member)

Danger Man 2-04. The Galloping Major (03-11-64)

Jimmy Fung (Cast Member)

Danger Man 1-22. The Honeymooners (02-04-61) 1-28. Sabotage (14-05-61)

Jimmy Gardner (Cast Member)

The Avengers 6-07. False Witness (06-1-68) Man In A Suitcase 03. Day Of Execution (11-10-67)

The Saint 3-10. The Imprudent Politician (10-12-64)

Jimmy Jewel (Cast Member)

The Avengers 6-11. Look (Stop Me If You've Heard This One) But There Were These Two Fellers

(04-12-68)
Jo Rowbottom (Cast Member)
The Baron 13. Portrait Of Louisa (21-12-67)
Doctor Who 36. The Evil Of The Daleks: Episode 2 (27-05-67)
Joan Crane (Cast Member)
Adam Adamant Lives! 07. To Set a Deadly Fashion (11-08-66)
Callan 2-02. The Most Promising Girl Of Her Year (15-01-69)
Joan Greenwood (Cast Member)
Danger Man: 3-22. The Paper Chase (31-03-66)
Joan Heath (Cast Member)
Undermind 07. Song Of Death (19-06-65)
Joan Hickson (Cast Member)
Danger Man: 2-01. Yesterday's Enemies (13-10-64)
Joan Ingram (Cast Member)
The Saint 3-12. The Unkind Philanthropist (24-12-64)
The Third Man 2-06. Barcelona Passage (01-10-59)
Joan Newell (Cast Member)
Danger Man 3-05. Loyalty Always Pays (28-10-65)
The Saint 6-13. The People Importers (22-12-68)
Strange Report 12. REPORT 7931 SNIPER When Is Your Cousin Not? (14-12-69)
Joan Paton (Cast Member)
Adam Adamant Lives! 13. The League Of Uncharitable Ladies (12-09-66)
Joan Young (Cast Member)
Danger Man 2-02. The Professionals (20-10-64)
Joanna Vogel (Cast Member)
The Avengers 5-09. The Correct Way To Kill (11-03-67) 6-08. All Done With Mirrors (13-11-68)
Department S: 14. Les Fleurs Du Mal (22-10-69)
Joanna Dunham (Cast Member)
Danger Man 1-38. Dead Man Walks (13-01-62)
The Third Man 3-01. A Question In Ice (27-06-64)
Joanna Wake (Cast Member)
The Avengers 4-14. Silent Dust (01-01-66)
Joanne Dainton (Cast Member)
The Avengers 5-22. The Positive Negative Man (4-11-67)
The Saint 6-01. The Best Laid Plans (29-09-68)
Joby Blanshard (Cast Member)
The Avengers 4-11. Man Eater Of Surrey Green (11-12-65)
Out Of The Unknown 1-03. Stranger In the Family (18-10-65)
Randall & Hopkirk (Deceased) 13. But What a Sweet Little Room (14-12-69)
The Saint 2-18. The Romantic Matron (16-01-64) 4-09. The Old Treasure Story (26-08-65)
Joe Baker (Cast Member)
Ghost Squad 2-04. The Golden Silence (08-06-63)
Strange Report 16. REPORT 4977 Square Root Of Evil (11-01-70)
Joe Beckett (Cast Member)
The Avengers 4-10. Dial a Deadly Number (04-12-65)
Joe Dunne (Cast Member)
The Avengers 4-03. The Cybernauts (16-10-65)
The Prisoner 09. Checkmate (14-11-67)
Joe Farrer (Cast Member)
The Avengers 4-02. The Gravediggers (09-01-65) 4-05. Castle De'ath (30-10-65) 4-06. The Master Minds (06-11-65)
Joe Gibbons (Cast Member)
The Saint 6-12. The Fiction Makers Part 2 (15-12-68)
Joe Gladwin (Cast Member)
The Prisoner 15. The Girl Who Was Death (18-01-67)
Joe Melia (Cast Member)
Man In A Suitcase 02. The Sitting Pigeon (04-10-67)
Public Eye 4-06. The Comedian's Graveyard (03-09-69)

Joe Phelps (Cast Member)
The Avengers 4-02. The Gravediggers (09-01-65)
Callan 2-01. Red Knight, White Knight (08-01-69)
Joe Ritchie (Cast Member)
The Avengers 4-11. Man Eater Of Surrey Green (11-12-65)
The Baron 20. The High Terrace (08-02-67)
Public Eye 1-02. Nobody Kill Santa Claus (30-01-65)
Joe Robinson (Cast Member)
The Avengers 3-06. November Five (02-11-63)
The Saint 2-11. The Saint Plays With Fire (28-11-63)
Joby Blanshard (Cast Member)
Adam Adamant Lives! 01 A Year For Scoundrels (20-06-66)
The Avengers 4-11, Man Eater Of Surrey Green (11-12-65)
Jocelyn Birdsall (Cast Member)
Doctor Who 13. The Web Planet: 6 Episodes (13-02-65)
Joel Fabiani (Cast Member)
Department S All Episodes (1969)
John Abineri (Cast Member)
The Baron 05. Enemy Of The State (26-10-66) 23. The Edge Of Fear (01-03-67)
The Protectors 03. Happy Is The Loser (11-04-64)
Out Of The Unknown 1-11. Thirteen To Centauraus
Strange Report 12. REPORT 7931 SNIPER When Is Your Cousin Not? (14-12-69)
John Acheson (Cast Member)
The Avengers 3-04. The Nutshell (19-10-63)
John Adams (Cast Member)
The Avengers 4-08. A Surfeit Of H2o (20-11-65)
John Alderson (Cast Member)
Doctor Who 25. The Gunfighters: 4 Episodes (30-04-66)
John Arnatt (Cast Member)
Randall & Hopkirk (Deceased) 18. Could You Recognise The Man Again (16-01-70)
The Saint 1-07. The Arrow Of God (15-11-62)
Strange Report 14. REPORT 2493 Whose Pretty Girl Are You? (28-12-69)
John Ashley Hamilton (Cast Member)
Strange Report 05. REPORT 8319 GRENADE What Price Change? (19-10-69)
John Atkinson (Cast Member)
The Avengers 6-07. False Witness (06-01-68)
Ghost Squad 2-25. The Thirteenth Girl (27-04-63)
John Atterbury (Cast Member)
Doctor Who 45. The Mind Robber: 5 Episodes (14-09-68)
John Baddeley (Cast Member)
Adam Adamant Lives! 12. Beauty Is An Ugly Word (15-09-66)
John Bailey (Cast Member)
Adam Adamant Lives! 15. The Village Of Evil (06-10-66)
The Avengers 2-26. Killer Whale (23-03-63) 4-01. The Town Of No Return (02-10-65) 4-10. Dial a Deadly Number (04-12-65) 6-17. Killer (22-01-69)
The Champions 17. A Case Of Lemmings (22-01-68)
Danger Man 2-03. Colony Three (27-10-64)
Department S: 07. Handicap Dead (20-04-69)
Doctor Who 36. The Evil Of The Daleks: Episode 2 (27-05-67)
Man Of The World 2-06. The Bullfighter (15-06-63)
The Saint 2-07. The Work Of Art (31-10-63)
John Baker (Cast Member)
The Avengers 5-21. You Have Just Been Murdered (28-10-67) 6-29. Requiem (16-04-69)
John Baldwin (Cast Member)
Public Eye 4-03. Paid In Full (13-08-69)
John Barcroft (Cast Member)
The Avengers 3-23. The Charmers (29-02-64)
The Baron 10. The Legends of Ammak (30-11-66)

Danger Man 3-18. The Hunting Party (27-01-66)
The Protectors 10. The Deadly Chameleon (30-5-64)
The Saint 6-07. The Time To Die (10-11-68)
Undermind 10. Waves Of Sound (10-07-65)
John Barrard (Cast Member)
The Avengers 6-24. Fog (12-03-69)
Doctor Who 08. The Reign Of Terror: 4 Episodes (08-08-64)
Interpol Calling 36. Desert Hijack (30-05-60)
The Saint 1-06. The Pearls Of Peace (08-11-62)
John Barrett (Cast Member)
The Baron 06. Masquerade (Part 1) (02-11-66)
Ghost Squad 2-01. Interrupted Requiem (02-02-63)
The Saint 2-01. The Fellow Traveller (19-09-63)
John Barrie (Cast Member)
Man In A Suitcase 06. Man From The Dead (01-11-67)
The Saint 2-15. The Benevolent Burglary (26-12-63) 5-12. Locate & Destroy (16-12-66)
John Barron (Cast Member)
The Avengers 4-24. A Sense Of History (12-03-66)
Department S: 24. The Bones Of Byrom Blain (28-01-70)
Ghost Squad 2-10. The Grand Duchess (11-05-63)
Out Of The Unknown 1-12. The Midas Plague (20-12-65)
The Saint 6-10. The Scales Of Justice (01-12-68)
Undermind 10. Waves Of Sound (10-07-65) 11. End Signal (17-07-65)
John Baskcomb (Cast Member)
The Protectors 01. Landscape With Bandits (28-03-64)
The Saint 3-08. The Man Who Liked Toys (26-11-64)
John Bennett (Cast Member)
The Avengers 2-05. Mission To Montreal (27-10-62) 6-07. False Witness (06-01-68)
The Baron 04. Red Horse, Red Rider (19-10-66)
Danger Man 2-07. The Colonels Daughter (24-11-64)
The Saint 2-16. The Wonderful War (02-01-64) 2-21. The Good Medicine (06-02-64) 3-14. The Contact (07-01-65) 5-23. The Gadget Lovers (21-04-67)
Strange Report 03. REPORT 2641 HOSTAGE If You Won't Learn Die (05-10-69)
John Benson (Cast Member)
Undermind 06. Intent To Destroy (12-06-65)
John Bentley (Cast Member)
Interpol Calling 37. Pipeline (06-06-60)
John Bindon (Cast Member)
Department S: 11. Who Plays The Dummy (01-10-69)
Public Eye 4-01. Welcome To Brighton? (30-07-69)
John Bloomfield (Cast Member)
The Saint 1-08. The Element Of Doubt (22-11-62) T2-26. The Ever Loving Spouse (12-03-64) 3-12. The Unkind Philanthropist (24-12-64)
John Bluthal (Cast Member)
The Avengers 4-12. Twos a Crowd (18-12-65)
The Baron 26. The Long, Long Day (22-03-67)
Man In A Suitcase 22. Jigsaw Man (21-02-67)
The Protectors 08. Freedom! (16-05-64)
The Saint 3-13. The Damsel In Distress (31-12-64) 3-23. The Happy Suicide (11-03-65)
John Bolt (Cast Member)
Randall & Hopkirk (Deceased) 26. The Smile Behind The Veil (13-03-70)
John Bonney (Cast Member)
Danger Man 1-29. The Contessa (21-05-61)
Ghost Squad 2-15. The Last Jump (23-02-63)
The Protectors 13. Cargo From Corinth (20-06-64)
John Bown (Cast Member)
The Baron 19. You Can't Win Them All (01-02-67)
The Champions 27. Nutcracker (02-04-69)

John Boxer (Cast Member)
Public Eye 4-04. My Lifes My Own (20-08-69) 4-05. Case For The Defence (27-08-69)
Randall & Hopkirk (Deceased) 21. The Ghost Talks (06-02-70)
John Boyd-Brent (Cast Member)
Doctor Who 29. The Tenth Planet: 3 Episodes (08-10-66)
Ghost Squad 2-03. Sentences Of Death (04-05-63)
John Brandon (Cast Member)
Man In A Suitcase 11. Dead Man's Shoes (06-12-67)
John Breslin (Cast Member)
Danger Man 2-16. A Room in The Basement (02-02-65)
John Brooking (Cast Member)
Danger Man 3-16. Dangerous Secret (13-01-66)
John Bown (Cast Member)
The Saint 5-25. The Power Artists (19-05-67)
John Boxer (Cast Member)
The Saint 6-10. The Scales Of Justice (01-12-68)
John Bryans (Cast Member)
The Baron 04. Red Horse, Red Rider (19-10-66) 26. The Long, Long Day (22-03-67)
The Champions 10. The Ghost Plane (27-11-68)
Danger Man 2-19. It's Up To The Lady (23-02-65)
The Protectors 02. The Bottle Shop (04-04-64)
Randall & Hopkirk (Deceased) 18. Could You Recognise The Man Again (16-01-70)
The Saint 3-10. The Imprudent Politician (10-12-64)
John Bull (Cast Member)
The Saint 5-25. The Power Artists (19-05-67)
John Cabot (Cast Member)
The Avengers 3-24. Concerto (07-03-64)
John Cairney (Cast Member)
The Avengers 6-29. Requiem (16-04-69)
Danger Man 2-14. Such Men Are Dangerous (12-01-65)
Ghost Squad 1-05. High Wire (30-09-61)
Interpol Calling 27. Ascent To Murder (28-03-60)
Man In A Suitcase 08. Essay In Evil (15-11-67)
John Carlin (Cast Member)
Ghost Squad 2-12. Quarantine At Kavar (01-06-63)
John Carlisle (Cast Member)
The Avengers 6-03. Super Secret Cypher Snatch (09-10-68)
Strange Report 16. REPORT 4977 Square Root Of Evil (11-01-70)
John Carney (Cast Member)
The Saint 5-25. The Power Artists (19-05-67)
John Carson (Cast Member)
Adam Adamant Lives! 13. The League Of Uncharitable Ladies (12-09-66)
The Avengers 2-24. A Chorus Of Frogs (09-03-63) 3-08. Second Sight (16-11-63) 4-10. Dial a Deadly Number (04-12-65)
The Baron 06. Masquerade (Part 1) (02-11-66) 07. The Killing (Part 2) (09-11-66)
Department S: 24. The Bones Of Byrom Blain (28-01-70)
Ghost Squad 1-07. Still Waters (21-10-61) 2-25. The Thirteenth Girl (27-04-63)
Man In A Suitcase 11. Dead Man's Shoes (06-12-67)
Credited Cast Members cont
Man Of The World 1-01. Death Of a Conference (29-09-62)
The Protectors 09. The Pirate (23-05-64)
The Saint 1-07. The Arrow Of God (15-11-62) 2-18. The Romantic Matron (16-01-64) 3-20. 3-21. Sibao (25-02-65) 5-16. The Fast Women (13-01-67)
John Castle (Cast Member)
The Prisoner 06. The General (03-11-67)
John Cater (Cast Member)
The Avengers 3-04. The Nutshell (19-10-63) 4-04. Death At Bargain Prices (23-10-65) 5-07. The Living Dead (25-02-67)

The Baron 19. You Can't Win Them All (01-02-67)
Danger Man 2-16. A Room in The Basement (02-02-65)
Department S: 17. Dead Men Die Twice (12-11-69)
John Cazabon (Cast Member)
The Avengers 6-20. Wish You Were Here (12-02-69)
The Baron 18. A Memory Of Evil (25-01-67)
Danger Man 2-09. No Marks For Servility (08-12-64) 2-18. The Ubiquitous Mr Lovegrove (16-02-65)
3-20. I Am Afraid You Have The Wrong Number (17-03-66)
Department S: 27. A Fish Out Of Water (25-02-70)
Ghost Squad 1-05. High Wire (30-09-61)
The Prisoner 04. Free For All (20-10-67) 16. Once Upon a Time (25-01-67)
Randall & Hopkirk (Deceased) 05. That's How Murder Snowballs (19-10-69)
The Saint 5-13. Flight Plan (23-12-66)
John Challis (Cast Member)
Strange Report 12. REPORT 7931 SNIPER When Is Your Cousin Not? (14-12-69)
John Chandos (Cast Member)
The Avengers 5-23. Murdersville (11-11-67)
Interpol Calling 30. A Foreign Body (18-04-60)
Man In A Suitcase 15. Burden Of Proof (03-01-67)
The Protectors 13. Cargo From Corinth (20-06-64)
John Church (Cast Member)
Adam Adamant Lives! 12. Beauty Is An Ugly Word (15-09-66)
The Avengers 2-23. Conspiracy Of Silence (02-03-63)
John Cleese (Cast Member)
The Avengers 6-11. Look (Stop Me If You've Heard This One) But There Were These Two Fellers
(04-12-68)
John Clive (Cast Member)
Man In A Suitcase 07. Sweet Sue (08-11-67)
The Saint 5-24. A Double In Diamonds (05-05-67)
John Cobner (Cast Member)
The Avengers 6-21. Love All (19-02-69)
John Collin (Cast Member)
The Baron 09. And Suddenly You're Dead (23-11-66) 20. The High Terrace (08-02-67)
Man In A Suitcase 22. Jigsaw Man (21-02-67)
Randall & Hopkirk (Deceased) 21. The Ghost Talks (06-02-70)
The Saint 5-21. Simon & Delilah (24-03-67) 6-05. The Organisation Man (27-10-67)
Undermind 03. The New Dimension (22-05-65)
John Collins (Cast Member)
The Saint 6-18. The Man Who Gambled With Life (26-01-68)
John Comer (Cast Member)
The Avengers 6-30. Take-Over (23-04-69)
John Cowley (Cast Member)
The Avengers 3-16. The Little Wonders (11-01-64)
John Crawford (Cast Member)
Danger Man 1-06. The Girl In Pink Pyjamas (16-10-60)
Ghost Squad 1-13. Death From a Distance (04-11-61)
Interpol Calling 04. The Sleeping Giant (05-10-59) 14. The Man's a Clown (21-12-59)
30. A Foreign Body (18-04-60)
The Third Man 3-01. A Question In Ice (27-06-64)
John Crocker (Cast Member)
Adam Adamant Lives! 29. A Sinister Sort Of Service (25-03-67)
The Avengers 2-02. Propellant 23 (06-10-62) 3-09. The Medicine Men (23-11-63) 5-06. The Winged
Avenger (18-02-67)
The Baron 20. The High Terrace (08-02-67)
The Protectors 14. The Reluctant Thief (27-06-64)
Public Eye 4-06. The Comedian's Graveyard (03-09-69)
The Saint 6-10. The Scales Of Justice (01-12-68)
Undermind 07. Song Of Death (19-06-65)

John Dawson (Cast Member)
Adam Adamant Lives! 08. The Last Sacrifice (18-08-66)
John Dearth (Cast Member)
The Avengers 2-02. Propellant 23 (06-10-62)
The Saint 1-05. The Loaded Tourist (01-11-62) 3-03. Jeannine (22-10-64)
John DeVaut (Cast Member)
Callan 2-09. Death Of a Friend (05-03-69)
John Drake (Cast Member)
The Prisoner 15. The Girl Who Was Death (18-01-67)
John Dunbar (Cast Member)
Adam Adamant Lives! 09. Sing a Song Of Murder (25-08-66)
Ghost Squad 2-20. P.G.7. (06-07-63)
Out Of The Unknown 3 -08. Little Black Bag (25-02-69)
The Saint 2-02. Starring The Saint (26-09-63)
John Edmunds (Cast Member)
Undermind 01. Instance One (08-05-65)
John Elsom (Cast Member)
The Avengers 6-17. Killer (22-01-69)
John Falconer (Cast Member)
The Avengers 2-21. The White Dwarf (16-02-63)
John Flint (Cast Member)
The Avengers 3-10. The Grandeur That Was Rome (30-11-63)
Doctor Who 14. The Crusade: 2 Episodes (27-03-65)
John Forbes-Robertson (Cast Member)
The Saint 1-11. The Man Who Was Lucky 3-22. The Crime Of The Century (04-03-65) 5-01. The
Queens Ransom (30-09-66)
John Forgeham (Cast Member)
The Avengers 4-07. The Murder Market (13-11-65)
John Fraser (Cast Member)
Danger Man 2-11. Don't Nail Him Yet (22-12-64)
Randall & Hopkirk (Deceased) 08. Whoever Heard Of a Ghost Dying (09-11-69)
John Franklyn-Robbins (Cast Member)
The Avengers 4-03. The Cybernauts (16-10-65)
The Baron 25. So Dark The Night (15-03-67)
The Champions 27. Nutcracker (02-04-69)
The Protectors 06. The Stamp Collection (02-05-64)
John Frawley (Cast Member)
The Avengers 2-04. Bullseye (20-10-62) 2-05. Mission To Montreal (27-10-62)
The Prisoner 08. Dance Of The Dead (17-11-67)
The Saint 5-26. When Spring Is Sprung (02-06-67)
John Gabriel (Cast Member)
The Baron 07. The Killing (Part 2) (09-11-66)
Danger Man 3-11. To Our Best Friend (09-12-65) 3-06. The Mercenaries (04-11-65)
Department S: 01. Six Days (09-03-69) 05. One Of Aircraft Is Empty (06-4-69)
Man In A Suitcase 28. Three Blinks Of The Eyes (03-04-67)
Out Of The Unknown 1-10. Some Lapse In Time (06-12-65)
The Saint 2-22. The Invisible Millionaire (13-2-64) 3-20. The Frightened Inn-Keeper (18-02-65)
John Garrie (Cast Member)
The Avengers 5-06. The Winged Avenger (18-02-67) 6-24. Fog (12-03-69)
The Baron 25. So Dark The Night (15-03-67)
Danger Man 3-24. Koroshi (12-02-67)
Man In A Suitcase 12. Find The Lady (13-12-67)
Public Eye 1-12. The Morning Wasn't So Hot (10-04-65)
The Saint 5-04. The Reluctant Revolution (21-10-66)
John Garvin (Cast Member)
Randall & Hopkirk (Deceased) 10. When Did You Start To Stop Seeing Things? (23-11-69)
Undermind 06. Intent To Destroy (12-06-65)
John Gatrell (Cast Member)

Adam Adamant Lives! 04. The Sweet Smell Of Disaster (14-07-66)
The Avengers 4-20. The Danger Makers (12-02-66)
The Baron 23. The Edge Of Fear (01-03-67)
Interpol Calling 35. Cargo Of Death (23-05-60)
John Gayford (Cast Member)
The Saint 2-02. Starring The Saint (26-09-63)
John Gill (Cast Member)
The Avengers 2-02. Propellant 23 (06-10-62)
The Baron 07. The Killing (Part 2) (09-11-66)
The Saint 2-12. The Well Meaning Mayor (05-12-63)
John Glyn-Jones (Cast Member)
The Avengers 4-24. A Sense Of History (12-03-66) 6-10. Noon Doomsday (27-11-68)
Danger Man 1-23. The Gallows Tree (09-04-61)
Man Of The World 1-10. Portrait Of a Girl (01-12-62)
Randall & Hopkirk (Deceased) 20. Money To Burn (30-01-70)
The Saint 2-14. The Bunco Artists (19-12-63)
John Gray (Cast Member)
The Saint 1-05. The Loaded Tourist (01-11-62)
John Gregson (Cast Member)
Man In A Suitcase 15. Burden Of Proof (03-01-67)
The Saint 5-14. Escape Route (30-12-66)
John Greenwood (Cast Member)
Adam Adamant Lives! 01 A Year For Scoundrels (20-06-66)
The Avengers 3-23. The Charmers (29-02-64)
John Grieve (Cast Member)
Public Eye 4-01. Welcome To Brighton? (30-07-69) 4-03. Paid In Full (13-08-69) 4-04. My Life's My Own (20-08-69) 4-07. A Fixed Address (19-06-69)
John Hallam (Cast Member)
Department S: 06. The Man In The Elegant Room (13-04-69)
Randall & Hopkirk (Deceased) 22. It's Supposed To Be Thicker Than Water (13-02-70)
John Hamblin (Cast Member)
The Prisoner 12. A Change Of Mind (15-12-67)
John Hart Dyke (Cast Member)
Adam Adamant Lives! 16. D Is For Destruction (13-06-66)
John Harvey (Cast Member)
Man In A Suitcase 27. Who's Mad Now (27-03-67)
Randall & Hopkirk (Deceased) 18. Could You Recognise The Man Again (16-01-70)
John Hatton (Cast Member)
Ghost Squad 2-12. Quarantine At Kavar (01-06-63)
John Heller (Cast Member)
The Avengers 4-11. Man Eater Of Surrey Green (11-12-65) 5-09. The Correct Way To Kill (11-03-67) 6-05. Split (23-10-68)
Danger Man 2-02. The Professionals (20-10-64) 2-09. No Marks For Servility (08-12-64) 3-15. Somebody Is Liable To Get Hurt (06-01-66)
Ghost Squad 1-04. Broken Doll (07-10-61)
The Saint 2-20. The Lawless Lady (30-01-64) 5-11. Paper Chase (09-12-66)
John Henderson (Cast Member)
Adam Adamant Lives! 15. The Village Of Evil (06-10-66)
John Herrington (Cast Member)
Danger Man 3-14. The Man Who Wouldn't Talk (30-12-65)
The Saint 5-11. Paper Chase (09-12-66)
John Hicks (Cast Member)
Doctor Who 44. The Dominators: 5 Episodes (10-08-68)
John Holland (Cast Member)
The Third Man 4-07. Diamond In the Rough (11-05-62)
John Hollis (Cast Member)
A For Andromeda 1-6. The Face Of The Tiger (07-11-61)
Adam Adamant Lives! 05. Allah Is Not Always With You (21-07-66)

The Andromeda Breakthrough 6 Episodes (1962)
The Avengers 2-18. Warlock (26-01-63) 4-03. The Cybernauts (16-10-65) 5-12. The Superlative Seven (01-04-67) 6-09. Legacy Of Death (20-11-68)
Man Of The World 1-06. The Sentimental Agent (03-11-62) 2-02. The Enemy (18-05-63)
The Saint 2-11. The Saint Plays With Fire (28-11-63) 5-16. The Fast Women (13-01-67)
John Horsley (Cast Member)
The Avengers 2-01. Mr Teddy Bear (29-09-62) 6-27. Thingamajig (16-04-69)
The Champions 24. Project Zero (12-03-69)
Department S: 15. The Shift That Never Was (25-10-69)
Interpol Calling 31. In The Swim (25-04-60)
John Hughes (Cast Member)
Randall & Hopkirk (Deceased) 20. Money To Burn (30-01-70)
John Hussey (Cast Member)
The Avengers 6-32. Get-a-Way (14-05-69)
John Junkin (Cast Member)
The Avengers 3-14. Dressed To Kill (28-12-63) 5-10. Never, Never Say Die (18-03-67)
John Kelland (Cast Member)
Department S: 04. The Pied Piper Of Hambledown (30-03-69)
The Saint 1-01. The Talented Husband (4-10-62) 2-11. The Saint Plays With Fire (28-11-63)
John Kidd (Cast Member)
Adam Adamant Lives! 10. The Doomsday Plan (01-09-66)
The Avengers 4-08. A Surfeit Of H2o (20-11-65) 6-05. Split (23-10-68)
Randall & Hopkirk (Deceased) 09. The House On Haunted Hill (16-11-69) 4-01. The Chequered Flag (01-07-65)
John Kirby (Cast Member)
Danger Man 2-05. Fair Exchange (10-11-64)
John F Landry (Cast Member)
Strange Report 07. REPORT 3424 EPIDEMIC A Most Curious Crime (02-11-69)
John Laurie (Cast Member)
The Avengers 2-08. Death Of Great Dane (17-11-62) 3-01. Brief For Murder (28-09-63) 5-13. A Funny Thing Happened On The Way To The Station (08-04-67) 6-31. Pandora (30-04-69)
Man Of The World 1-07. The Highland Story (10-11-62)
Strange Report 13. REPORT 4821 X-RAY Who Weeps For The Doctor (21-12-69)
John Law (Cast Member)
Adam Adamant Lives! 15. The Village Of Evil (06-10-66)
Doctor Who 08. The Reign Of Terror: 4 Episodes (08-08-64)
John Le Mesuirer (Cast Member)
Adam Adamant Lives! 06. The Happy Embalmers (04-06-66)
The Avengers 3-18. Mandrake (25-01-64) 4-22. What The Butler Saw (26-02-66)
Danger Man 1-10. An Affair Of State (13-11-60)
Ghost Squad 1-13. Death From a Distance (04-11-61)
Interpol Calling 06. The Long Weekend (19-10-59)
John Lee (Cast Member)
The Avengers 5-05. The Bird Who Knew Too Much (11-2-67) 5-17. Return Of The Cybernauts (30-9-67)
The Champions 08. To Trap a Rat (13-11-68)
Man In A Suitcase 04. Variation On a Million Bucks Part 1 (18-10-67) 17. Why They Killed Nolan (17-01-67)
Danger Man 1-01. View From The Villa (11-09-60)
Doctor Who 02. The Daleks: 5 Episodes (21-12-63)
John Levene (Cast Member)
Doctor Who 41. The Web Of Fear: 5 Episodes (3-2-68) 46. The Invasion: 6 Episodes (09-11-68)
John Livesey (Cast Member)
Doctor Who 50. The War Games: 10 Episodes (19-04-69)
John Longden (Cast Member)
Ghost Squad 2-19. Death of a Sportsman (26-01-63)
Interpol Calling 38. The Absent Assassin (13-06-60)
John Louis Mansi (Cast Member)

Department S: 12. The Treasure Of the Costa Del Sol (08-10-69)
John Lowe (Cast Member)
The Avengers 3-21. Build a Better Mousetrap (15-02-64)
John Lynn (Cast Member)
The Avengers 3-21. Build a Better Mousetrap (15-02-64)
John Martin (Cast Member)
The Saint 2-02. Starring The Saint (26-09-63)
John Maxim (Cast Member)
The Prisoner 02. The Chimes Of Big Ben (06-10-67) 16. Once Upon a Time (25-01-67)
John McArdle (Cast Member)
Out Of The Unknown 1-07. Sucker Bait (15-11-65)
John McCarthy (Cast Member)
Man Of The World 2-01. The Bandit (11-05-63)
John McLaren (Cast Member)
The Saint 2-03. Judith (03-10-63) 3-21. Sibao (25-02-65)
John McKelvey (Cast Member)
Adam Adamant Lives! 12. Beauty Is An Ugly Word (15-09-66)
The Protectors 06. The Stamp Collection (02-05-64) 14. The Reluctant Thief (27-06-64)
John McLaren (Cast Member)
The Avengers 2-14. Dead On Course (29-12-62)
Ghost Squad 1-09. Million Dollar Ransom (11-11-61)
John Meillon (Cast Member)
Man Of The World 2-02. The Enemy (18-05-63)
Out Of The Unknown 1-07. Sucker Bait (15-11-65)
John Miller (Cast Member)
Danger Man 3-10. Are You Going To Be More Permanent? (02-12-65)
John Moore (Cast Member)
The Avengers 4-07. The Murder Market (13-11-65) 5-08. The Hidden Tiger (04-03-67)
6-27. Thingamajig (16-04-69)
The Champions 24. Project Zero (12-03-69)
Out Of The Unknown 1-11. Thirteen To Centauraus
John Murray Scott (Cast Member)
A For Andromeda 1-6. The Face Of The Tiger (07-11-61)
The Avengers 3-06. November Five (02-11-63)
John Nettleton (Cast Member)
The Avengers 5-04. The See Through Man (04-02-67) 6-14. The Interrogators (01-01-69)
The Champions 26. Full Circle (26-03-69)
Department S: 16. The Man From X (05-11-69)
John Nolan (Cast Member)
Strange Report 05. REPORT 8319 GRENADE What Price Change? (19-10-69)
John Orchard (Cast Member)
The Baron 12. The Maze (14-12-67)
John Paul (Cast Member)
The Avengers 6-29. Requiem (16-04-69)
Ghost Squad 2-26. Sabotage (20-04-63)
The Saint 3-08. The Man Who Liked Toys (26-11-64)
Out Of The Unknown 1-03. Stranger In the Family (18-10-65)
John Phillips (Cast Member)
The Avengers 5-08. The Hidden Tiger (04-03-67)
Danger Man 1-07. Position Of Trust (23-10-60) 1-34. The Deputy Coyannis Story (16-12-61) 3-13.
Say It With Flowers (23-12-65)
Man Of The World 1-01. Death Of a Conference (29-09-62)
John Porter-Davison (Cast Member)
Adam Adamant Lives! 16. D Is For Destruction (13-06-66)
The Avengers 6-06. Whoever Shot George Oblique Stroke XR40? (30-10-68)
The Champions 07. The Survivors (06-11-68)
Department S: 14. Les Fleurs Du Mal (22-10-69)
John Rae (Cast Member)

Danger Man 1-23. The Gallows Tree (09-04-61) 1-09. The Sanctuary (06-11-60)
Ghost Squad 2-03. Sentences Of Death (04-05-63)
Man Of The World 1-07. The Highland Story (10-11-62)
Randall & Hopkirk (Deceased) 19. A Sentimental Journey (23-01-70)
John Railton (Cast Member)
Man In A Suitcase 15. Burden Of Proof (03-01-67)
John Rapley (Cast Member)
The Avengers 6-26. Homicide & Old Lace (26-03-69)
Undermind 09. Test For The Future (03-07-65)
John Rees (Cast Member)
The Prisoner 15. The Girl Who Was Death (18-01-67)
Strange Report 06. REPORT 3906 COVER-GIRLS Last Years Model (26-10-69)
John Richmond (Cast Member)
Randall & Hopkirk (Deceased) 08. Whoever Heard Of a Ghost Dying (09-11-69)
John Ringham (Cast Member)
The Avengers 3-19. The Secrets Broker (01-02-64) 4-24. A Sense Of History (12-03-66)
The Baron 28. The Man Outside (05-04-67)
Ghost Squad 2-10. The Grand Duchess (11-05-63)
The Protectors 03. Happy Is The Loser (11-04-64)
The Saint 6-01. The Best Laid Plans (29-09-68)
John Robinson (Cast Member)
The Protectors 08. Freedom! (16-05-64)
The Saint 2-11. The Saint Plays With Fire (28-11-63) 6-04. The Desperate Diplomat (20-10-68)
John Rolfe (Cast Member)
Adam Adamant Lives!: 02. Death Has a Thousand Faces (30-06-66)
Doctor Who 33. The Moonbase: 2 Episodes (18-02-67)
John Ronane (Cast Member)
The Avengers 5-23. Murdersville (11-11-67) 6-23. Take Me To Your Leader (05-03-69)
Department S: 28. The Soup Of The Day (04-03-70)
Ghost Squad 2-25. The Thirteenth Girl (27-04-63)
The Saint 2-08. Iris (07-11-63) 6-20. The World Beater (09-02-69)
Strange Report 01. REPORT 5055 CULT Murder Shrieks Out (21-09-69)
John Ruddock (Cast Member)
The Avengers 2-01. Mr Teddy Bear (29-09-62)
John Rutland (Cast Member)
The Avengers 4-17. The Girl From AUNTIE (22-01-66)
John Salew (Cast Member)
The Avengers 1-20. Tunnel Of Fear (05-08-61)
Ghost Squad 1-08. Assassin (28-10-61)
Interpol Calling 24. Finger Of Guilt (07-03-60) 36. Desert Hijack (30-05-60)
John Savident (Cast Member)
The Avengers 6-28. My Wildest Dream (07-04-69)
Callan 2-01. Red Knight, White Knight (08-01-69)
Department S: 10. Double Death Of Charlie Crippen (14-09-69)
Man In A Suitcase 23. Web With Four Spiders (28-02-67)
The Saint 6-14. Where The Money Is (29-12-68)
John Scott (Cast Member)
Adam Adamant Lives! 06. The Happy Embalmers (04-06-66)
The Avengers 6-14. The Interrogators (01-01-69)
Ghost Squad 2-09. Hot Money (25-05-63)
John Scott Martin (Cast Member)
Ghost Squad 2-07. Lost in Transit (15-06-63)
John Serret (Cast Member)
Danger Man 2-08. The Battle Of The Cameras (01-12-64)
Department S: 02. The Trojan Tanker (16-03-69) 17. Dead Men Die Twice (12-11-69)
The Saint 2-3. Judith (3-10-63) 5-1. The Queens Ransom (30-9-66) 5-19. To Kill a Saint (24-2-67)
John Sharp (Cast Member)
The Avengers 2-11 Traitor In Zebra (8-12-62) 5-23 Murdersville (11-11-67) 6-33. Bizarre (21-5-69)

The Corridor People All Episodes (1966)
The Prisoner 12. A Change Of Mind (15-12-67)
Randall & Hopkirk (Deceased) 11. The Ghost Who Saved The Bank At Monte Carlo (30-11-69)
The Saint 4-02. The Abductors (08-07-65)
John Slater (Cast Member)
Danger Man 3-06. The Mercenaries (04-11-65)
John Southworth (Cast Member)
Danger Man 2-13. That's Two Of Us Sorry (05-01-64)
John Standing (Cast Member)
The Avengers 2-20. School For Traitors (09-02-63)
Danger Man 3-03. Sting In The Tail (14-10-65)
The Saint 2-14. The Bunco Artists (19-12-63)
John Slavid (Cast Member)
Danger Man 1-13. The Prisoner (04-12-60)
John Steiner (Cast Member)
Department S: 08. A Ticket To Nowhere (27-04-69)
The Saint 5-17. The Death Game (20-01-67)
John Sterland (Cast Member)
Danger Man 1-28. Sabotage (14-05-61)
John Stone (Cast Member)
The Avengers 3-19. The Secrets Broker (01-02-64) 5-15. The Joker (22-04-67) 6-14. The Interrogators (01-01-69)
The Champions 13. Twelve Hours (18-12-68)
The Saint 3-15. The Set-Up (14-01-65)
John Styles (Cast Member)
Randall & Hopkirk (Deceased) 05. That's How Murder Snowballs (19-10-69)
John Sullivan (Cast Member)
The Saint 1-11. The Man Who Was Lucky (13-12-62)
John Tate (Cast Member)
The Avengers 2-26. Killer Whale (23-03-63)
The Baron 18. A Memory Of Evil (25-01-67)
The Champions 07. The Survivors (06-11-68)
Danger Man 3-23. Not So Jolly Roger (07-04-66)
Department S: 14. Les Fleurs Du Mal (22-10-69)
Man Of The World 2-03. Double Exposure (25-05-63)
The Saint 3-07. The Loving Brothers (19-11-64) 4-03. The Crooked Ring (15-07-65) 6-01. The Best Laid Plans (29-09-68)
Strange Report 16. REPORT 4977 Square Root Of Evil (11-01-70)
John Thaw (Cast Member)
The Avengers 3-25. Espirit de Corps (14-03-64)
Strange Report 08. REPORT 2475 REVENGE When a Man Hates (09-11-69)
John Timberlake (Cast Member)
The Avengers 4-08. A Surfeit Of H2o (20-11-65)
John Tinn (Cast Member)
Ghost Squad 1-01. Hong Kong Story (23-09-61)
Randall & Hopkirk (Deceased) 22. It's Supposed To Be Thicker Than Water (13-02-70)
John Trenaman (Cast Member)
City Beneath The Sea All episodes (1962)
John Turner (Cast Member)
The Champions 13. Twelve Hours (18-12-68)
The Saint 6-08. The Master Plan (17-11-68)
John Van Eyssen (Cast Member)
Interpol Calling 11. Air Switch (23-11-59)
John Walker (Cast Member)
Adam Adamant Lives! 11. Death By Appointment Only (08-09-66)
John Watson (Cast Member)
The Corridor People 2 Episodes (1966)
John Welsh (Cast Member)

Danger Man 2-02. The Professionals (20-10-64) 2-16. A Room in The Basement (02-02-65)
3-18. The Hunting Party (27-01-66)
Ghost Squad 1-11 The Green Shoes (29-12-62)
John Wentworth (Cast Member)
The Avengers 2-25. Six Hands Across a Table (16-03-63) 4-06. The Master Minds (06-11-65)
Callan 2-06. Heir Apparent (12-02-69) 2-13. The Worst Soldier I Ever Saw (02-04-69)
Ghost Squad 2-25. The Thirteenth Girl (27-04-63)
The Saint 2-24. Sophia (24-02-64)
Undermind 07. Song Of Death (19-06-65)
John Whitney (Cast Member)
Ghost Squad 2-03. Sentences Of Death (04-05-63)
John Wilding (Cast Member)
Public Eye 4-06. The Comedian's Graveyard (03-09-69)
John Wood (Cast Member)
The Avengers 5-05. The Bird Who Knew Too Much (11-02-67)
John Woodnutt (Cast Member)
Adam Adamant Lives! 05. Allah Is Not Always With You (21-07-66)
The Avengers 4-19. Quick-Quick Slow Death (05-02-66)
The Corridor People Victim as Red (1966)
Out Of The Unknown 3 -08. Little Black Bag (25-02-69)
The Saint 2-19. Luella (23-01-64)
John Woodvine (Cast Member)
The Avengers 4-07. The Murder Market (13-11-65) 6-11. Look (Stop Me If You've Heard This One)
But There Were These Two Fellers (04-12-68)
The Baron 15. Storm Warning (Part 1) (04-01-67)
The Champions 14. The Search (01-01-68)
Danger Man 1-25. The Brothers (23-04-61) 3-07. Judgement Day (11-11-65) 3-19. Two Birds With
One Bullet (10-03-66)
Ghost Squad 2-07. Lost in Transit (15-06-63)
Man Of The World 2-01. The Bandit (11-05-63)
The Saint 5-01. The Queens Ransom (30-09-66)
John Wynyard (Cast Member)
Danger Man 1-20. The Vacation (29-01-61)
John Wyse (Cast Member)
Danger Man 1-29. The Contessa (21-05-61)
Johnny Briggs (Cast Member)
Department S: 18. The Perfect Operation (26-12-69)
The Saint 2-06. Marcia (24-10-63)
Johnny Sekka (Cast Member)
The Avengers 6-12. Have Guns - Will Haggle (11-12-68)
Danger Man 3-05. Loyalty Always Pays (28-10-65)
Johnny Vyvyan (Cast Member)
The Avengers 6-11. Look (Stop Me If You've Heard This One) But There Were These Two Fellers
(04-12-68)
Johnson Bayly (Cast Member)
The Avengers 2-12. The Big Thinker (15-12-62)
Doctor Who 44. The Dominators: 5 Episodes (10-08-68)
Jolyon Booth (Cast Member)
The Baron 01. Diplomatic Immunity (28-09-66)
Doctor Who 13. The Web Planet: 6 Episodes (13-02-65)
Jon Croft (Cast Member)
Callan 2-01. Red Knight, White Knight (08-01-69)
Public Eye 2-07. Works With Chess, Not With Life (13-08-66)
Jon Laurimore (Cast Member)
The Avengers 4-26. Honey For The Prince (26-03-66) 5-19. The £50,000 Breakfast (14-10-67)
Callan 1-06. You Should Have Got Here Sooner (12-08-67)
The Prisoner 07. Many Happy Returns (10-11-67)
Jon Pertwee (Cast Member)

The Avengers 5-01. From Venus With Love (14-01-67)
Jon Rollason (Cast Member)
The Avengers 2-05. Mission To Montreal (27-0-62) 2-09. The Sell Out (24-11-62) 2-14. Dead On Course (29-12-62)
The Baron 18. A Memory Of Evil (25-01-67)
Danger Man 3-23. Not So Jolly Roger (07-04-66)
Doctor Who 41. The Web Of Fear: 5 Episodes (03-02-68)
Jonathan Burn (Cast Member)
The Avengers 6-12. Have Guns - Will Haggle (11-12-68)
Callan 2-14. Nice People Die At Home (09-04-69)
Jonathon Elsom (Cast Member)
The Avengers 5-04. The See Through Man (04-02-67)
The Baron 24. Long Ago & Far Away (08-03-67)
The Saint 6-01. The Best Laid Plans (29-09-68)
Jonathan Hansen (Cast Member)
Out Of The Unknown 2-01. The Machine Stops (06-10-66)
Jonathan Harris (Cast Member)
The Third Man 2-06. Barcelona Passage (01-10-59) 2-10. Toys Of The Dead (03-11-59) 4-07. Diamond In the Rough (11-05-62) 3-01. A Question In Ice (27-06-64)
Jonathon Holt (Cast Member)
Strange Report 03. REPORT 2641 HOSTAGE If You Won't Learn Die (05-10-69)
Jonathan Scott (Cast Member)
The Avengers 6-18. The Morning After (29-10-69)
Jose Berlinka (Cast Member)
Danger Man 2-08. The Battle Of The Cameras (01-12-64) 2-16. A Room in The Basement (02-02-65) 3-03. Sting In The Tail (14-10-65)
Man In A Suitcase 18. The Boston Square (24-01-67)
Josef Zaranoff (Cast Member)
Adam Adamant Lives! 18. Black Echo (07-01-67) 29. A Sinister Sort Of Service (25-03-67)
Joseph Conrad (Cast Member)
Callan 2-04. The Little Bits & Pieces Of Love (29-01-69)
Joseph Cuby (Cast Member)
Danger Man 1-04. The Blue Veil (02-10-60) 1-29. The Contessa (21-05-61)
Man Of The World 2-06. The Bullfighter (15-06-63)
The Prisoner 12. A Change Of Mind (15-12-67)
The Saint 1-05. The Loaded Tourist (01-11-62)
Joseph Furst (Cast Member)
The Barron 05. Enemy Of The State (26-10-66)
The Champions 01. The Beginning (25-09-68) 14. The Search (01-01-68)
Ghost Squad 1-08. Assassin (28-10-61)
Doctor Who 32. The Underwater Menace: 2 Episodes (21-01-67)
Man Of The World 1-13. Shadow Of the Wall (22-12-62)
The Saint 2-11. The Saint Plays With Fire (28-11-63) 2-27. The Saint Sees It Through (19-03-64) 5-03. The Russian Prisoner (14-10-66)
Joseph Greig (Cast Member)
The Avengers 5-23. Murdersville (11-11-67)
The Baron 28. The Man Outside (05-04-67)
The Saint 5-15. The Persistent Patriots (06-01-67)
Joseph Layode (Cast Member)
Danger Man 2-22. Parallel Lines Sometimes Meet (16-03-65)
Joseph O'Conor (Cast Member)
Out Of The Unknown 1-01. No Place Like Earth (04-10-65)
Public Eye 4-03. Paid In Full (13-08-69)
Joseph Wise (Cast Member)
Man In A Suitcase 29. Castle In The Clouds (10-04-67)
Josephine Brown (Cast Member)
The Saint 1-04. The Covetous Headsman (25-10-62)
Joss Ackland (Cast Member)

The Avengers 6-18. The Morning After (29-10-69)
Joyce Blair (Cast Member)
Ghost Squad 1-11 The Green Shoes (29-12-62)
The Saint 5-02. Interlude In Venice (07-10-66)
Joyce Carey (Cast Member)
The Avengers 6-26. Homicide & Old Lace (26-03-69)
Danger Man 2-15. Whatever Happened To George Foster (19-01-65)
Randall & Hopkirk (Deceased) 07. Murder Ain't What It Used To Be (02-11-69)
Joyce Carpenter (Cast Member)
Adam Adamant Lives! 13. The League Of Uncharitable Ladies (12-09-66)
Joyce Donaldson (Cast Member)
Out Of The Unknown 1-11. Thirteen To Centauraus
Joyce Heron (Cast Member)
The Avengers 3-25. Espirit de Corps (14-03-64)
Judee Morton (Cast Member)
The Saint 6-14. Where The Money Is (29-12-68)
Judith Arthy (Cast Member)
The Baron 12. The Maze (14-12-67)
Man In A Suitcase 13. The Bridge (20-12-67)
Randall & Hopkirk 02. A Disturbing Case (28-9-69) 09. The House On Haunted Hill (16-11-69)
Judith Bruce (Cast Member)
The Avengers 3-08. Second Sight (16-11-63)
Judy Carne (Cast Member)
Danger Man 1-33. Hired Assassin (18-06-61)
Judy Geeson (Cast Member)
Danger Man 3-08. The Outcast (18-11-65)
Man In A Suitcase 07. Sweet Sue (08-11-67)
Judy Huxtable (Cast Member)
Danger Man 3-09. English Lady Take Lodgers (25-11-65)
Judy Parfitt (Cast Member)
Adam Adamant Lives! 18. Black Echo (07-01-67)
The Avengers 2-04. Bullseye (20-10-62) 3-15. The White Elephant (04-01-64) 5-03. Escape In Time (26-01-67) 6-06. Whoever Shot George Oblique Stroke XR40? (30-10-68)
Out Of The Unknown 1-05. Time In Advance (01-11-65)
The Saint 5-15. The Persistent Patriots (06-01-67)
Undermind 03. The New Dimension (22-05-65)
Julia Arnall (Cast Member)
The Avengers 2-15. Intercrime (05-01-63)
Danger Man 1-03. Josetta (25-09-60) 1-38. Dead Man Walks (13-01-62)
Ghost Squad 1-04. Broken Doll (07-10-61)
The Saint 5-12. Locate & Destroy (16-12-66)
Julia Lockwood (Cast Member)
Interpol Calling 22. The Heiress (15-02-60)
Julia McCarthy (Cast Member)
Callan 2-13. The Worst Soldier I Ever Saw (02-04-69)
Julian Chagrin (Cast Member)
The Avengers 6-11. Look (Stop Me If You've Heard This One) But There Were These Two Fellers (04-12-68)
Julian Curry (Cast Member)
Out Of The Unknown 1-12. The Midas Plague (20-12-65)
Julian Glover (Cast Member)
The Avengers 4-12. Twos a Crowd (18-12-65) 5-07. The Living Dead (25-02-67) 6-05. Split (23-10-68) 6-31. Pandora (30-04-69)
Doctor Who 14. The Crusade: 2 Episodes (27-03-65)
The Saint 2-20. The Lawless Lady (30-01-64) 6-02. Invitation To Danger (06-10-68)
Strange Report 08. REPORT 2475 REVENGE When a Man Hates (09-11-69)
Julian Herrington (Cast Member)
Department S: 24. The Bones Of Byrom Blain (28-01-70)

Julian Holloway (Cast Member)
The Avengers 1-20. Tunnel Of Fear (05-08-61)
The Saint 2-19. Luella (23-01-64)
Julian Sherrier (Cast Member)
The Baron 03. Something For a Rainy Day (12-10-66)
Danger Man 3-11. To Our Best Friend (09-12-65)
Doctor Who 21. The Daleks' Master Plan: 3 Episodes (20-11-65)
Ghost Squad 2-18. The Heir Apparent (09-03-63) 2-12. Quarantine At Kavar (01-06-63)
Interpol Calling 01. The Angola Brights (14-09-59) 27. Ascent To Murder (28-03-60)
The Saint 6-13. The People Importers (22-12-68)
Julian Somors (Cast Member)
The Avengers 2-22. Man In The Mirror (23-02-63)
Danger Man 3-03. Sting In The Tail (14-10-65)
Interpol Calling 05. The Two Headed Monster (12-10-59)
Julie Allan (Cast Member)
Danger Man 1-32. The Actor (11-06-61)
Ghost Squad 1-01. Hong Kong Story (23-09-61)
Julie Bevan (Cast Member)
Man In A Suitcase 02. The Sitting Pigeon (04-10-67)
Julie Christie (Cast Member)
A For Andromeda 1-6. The Face Of The Tiger (07-11-61)
The Saint 2-03. Judith (03-10-63)
Julie Collins (Cast Member)
Strange Report 02. REPORT 0649 SKELETON Let Sleeping Heroes Lie (28-09-69)
Julie Hopkins (Cast Member)
Danger Man 1-34. The Deputy Coyannis Story (16-12-61)
Julie La Rousee (Cast Member)
The Avengers 2-10. Death On The Rocks (01-12-62) 2-12. The Big Thinker (15-12-62)
Julie May (Cast Member)
Out Of The Unknown 1-06. Come Buttercup, Come Daisy, Come…? (08-11-65)
Strange Report 02. REPORT 0649 SKELETON Let Sleeping Heroes Lie (28-09-69)
Julie Paulle (Cast Member)
The Avengers 2-26. Killer Whale (23-03-63)
Julie Samuel (Cast Member)
The Avengers 1-20. Tunnel Of Fear (05-08-61)
Strange Report 15. REPORT 4407 No Choice For The Donor (04-01-70)
Julie Stevens (Cast Member)
The Avengers 2-03. The Decapod (13-10-62) 2-06. The Removal Men (03-11-62) 2-17. Box Of Tricks (19-01-63) 2-20. School For Traitors (09-02-63) 2-22. Man In The Mirror (23-02-63) 2-24. A Chorus Of Frogs (09-03-63)
Julie Wallace (Cast Member)
Danger Man 2-13. That's Two Of Us Sorry (05-01-64)
Juliet Harmer (Cast Member)
Adam Adamant Lives! 17 Episodes
The Avengers 4-01. The Town Of No Return (02-10-65)
Danger Man 3-03. Sting In The Tail (14-10-65) 3-12. The Man On The Beach (16-12-65)
Department S: 06. The Man In The Elegant Room (13-4-69) 08. A Ticket To Nowhere (27-4-69)
Randall & Hopkirk (Deceased) 25. You Can Always Find a Fall Guy (06-03-70)
Juliet Mills (Cast Member)
Man Of The World 1-09. The Mindreader (24-11-62)
Juliet Winsor (Cast Member)
Ghost Squad 1-07. Still Waters (21-10-61)
Juliette Manet (Cast Member)
Ghost Squad 2-17. Mr Five Per Cent (06-04-63)
June Abbott (Cast Member)
Department S: 12. The Treasure Of the Costa Del Sol (08-10-69)
The Saint 6-06. The Double Take (03-11-68)
June Barry (Cast Member)

Out Of The Unknown 3-03. The Last Lonely Man (21-01-69)
Public Eye 1-02. Nobody Kill Santa Claus (30-01-65)
June Cunningham (Cast Member)
Man Of The World 1-10. Portrait Of a Girl (01-12-62)
June Ellis (Cast Member)
The Prisoner 12. A Change Of Mind (15-12-67)
June Hodgson (Cast Member)
The Avengers 2-26. Killer Whale (23-03-63)
June Merlin (Cast Member)
Interpol Calling 24. Finger Of Guilt (07-03-60)
June Murphy (Cast Member)
The Avengers 2-11. Traitor In Zebra (08-12-62)
June Ritchie (Cast Member)
The Baron 27. Roundabout (29-03-67)
The Saint 5-10. Little Girl Lost (02-12-66)
June Shaw (Cast Member)
Ghost Squad 2-04. The Golden Silence (08-06-63)
June Smith (Cast Member)
The Saint 2-07. The Work Of Art (31-10-63)
June Thody (Cast Member)
The Avengers 3-01. Brief For Murder (28-09-63)
June Throburn (Cast Member)
Danger Man 1-13. The Prisoner (04-12-60)
Juno (Cast Member)
The Avengers 1-20. Tunnel Of Fear (05-08-61)
Justine Lord (Cast Member)
The Avengers 2-01. Mr Teddy Bear (29-09-62) 2-02. Propellant 23 (06-10-62)
Man In A Suitcase 25. Property Of A Gentleman (13-03-67)
Out Of The Unknown 1-03. Stranger In the Family (18-10-65)
The Prisoner 15. The Girl Who Was Death (18-01-67)
The Saint 2-11. The Saint Plays With Fire (28-11-63) 2-14. The Bunco Artists (19-12-63) 3-06. The Saint Steps In (12-11-64) 3-10. The Imprudent Politician (10-12-64) 4-01. The Chequered Flag (1-7-65) 6-11. The Fiction Makers Pt 1 (8-12-68) 6-12. The Fiction Makers Pt 2 (15-12-68)

K

Kaplan Kaye (Cast Member)
The Saint 2-18. The Romantic Matron (16-01-64)
Karen Clare (Cast Member)
Danger Man 2-06. Fish On The Hook (17-11-64)
Undermind 07. Song Of Death (19-06-65)
Karen Ford (Cast Member)
The Avengers 5-10. Never, Never Say Die (18-03-67)
The Saint 5-17. The Death Game (20-01-67)
Karl Held (Cast Member)
Strange Report 11. REPORT 1553 RACIST A Most Dangerous Proposal (07-12-69)
Karl Lanchbury (Cast Member)
Out Of The Unknown 1-11. Thirteen To Centauraus
Kate Newman (Cast Member)
Doctor Who 23. The Ark: 4 Episodes (05-03-66)
Kate O'Mara (Cast Member)
The Avengers 6-22. Stay Tuned (26-02-69)
The Champions 08. To Trap a Rat (13-11-68)
Danger Man 2-16. A Room in The Basement (02-02-65)
Department S: 11. Who Plays The Dummy (01-10-69)
The Saint 5-16. The Fast Women (13-01-67) 5-20. The Counterfeit Countess (03-03-67) 6-06. The Double Take (03-11-68)
Kate Story (Cast Member)
Out Of The Unknown 2-03. Lambda One (20-10-66)
Katherina Holden (Cast Member)
The Saint 5-12. Locate & Destroy (16-12-66)
Katherine Blake (Cast Member)
The Baron 22. Night Of The Hunter (22-02-67)
Public Eye 4-04. My Lifes My Own (20-08-69)
The Saint 2-22. The Invisible Millionaire (13-02-64)
Undermind 08. Puppets Of Evil (26-06-65)
Katherine Kath (Cast Member)
The Prisoner 03. A.B. & C. (13-10-67)
Katherine Kessey (Cast Member)
Out Of The Unknown 3 -08. Little Black Bag (25-02-69)
Katherine Schofield (Cast Member)
The Avengers 4-03. The Cybernauts (16-10-65)
Department S: 24. The Bones Of Byrom Blain (28-01-70)
The Saint 5-07. The Angel's Eye (11-11-66) 5-17. The Death Game (20-01-67)
Katherine Woodville (Cast Member)
The Avengers 2-02. Propellant 23 (06-10-62)
Danger Man 2-03. Colony Three (27-10-64)
The Saint 3-04. The Scorpion (29-10-64) 3-13. The Damsel In Distress (31-12-64)
Kathleen Breck (Cast Member)
Danger Man 2-20. Have a Glass of Wine (02-03-65)
The Prisoner 12. A Change Of Mind (15-12-67)
Kathleen Byron (Cast Member)
The Avengers 6-31. Pandora (30-04-69)
Danger Man 1-19. Name, Date & Place (22-01-61)
Kathleen St John (Cast Member)
Man In A Suitcase 10. All That Glitters (29-11-67)
Katy Greenwood (Cast Member)
The Avengers 3-05. Death Of a Batman (26-01-63)
Katy Wild (Cast Member)
The Avengers 2-11. Traitor In Zebra (08-12-62)
Katya Wyeth (Cast Member)

The Avengers 6-29. Requiem (16-04-69)
Randall & Hopkirk (Deceased) 06. Just For The Record (26-10-69)
Kay Patrick (Cast Member)
Doctor Who 12. The Romans: 4 Episodes (16-01-65)
Kay Walsh (Cast Member)
The Baron 09. And Suddenly You're Dead (23-11-66)
Kas Garas (Cast Member)
Strange Report all episodes (1969)
Keith Anderson (Cast Member)
Adam Adamant Lives! 07. To Set a Deadly Fashion (11-08-66)
Doctor Who 08. The Reign Of Terror: 4 Episodes (08-08-64)
Ghost Squad 2-11. A First Class Way To Die (13-07-63)
Keith Ball (Cast Member)
Danger Man 2-11. Don't Nail Him Yet (22-12-64)
Keith Barron (Cast Member)
Randall & Hopkirk (Deceased) 10. When Did You Start To Stop Seeing Things? (23-11-69)
Strange Report 10. REPORT 8944 HAND A Matter Of Witchcraft (30-11-69)
Keith Baxter (Cast Member)
The Avengers 6-26. Homicide & Old Lace (26-03-69)
Out Of The Unknown 2-04. Level Seven (27-10-66)
Public Eye 1-02. Nobody Kill Santa Claus (30-01-65)
Keith Buckley (Cast Member)
The Avengers 6-30. Take-Over (23-04-69)
Out Of The Unknown 1-02. The Counterfeit Man (11-10-65)
Randall & Hopkirk (Deceased) 09. The House On Haunted Hill (16-11-69)
Keith Goodman (Cast Member)
Danger Man 1-13. The Prisoner (04-12-60)
Keith Grenville (Cast Member)
Randall & Hopkirk (Deceased) 23. The Trouble With Women (20-02-70)
Keith Marsh (Cast Member)
Ghost Squad 2-08. The Man With The Delicate Hands (22-06-63)
Man In A Suitcase 20. Blind Spot (07-02-67)
Keith Peacock (Cast Member)
Out Of The Unknown 1-07. Sucker Bait (15-11-65)
Keith Pyott (Cast Member)
The Avengers 2-21. The White Dwarf (16-02-63) 4-23. The House That Jack Built (05-03-66)
Ghost Squad 1-09. Million Dollar Ransom (11-11-61)
Man Of The World 1-12. A Family Affair (15-12-62)
The Prisoner 06. The General (03-11-67)
Keith Rawlings (Cast Member)
Danger Man 1-17. Find & Return (08-01-61)
Keith Smith (Cast Member)
The Saint 4-05. The Persistent Parasites (29-07-65)
Ken Barker (Cast Member)
The Avengers 6-25. Who Was That Man I Saw You With (19-03-69)
The Baron 19. You Can't Win Them All (01-02-67)
Danger Man 3-14. The Man Who Wouldn't Talk (30-12-65)
Ken Hayward (Cast Member)
The Protectors 05. The Loop Men (25-04-64)
Ken Lawrence (Cast Member)
Doctor Who 08. The Reign Of Terror: 4 Episodes (08-08-64)
Ken Norris (Cast Member)
Doctor Who 15. The Space Museum: 4 Episodes (24-04-65)
Ken Parry (Cast Member)
The Avengers 3-13. Death a La Carte (21-12-63) 4-26. Honey For The Prince (26-03-66)
The Baron 14. There's Someone Close Behind You (28-12-67)
Out Of The Unknown 1-05. Time In Advance (01-11-65)
Ken Watson (Cast Member)

Randall & Hopkirk (Deceased) 06. Just For The Record (26-10-69)
Ken Wayne (Cast Member)
The Saint 1-08. The Element Of Doubt (22-11-62)
Ken Wynne (Cast Member)
A For Andromeda 1-6. The Face Of The Tiger (07-11-61)
Kenjin Takeri (Cast Member)
The Saint 3-18. The Sign Of The Claw (04-02-65)
Kenneth Adams (Cast Member)
Danger Man 2-05. Fair Exchange (10-11-64) 2-07. The Colonels Daughter (24-11-64)
Kenneth Benda (Cast Member)
Adam Adamant Lives! 01 A Year For Scoundrels (20-06-66)
The Avengers 5-01. From Venus With Love (14-01-67)
Callan 2-14. Nice People Die At Home (09-04-69)
The Prisoner 04. Free For All (20-10-67)
The Saint 2-20. The Lawless Lady (30-01-64)
Kenneth Colley (Cast Member)
The Avengers 3-12. Don't Look Behind You (14-12-63)
The Baron 10. The Legends of Ammak (30-11-66)
Ghost Squad 2-09. Hot Money (25-05-63)
Kenneth Cope (Cast Member)
The Avengers 5-05. The Bird Who Knew Too Much (11-02-67) 6-19. The Curious Case Of The Countless Clues (05-02-69)
Randall & Hopkirk (Deceased) All episodes (1969)
Kenneth Cowan (Cast Member)
Man In A Suitcase 24. Which Way Did He Go, McGill (06-03-67)
Kenneth Edwards (Cast Member)
The Saint 5-26. When Spring Is Sprung (02-06-67)
Kenneth Farrington (Cast Member)
The Avengers 2-26. Killer Whale (23-03-63)
Man Of The World 2-04. Jungle Mission (01-06-63)
The Saint 6-03. Legacy For The Saint (13-10-68)
Kenneth Gardiner (Cast Member)
The Champions 16. Shadow Of The Panther (15-01-68)
The Saint 5-22. Island Of Chance (07-04-67) 6-04. The Desperate Diplomat (20-10-68)
Strange Report 11. REPORT 1553 RACIST A Most Dangerous Proposal (07-12-69)
Kenneth Gilbert (Cast Member)
Callan 2-05. Let's Kill Everybody (05-02-69)
Kenneth Griffith (Cast Member)
Danger Man 3-25. Shinda Shima (26-02-67)
The Prisoner 15. The Girl Who Was Death (18-01-67) 17. Fall Out (01-02-68)
Strange Report 15. REPORT 4407 No Choice For The Donor (04-01-70)
Kenneth Haigh (Cast Member)
Danger Man 1-03. Josetta (25-09-60)
Strange Report 03. REPORT 2641 HOSTAGE If You Won't Learn Die (05-10-69)
Kenneth Henry (Cast Member)
The Saint 2-12. The Well Meaning Mayor (05-12-63)
Kenneth Ives (Cast Member)
Adam Adamant Lives! 08. The Last Sacrifice (18-08-66) 18. Black Echo (07-01-67)
Doctor Who 44. The Dominators: 5 Episodes (10-08-68)
Strange Report 15. REPORT 4407 No Choice For The Donor (04-01-70)
Kenneth Keeling (Cast Member)
The Avengers 2-01. Mr Teddy Bear (29-09-62) 3-10. The Grandeur That Was Rome (30-11-63)
Kenneth Kendall (Cast Member)
Adam Adamant Lives! 10. The Doomsday Plan (01-09-66)
Kenneth MacKintosh (Cast Member)
The Saint 2-06. Marcia (24-10-63)
Kenneth Warren (Cast Member)
The Avengers 1-06. Girl On The Trapeze (11-02-61) 2-15. Intercrime (05-01-63) 3-16. The Little

Wonders (11-01-64) 5-11. Epic (25-03-67)
The Baron 06. Masquerade (Part 1) (02-11-66) 07. The Killing (Part 2) (09-11-66)
The Champions 01. The Beginning (25-09-68)
Danger Man: 3-22. The Paper Chase (31-03-66)
The Saint 6-11. The Fiction Makers Part 1 (08-12-68) 6-12. The Fiction Makers Part 2 (15-12-68) 6-14. Where The Money Is (29-12-68)
Kenneth Watson (Cast Member)
Doctor Who 43. The Wheel in Space: 2 Episodes (11-05-68)
Man Of The World 1-07. The Highland Story (10-11-62)
Public Eye 4-03. Paid In Full (13-08-69)
Kenny Baker (Cast Member)
The Avengers 1-06. Girl On The Trapeze (11-02-61)
Man Of The World 1-11. Specialist For the Kill (08-12-62)
Kerrigan Prescott (Cast Member)
Danger Man 1-22. The Honeymooners (02-04-61)
Kerry Marsh (Cast Member)
The Baron 10. The Legends of Ammak (30-11-66)
Kevin Barry (Cast Member)
The Avengers 2-08. Death Of Great Dane (17-11-62)
Kevin Brennan (Cast Member)
Adam Adamant Lives! 05. Allah Is Not Always With You (21-07-66)
The Avengers 4-25. How To Succeed…. At Murder (19-03-66)
The Corridor People Victim as White (1966)
The Saint 3-23. The Happy Suicide (11-03-65)
Kevin Flood (Cast Member)
The Saint 5-10. Little Girl Lost (02-12-66)
Kevin Scott (Cast Member)
The Saint 1-09. The Effete Angler (29-11-62) 3-11. The Hijackers (17-12-64)
Kevin Stoney (Cast Member)
The Avengers 5-24. Mission, Highly Improbable (18-11-67)
Danger Man 3-13. Say It With Flowers (23-12-65)
Doctor Who 21. The Daleks' Master Plan: 3 Episodes (20-11-65)
Doctor Who 46. The Invasion: 6 Episodes (09-11-68)
Interpol Calling 16. No Flowers For Onno (04-01-59)
Man In A Suitcase 10. All That Glitters (29-11-67)
The Prisoner 02. The Chimes Of Big Ben (06-10-67)
The Saint 3-21. Sibao (25-02-65)
Kevork Malikyan (Cast Member)
The Avengers 6-26. Homicide & Old Lace (26-03-69)
Doctor Who 43. The Wheel in Space: 2 Episodes (11-05-68)
Kieron Moore (Cast Member)
Danger Man 1-09. The Sanctuary (06-11-60)
Department S: 17. Dead Men Die Twice (12-11-69)
Randall & Hopkirk (Deceased) 16. When The Spirit Moves You (02-01-70)
Kika Markham (Cast Member)
Strange Report 12. REPORT 7931 SNIPER When Is Your Cousin Not? (14-12-69)
Kit Williams (Cast Member)
Danger Man 3-24. Koroshi (12-02-67)
Kitty Atwood (Cast Member)
The Avengers 3-05. Death Of a Batman (26-01-63)
Kristopher Kum (Cast Member)
The Avengers 6-26. Homicide & Old Lace (26-03-69)
Danger Man 3-25. Shinda Shima (26-02-67)
The Saint 3-18. The Sign Of The Claw (04-02-65)
Kumar Ranji (Cast Member)
Danger Man 2-07. The Colonels Daughter (24-11-64)
Kynaston Reeves (Cast Member)
The Avengers 4-22. What The Butler Saw (26-02-66) 6-09. Legacy Of Death (20-11-68)

L

L.W. Clarke (Cast Member)
Adam Adamant Lives! 16. D Is For Destruction (13-06-66)
Laidlaw Dalling (Cast Member)
Doctor Who 08. The Reign Of Terror: 4 Episodes (08-08-64)
Out Of The Unknown 1-10. Some Lapse In Time (06-12-65)
Lally Bowers (Cast Member)
The Avengers 3-02. The Undertakers (05-10-63)
Undermind 06. Intent To Destroy (12-06-65)
Lana Morris (Cast Member)
The Saint 2-04. Teresa (10-10-63)
Lance George (Cast Member)
The Avengers 2-09. The Sell Out (24-11-62)
Langton Jones (Cast Member)
The Avengers 5-23. Murdersville (11-11-67)
Larry Burns (Cast Member)
The Avengers 6-07. False Witness (06-01-68)
Interpol Calling 02. The Thirteen Innocents (21-09-59)
Larry Cross (Cast Member)
The Avengers 4-19. Quick-Quick Slow Death (05-02-66)
Callan 2-13 The Worst Soldier I Ever Saw (2-4-69)
Man In A Suitcase 10. All That Glitters (29-11-67)
Man Of The World 2-07. The Prince (22-06-63)
The Saint 2-27. The Saint Sees It Through (19-03-64)
Larry Martyn (Cast Member)
Department S: 23. A Small War Of Nerves (21-01-70)
Man In A Suitcase 11. Dead Man's Shoes (06-12-67)
Larry Noble (Cast Member)
Adam Adamant Lives! 13. The League Of Uncharitable Ladies (12-09-66)
Larry Taylor (Cast Member)
The Avengers 6-21. Love All (19-02-69)
The Baron 11. Samurai West (07-12-66)
Danger Man 2-20. Have a Glass of Wine (02-03-65)
Department S: 02. The Trojan Tanker (16-03-69)
Man In A Suitcase 15. Burden Of Proof (03-01-67)
The Prisoner 07. Many Happy Returns (10-11-67) 14. Living In Harmony (29-12-67)
Randall & Hopkirk (Deceased) 19. A Sentimental Journey (23-01-70)
The Saint 2-18. Romantic Matron (16-1-64) 3-12 The Unkind Philanthropist (24-12-64) 4-04. The Smart Detective (22-7-65) 5-01 Queens Ransom (30-9-66) 6-19. Portrait Of Brenda (2-2-69)
Laurence Hardy (Cast Member)
The Avengers 4-06. The Master Minds (06-11-65)
Callan 2-04. The Little Bits & Pieces Of Love (29-01-69)
Ghost Squad 2-11. A First Class Way To Die (13-07-63)
Public Eye 2-07. Works With Chess, Not With Life (13-08-66)
Laurence Herder (Cast Member)
Danger Man 2-03. Colony Three (27-10-64)
The Saint 4-07. The Saint Bids Diamonds (12-08-65) 5-05. The Helpful Pirate (28-10-66)
Laurence Naismith (Cast Member)
Danger Man 1-04. The Blue Veil (02-10-60)
Laurence Payne (Cast Member)
Interpol Calling 35. Cargo Of Death (23-05-60)
The Saint 5-06. The Convenient Monster (04-11-66)
Laurie Asprey (Cast Member)
The Champions 13. Twelve Hours (18-12-68)
Department S: 15. The Shift That Never Was (25-10-69)
Man In A Suitcase 11. Dead Man's Shoes (06-12-67)

Laurie Leigh (Cast Member)
The Avengers 2-04. Bullseye (20-10-62)
Lawrence Dane (Cast Member)
The Saint 2-04. Teresa (10-10-63)
Lawrence Davidson
Danger Man 1-20. The Vacation (29-01-61) 1-29. The Contessa (21-05-61)
The Saint 5-19. To Kill a Saint (24-02-67)
Lawrence Dean (Cast Member)
Doctor Who 15. The Space Museum: 4 Episodes (24-04-65)
Lawrence James (Cast Member)
The Avengers 6-10. Noon Doomsday (27-11-68)
The Champions 26. Full Circle (26-03-69)
Man In A Suitcase 23. Web With Four Spiders (28-02-67)
Lawrence Trimble (Cast Member)
Callan 2-09. Death Of a Friend (05-03-69)
Lee Fox (Cast Member)
The Protectors 09. The Pirate (23-05-64)
Lee Montague (Cast Member)
The Baron 11. Samurai West (07-12-66)
Danger Man 1-22. The Honeymooners (02-04-61) 2-14. Such Men Are Dangerous (12-01-65)
Department S: 27. A Fish Out Of Water (25-02-70)
Interpol Calling 10. Dead On Arrival (16-11-59)
Lee Patterson (Cast Member)
The Avengers 3-02. The Undertakers (05-10-63)
Lee Richardson (Cast Member)
Ghost Squad 2-08. The Man With The Delicate Hands (22-06-63)
Leela Naidu (Cast Member)
Man Of The World 1-05. The Frontier (27-10-62)
Leigh Madison (Cast Member)
Interpol Calling 16. No Flowers For Onno (04-01-59)
Leila Forde (Cast Member)
Ghost Squad 2-17. Mr Five Per Cent (06-04-63)
Leila Goldini (Cast Member)
Danger Man 2-05. Fair Exchange (10-11-64) 3-19. Two Birds With One Bullet (10-03-66)
Strange Report 12. REPORT 7931 SNIPER When Is Your Cousin Not? (14-12-69)
Len Belmont (Cast Member)
The Avengers 6-11. Look (Stop Me If You've Heard This One) But There Were These Two Fellers (04-12-68)
Len Jones (Cast Member)
Adam Adamant Lives! 15. The Village Of Evil (06-10-66)
Lennard Pearce (Cast Member)
Undermind 09. Test For The Future (03-07-65)
Leo Carera (Cast Member)
Ghost Squad 2-19. Death of a Sportsman (26-01-63)
Man Of The World 2-04. Jungle Mission (01-06-63)
Leo Kayne (Cast Member)
The Baron 13. Portrait Of Louisa (21-12-67)
Leo Leyden (Cast Member)
The Saint 5-10. Little Girl Lost (02-12-66)
Leo McKern
The Prisoner 02 (Cast Member). The Chimes Of Big Ben (06-10-67) 16. Once Upon a Time (25-01-67) 17. Fall Out (01-02-68)
Leon Cortez (Cast Member)
Out Of The Unknown 3 -08. Little Black Bag (25-02-69)
The Saint 3-04. The Scorpion (29-10-64) 6-10. The Scales Of Justice (01-12-68)
Leon Eagles (Cast Member)
The Avengers 3-14. Dressed To Kill (28-12-63)
Leon Greene (Cast Member)

The Avengers 5-12. The Superlative Seven (01-04-67)
The Saint 5-21. Simon & Delilah (24-03-67)
Leon Lisssek (Cast Member)
The Avengers 5-17. Return Of The Cybernauts (30-09-67)
Leon Maybank (Cast Member)
Doctor Who 33. The Moonbase: 2 Episodes (18-02-67)
Leon Peters (Cast Member)
Man Of The World 1-04. The Runaways (20-10-62)
Leon Sinden (Cast Member)
The Avengers 4-22. What The Butler Saw (26-02-66)
Leon Thau (Cast Member)
The Avengers 6-09. Legacy Of Death (20-11-68)
Leonard Kingston (Cast Member)
The Avengers 2-16. Immortal Clay (12-01-63) 3-23. The Charmers (29-02-64)
Leonard Llewellen (Cast Member)
The Avengers 4-09. The Hour That Never Was (27-11-65)
Leonard Monaghan (Cast Member)
Danger Man 2-11. Don't Nail Him Yet (22-12-64)
Leonard Rossiter (Cast Member)
The Avengers 3-14. Dressed To Kill (28-12-63)
Leonard Sachs (Cast Member)
Danger Man 1-34. The Deputy Coyannis Story (16-12-61)
Ghost Squad 1-01. Hong Kong Story (23-09-61) 2-01. Interrupted Requiem (02-02-63)
Interpol Calling 07. You Can't Die Twice (26-10-59) 21. The Collector (08-02-60)
The Saint 4-08. The Spanish Cow (19-08-65)
Leonardo Pierni (Cast Member)
Department S: 25. Spencer Bodily Is 60 Years Old (11-02-70)
Les White (Cast Member)
The Baron 29. Countdown (12-04-67)
Danger Man 3-13. Say It With Flowers (23-12-65) 3-20. I Am Afraid You Have The Wrong Number (17-03-66)
Randall & Hopkirk (Deceased) 02. A Disturbing Case (28-09-69)
The Saint 6-17. The Ex-King Of Diamonds (19-01-68)
Lesley Allen (Cast Member)
Danger Man 3-10. Are You Going To Be More Permanent? (02-12-65)
Lesley Nunnerley (Cast Member)
Undermind 04. Death In England (29-05-65) 05. Too Many Enemies (05-06-65)
Leslie Anderson (Cast Member)
The Saint 5-26. When Spring Is Sprung (02-06-67) 6-08. The Master Plan (17-11-68)
Leslie Bates (Cast Member)
Adam Adamant Lives! 16. D Is For Destruction (13-06-66)
Leslie Crawford (Cast Member)
The Avengers 5-21. You Have Just Been Murdered (28-10-67)
The Prisoner 14. Living In Harmony (29-12-67)
The Saint 5-26. When Spring Is Sprung (02-06-67) 6-02. Invitation To Danger (06-10-68) 6-04. The Desperate Diplomat (20-10-68)
Leslie Dwyer (Cast Member)
Public Eye 4-06. The Comedian's Graveyard (03-09-69)
Leslie French (Cast Member)
The Avengers 2-08 The Death Of Great Dane (17-11-62) 5-21 You Have Just Been Murdered (28-10-67)
Interpol Calling 09. Private View (09-11-59)
Man Of The World 1-09. The Mindreader (24-11-62)
The Protectors 09. The Pirate (23-05-64)
Leslie Glazer (Cast Member)
The Avengers 3-24. Concerto (07-03-64)
Leslie Lawton (Cast Member)
Public Eye 4-03. Paid In Full (13-08-69) 4-04. My Life's My Own (20-08-69) 4-05. Case For The

Defence (27-08-69)
Leslie Pitt (Cast Member)
The Avengers 2-05. Mission To Montreal (27-10-62)
Leslie Sands (Cast Member)
The Avengers 3-26. Lobster Quadrille (21-03-64)
Department S: 22. Last Train to Redbridge (14-01-70)
The Saint 2-12. The Well Meaning Mayor (05-12-63)
Leslie Sarony (Cast Member)
Strange Report 02. REPORT 0649 SKELETON Let Sleeping Heroes Lie (28-09-69)
Leslie Schofield (Cast Member)
Department S: 15. The Shift That Never Was (25-10-69)
Randall & Hopkirk (Deceased) 14. Who Killed Cock Robin? (21-12-69)
Leslie Weston (Cast Member)
Interpol Calling 26. Trial At Cranby's Creek (21-03-60)
Lew Luton (Cast Member)
Out Of The Unknown 1-02. The Counterfeit Man (11-10-65)
Lewis Alexander (Cast Member)
The Avengers 4-04. Death At Bargain Prices (23-10-65)
The Baron 02. Epitaph For a Hero (05-10-66)
Strange Report 07. REPORT 3424 EPIDEMIC A Most Curious Crime (02-11-69)
Lewis Teasdale (Cast Member)
Man In A Suitcase 07. Sweet Sue (08-11-67)
Liam Gaffney (Cast Member)
The Avengers 2-14. Dead On Course (29-12-62)
Danger Man 1-34. The Deputy Coyannis Story (16-12-61)
Liam Redmond (Cast Member)
The Avengers 4-16 Small Game For Big Hunters (15-1-65) 6-20 Wish You Were Here (12-2-69)
The Saint 5-07. The Angel's Eye (11-11-66)
Lian-Shin Yang (Cast Member)
Danger Man 1-26. The Journey Ends Halfway (30-04-61)
Liane Aukin (Cast Member)
The Avengers 6-08. All Done With Mirrors (13-11-68)
Lila Kaye (Cast Member)
The Saint 6-12. The Fiction Makers Part 2 (15-12-68)
Lilani Young (Cast Member)
Danger Man 3-24. Koroshi (12-02-67)
Lillias Walker (Cast Member)
Out Of The Unknown 3-03. The Last Lonely Man (21-01-69)
Linbert Spencer (Cast Member)
The Champions 03. Reply Box 666 (09-10-68)
Linda Cole (Cast Member)
Randall & Hopkirk (Deceased) 20. Money To Burn (30-01-70)
Linda Marlowe (Cast Member)
Callan 1-01. The Good Ones Are Dead (08-07-67)
The Saint 6-07. The Time To Die (10-11-68)
Linda Renick (Cast Member)
Strange Report 13. REPORT 4821 X-RAY Who Weeps For The Doctor (21-12-69)
Linda Thorson (Cast Member)
The Avengers 33 Episodes
Linda Watkins (Cast Member)
The Third Man 4-07. Diamond In the Rough (11-05-62)
Ling Ling (Cast Member)
Adam Adamant Lives! 03. More Deadly Than The Sword (07-07-66)
Lionel Gamlin (Cast Member)
Adam Adamant Lives! 01 A Year For Scoundrels (20-06-66)
Lionel Murton (Cast Member)
Danger Man 1-02. Time to Kill (18-11-60) 1-29. The Contessa (21-05-61) 1-36. Under the Lake (30-12-61)

Ghost Squad 1-06. Eyes Of The Bat (14-10-61)
Interpol Calling 32. The Three Keys (02-05-60)
Man In A Suitcase 06. Man From The Dead (01-11-67)
Strange Report 05. REPORT 8319 GRENADE What Price Change? (19-10-69)
Lionel Ngakane (Cast Member)
Danger Man 1-39. Deadline (20-01-62)
Lionel Stevens (Cast Member)
Out Of The Unknown 1-11. Thirteen To Centauraus
Lionel Wheeler (Cast Member)
The Avengers 6-03. Super Secret Cypher Snatch (09-10-68)
Department S: 22. Last Train to Redbridge (14-01-70)
Lisa Daniely (Cast Member)
The Baron 27. Roundabout (29-03-67)
Danger Man 3-23. Not So Jolly Roger (07-04-66)
Doctor Who 49. The Space Pirates: Episode 2 (15-03-69)
Interpol Calling 08. Diamond S.O.S. (02-11-59) 14. The Man's a Clown (21-12-59)
The Saint 5-09. The Better Mouse Trap (25-11-66)
Strange Report 06. REPORT 3906 COVER-GIRLS Last Years Model (26-10-69)
Lisa Gastoni (Cast Member)
Danger Man 1-04. The Blue Veil (02-10-60) 1-25. The Brothers (23-04-61)
Lisa Langdon (Cast Member)
Callan 1-01. The Good Ones Are Dead (08-07-67) 1-06. You Should Have Got Here Sooner (12-08-67)
2-01. Red Knight, White Knight (08-01-69) 2-04. The Little Bits & Pieces Of Love
(29-01-69) 2-06. Heir Apparent (12-02-69) 2-09. Death Of a Friend (05-03-69) 2-13. The Worst
Soldier I Ever Saw (02-04-69) 2-14. Nice People Die At Home (09-04-69)
Lisa Page (Cast Member)
Man Of The World 1-12. A Family Affair (15-12-62)
Lisa Peake (Cast Member)
The Avengers 3-11. The Golden Fleece (07-12-63)
Lisa Thomas (Cast Member)
The Baron 06. Masquerade (Part 1) (02-11-66) 13. Portrait Of Louisa (21-12-67) 27. Roundabout
(29-03-67)
Liz Fraser (Cast Member)
The Avengers 4-17. The Girl From AUNTIE (22-01-66)
Randall & Hopkirk (Deceased) 22. It's Supposed To Be Thicker Than Water (13-02-70)
Liz Lanchbury (Cast Member)
Danger Man 1-08 The Lonely Chair (30-10-60)
Llewellyn Rees (Cast Member)
Strange Report 08. REPORT 2475 REVENGE When a Man Hates (09-11-69)
Lloyd Lamble (Cast Member)
The Avengers 4-02. The Gravediggers (09-01-65)
Ghost Squad 2-09. Hot Money (25-05-63)
Interpol Calling 11. Air Switch (23-11-59)
Lloyd Reckord (Cast Member)
Danger Man 1-15. Colonel Rodriguez (18-12-60) 1-39. Deadline (20-01-62) 2-04. The Galloping
Major (03-11-64) 3-05. Loyalty Always Pays (28-10-65)
Interpol Calling 19. Act Of Piracy (25-01-60)
Lookwood West (Cast Member)
Strange Report 03. REPORT 2641 HOSTAGE If You Won't Learn Die (05-10-69)
Lois Daine (Cast Member)
Man In A Suitcase 02. The Sitting Pigeon (04-10-67)
Lois Maxwell (Cast Member)
The Avengers 3-16. The Little Wonders (11-01-64)
The Baron 03. Something For a Rainy Day (12-10-66)
Danger Man 1-07. Position Of Trust (23-10-60)
Randall & Hopkirk (Deceased) 12. For The Girl Who Has Everything (07-12-69)
The Saint 5-02. Interlude In Venice (07-10-66) 5-21. Simon & Delilah (24-03-67)
Loretta Parry (Cast Member)

The Saint 1-12. The Charitable Countess (20-12-62)
Lorne Cossette (Cast Member)
Doctor Who 07. The Sensorites: 3 Episodes (20-06-64)
Louie Ramsay (Cast Member)
The Avengers 5-14. Something Nasty In The Nursery (15-04-67)
Louis Haslar (Cast Member)
The Avengers 2-19. The Golden Egg (02-02-63)
Louis Mahoney (Cast Member)
Danger Man 2-22. Parallel Lines Sometimes Meet (16-03-65)
Louis Marks (Cast Member)
Ghost Squad 2-17. Mr Five Per Cent (06-04-63)
Louis Negin (Cast Member)
Man In A Suitcase 26. The Revolutionaries (20-03-67)
Louis Raynor (Cast Member)
The Saint 2-16. The Wonderful War (02-01-64) 5-04. The Reluctant Revolution (21-10-66)
Lois Maxwell (Cast Member)
Department S: 26. The Ghost Of Mary Burnham (18-02-70)
Louise Collins (Cast Member)
Danger Man 1-02. Time to Kill (18-11-60) 1-29. The Contessa (21-05-61)
The Saint 2-14. The Bunco Artists (19-12-63)
Louise Nolan (Cast Member)
The Avengers 4-04. Death At Bargain Prices (23-10-65)
Louise Pajo (Cast Member)
The Avengers 6-20. Wish You Were Here (12-02-69)
Doctor Who 48. The Seeds Of Death: 6 Episodes (25-01-69)
Strange Report 16. REPORT 4977 Square Root Of Evil (11-01-70)
Luan Petters (Cast Member)
Strange Report 07. REPORT 3424 EPIDEMIC A Most Curious Crime (02-11-69)
Luanshya Greer (Cast Member)
Man In A Suitcase 27. Who's Mad Now (27-03-67) 30. Night Flight To Andorra (17-04-67)
Lucille Soong (Cast Member)
Adam Adamant Lives! 03. More Deadly Than The Sword (07-07-66)
The Avengers 4-03. The Cybernauts (16-10-65)
Ghost Squad 2-26. Sabotage (20-04-63)
The Prisoner 03. A.B. & C. (13-10-67)
Lucinda Curtis (Cast Member)
The Avengers 3-21. Build a Better Mousetrap (15-02-64)
Lucy Fleming (Cast Member)
The Avengers 6-16. Invasion Of The Earthman (15-01-69)
Lucy Griffiths (Cast Member)
Adam Adamant Lives! 13. The League Of Uncharitable Ladies (12-09-66)
The Prisoner 02. The Chimes Of Big Ben (06-10-67) 08. Dance Of The Dead (17-11-67)
Lucy Hill (Cast Member)
Out Of The Unknown 2-01. The Machine Stops (06-10-66)
Lucy Young (Cast Member)
Out Of The Unknown 1-10. Some Lapse In Time (06-12-65)
Lyn Ashley (Cast Member)
Danger Man 1-28. Sabotage (14-05-61)
Doctor Who 18. Galaxy 4: Air Lock (25-09-65)
The Saint 6-08. The Master Plan (17-11-68)
Lyn Pinkney (Cast Member)
Strange Report 03. REPORT 2641 HOSTAGE If You Won't Learn Die (05-10-69)
Lyndall Goodman (Cast Member)
The Avengers 2-26. Killer Whale (23-03-63)
Lyndon Brook (Cast Member)
The Avengers 5-08. The Hidden Tiger (04-03-67) 6-10. Noon Doomsday (27-11-68)
Danger Man 3-16. Dangerous Secret (13-01-66)
Lynn Furlong (Cast Member)

The Avengers 2-03. The Decapod (13-10-62)
Lynn Taylor (Cast Member)
The Avengers 2-17. Box Of Tricks (19-01-63)
Danger Man: 2-01. Yesterday's Enemies (13-10-64)

M

Mabel Etherington (Cast Member)
The Avengers 4-10. Dial a Deadly Number (04-12-65)
Magdalena Nicol (Cast Member)
The Champions 04. The Experiment (16-10-68)
Madge Brindley (Cast Member)
The Saint 2-18. The Romantic Matron (16-01-64)
Madge Ryan (Cast Member)
The Avengers 3-18. Mandrake (25-01-64)
The Champions 17. A Case Of Lemmings (22-01-68)
Randall & Hopkirk (Deceased) 18. Could You Recognise The Man Again (16-01-70)
The Saint 5-09. The Better Mouse Trap (25-11-66)
Madeleine Kasket (Cast Member)
Danger Man 1-07. Position Of Trust (23-10-60)
Madeline Mills (Cast Member)
Doctor Who 47. The Krotons: 4 Episodes (28-12-68)
Magda Konopka (Cast Member)
Danger Man 2-12. A Date With Doris (29-12-64)
Department S: 27. A Fish Out Of Water (25-02-70)
Man Of The World 1-09. The Mindreader (24-11-62)
Maggie Fitzgibbon (Cast Member)
Danger Man 1-28. Sabotage (14-05-61)
Maggie Lee (Cast Member)
The Avengers 2-18. Warlock (26-01-63)
Maggie London (Cast Member)
Randall & Hopkirk (Deceased) 25. You Can Always Find a Fall Guy (06-03-70)
The Saint 6-04. The Desperate Diplomat (20-10-68)
Maggie Vieler (Cast Member)
Man In A Suitcase 28. Three Blinks Of The Eyes (03-04-67)
Maggie Wright (Cast Member)
The Baron 01. Diplomatic Immunity (28-09-66)
Department S: 27. A Fish Out Of Water (25-02-70)
Man In A Suitcase 03. Day Of Execution (11-10-67)
The Saint 3-02. Lida (15-10-64) 3-03. Jeannine (22-10-64) 3-22. The Crime Of The Century (04-03-65) 5-19. To Kill a Saint (24-02-67)
Mai Zetterling (Cast Member)
Danger Man 1-12. The Sisters (27-11-60)
Interpol Calling 08. Diamond S.O.S. (02-11-59)
The Third Man 2-02. One Kind Word (07-09-59)
Mairhi Russell (Cast Member)
Undermind 02. Flowers Of Havoc (15-05-65)
Maitland Moss (Cast Member)
Out Of The Unknown 1-10. Some Lapse In Time (06-12-65)
Makki Marseilles (Cast Member)
The Avengers 2-24. A Chorus Of Frogs (09-03-63)
Department S: 20. The Mysterious Man In The Flying Machine (10-12-69)
Man In A Suitcase 05. Variation On a Million Bucks Part 2 (25-10-67)
Randall & Hopkirk (Deceased) 01. My Late Lamented Friend & Partner (21-09-69)
Strange Report 01. REPORT 5055 CULT Murder Shrieks Out (21-09-69)
Malcolm Farquhar (Cast Member)
The Baron 29. Countdown (12-04-67)
Malcolm Howard (Cast Member)
Public Eye 4-04. My Life's My Own (20-08-69) 4-05. Case For The Defence (27-08-69)
Malcolm Johns (Cast Member)
The Avengers 5-16. Who's Who (29-04-67)
Malcolm Rogers (Cast Member)

Danger Man 3-19. Two Birds With One Bullet (10-03-66)
Malcolm Russell (Cast Member)
The Avengers 3-23. The Charmers (29-02-64)
Malcolm Taylor (Cast Member)
The Avengers 2-05. Mission To Montreal (27-10-62) 5-16. Who's Who (29-04-67)
Malcolm Terris (Cast Member)
Doctor Who 44. The Dominators: 5 Episodes (10-08-68)
Malou Pantera (Cast Member)
Man Of The World 1-02. Masquerade In Spain (06-10-62)
Malya Nappi (Cast Member)
The Saint 6-15. Vendetta For The Saint Part 1 (05-01-68)
Strange Report 10. REPORT 8944 HAND A Matter Of Witchcraft (30-11-69)
Mandy Mayer (Cast Member)
The Saint 5-16. The Fast Women (13-01-67)
Mandy Miller (Cast Member)
The Avengers 3-02. The Undertakers (05-10-63)
The Saint 2-12. The Well Meaning Mayor (05-12-63)
Mandy Morris (Cast Member)
A For Andromeda 1-6. The Face Of The Tiger (07-11-61)
Manning Wilson (Cast Member)
The Avengers 4-06. The Master Minds (06-11-65)
The Saint 2-07. The Work Of Art (31-10-63) 3-03. Jeannine (22-10-64)
Marcella Markham (Cast Member)
The Avengers 3-02. The Undertakers (05-10-63)
Marcus Hammond (Cast Member)
Doctor Who 02. The Daleks: 5 Episodes (21-12-63)
Marga Roche (Cast Member)
Man In A Suitcase 26. The Revolutionaries (20-03-67)
Margaret Courtenay (Cast Member)
Ghost Squad 2-15. The Last Jump (23-02-63)
Margaret Diamond (Cast Member)
Interpol Calling 18. The Thousand Mile Alibi (18-01-60)
Margaret Gordon (Cast Member)
Undermind 06. Intent To Destroy (12-06-65)
Margaret John (Cast Member)
Ghost Squad 2-25. The Thirteenth Girl (27-04-63)
Margaret Neale (Cast Member)
The Avengers 5-12. The Superlative Seven (01-04-67)
Margaret Nolan (Cast Member)
Adam Adamant Lives! 03. More Deadly Than The Sword (07-07-66)
Danger Man 2-22. Parallel Lines Sometimes Meet (16-03-65)
Margaret Vines (Cast Member)
Ghost Squad 2-05. The Retirement Of The Gentle Dove (30-03-63)
The Saint 1-08. The Element Of Doubt (22-11-62)
Margaret Whiting (Cast Member)
Undermind 04. Death In England (29-05-65) 05. Too Many Enemies (05-06-65)
Margaretta Scott (Cast Member)
The Saint 2-11. The Saint Plays With Fire (28-11-63)
Margit Saad (Cast Member)
The Saint 2-27. The Saint Sees It Through (19-03-64)
Margo Andrew (Cast Member)
The Prisoner 10. Hammer & Anvil (01-12-67)
Margo Cunningham (Cast Member)
The Avengers 3-07. The Gilded Cage (09-11-63)
Margo Jenkins (Cast Member)
The Avengers 2-14. Dead On Course (29-12-62)
Margo Johns (Cast Member)
Danger Man 2-16. A Room in The Basement (02-02-65)

The Saint 2-03. Judith (03-10-63)
Margo McLennan (Cast Member)
Danger Man 1-12. The Sisters (27-11-60)
Margot Thomas (Cast Member)
Doctor Who 12. The Romans: 4 Episodes (16-01-65)
Maria Antipass (Cast Member)
The Avengers 2-13. Death Dispatch (22-12-62)
Maria Machado (Cast Member)
The Avengers 4-12 Twos a Crowd (18-12-65)
Maria Roza (Cast Member)
The Saint 5-04. The Reluctant Revolution (21-10-66)
Maria Warburg (Cast Member)
Man In A Suitcase 19. Somebody Loses, Somebody… Wins? (31-01-67)
Marian Spencer (Cast Member)
The Corridor People Victim as Black (1966)
Marianne Deeming (Cast Member)
Man Of The World 1-11. Specialist For the Kill (08-12-62)
Marie Burke (Cast Member)
Danger Man 1-01. View From The Villa (11-09-60) 1-29. The Contessa (21-05-61)
The Saint 1-02 The Latin Touch (11-10-62) 1-12 The Charitable Countess (20-12-62) 2-04 Teresa (10-10-63) 6-15 Vendetta For The Saint 1 (5-1-68) 6-16 Vendetta For The Saint Part 2 (12-1-68)
Marie France (Cast Member)
Man Of The World 1-02. Masquerade In Spain (06-10-62
Marie Makino (Cast Member)
Randall & Hopkirk (Deceased) 05. That's How Murder Snowballs (19-10-69)
The Saint 2-14. The Bunco Artists (19-12-63)
Marie Sutherland (Cast Member)
Public Eye 4-07. A Fixed Address (19-06-69)
Marie Yang (Cast Member)
Man Of The World 2-07. The Prince (22-06-63)
Marika Mann (Cast Member)
The Avengers 5-23. Murdersville (11-11-67)
Marika Rivera (Cast Member)
The Saint 5-09. The Better Mouse Trap (25-11-66)
Marina Martin (Cast Member)
The Avengers 2-12. The Big Thinker (15-12-62)
Doctor Who 18. Galaxy 4: Air Lock (25-09-65)
Marina Vasquez (Cast Member)
Danger Man 3-08. The Outcast (18-11-65)
Mario Zappellini (Cast Member)
Callan 2-06. Heir Apparent (12-02-69**)**
Marion Mathie (Cast Member)
The Saint 2-06. Marcia (24-10-63)
Marius Goring (Cast Member)
Doctor Who 36. The Evil Of The Daleks: Episode 2 (27-05-67)
The Third Man 3-01. A Question In Ice (27-06-64)
Marjie Lawrence (Cast Member)
Ghost Squad 2-06. The Missing People (29-06-63)
The Protectors 04. No Forwarding Address (18-04-64)
Marjorie Keys (Cast Member)
The Avengers 3-21. Build a Better Mousetrap (15-02-64)
Undermind 02. Flowers Of Havoc (15-05-65)
Marjorie Rhodes (Cast Member)
Randall & Hopkirk (Deceased) 12. For The Girl Who Has Everything (07-12-69)
Mark Burns (Cast Member)
The Baron 13. Portrait Of Louisa (21-12-67)
The Prisoner 11. It's Your Funeral (08-12-67)
The Saint 6-10. The Scales Of Justice (01-12-68)

Undermind 03. The New Dimension (22-05-65)
Mark Dignam (Cast Member)
The Baron 19. You Can't Win Them All (01-02-67)
Danger Man 2-16. A Room in The Basement (02-02-65)
The Saint 6-05. The Organisation Man (27-10-67)
Mark Eden (Cast Member)
The Avengers 2-05. Mission To Montreal (27-10-62)
Man In A Suitcase 02. The Sitting Pigeon (04-10-67)
The Prisoner 11. It's Your Funeral (08-12-67)
The Saint 2-22. The Invisible Millionaire (13-02-64)
Mark Elwes (Cast Member)
The Avengers 6-14. The Interrogators (01-01-69)
Department S: 23. A Small War Of Nerves (21-01-70)
Man In A Suitcase 17. Why They Killed Nolan (17-01-67)
Mark Hawkins (Cast Member)
Strange Report 15. REPORT 4407 No Choice For The Donor (04-01-70)
Mark Heath (Cast Member)
The Avengers 3-16. The Little Wonders (11-01-64)
Danger Man 3-05. Loyalty Always Pays (28-10-65)
Mark Kelly (Cast Member)
Ghost Squad 2-23. The Menacing Mazurka (23-03-63)
Mark Kingston (Cast Member)
The Protectors 02. The Bottle Shop (04-04-64)
Mark London (Cast Member)
The Avengers 6-26. Homicide & Old Lace (26-03-69)
Mark Moss (Cast Member)
Adam Adamant Lives! 29. A Sinister Sort Of Service (25-03-67)
The Avengers 2-13. Death Dispatch (22-12-62)
Mark Peterson (Cast Member)
The Baron 18. A Memory Of Evil (25-01-67)
Man In A Suitcase 26. The Revolutionaries (20-03-67)
The Protectors 09. The Pirate (23-05-64)
Mark Singleton (Cast Member)
Department S: 09. Black Out (17-09-69)
Marla Corvin (Cast Member)
Man Of The World 1-12. A Family Affair (15-12-62)
Marla Landi (Cast Member)
Danger Man 1-38. Dead Man Walks (13-01-62)
Interpol Calling 05. The Two Headed Monster (12-10-59)
Man Of The World 2-06. The Bullfighter (15-06-63)
The Protectors 13. Cargo From Corinth (20-06-64)
Marlene Domanska (Cast Member)
Man In A Suitcase 28. Three Blinks Of The Eyes (03-04-67)
Marlon Mathie (Cast Member)
Department S: 01. Six Days (09-03-69)
Marlus Goring (Cast Member)
Man In A Suitcase 20. Blind Spot (07-02-67)
Marne Maitland (Cast Member)
The Avengers 5-18. Death's Door (07-10-67)
The Champions 20. The Silent Enemy (12-02-69)
Danger Man 1-29. The Contessa (21-05-61)
Department S: 18. The Perfect Operation (26-12-69)
Interpol Calling 35. Cargo Of Death (23-05-60)
Randall & Hopkirk (Deceased) 21. The Ghost Talks (06-02-70)
The Saint 2-04. Teresa (10-10-63) 3-02. Lida (15-10-64) 5-13. Flight Plan (23-12-66) 6-19.
Portrait Of Brenda (02-02-69)
The Third Man 2-10. Toys Of The Dead (03-11-59)
Marrianne Stone (Cast Member)

Man In A Suitcase 08. Essay In Evil (15-11-67)
Marshall Jones (Cast Member)
City Beneath The Sea 1 episode (1962)
Man Of The World 2-03. Double Exposure (25-05-63)
Martin Benson (Cast Member)
The Champions 26. Full Circle (26-03-69)
Danger Man 1-07. Position Of Trust (23-10-60) 2-17. The Affair At Castelevara (09-02-65)
Ghost Squad 2-19. Death of a Sportsman (26-01-63)
Interpol Calling 17. Mr George (11-01-60)
The Saint 2-07. The Work Of Art (31-10-63) 5-03. The Russian Prisoner (14-10-66) 5-04. The Reluctant Revolution (21-10-66) 5-27. The Gadic Collection (22-06-67)
Martin Boddey (Cast Member)
The Champions 06. Operation Deep Freeze (30-10-68)
Danger Man 1-26. The Journey Ends Halfway (30-04-61)
Department S: 06. The Man In The Elegant Room (13-04-69)
Martin Carroll (Cast Member)
Randall & Hopkirk (Deceased) 21. The Ghost Talks (06-02-70)
Martin Cort (Cast Member)
Doctor Who 48. The Seeds Of Death: 6 Episodes (25-01-69)
Martin Dempsey (Cast Member)
Public Eye 4-01. Welcome To Brighton? (30-07-69)
Martin Friend (Cast Member)
The Avengers 3-07. The Gilded Cage (09-11-63) 3-15. The White Elephant (04-01-64)
The Protectors 10. The Deadly Chameleon (30-5-64)
Martin Jarvis (Cast Member)
Doctor Who 13. The Web Planet: 6 Episodes (13-02-65)
Martin Lyder (Cast Member)
Callan 2-06. Heir Apparent (12-02-69**)**
Martin Miller (Cast Member)
The Avengers 4-06. The Master Minds (06-11-65)
Danger Man 1-05. The Lovers (09-10-60) 2-06. Fish On The Hook (17-11-64)
Department S: 18. The Perfect Operation (26-12-69)
Ghost Squad 1-11 The Green Shoes (29-12-62)
Man Of The World 1-03. Blaze Of Glory (13-10-62)
The Protectors 01. Landscape With Bandits (28-03-64)
The Saint 3-03. Jeannine (22-10-64) 4-04. The Smart Detective (22-07-65)
Martin Ripper (Cast Member)
Danger Man 1-05. The Lovers (09-10-60)
Martin Shaw (Cast Member)
Strange Report 12. REPORT 7931 SNIPER When Is Your Cousin Not? (14-12-69)
Martin Sterndale (Cast Member)
Danger Man 1-11. The Key (20-11-60)
Martin Wyldeck (Cast Member)
The Baron 08. The Persuaders (16-11-66)
Danger Man 1-12. The Sisters (27-11-60)
Ghost Squad 2-12. Quarantine At Kavar (01-06-63)
The Protectors 07. It Could Happen Here (09-05-64)
The Saint 2-17. The Noble Sportsman (09-01-64) 4-02. The Abductors (08-07-65) 5-07. The Angel's Eye (11-11-66)
Mary Abbott (Cast Member)
Ghost Squad 2-17. Mr Five Per Cent (06-04-63) 2-07. Lost in Transit (15-06-63)
Mary Chester (Cast Member)
Public Eye 4-06. The Comedian's Graveyard (03-09-69)
Mary Hignett (Cast Member)
Adam Adamant Lives! 01 A Year For Scoundrels (20-06-66)
Mary Jones (Cast Member)
The Saint 3-14. The Contact (07-01-65) 4-06. The Man Who Could No Die (05-08-65) 5-13. Flight Plan (23-12-66)

Mary Kenton (Cast Member)
The Protectors 12. Channel Crossing (13-06-64)
The Saint 2-12. The Well Meaning Mayor (05-12-63)
Mary Laura Wood (Cast Member)
Interpol Calling 25. The Girl With The Grey Hair (14-03-60)
Mary Mackenzie (Cast Member)
Ghost Squad 2-24. Gertrude (13-04-63)
Mary Maude (Cast Member)
Man In A Suitcase 24. Which Way Did He Go, McGill (06-03-67)
Mary Maxwell (Cast Member)
The Avengers 4-17. The Girl From AUNTIE (22-01-66)
Mary Merrall (Cast Member)
The Avengers 6-26. Homicide & Old Lace (26-03-69)
The Saint 2-14. The Bunco Artists (19-12-63)
Mary Miller (Cast Member)
The Protectors 08. Freedom! (16-05-64)
Mary Mitchell (Cast Member)
Department S: 17. Dead Men Die Twice (12-11-69)
Mary Morris (Cast Member)
The Andromeda Breakthrough 6 Episodes (1962)
Ghost Squad 2-22. The Magic Bullet (16-03-63)
Interpol Calling 29. White Blackmail (11-04-60)
The Prisoner 08. Dance Of The Dead (17-11-67)
Mary Peach (Cast Member)
Doctor Who 40. The Enemy Of The World: 6 Episodes (23-12-67)
The Saint 5-23. The Gadget Lovers (21-04-67)
Mary Webster (Cast Member)
Adam Adamant Lives! 03. More Deadly Than The Sword (07-07-66)
Danger Man: 3-03. Sting In The Tail (14-10-65) 3-03. Sting In The Tail (14-10-65)
Out Of The Unknown 2-03. Lambda One (20-10-66)
Mary Yeomans (Cast Member)
Danger Man 2-21. The Mirror's New (09-03-65)
Maryann Turner (Cast Member)
Callan 2-09. Death Of a Friend (05-03-69)
Matthew Long (Cast Member)
The Avengers 6-23. Take Me To Your Leader (05-03-69)
Maureen Connell (Cast Member)
Danger Man: 2-01. Yesterday's Enemies (13-10-64)
Maureen Moore (Cast Member)
The Third Man 2-10. Toys Of The Dead (03-11-59)
Maureen O'Brien (Cast Member)
Doctor Who 11 The Rescue: 2 Episodes (2-1-65) 12 The Romans: 4 Episodes (16-1-65) 13. The Web Planet: 6 Episodes (13-02-65) 15. The Space Museum: 4 Episodes (24-04-65)16. The Chase: 6 Episodes (22-05-65) 17. The Time Meddler: 4 Episodes (3-7-65) 18. Galaxy 4: Air Lock (25-09-65)
Maureen Pryor (Cast Member)
Man In A Suitcase 13. The Bridge (20-12-67)
Maurice Browning (Cast Member)
The Avengers 4-17. The Girl From AUNTIE (22-01-66)
The Champions 24. Project Zero (12-03-69)
The Saint 5-23. The Gadget Lovers (21-04-67)
Maurice Colbourne (Cast Member)
Ghost Squad 2-26. Sabotage (20-04-63)
Maurice Denham (Cast Member)
Danger Man 3-15. Somebody Is Liable To Get Hurt (06-01-66)
Maurice Durant (Cast Member)
Ghost Squad 2-26. Sabotage (20-04-63)
Pathfinders To Mars 1 Episode (1961)
Maurice Good (Cast Member)

The Avengers 3-12. Don't Look Behind You (14-12-63) 6-05. Split (23-10-68)
Doctor Who 25. The Gunfighters: 4 Episodes (30-04-66)
Man In A Suitcase 08. Essay In Evil (15-11-67)
Public Eye 4-03. Paid In Full (13-08-69)
The Saint 5-10. Little Girl Lost (02-12-66) 6-07. The Time To Die (10-11-68)
Maurice Hedley (Cast Member)
A For Andromeda 1-6. The Face Of The Tiger (07-11-61)
Adam Adamant Lives! 03. More Deadly Than The Sword (07-07-66)
The Andromeda Breakthrough 3 Episodes (1962)
The Avengers 2-17. Box Of Tricks (19-01-63)
Ghost Squad 2-22. The Magic Bullet (16-03-63)
The Protectors 12. Channel Crossing (13-06-64)
Public Eye 1-02. Nobody Kill Santa Claus (30-01-65)
The Saint 3-17. The Inescapable World (28-01-65)
The Third Man 2-06. Barcelona Passage (01-10-59)
Maurice Kaufmann (Cast Member)
The Avengers 4-19. Quick-Quick Slow Death (05-02-66)
Danger Man 3-07. Judgement Day (11-11-65)
Ghost Squad 2-12. Quarantine At Kavar (01-06-63)
Interpol Calling 22. The Heiress (15-02-60)
Man In A Suitcase 22. Jigsaw Man (21-02-67)
Man Of The World 2-05. In The Picture (08-06-63)
The Saint 3-08. The Man Who Liked Toys (26-11-64) 5-12. Locate & Destroy (16-12-66)
Maurice Podbrey (Cast Member)
Out Of The Unknown 1-03. Stranger In the Family (18-10-65)
Maurice Selwyn (Cast Member)
Doctor Who 47. The Krotons: 4 Episodes (28-12-68)
Maurie Taylor (Cast Member)
The Protectors 14. The Reluctant Thief (27-06-64)
Undermind 09. Test For The Future (03-07-65)
Mavis Villiers (Cast Member)
The Saint 3-23. The Happy Suicide (11-03-65)
Max Adrian (Cast Member)
The Baron 20. The High Terrace (08-02-67)
Max Bacon (Cast Member)
Ghost Squad 2-09. Hot Money (25-05-63)
Max Butterfield (Cast Member)
Ghost Squad 1-07. Still Waters (21-10-61)
Max Faulkner (Cast Member)
The Prisoner 14. Living In Harmony (29-12-67) 15. The Girl Who Was Death (18-01-67)
Randall & Hopkirk (Deceased) 02. A Disturbing Case (28-09-69)
Maxine Audley (Cast Member)
Danger Man 1-05. The Lovers (09-10-60) 1-15. Colonel Rodriguez (18-12-60)
3-25. Shinda Shima (26-02-67)
Out Of This World 02. Little Lost Robot (07-07-1962)
Maxine Casson (Cast Member)
Strange Report 10. REPORT 8944 HAND A Matter Of Witchcraft (30-11-69)
Maxwell Craig (Cast Member)
Ghost Squad 1-12. Princess (12-01-61)
Maxwell Foster (Cast Member)
Ghost Squad 2-05. The Retirement Of The Gentle Dove (30-03-63)
Maxwell Shaw (Cast Member)
Danger Man 1-37. The Nurse (06-01-61) 2-19. It's Up To The Lady (23-02-65) 3-10. Are You Going
To Be More Permanent? (02-12-65)
Man In A Suitcase 12. Find The Lady (13-12-67)
Man Of The World 2-05. In The Picture (08-06-63) 3-10. The Imprudent Politician (10-12-64)
Maya Sorell (Cast Member)
Ghost Squad 2-04. The Golden Silence (08-06-63)

Meadows White (Cast Member)
Danger Man 2-19. It's Up To The Lady (23-02-65)
The Saint 2-08. Iris (07-11-63) 2-14. The Bunco Artists (19-12-63)
Meier Tzelniker (Cast Member)
The Avengers 2-10. Death On The Rocks (01-12-62)
Melissa Stribling (Cast Member)
The Avengers 2-20. School For Traitors (09-02-63)
Mellan Mitchell (Cast Member)
Ghost Squad 2-02. East Of Mandalay (09-02-63)
Man Of The World 1-05. The Frontier (27-10-62)
Melvyn Mordant (Cast Member)
The Avengers 2-11. Traitor In Zebra (08-12-62)
Meredith Edwards (Cast Member)
The Baron 13. Portrait Of Louisa (21-12-67)
Interpol Calling 13. Slave Ship (14-12-59)
Randall & Hopkirk (Deceased) 22. It's Supposed To Be Thicker Than Water (13-02-70)
The Saint 4-03. The Crooked Ring (15-07-65) 4-06. The Man Who Could No Die (05-08-65)
Merrill Colebrook (Cast Member)
Man In A Suitcase 02. The Sitting Pigeon (04-10-67)
Mervyn Johns (Cast Member)
The Avengers 4-13. Too Many Christmas Trees (25-12-65)
Danger Man 2-09. No Marks For Servility (08-12-64)
The Saint 6-09. The House On Dragons Rock (24-11-68)
Mia Karam (Cast Member)
The Avengers 1-06. Girl On The Trapeze (11-02-61)
Ghost Squad 2-05. The Retirement Of The Gentle Dove (30-03-63)
Michael Anthony (Cast Member)
Danger Man 3-16. Dangerous Secret (13-01-66)
The Saint 3-03. Jeannine (22-10-64) 5-17. The Death Game (20-01-67)
Michael Atkinson (Cast Member)
The Protectors All Episodes (1964)
Michael Balfour (Cast Member)
The Avengers 6-33. Bizarre (21-05-69)
Danger Man 2-20. Have a Glass of Wine (02-03-65)
Department S: 02. The Trojan Tanker (16-03-69)
Interpol Calling 26. Trial At Cranby's Creek (21-03-60) 30. A Foreign Body (18-04-60)
The Prisoner 14. Living In Harmony (29-12-67)
Michael Barker (Cast Member)
Undermind 02. Flowers Of Havoc (15-05-65)
Michael Barrington (Cast Member)
The Avengers 4-10. Dial a Deadly Number (04-12-65)
The Champions 27. Nutcracker (02-04-69)
Department S: 21. Death On Reflection (17-12-69)
Michael Bates (Cast Member)
Man In A Suitcase 20. Blind Spot (07-02-67)
The Saint 2-01. The Fellow Traveller (19-09-63)
Michael Beint (Cast Member)
Adam Adamant Lives! 09. Sing a Song Of Murder (25-08-66)
The Avengers 2-02. Propellant 23 (06-10-62)
Randall & Hopkirk (Deceased) 06. Just For The Record (26-10-69)
Michael Billington (Cast Member)
The Prisoner 12. A Change Of Mind (15-12-67)
Michael Bilton (Cast Member)
The Avengers 6-09. Legacy Of Death (20-11-68)
The Champions 23. The Night People (05-03-69)
The Prisoner 11. It's Your Funeral (08-12-67)
The Saint 5-19. To Kill a Saint (24-02-67)
Michael Bird (Cast Member)

Danger Man 1-23. The Gallows Tree (09-04-61)
Randall & Hopkirk (Deceased) 19. A Sentimental Journey (23-01-70)
Michael Brennen (Cast Member)
Interpol Calling 15. Last Man Lucky (28-12-59)
The Prisoner 15. The Girl Who Was Death (18-01-67)
Michael Browning (Cast Member)
The Avengers 2-11. Traitor In Zebra (08-12-62)
Ghost Squad 2-11. A First Class Way To Die (13-07-63)
Michael Chow (Cast Member)
The Baron 15. Storm Warning (Part 1) (04-01-67)
The Prisoner 12. A Change Of Mind (15-12-67)
The Saint 3-18. The Sign Of The Claw (04-02-65)
Michael Coles (Cast Member)
The Avengers 5-05. The Bird Who Knew Too Much (11-02-67)
The Baron 28. The Man Outside (05-04-67)
Department S: 28. The Soup Of The Day (04-03-70)
Ghost Squad 2-09. Hot Money (25-05-63)
Randall & Hopkirk (Deceased) 12. For The Girl Who Has Everything (07-12-69)
The Saint 5-09. The Better Mouse Trap (25-11-66)
Michael Collins (Cast Member)
The Avengers 2-01. Mr Teddy Bear (29-09-62)
Danger Man 2-15. Whatever Happened To George Foster (19-01-65)
The Protectors 08. Freedom! (16-05-64)
The Saint 3-11. The Hijackers (17-12-64)
Michael Corcoran (Cast Member)
The Avengers 4-08. A Surfeit Of H2o (20-11-65) 6-13. They Keep Killing Steed (18-12-68)
Danger Man 2-20. Have a Glass of Wine (02-03-65)
Michael Craze (Cast Member)
Doctor Who 29. The Tenth Planet: 3 Episodes (08-10-66) 32. The Underwater Menace: 2 Episodes (21-01-67) 33. The Moonbase: 2 Episodes (18-02-67) 35. The Faceless Ones: Episode 1 (08-04-67)
Michael Crockett (Cast Member)
Undermind 06. Intent To Destroy (12-06-65)
Michael Culver (Cast Member)
Man In A Suitcase 13. The Bridge (20-12-67)
Michael Danvers-Walker (Cast Member)
The Avengers 2-11. Traitor In Zebra (08-12-62)
The Baron 18. A Memory Of Evil (25-01-67)
Out Of The Unknown 1-05. Time In Advance (01-11-65) 2-03. Lambda One (20-10-66)
The Prisoner 09. Checkmate (14-11-67)
Michael David (Cast Member)
The Avengers 6-28. My Wildest Dream (07-04-69)
Michael Davis (Cast Member)
Doctor Who 10. Dalek Invasion Of Earth (1964)
Michael Earl (Cast Member)
Out Of The Unknown 1-12. The Midas Plague (20-12-65)
Michael Elwyn (Cast Member)
The Avengers 6-32. Get-a-Way (14-05-69)
Michael Forrest (Cast Member)
The Avengers 2-13. Death Dispatch (22-12-62) 5-08. The Hidden Tiger (04-03-67)
The Baron 24. Long Ago & Far Away (08-03-67)
Danger Man 3-21. The Man With The Foot (24-03-66)
Ghost Squad 2-18. The Heir Apparent (09-03-63)
Randall & Hopkirk (Deceased) 11. The Ghost Who Saved The Bank At Monte Carlo (30-11-69)
The Saint 5-08. The Man Who Liked Lions (18-11-66)
Strange Report 16. REPORT 4977 Square Root Of Evil (11-01-70)
Michael Godfrey (Cast Member)
The Baron 10. The Legends of Ammak (30-11-66)
The Champions 06. Operation Deep Freeze (30-10-68)

Danger Man 2-06. Fish On The Hook (17-11-64) 3-18. The Hunting Party (27-01-66)
Department S: 10. Double Death Of Charlie Crippen (14-09-69)
The Saint 3-05. The Revolution Racket (05-11-64) 5-04. The Reluctant Revolution (21-10-66)
Michael Goldie (Cast Member)
The Avengers 3-01. Brief For Murder (28-09-63)
Doctor Who 10. Dalek Invasion Of Earth (1964) 43. The Wheel in Space: 2 Episodes (11-05-68)
The Protectors 06. The Stamp Collection (02-05-64)
Randall & Hopkirk (Deceased) 14. Who Killed Cock Robin? (21-12-69)
Strange Report 11. REPORT 1553 RACIST A Most Dangerous Proposal (07-12-69)
Michael Goodliffe (Cast Member)
The Avengers 4-23. The House That Jack Built (05-03-66)
Callan 2-01. Red Knight, White Knight (8-1-69) 2-02. The Most Promising Girl Of Her Year (15-1-69)
2-04. The Little Bits & Pieces Of Love (29-1-69) 2-05. Let's Kill Everybody (5-02-69)
Ghost Squad 1-10. Catspaw (05-01-61)
Interpol Calling 09. Private View (09-11-59)
Man In A Suitcase 10. All That Glitters (29-11-67)
Man Of The World 1-10. Portrait Of a Girl (01-12-62)
Randall & Hopkirk (Deceased) 13. But What a Sweet Little Room (14-12-69)
The Saint 2-22. The Invisible Millionaire (13-02-64)
Michael Gothard (Cast Member)
Department S: 14. Les Fleurs Du Mal (22-10-69)
Randall & Hopkirk (Deceased) 16. When The Spirit Moves You (02-01-70)
Out Of The Unknown 2-01. The Machine Stops (06-10-66)
Michael Gough (Cast Member)
The Avengers 4-03. The Cybernauts (16-10-65) 5-09. The Correct Way To Kill (11-03-67)
The Champions 05. Happening (23-10-68)
Doctor Who 24. The Celestial Toymaker: The Final Test (23-04-66)
The Saint 3-10. The Imprudent Politician (10-12-64)
Undermind 02. Flowers Of Havoc (15-05-65)
Michael Gover (Cast Member)
The Avengers 2-22. Man In The Mirror (23-02-63) 2-24. A Chorus Of Frogs (09-03-63)
The Protectors 01. Landscape With Bandits (28-03-64)
Randall & Hopkirk (Deceased) 18. Could You Recognize The Man Again (16-01-70)
Michael Graham (Cast Member)
The Champions 17. A Case Of Lemmings (22-01-68)
Danger Man 1-03. Josetta (25-09-60)
Randall & Hopkirk (Deceased) 25. You Can Always Find a Fall Guy (06-03-70)
The Saint 5-06. The Convenient Monster (04-11-66) 5-15. The Persistent Patriots (06-01-67)
Michael Graham Cox (Cast Member)
Public Eye 4-01. Welcome To Brighton? (30-07-69)
Undermind 02. Flowers Of Havoc (15-05-65)
Michael Griffiths (Cast Member)
Department S: 24. The Bones Of Byrom Blain (28-01-70)
Randall & Hopkirk (Deceased) 02. A Disturbing Case (28-09-69) 05. That's How Murder Snowballs
(19-10-69)
Michael Guest (Cast Member)
The Champions 08. To Trap a Rat (13-11-68)
Doctor Who 17. The Time Meddler: 4 Episodes (03-07-65)
Pathfinders In Space 7 Episodes (1960)
Michael Gwynn (Cast Member)
The Avengers 6-30. Take-Over (23-04-69)
The Baron 03. Something For a Rainy Day (12-10-66)
Danger Man 2-16. A Room in The Basement (02-02-65)
Department S: 08. A Ticket To Nowhere (27-04-69)
Randall & Hopkirk (Deceased) 15. The Man From Nowhere (28-12-69)
The Saint 3-20. The Frightened Inn-Keeper (18-02-65)
Michael Harding (Cast Member)
Out Of The Unknown 1-05. Time In Advance (01-11-65)

Michael Harrison (Cast Member)
The Avengers 3-21. Build a Better Mousetrap (15-02-64)
Michael Hawkins (Cast Member)
The Avengers 3-11. The Golden Fleece (07-12-63) 6-23. Take Me To Your Leader (05-03-69)
The Baron 16. The Island (Part 2) (11-01-67)
Man In A Suitcase 24. Which Way Did He Go, McGill (06-03-67)
The Protectors 09. The Pirate (23-05-64)
Michael Hitchman (Cast Member)
Danger Man 1-10. An Affair Of State (13-11-60)
Michael Hunt (Cast Member)
Danger Man 1-12. The Sisters (27-11-60)
The Corridor People 2 Episodes (1966)
Michael Jacques (Cast Member)
Danger Man 1-12. The Sisters (27-11-60)
Michael Jenkinson (Cast Member)
Ghost Squad 2-20. P.G..7. (06-07-63)
Michael Latimer (Cast Member)
The Avengers 4-21 A Touch Of Brimstone (19-2-66) 5-22. The Positive Negative Man (4-11-67)
Michael Lees (Cast Member)
The Avengers 6-07. False Witness (06-01-68)
The Champions 28. The Final Countdown (16-04-69)
Out Of The Unknown 2-03. Lambda One (20-10-66)
Undermind 11. End Signal (17-07-65)
Michael Lynch (Cast Member)
The Avengers 5-01. From Venus With Love (14-01-67)
The Saint 3-05. The Revolution Racket (05-11-64)
Michael Martin (Cast Member)
Strange Report 15. REPORT 4407 No Choice For The Donor (04-01-70)
Michael McKevitt (Cast Member)
The Avengers 6-27. Thingamajig (16-04-69)
The Saint 2-22. The Invisible Millionaire (13-02-64)
Michael McStay (Cast Member)
The Avengers 6-17. Killer (22-01-69)
Michael Meacham (Cast Member)
The Saint 2-09. The King Of The Beggars (14-11-63)
Michael Mellinger (Cast Member)
The Avengers 2-09. The Sell Out (24-11-62)
The Champions 09. The Iron Man (20-11-68)
Department S: 09. Black Out (17-09-69)
Man Of The World 1-08. The Nature Of Justice (17-11-62)
The Saint 6-06. The Double Take (03-11-68)
Michael Miller (Cast Member)
Doctor Who 17. The Time Meddler: 4 Episodes (03-07-65)
The Prisoner 06. The General (3-11-67) 12. A Change Of Mind (15-12-67) 17. Fall Out (1-2-68)
Michael Moyer (Cast Member)
The Avengers 2-08. Death Of Great Dane (17-11-62)
Michael Nightingale (Cast Member)
The Avengers 5-13. A Funny Thing Happened On The Way To The Station (08-04-67) 6-08. All Done With Mirrors (13-11-68)
Danger Man 2-07. The Colonels Daughter (24-11-64)
The Prisoner 08. Dance Of The Dead (17-11-67)
Michael Peake (Cast Member)
Danger Man 1-13. The Prisoner (04-12-60) 1-22. The Honeymooners (02-04-61) 3-18. The Hunting Party (27-01-66)
Doctor Who 12. The Romans: 4 Episodes (16-01-65)
Man Of The World 2-06. The Bullfighter (15-06-63)
The Saint 2-01. The Fellow Traveler (19-09-63) 3-14. The Contact (07-01-65)
Michael Pearce (Cast Member)

174

Undermind 06. Intent To Destroy (12-06-65)
Michael Pemberton (Cast Member)
The Saint 5-25. The Power Artists (19-05-67) 6-06. The Double Take (03-11-68)
Michael Quinn (Cast Member)
Ghost Squad 28 Episodes
Michael Radford (Cast Member)
Randall & Hopkirk (Deceased) 26. The Smile Behind The Veil (13-03-70)
Michael Rennie (Cast Member)
The Third Man all episodes
Michael Ripper (Cast Member)
Adam Adamant Lives! 16. D Is For Destruction (13-06-66)
Danger Man 1-16. The Island (01-01-61) 1-38. Dead Man Walks (13-01-62)
Randall & Hopkirk (Deceased) 22. It's Supposed To Be Thicker Than Water (13-02-70)
The Saint 5-27. The Gadic Collection (22-06-67)
Michael Ritterman (Cast Member)
Ghost Squad 2-06. The Missing People (29-06-63) 2-23. The Menacing Mazurka (23-03-63)
Man Of The World 2-01. The Bandit (11-05-63)
The Saint 1-05. The Loaded Tourist (01-11-62) 2-18. The Romantic Matron (16-01-64)
Michael Robbins (Cast Member)
Adam Adamant Lives!: 02. Death Has a Thousand Faces (30-06-66)
The Avengers: 2-01. Mr Teddy Bear (29-09-62) 6-23. Take Me To Your Leader (05-03-69)
The Baron: 14. There's Someone Close Behind You (28-12-67)
Department S: 06. The Man In The Elegant Room (13-04-69)
Ghost Squad: 2-10. The Grand Duchess (11-05-63)
The Saint; 3-06. The Saint Steps In (12-11-64) 6-06. The Double Take (03-11-68) 6-13. The People Importers (22-12-68)
Michael Rothwell (Cast Member)
The Avengers 5-19. The £50,000 Breakfast (14-10-67)
Michael Sarne (Cast Member)
Man In A Suitcase 22. Jigsaw Man (21-02-67)
Michael Segal (Cast Member)
The Baron 21. The Seven Eyes Of Night (15-02-67)
Man Of The World 2-03. Double Exposure (25-05-63)
The Prisoner 10. Hammer & Anvil (01-12-67)
Michael Sheard (Cast Member)
Adam Adamant Lives! 16. D Is For Destruction (13-06-66)
Randall & Hopkirk (Deceased) 17. Somebody Just Walked Over My Grave (09-01-70)
Strange Report 12. REPORT 7931 SNIPER When Is Your Cousin Not? (14-12-69)
Michael Sirr (Cast Member)
Man Of The World 2-07. The Prince (22-06-63)
Michael Slater (Cast Member)
The Champions 17. A Case Of Lemmings (22-01-68)
Michael Spear (Cast Member)
The Saint 1-04. The Covetous Headsman (25-10-62)
Michael Standing (Cast Member)
Adam Adamant Lives! 09. Sing a Song Of Murder (25-08-66)
The Champions 08. To Trap a Rat (13-11-68)
Micheal Stevens (Cast Member)
The Avengers 4-02. The Gravediggers (09-01-65) 4-05. Castle De'ath (30-10-65)
Man In A Suitcase 15. Burden Of Proof (03-01-67)
Michael Trubshawe (Cast Member)
The Avengers 4-10. Dial a Deadly Number (04-12-65) 6-08. All Done With Mirrors (13-11-68)
Danger Man 2-07. The Colonels Daughter (24-11-64)
Michael Turner (Cast Member)
The Avengers 6-12. Have Guns - Will Haggle (11-12-68)
Doctor Who 43. The Wheel in Space: 2 Episodes (11-05-68)
Strange Report 12. REPORT 7931 SNIPER When Is Your Cousin Not? (14-12-69)
Michael Tye-Walker (Cast Member)

Man In A Suitcase 28. Three Blinks Of The Eyes (03-04-67)
Michael Ward (Cast Member)
The Avengers 6-17. Killer (22-01-69)
Michael Williamson (Cast Member)
Man In A Suitcase 16. The Whisper (10-01-67)
Michael Wolf (Cast Member)
The Baron 01. Diplomatic Immunity (28-09-66) 05. Enemy Of The State (26-10-66)
Doctor Who 33. The Moonbase: 2 Episodes (18-02-67)
The Saint 5-05. The Helpful Pirate (28-10-66)
Michael Wynne (Cast Member)
The Avengers 4-23. The House That Jack Built (05-03-66)
The Baron 29. Countdown (12-04-67)
The Champions 10. The Ghost Plane (27-11-68)
The Protectors 04. No Forwarding Address (18-04-64)
The Saint 2-19.Luella (23-01-64) 4-08 Spanish Cow (19-08-65) 5-08 Man Who Liked Lions (18-11-66)
Michel Faure (Cast Member)
The Avengers 5-18. Death's Door (07-10-67)
Department S: 20. The Mysterious Man In The Flying Machine (10-12-69)
Michele Dotrice (Cast Member)
Out Of The Unknown 2-04. Level Seven (27-10-66)
Michelle Karlli (Cast Member)
Department S 26. The Ghost Of Mary Burnham (18-02-70)
Micky Ventura (Cast Member)
Danger Man 2-12. A Date With Doris (29-12-64)
Mike Lewin (Cast Member)
The Avengers 6-29. Requiem (16-04-69)
Mike Oxley (Cast Member)
Ghost Squad 2-07. Lost in Transit (15-06-63)
Mike Pratt (Cast Member)
The Baron 14. There's Someone Close Behind You (28-12-67)
The Champions 13. Twelve Hours (18-12-68)
Danger Man 2-18. The Ubiquitous Mr Lovegrove (16-02-65) 3-01. The Black Book (30-09-65) 3-02.
A Very Dangerous Game (07-10-65) 3-14. The Man Who Wouldn't Talk (30-12-65)
Man In A Suitcase 04. Variation On a Million Bucks Part 1 (18-10-67)
Out Of The Unknown 1-05. Time In Advance (01-11-65)
The Protectors 07. It Could Happen Here (09-05-64)
Randall & Hopkirk (Deceased) All episodes (1969)
The Saint 3-10. The Imprudent Politician (10-12-64) 5-15. The Persistent Patriots (06-01-67)
Mike Reid (Cast Member)
The Avengers 4-03. The Cybernauts (16-10-65)
The Saint 6-12. The Fiction Makers Part 2 (15-12-68)
Miki Iveria (Cast Member)
Danger Man 1-29. The Contessa (21-05-61)
The Saint 2-07. The Work Of Art (31-10-63)
Milo O'Shea (Cast Member)
Out Of The Unknown 1-06. Come Buttercup, Come Daisy, Come…? (08-11-65)
Milton Johns (Cast Member)
The Saint 5-22. Island Of Chance (07-04-67)
Milton Reid (Cast Member)
Department S: 25. Spencer Bodily Is 60 Years Old (11-02-70)
Miranda Connell (Cast Member)
The Avengers 1-20. Tunnel Of Fear (05-08-61)
Miranda Hampton (Cast Member)
Adam Adamant Lives! 05. Allah Is Not Always With You (21-07-66)
Mitzi Rogers (Cast Member)
The Avengers 2-04. Bullseye (20-10-62)
Ghost Squad 2-11. A First Class Way To Die (13-07-63)
Mo Kiki (Cast Member)

Adam Adamant Lives! 18. Black Echo (07-01-67)
Mohammad Shamsi (Cast Member)
Danger Man 3-07. Judgment Day (11-11-65)
Moira Lister (Cast Member)
The Avengers 5-04. The See Through Man (04-02-67)
Danger Man 1-17. Find & Return (08-01-61) 3-18. The Hunting Party (27-01-66)
Moira Redmond (Cast Member)
The Baron 13. Portrait Of Louisa (21-12-67)
Danger Man 1-24. The Relaxed Informer (16-04-61) 1-36. Under the Lake (30-12-61) 2-22. Parallel Lines Sometimes Meet (16-03-65)
Ghost Squad 1-13. Death From a Distance (04-11-61)1-10. Catspaw (05-01-61)
Interpol Calling 09. Private View (09-11-59)
Man Of The World 1-09. The Mindreader (24-11-62)
Mollie Maureen (Cast Member)
The Avengers 2-14. Dead On Course (29-12-62)
Molly Weir (Cast Member)
Ghost Squad 2-25. The Thirteenth Girl (27-04-63)
Mona Bruce (Cast Member)
Public Eye 4-06. The Comedian's Graveyard (03-09-69)
Mona Chong (Cast Member)
Adam Adamant Lives! 03. More Deadly Than The Sword (07-07-66)
Danger Man 3-02. A Very Dangerous Game (07-10-65) 3-25. Shinda Shima (26-02-67)
Monica Grey (Cast Member)
The Saint 6-07. The Time To Die (10-11-68)
Monica Stevenson (Cast Member)
The Avengers 3-09. The Medicine Men (23-11-63)
The Saint 2-02. Starring The Saint (26-09-63)
Monika Dietrich (Cast Member)
Department S: 02. The Trojan Tanker (16-03-69)
Monique Ahrens (Cast Member)
Danger Man 1-11. The Key (20-11-60)
Monti DeLyle (Cast Member)
The Prisoner 14. Living In Harmony (29-12-67)
Moray Watson (Cast Member)
The Avengers 4-20. The Danger Makers (12-02-66)
The Saint 3-10. The Imprudent Politician (10-12-64)
Morris Perry (Cast Member)
The Avengers 1-20. Tunnel Of Fear (05-08-61) 2-26. Killer Whale (23-03-63)
City Beneath The Sea 4 episodes (1962)
The Protectors 05. The Loop Men (25-04-64)
Moultrie Kelsall (Cast Member)
The Saint 3-06. The Saint Steps In (12-11-64) 5-06. The Convenient Monster (04-11-66)
Out Of The Unknown 1-10. Some Lapse In Time (06-12-65)
Moya O'Sullivan (Cast Member)
Undermind 01. Instance One (08-05-65)
Murray Evans (Cast Member)
Man In A Suitcase 11. Dead Man's Shoes (06-12-67)
Murray Hayne (Cast Member)
The Avengers 6-28. My Wildest Dream (07-04-69)
Danger Man 3-14. The Man Who Wouldn't Talk (30-12-65)
Out Of This World 02. Little Lost Robot (07-07-1962)
Murray Kash (Cast Member)
Danger Man 3-10. Are You Going To Be More Permanent? (02-12-65)
Out Of The Unknown 2-03. Lambda One (20-10-66)
Myo Toon (Cast Member)
Danger Man 1-22. The Honeymooners (02-04-61)
Myrtle Reed (Cast Member)
Ghost Squad 2-04. The Golden Silence (08-06-63)

N

Nadia Baker (Cast Member)
Adam Adamant Lives!: 02. Death Has a Thousand Faces (30-06-66)
Nadia Gray (Cast Member)
The Prisoner 02. The Chimes Of Big Ben (06-10-67)
Nadim Sawalha (Cast Member)
Danger Man: 2-01. Yesterday's Enemies (13-10-64)
Nadja Regin (Cast Member)
Danger Man 1-35. Find & Destroy (23-12-61)
Man Of The World 2-05. In The Picture (08-06-63)
The Saint 5-18. The Art Collectors (27-01-67)
Nan Brauton (Cast Member)
Strange Report 03. REPORT 2641 HOSTAGE If You Won't Learn Die (05-10-69)
Nan Marriott-Watson (Cast Member)
The Saint 2-13. The Sporting Chance (12-12-63)
Nancy Beckh (Cast Member)
Danger Man 1-25. The Brothers (23-04-61)
Nancy Nevinson (Cast Member)
Adam Adamant Lives! 07. To Set a Deadly Fashion (11-08-66)
Man Of The World 1-13. Shadow Of the Wall (22-12-62)
The Saint 4-08. The Spanish Cow (19-08-65)
Nancy Seabrooke (Cast Member)
Danger Man 1-17. Find & Return (08-01-61)
Nanette Newman (Cast Member)
Interpol Calling 29. White Blackmail (11-04-60)
The Saint 3-01. The Miracle Tea Party (8-10-64)
Naomi Chance (Cast Member)
The Avengers 2-10. Death On The Rocks (01-12-62) 4-07. The Murder Market (13-11-65)
Ghost Squad 2-17. Mr Five Per Cent (06-04-63) 2-13. The Desperate Diplomat (18-05-63)
The Third Man 2-10. Toys Of The Dead (03-11-59)
Natalie Benesh (Cast Member)
The Saint 1-04. The Covetous Headsman (25-10-62)
Natasha Parry (Cast Member)
Man Of The World 2-01. The Bandit (11-05-63)
Neal Ardan (Cast Member)
Department S: 22. Last Train to Redbridge (14-01-70)
Ghost Squad 1-03. Ticket For Blackmail (09-09-61)
Interpol Calling 36. Desert Hijack (30-05-60)
Randall & Hopkirk (Deceased) 23. The Trouble With Women (20-02-70)
The Saint 2-15. The Benevolent Burglary (26-12-63)
Neil Curnow (Cast Member)
Adam Adamant Lives! 29. A Sinister Sort Of Service (25-03-67)
Neil Hallett (Cast Member)
The Avengers 5-06. The Winged Avenger (18-02-67) 6-32. Get-a-Way (14-05-69)
Department S: 09. Black Out (17-09-69)
Ghost Squad 25 Episodes
The Saint 1-05. The Loaded Tourist (01-11-62) 6-13. The People Importers (22-12-68)
Neil McCallum (Cast Member)
Department S: 07. Handicap Dead (20-04-69)
Randall & Hopkirk (Deceased) 22. It's Supposed To Be Thicker Than Water (13-02-70)
The Saint 2-01. The Fellow Traveler (19-09-63)
Neil McCarthy (Cast Member)
The Avengers 5-20. Dead Man's Treasure (21-10-67) 6-14. The Interrogators (01-01-69)
Danger Man 1-21. The Conspirators (05-02-61)
Department S: 08. A Ticket To Nowhere (27-04-69)
Ghost Squad 1-11 The Green Shoes (29-12-62)

Man Of The World 1-10. Portrait Of a Girl (01-12-62)
Randall & Hopkirk (Deceased) 15. The Man From Nowhere (28-12-69)
The Saint 3-06. The Saint Steps In (12-11-64) 3-11 Hijackers (17-12-64) 4-01.Chequered Flag (1-7-65)
Neil Robinson (Cast Member)
The Avengers 3-17. The Wringer (18-01-64)
The Baron 26. The Long, Long Day (22-03-67)
Neil Stacy (Cast Member)
The Avengers 6-14. The Interrogators (01-01-69)
Neil Wilson (Cast Member)
The Avengers 1-15. The Frighteners (27-11-61) 3-07. The Gilded Cage (09-11-63) 6-14. The Interrogators (01-01-69)
Neville Barber (Cast Member)
Strange Report 14. REPORT 2493 Whose Pretty Girl Are You? (28-12-69)
Neville Becker (Cast Member)
Adam Adamant Lives! 04. The Sweet Smell Of Disaster (14-07-66)
Danger Man 1-15. Colonel Rodriguez (18-12-60) 3-03. Sting In The Tail (14-10-65) 3-07. Judgement Day (11-11-65)
Man In A Suitcase 14. The Man Who Stood Still (27-12-67)
Man Of The World 1-06. The Sentimental Agent (03-11-62)
The Protectors 03. Happy Is The Loser (11-04-64)
The Saint 1-12. The Charitable Countess (20-12-62) 2-07. The Work Of Art (31-10-63) 4-07. The Saint Bids Diamonds (12-08-65) 5-01. The Queens Ransom (30-09-66)
Neville Hughes (Cast Member)
The Avengers 6-27. Thingamajig (16-04-69)
Neville Marten (Cast Member)
The Avengers 6-25. Who Was That Man I Saw You With (19-03-69)
Neville Smith (Cast Member)
Doctor Who 08. The Reign Of Terror: 4 Episodes (08-08-64)
Newton Black (Cast Member)
The Avengers 3-09. The Medicine Men (23-11-63)
Niall MacGinnis (Cast Member)
Danger Man 2-03. Colony Three (27-10-64) 2-08. The Battle Of The Cameras (01-12-64)
The Saint 5-11. Paper Chase (09-12-66)
Nicola Pagett (Cast Member)
Man In A Suitcase 15. Burden Of Proof (03-01-67)
Nicholas Chagrin (Cast Member)
Randall & Hopkirk (Deceased) 11. The Ghost Who Saved The Bank At Monte Carlo (30-11-69)
Nicholas Courtney (Cast Member)
The Avengers 2-02. Propellant 23 (06-10-62) 5-24. Mission, Highly Improbable (18-11-67)
The Champions 04. The Experiment (16-10-68)
Doctor Who 21. The Daleks' Master Plan: 3 Episodes (20-11-65) 46. The Invasion: 6 Episodes (09-11-68) 46. The Invasion: 6 Episodes (09-11-68)
Randall & Hopkirk (Deceased) 11. The Ghost Who Saved The Bank At Monte Carlo (30-11-69)
The Saint 4-02. The Abductors (08-07-65)
Nicholas Donnelly (Cast Member)
The Saint 5-23. The Gadget Lovers (21-04-67)
Nicholas Evans (Cast Member)
Doctor Who 12. The Romans: 4 Episodes (16-01-65)
Nicholas Hawtrey (Cast Member)
Danger Man 2-11. Don't Nail Him Yet (22-12-64)
Nicholas Pennell (Cast Member)
The Saint 2-05. The Elusive Elishaw (17-10-63) 3-06. The Saint Steps In (12-11-64)
Nicholas Selby (Cast Member)
The Saint 1-11. The Man Who Was Lucky (13-12-62)
Strange Report 13. REPORT 4821 X-RAY Who Weeps For The Doctor (21-12-69)
Nicholas Smith (Cast Member)
The Avengers 5-03. Escape In Time (26-01-67) 6-03. Super Secret Cypher Snatch (09-10-68)
The Champions 24. Project Zero (12-03-69)

Doctor Who 10. Dalek Invasion Of Earth (1964)
The Saint 6-11. The Fiction Makers Part 1 (08-12-68)
Nicholas Stewart (Cast Member)
The Saint 1-03. The Careful Terrorist (18-10-62) 2-13. The Sporting Chance (12-12-63) 3-20. 3-21. Sibao (25-02-65)
Nicky Henson (Cast Member)
The Avengers 1-20. Tunnel Of Fear (05-08-61)
Nicola Pagett (Cast Member)
The Avengers 6-12. Have Guns - Will Haggle (11-12-68)
Danger Man 2-21. The Mirror's New (09-03-65)
Nicolas Chagrin (Cast Member)
The Champions 29. The Gun Runners (23-04-69)
Department S: 10. Double Death Of Charlie Crippen (14-09-69)
Nicole Shelby (Cast Member)
The Avengers 5-24 Mission Highly Improbable (18-11-67) 6-13 They Keep Killing Steed (18-12-68)
Danger Man 3-16. Dangerous Secret (13-01-66)
The Saint 5-27. The Gadic Collection (22-06-67)
Nicolette Pendrell (Cast Member)
Doctor Who 44. The Dominators: 5 Episodes (10-08-68)
Nigel Arkwright (Cast Member)
The Avengers 2-14. Dead On Course (29-12-62)
Nigel Davenport (Cast Member)
The Avengers 4-20. The Danger Makers (12-02-66) 6-05. Split (23-10-68)
Man Of The World 2-03. Double Exposure (25-05-63)
The Saint 1-12. The Charitable Countess (20-12-62) 3-16. The Rhine Maiden (21-01-65)
Nigel Green (Cast Member)
The Avengers 5-06. The Winged Avenger (18-02-67) 6-24. Fog (12-03-69)
Danger Man 1-18. The Girl Who Likes G.I.'s (15-1-61) 2-13. That's Two Of Us Sorry (5-1-64)
Ghost Squad 2-06. The Missing People (29-06-63)
Nigel Hawthorne (Cast Member)
Man Of The World 2-01. The Bandit (11-05-63)
Nigel Lambert (Cast Member)
The Avengers 4-06. The Master Minds (06-11-65) 5-19. The £50,000 Breakfast (14-10-67)
Out Of The Unknown 1-06. Come Buttercup, Come Daisy, Come…? (08-11-65)
Nigel Stock (Cast Member)
The Avengers 3-24. Concerto (07-03-64) 4-24. A Sense Of History (12-03-66)
Danger Man 3-05. Loyalty Always Pays (28-10-65)
The Prisoner 13. Do Not Forsake Me Oh My Darling (22-12-67)
The Saint 2-22. The Invisible Millionaire (13-02-64)
Nigel Rideout (Cast Member)
The Avengers 5-24. Mission, Highly Improbable (18-11-67)
Nigel Terry (Cast Member)
Randall & Hopkirk (Deceased) 17. Somebody Just Walked Over My Grave (09-01-70)
Nik Zaran (Cast Member)
The Champions 25. Desert Journey (19-03-69)
Danger Man 2-10. A Man To Be Trusted (15-12-64)
Department S: 13. The Man Who Got a New Face (15-10-69) 18. The Perfect Operation (26-12-69)
Man In A Suitcase 26. The Revolutionaries (20-03-67)
Randall & Hopkirk (Deceased) 23. The Trouble With Women (20-02-70)
The Saint 3-21. Sibao (25-02-65) 6-13. The People Importers (22-12-68)
Nike Arighi (Cast Member)
The Champions 03. Reply Box 666 (09-10-68)
Man In A Suitcase 17. Why They Killed Nolan (17-01-67) 22. Jigsaw Man (21-02-67)
Out Of The Unknown 2-01. The Machine Stops (06-10-66)
The Prisoner 07. Many Happy Returns (10-11-67)
The Saint 5-08. The Man Who Liked Lions (18-11-66)
Nina Huby (Cast Member)
Man In A Suitcase 20. Blind Spot (07-02-67)

Nita Lorraine (Cast Member)
The Avengers 6-25. Who Was That Man I Saw You With (19-03-69)
Man In A Suitcase 30. Night Flight To Andorra (17-04-67)
The Saint 5-19. To Kill a Saint (24-02-67)
Noel Coleman (Cast Member)
The Avengers 2-11. Traitor In Zebra (08-12-62) 5-17. Return Of The Cybernauts (30-09-67)
Doctor Who 50. The War Games: 10 Episodes (19-04-69)
Man Of The World 1-02. Masquerade In Spain (06-10-62)
Noel Davis (Cast Member)
The Avengers 6-14. The Interrogators (01-01-69) 5-13. A Funny Thing Happened On The Way To The Station (08-04-67)
Randall & Hopkirk (Deceased) 03. All Work & No Pay (05-10-69)
Noel Harrison (Cast Member)
Man Of The World 1-04. The Runaways (20-10-62)
Noel Howlett (Cast Member)
The Avengers 5-24. Mission, Highly Improbable (18-11-67)
Danger Man 2-05. Fair Exchange (10-11-64)
Ghost Squad 2-19. Death of a Sportsman (26-01-63)
Man In A Suitcase 11. Dead Man's Shoes (06-12-67)
Noel Johnson (Cast Member)
Danger Man 2-02. The Professionals (20-10-64)
Doctor Who 32. The Underwater Menace: 2 Episodes (21-01-67)
The Andromeda Breakthrough 6 Episodes (1962)
Out Of The Unknown 1-11. Thirteen To Centauraus
Noel Purcell (Cast Member)
The Avengers 4-08. A Surfeit Of H2o (20-11-65)
The Saint 2-16. The Wonderful War (02-01-64) 5-10. Little Girl Lost (02-12-66)
Noel Trevarthen (Cast Member)
Danger Man 1-29. The Contessa (21-05-61)
The Saint 2-12. The Well Meaning Mayor (05-12-63) 3-07. The Loving Brothers (19-11-64)
Noel Willman (Cast Member)
Danger Man 1-15. Colonel Rodriguez (18-12-60)
Noelle Middleton (Cast Member)
Man Of The World 2-04. Jungle Mission (01-06-63)
Nora Nicholson (Cast Member)
The Avengers 6-08. All Done With Mirrors (13-11-68)
Danger Man 2-04. The Galloping Major (03-11-64)
The Saint 5-01. The Queens Ransom (30-09-66)
Norma Foster (Cast Member)
Man In A Suitcase 12. Find The Lady (13-12-67)
Norma Parnell (Cast Member)
The Protectors 04. No Forwarding Address (18-04-64)
Norma West (Cast Member)
Danger Man 3-02. A Very Dangerous Game (07-10-65)
The Prisoner 08. Dance Of The Dead (17-11-67)
The Saint 5-11. Paper Chase (09-12-66)
Norman Beaton (Cast Member)
Randall & Hopkirk (Deceased) 20. Money To Burn (30-01-70)
Norman Bird (Cast Member)
The Avengers 4-14. Silent Dust (01-01-66)
The Baron 27. Roundabout (29-03-67)
Department S. 26. The Ghost Of Mary Burnham (18-02-70)
Ghost Squad 1-08. Assassin (28-10-61)
The Protectors 04. No Forwarding Address (18-04-64)
Randall & Hopkirk (Deceased) 13. But What a Sweet Little Room (14-12-69)
The Saint 2-12. The Well Meaning Mayor (05-12-63) 3-20. The Frightened Inn-Keeper (18-02-65) 6-01. The Best Laid Plans (29-09-68) 6-05. The Organization Man (27-10-67)
Norman Bowler (Cast Member)

The Avengers 5-20. Dead Man's Treasure (21-10-67)
Norman Chancer (Cast Member)
Department S: 16. The Man From X (05-11-69)
Norman Chappell (Cast Member)
The Avengers 3-07. The Gilded Cage (09-11-63) 4-10. Dial a Deadly Number (04-12-65) 5-23.
Murdersville (11-11-67) 6-24. Fog (12-03-69)
Ghost Squad 2-03. Sentences Of Death (04-05-63)
Undermind 08. Puppets Of Evil (26-06-65)
Norman Claridge (Cast Member)
Ghost Squad 2-22. The Magic Bullet (16-03-63)
Norman Eshley (Cast Member)
Department S: 07. Handicap Dead (20-04-69)
Randall & Hopkirk (Deceased) 18. Could You Recognize The Man Again (16-01-70)
Norman Florence (Cast Member)
The Champions 09. The Iron Man (20-11-68) 22. Get Me Out Of Here (26-02-69)
Danger Man 1-33. Hired Assassin (18-06-61) 1-36. Under the Lake (30-12-61)
Ghost Squad 1-01. Hong Kong Story (23-09-61)
Man Of The World 1-03. Blaze Of Glory (13-10-62)
The Saint 1-05. The Loaded Tourist (01-11-62) 3-15. The Set-Up (14-01-65) 5-04. The Reluctant
Revolution (21-10-66)
Norman Hartley (Cast Member)
Adam Adamant Lives! 05. Allah Is Not Always With You (21-07-66)
Doctor Who 39. The Ice Warriors: 4 Episodes (11-11-67)
Man In A Suitcase 17. Why They Killed Nolan (17-01-67)
Out Of The Unknown 3-03. The Last Lonely Man (21-01-69)
Norman Jones (Cast Member)
The Avengers 6-13. They Keep Killing Steed (18-12-68)
Doctor Who 39. The Ice Warriors: 4 Episodes (11-11-67)
The Saint 5-22. Island Of Chance (07-04-67)
Norman Johns (Cast Member)
The Avengers 2-24. A Chorus Of Frogs (09-03-63)
The Champions 28. The Final Countdown (16-04-69)
Ghost Squad 1-01. Hong Kong Story (23-09-61)
Norman Mitchell (Cast Member)
Man In A Suitcase 11. Dead Man's Shoes (06-12-67)
The Prisoner 06. The General (03-11-67)
The Saint 1-01. The Talented Husband (4-10-62)
Norman Pitt (Cast Member)
The Avengers 6-21. Love All (19-02-69)
The Saint 2-05. The Elusive Elishaw (17-10-63)
Norman Rodway (Cast Member)
Danger Man 3-14. The Man Who Wouldn't Talk (30-12-65)
Norman Rossington (Cast Member)
Man In A Suitcase 05. Variation On a Million Bucks Part 2 (25-10-67)
Norman Scace (Cast Member)
The Andromeda Breakthrough 2 Episodes (1962)
The Avengers 4-22. What The Butler Saw (26-02-66)
The Baron 14. There's Someone Close Behind You (28-12-67)
Ghost Squad 2-01. Interrupted Requiem (02-02-63)
The Prisoner 10. Hammer & Anvil (01-12-67)
Norman Wynne (Cast Member)
The Avengers 4-18. The Thirteenth Hole (29-01-66)
Man In A Suitcase 10. All That Glitters (29-11-67)
Nosher Powell (Cast Member)
Adam Adamant Lives! 05. Allah Is Not Always With You (21-07-66)
The Avengers 5-24. Mission, Highly Improbable (18-11-67)
The Baron 02. Epitaph For a Hero (05-10-66)
Department S: 23. A Small War Of Nerves (21-01-70)

Randall & Hopkirk (Deceased) 06. Just For The Record (26-10-69)
The Saint 4-03. The Crooked Ring (15-07-65) 5-15. The Persistent Patriots (06-01-67)
Nyree Dawn Porter (Cast Member)
Danger Man 1-16. The Island (01-01-61)
The Saint 3-04. The Scorpion (29-10-64)

O

Olaf Pooley (Cast Member)
Ghost Squad 1-09. Million Dollar Ransom (11-11-61) 2-23. The Menacing Mazurka (23-03-63)
Olga Lowe (Cast Member)
Randall & Hopkirk (Deceased) 20. Money To Burn (30-01-70)
Olive Burt (Cast Member)
Danger Man 1-28. Sabotage (14-05-61) Interpol Calling 04. The Sleeping Giant (05-10-59)
Olive Lucius (Cast Member)
The Saint 3-12. The Unkind Philanthropist (24-12-64)
Olive McFarland (Cast Member)
The Champions 17. A Case Of Lemmings (22-01-68) Danger Man 1-19. Name, Date & Place (22-01-61)
Olive Milborne (Cast Member)
The Avengers 2-18. Warlock (26-01-63)
The Saint 6-01. The Best Laid Plans (29-09-68)
Oliver Cotton (Cast Member)
Strange Report 12. REPORT 7931 SNIPER When Is Your Cousin Not? (14-12-69)
Oliver Johnston (Cast Member)
Danger Man 3-18. The Hunting Party (27-01-66)
Oliver Hamnett (Cast Member)
Department S: 12. The Treasure Of the Costa Del Sol (08-10-69)
Oliver Johnston (Cast Member)
Man Of The World 1-10. Portrait Of a Girl (01-12-62)
Oliver MacGreevy (Cast Member)
The Avengers 6-17. Killer (22-01-69)
Danger Man: 3-22. The Paper Chase (31-03-66)
Department S: 19. The Duplicated Man (03-12-69)
Ghost Squad 2-11. A First Class Way To Die (13-07-63)
Out Of The Unknown 1-05. Time In Advance (01-11-65)
The Prisoner 01. Arrival (29-09-67)
Strange Report 16. REPORT 4977 Square Root Of Evil (11-01-70)
Oliver Reed (Cast Member)
The Saint 2-24. Sophia (24-02-64)
The Third Man 3-01. A Question In Ice (27-06-64)
Olivia Hamnett (Cast Member)
Randall & Hopkirk (Deceased) 06. Just For The Record (26-10-69)
Olwen Brookes (Cast Member)
Ghost Squad 2-05. The Retirement Of The Gentle Dove (30-03-63)
Oscar Quitak (Cast Member)
Interpol Calling 13. Slave Ship (14-12-59)
Man In A Suitcase 15. Burden Of Proof (03-01-67)
Man Of The World 1-11. Specialist For the Kill (08-12-62)
Oswald Laurence (Cast Member)
The Saint 6-11. The Fiction Makers Part 1 (08-12-68)
Otto Diamant (Cast Member)
The Saint 5-05. The Helpful Pirate (28-10-66)
Otto Waldis (Cast Member)
The Third Man 1-25. How To Buy a Country (24-09-59)

P

P.G. Stephens (Cast Member)
Doctor Who 32. The Underwater Menace: 2 Episodes (21-01-67)
The Saint 5-16. The Fast Women (13-01-67)
Pamela Ann Davy (Cast Member)
The Avengers 2-05. Mission To Montreal (27-10-62) 5-07. The Living Dead (25-02-67)
Department S: 28. The Soup Of The Day (04-03-70)
Ghost Squad 2-06. The Missing People (29-06-63)
The Saint 5-19. To Kill a Saint (24-02-67)
Pamela Barney (Cast Member)
Pathfinders In Space 7 Episodes (1960)
Pathfinders To Mars 6 Episodes (1961)
Pathfinders To Venus 8 Episodes (1961)
Pamela Conway (Cast Member)
The Avengers 2-03. The Decapod (13-10-62)
Ghost Squad 2-11. A First Class Way To Die (13-07-63)
The Saint 4-01. The Checkered Flag (01-07-65) 6-04. The Desperate Diplomat (20-10-68)
Pamela Franklin (Cast Member)
Strange Report 01. REPORT 5055 CULT Murder Shrieks Out (21-09-69)
Pamela Gale (Cast Member)
Ghost Squad 2-21. Polsky (02-03-63)
Pamela Plant (Cast Member)
The Avengers 3-08. Second Sight (16-11-63)
Pamela Ryan (Cast Member)
Randall & Hopkirk (Deceased) 08. Whoever Heard Of a Ghost Dying (09-11-69)
Pamela Wardel (Cast Member)
The Avengers 3-01. Brief For Murder (28-09-63)
Pamela Sholto (Cast Member)
Adam Adamant Lives! 01 A Year For Scoundrels (20-06-66)
Pat Connell (Cast Member)
Man In A Suitcase 21. No Friend Of Mine (14-02-67)
Pat Goh (Cast Member)
Man Of The World 2-02. The Enemy (18-05-63)
Pat Gorman (Cast Member)
Adam Adamant Lives! 12. Beauty Is An Ugly Word (15-9-66) 15. The Village Of Evil (6-10-66)
Pat Keen (Cast Member)
The Prisoner 05. The Schizoid Man (27-10-67)
Pat Ryan (Cast Member)
Ghost Squad 1-04. Broken Doll (07-10-61)
Pat Spencer (Cast Member)
The Avengers 2-18. Warlock (26-01-63)
Patricia Clapton (Cast Member)
Ghost Squad 2-06. The Missing People (29-06-63)
Patricia Cutts (Cast Member)
The Third Man 1-25. How To Buy a Country (24-09-59)
Patricia Denys (Cast Member)
The Avengers 2-06. The Removal Men (03-11-62)
Patricia Donahue (Cast Member)
Danger Man 2-10. A Man To Be Trusted (15-12-64) 3-06. The Mercenaries (04-11-65)
Department S: 25. Spencer Bodily Is 60 Years Old (11-02-70)
Man Of The World 1-03. Blaze Of Glory (13-10-62)
The Saint 1-12. The Charitable Countess (20-12-62) 5-22. Island Of Chance (07-04-67)
Patricia Driscoll (Cast Member)
Danger Man 1-21. The Conspirators (05-02-61) 2-01. Yesterday's Enemies (13-10-64)
Patricia English (Cast Member)
The Avengers 2-05. Mission To Montreal (27-10-62) 3-19. The Secrets Broker (01-02-64)

5-10. Never, Never Say Die (18-03-67)
The Baron 21. The Seven Eyes Of Night (15-02-67)
The Champions 14. The Search (01-01-68)
Department S: 22. Last Train to Redbridge (14-01-70)
The Protectors 11. Who Killed Lazoryck? (06-06-64)
Patricia Haines (Cast Member)
Adam Adamant Lives! 11. Death By Appointment Only (08-09-66)
The Avengers 3-04. The Nutshell (19-10-63) 4-06. The Master Minds (6-11-65) 5-16. Who's Who (29-04-67)
The Baron 02. Epitaph For a Hero (05-10-66)
The Champions 19. The Mission (05-02-69)
Danger Man 3-01. The Black Book (30-09-65) 3-08. The Outcast (18-11-65)
Department S: 02. The Trojan Tanker (16-03-69)
Ghost Squad 2-19. Death of a Sportsman (26-01-63)
The Saint 6-20. The World Beater (09-02-69)
Randall & Hopkirk (Deceased) 17. Somebody Just Walked Over My Grave (09-01-70)
Patricia Jessel (Cast Member)
The Prisoner 09. Checkmate (14-11-67)
Patricia Kneale (Cast Member)
A For Andromeda 1-6. The Face Of The Tiger (07-11-61)
Patricia Marmont (Cast Member)
Danger Man 1-19. Name, Date & Place (22-01-61)
Ghost Squad 1-07. Still Waters (21-10-61)
Patricia Michon (Cast Member)
The Saint 3-12. The Unkind Philanthropist (24-12-64)
Patricia Mort (Cast Member)
Ghost Squad 2-06. The Missing People (29-06-63) 2-19. Death of a Sportsman (26-01-63) 2-25. The Thirteenth Girl (27-04-63)
Patricia Roc (Cast Member)
The Saint 1-01. The Talented Husband (4-10-62)
Patrick Allen (Cast Member)
The Avengers 4-18. The Thirteenth Hole (29-01-66)
The Baron 03. Something For a Rainy Day (12-10-66)
The Champions 26. Full Circle (26-03-69)
Man In A Suitcase 16. The Whisper (10-01-67)
The Saint 4-06. The Man Who Could No Die (05-08-65)
Undermind 03. The New Dimension (22-05-65)
Patrick Barr (Cast Member)
The Avengers 6-22. Stay Tuned (26-02-69) 6-23. Take Me To Your Leader (05-03-69)
Department S: 24. The Bones Of Byrom Blain (28-01-70)
Doctor Who 33. The Moonbase: 2 Episodes (18-02-67)
Randall & Hopkirk (Deceased) 25. You Can Always Find a Fall Guy (06-03-70)
Patrick Bedford (Cast Member)
The Baron 30. Farewell To Yesterday (19-04-67)
Undermind 03. The New Dimension (22-05-65)
Patrick Boxill (Cast Member)
Ghost Squad 2-08. The Man With The Delicate Hands (22-06-63)
Patrick Cargill (Cast Member)
The Avengers 4-07. The Murder Market (13-11-65) 5-02. The Fear Merchants (21-01-67)
Man In A Suitcase 12. Find The Lady (13-12-67)
The Prisoner 07. Many Happy Returns (10-11-67) 10. Hammer & Anvil (01-12-67)
Patrick Carter (Cast Member)
Ghost Squad 2-01. Interrupted Requiem (02-02-63) 2-12. Quarantine At Kavar (01-06-63)
Patrick Conner (Cast Member)
The Avengers 6-33. Bizarre (21-05-69)
Danger Man 2-14. Such Men Are Dangerous (12-1-65) 2-18. The Ubiquitous Mr Lovegrove (16-02-65)
Randall & Hopkirk (Deceased) 07. Murder Ain't What It Used To Be (02-11-69)

Patricia Denys (Cast Member)
Out Of The Unknown 2-04. Level Seven (27-10-66)
Patrick Durkin (Cast Member)
Adam Adamant Lives! 10. The Doomsday Plan (01-09-66)
The Baron 01. Diplomatic Immunity (28-09-66) 12. The Maze (14-12-67)
Department S: 28. The Soup Of The Day (04-03-70)
The Protectors 01. Landscape With Bandits (28-03-64)
The Saint 5-16. The Fast Women (13-01-67)
Patrick Halpin (Cast Member)
The Avengers 4-04. Death At Bargain Prices (23-10-65)
Patrick Holt (Cast Member)
The Avengers 3-02. The Undertakers (05-10-63)
Randall & Hopkirk (Deceased) 05. That's How Murder Snowballs (19-10-69)
The Saint 5-21. Simon & Delilah (24-03-67)
Patrick Jordan (Cast Member)
Danger Man 3-06. The Mercenaries (04-11-65)
Interpol Calling 36. Desert Hijack (30-05-60)
Man In A Suitcase 16. The Whisper (10-01-67)
Randall & Hopkirk (Deceased) 02. A Disturbing Case (28-09-69)
Patrick Kavanagh (Cast Member)
The Avengers 5-17. Return Of The Cybernauts (30-09-67)
Patrick Madden (Cast Member)
Danger Man 2-14. Such Men Are Dangerous (12-01-65)
Out Of The Unknown 2-08. Tunnel Under The World (01-12-66)
Patrick McAlinney (Cast Member)
The Saint 1-09. The Effete Angler (29-11-62)
Patrick McGoohan (Cast Member)
Danger Man All Episodes
The Prisoner All Episodes
Patrick MacNee (Cast Member)
The Avengers All Episodes
Patrick Magee (Cast Member)
The Avengers 3-07. The Gilded Cage (09-11-63)
The Champions 09. The Iron Man (20-11-68)
Patrick Marley (Cast Member)
Doctor Who 08. The Reign Of Terror: 4 Episodes (08-08-64)
Patrick Mower (Cast Member)
The Avengers 4-24. A Sense Of History (12-03-66)
Department S: 28. The Soup Of The Day (04-03-70)
Patrick Mynhardt (Cast Member)
Danger Man 1-29. The Contessa (21-05-61)
Patrick Newell (Cast Member)
The Avengers 4-01. The Town Of No Return (02-10-65) 5-14. Something Nasty In The Nursery (15-04-67) 5-17. Return Of The Cybernauts (30-09-67) 6-03. Super Secret Cypher Snatch (09-10-68) 6-04. You'll Catch Your Death (16-10-68) 6-07. False Witness (06-01-68) 6-08. All Done With Mirrors (13-11-68) 6-10. Noon Doomsday (27-11-68) 6-13. They Keep Killing Steed (18-12-68) 6-14. The Interrogators (01-01-69) 6-17. Killer (22-01-69) 6-20. Wish You Were Here (12-02-69) 6-14. The Interrogators (01-01-69) 6-21. Love All (19-02-69) 6-22. Stay Tuned (26-02-69) 6-23. Take Me To Your Leader (05-03-69) 6-24. Fog (12-03-69) 6-25. Who Was That Man I Saw You With (19-03-69) 6-26. Homicide & Old Lace (26-03-69) 6-29. Requiem (16-04-69) 6-31. Pandora (30-04-69) 6-33. Bizarre (21-05-69)
Danger Man 2-08. The Battle Of The Cameras (01-12-64)
Randall & Hopkirk (Deceased) 15. The Man From Nowhere (28-12-69)
Patrick O'Connell (Cast Member)
Adam Adamant Lives!: 02. Death Has a Thousand Faces (30-06-66)
Doctor Who 10. Dalek Invasion Of Earth (1964)
The Saint: 5-15. The Persistent Patriots (06-01-67)
Strange Report 16. REPORT 4977 Square Root Of Evil (11-01-70)

186

Patrick Parnell (Cast Member)
Out Of The Unknown 2-08. Tunnel Under The World (01-12-66)
Patrick Scanlon (Cast Member)
Out Of The Unknown 1-05. Time In Advance (01-11-65)
Patrick Troughton (Cast Member)
Adam Adamant Lives! 16. D Is For Destruction (13-06-66)
Danger Man 1-08, The Lonely Chair (30-10-60) 1-27. Bury The Dead (07-05-61)
Doctor Who all episodes (1968-1969)
Interpol Calling 02. The Thirteen Innocents (21-09-59)
Man Of The World 1-01. Death Of a Conference (29-09-62)
The Saint 2-18. The Romantic Matron (16-01-64) 5-02. Interlude In Venice (07-10-66)
The Third Man 3-01. A Question In Ice (27-06-64)
Patrick Waddington (Cast Member)
Department S: 11. Who Plays The Dummy (01-10-69)
Patrick Westwood (Cast Member)
The Avengers 6-22. Stay Tuned (26-02-69)
Department S: 19. The Duplicated Man (03-12-69)
The Saint 2-16. The Wonderful War (02-01-64) 3-01. The Miracle Tea Party (8-10-64) 5-01. The Queens Ransom (30-09-66)
Patrick Whyte (Cast Member)
The Saint 5-09. The Better Mouse Trap (25-11-66)
Patrick Wymark (Cast Member)
The Champions 06. Operation Deep Freeze (30-10-68)
Danger Man 1-10. An Affair Of State (13-11-60)
Man Of The World 1-09. The Mindreader (24-11-62)
Patsy Rowlands (Cast Member)
The Avengers 6-21. Love All (19-02-69)
Danger Man 1-32. The Actor (11-06-61) 2-18. The Ubiquitous Mr Lovegrove (16-02-65)
Out Of The Unknown 1-06. Come Buttercup, Come Daisy, Come…? (08-11-65)
Patsy Smart (Cast Member)
The Avengers 6-24. Fog (12-03-69)
Danger Man 1-29 The Contessa (21-5-61) 2-15 Whatever Happened To George Foster (19-1-65)
Man Of The World 1-07. The Highland Story (10-11-62)
The Prisoner 01. Arrival (29-09-67) 08. Dance Of The Dead (17-11-67)
Patti Brooks (Cast Member)
Strange Report 02. REPORT 0649 SKELETON Let Sleeping Heroes Lie (28-09-69)
Paul Anil (Cast Member)
The Avengers 2-21. The White Dwarf (16-02-63)
Doctor Who 32. The Underwater Menace: 2 Episodes (21-01-67)
Paul Armstron (Cast Member)
Danger Man 2-17. The Affair At Castelevara (09-02-65) 3-08. The Outcast (18-11-65)
Paul Beradi (Cast Member)
Department S: 21. Death On Reflection (17-12-69)
Paul Bertoya (Cast Member)
Man In A Suitcase 22. Jigsaw Man (21-02-67)
Randall & Hopkirk (Deceased) 12. For The Girl Who Has Everything (07-12-69)
Paul Blomey (Cast Member)
The Avengers 3-22. The Outside-In Man (22-02-64)
Paul Carpenter (Cast Member)
The Saint 2-26. The Ever Loving Spouse (12-03-64)
Paul Curran (Cast Member)
Danger Man 3-19 Two Birds With One Bullet (10-3-66) 3-21 The Man With The Foot (24-3-66)
The Saint 2-17. The Noble Sportsman (09-01-64)
Undermind 03. The New Dimension (22-05-65)
Paul Daneman (Cast Member)
Danger Man 1-26. The Journey Ends Halfway (30-04-61)
The Saint 6-01. The Best Laid Plans (29-09-68)
Paul Danquah (Cast Member)

The Avengers 4-16. Small Game For Big Hunters (15-01-65)
Danger Man 2-22. Parallel Lines Sometimes Meet (16-03-65) 3-06. The Mercenaries (04-11-65) 3-12. The Man On The Beach (16-12-65)
Paul Darrow (Cast Member)
The Saint 5-27. The Gadic Collection (22-06-67)
Paul Dawkins (Cast Member)
The Avengers 3-13. Death a La Carte (21-12-63) 5-18. Death's Door (07-10-67)
The Baron 23. The Edge Of Fear (01-03-67)
Public Eye 2-02. Don't Forget You're Mine (09-07-66)
Paul Duval (Cast Member)
The Avengers 2-06. The Removal Men (03-11-62)
Paul Eden (Cast Member)
The Avengers 2-03. The Decapod (13-10-62) 2-17. Box Of Tricks (19-01-63)
The Protectors 08. Freedom! (16-05-64)
Paul Eddington (Cast Member)
The Avengers 2-16. Immortal Clay (12-01-63) 5-14. Something Nasty In The Nursery (15-4-67)
The Champions 30. Autokill (30-04-69)
Danger Man 3-20. I Am Afraid You Have The Wrong Number (17-03-66)
Interpol Calling 18. The Thousand Mile Alibi (18-01-60)
The Prisoner 01. Arrival (29-09-67)
Paul Elliott (Cast Member)
Ghost Squad 2-17. Mr Five Per Cent (06-04-63)
Paul Ferris (Cast Member)
The Baron 01. Diplomatic Immunity (28-09-66) Epitaph For a Hero (05-10-66) 04. Red Horse, Red Rider (19-10-66) 08. The Persuaders (16-11-66) 10. The Legends of Ammak (30-11-66) 11. Samurai West (07-12-66) 13. Portrait Of Louisa (21-12-67) 30. Farewell To Yesterday (19-4-67)
Paul Gillard (Cast Member)
The Avengers 5-01. From Venus With Love (14-01-67)
Paul Greenhalgh (Cast Member)
The Saint 6-08. The Master Plan (17-11-68)
Paul Grist (Cast Member)
The Champions 10. The Ghost Plane (27-11-68)
Paul Hansard (Cast Member)
The Avengers 2-15. Intercrime (05-01-63)
The Champions 19. The Mission (05-02-69)
Man In A Suitcase 19. Somebody Loses, Somebody… Wins? (31-01-67)
Paul Hardtmuth (Cast Member)
Danger Man 1-26. The Journey Ends Halfway (30-04-61)
Paul Hardwick (Cast Member)
The Avengers 5-14. Something Nasty In The Nursery (15-04-67)
Paul Harris (Cast Member)
The Baron 14. There's Someone Close Behind You (28-12-67)
Paul Massie (Cast Member)
The Avengers 4-02. The Gravediggers (09-01-65)
Paul Maxwell (Cast Member)
The Baron 02. Epitaph For a Hero (05-10-66) 28. The Man Outside (05-04-67)
The Champions 20. The Silent Enemy (12-02-69)
Danger Man 1-18. The Girl Who Likes G.I.'s (15-01-61) 1-24. The Relaxed Informer (16-04-61)
Ghost Squad 1-08. Assassin (28-10-61)
Man Of The World 1-11. Specialist For the Kill (08-12-62) 1-13. Shadow Of the Wall (22-12-62) 2-04. Jungle Mission (01-06-63)
Randall & Hopkirk (Deceased) 23. The Trouble With Women (20-02-70)
The Saint 5-05. The Helpful Pirate (28-10-66)
Undermind 01. Instance One (08-05-65)
Paul Mead (Cast Member)
The Avengers 2-11. Traitor In Zebra (08-12-62) 3-23. The Charmers (29-02-64)
Paul Rogers (Cast Member)
Danger Man 1-23. The Gallows Tree (09-04-61)

Paul Stanton (Cast Member)
The Baron 07. The Killing (Part 2) (09-11-66)
Paul Stassino (Cast Member)
The Avengers 2-03. The Decapod (13-10-62)
The Baron 24. Long Ago & Far Away (08-03-67)
The Champions 29. The Gun Runners (23-04-69)
Danger Man 1-17. Find & Return (08-01-61) 1-27. Bury The Dead (07-05-61)
Department S: 09. Black Out (17-09-69)
Ghost Squad 1-03. Ticket For Blackmail (09-09-61) 1-10. Catspaw (05-01-61)
Interpol Calling 21. The Collector (08-02-60)
The Saint 1-09. The Effete Angler (29-11-62) 2-09. The King Of The Beggars (14-11-63) 3-09. The
Death Penalty (3-12-64) 5-02. Interlude In Venice (7-10-66) 6-17. The Ex-King Of Diamonds (19-1-68)
Paul Tann (Cast Member)
Danger Man 3-02. A Very Dangerous Game (07-10-65)
Paul Whitsun-Jones (Cast Member)
The Avengers 3-03. Man With Two Shadows (12-10-63) 3-17. The Wringer (18-01-64) 4-15. Room
Without a View (08-01-65) 6-24. Fog (12-03-69)
Department S: 03. Cellar Full Of Silence (23-03-69) 21. Death On Reflection (17-12-69)
Man Of The World 1-12. A Family Affair (15-12-62)
The Saint 1-10. The Golden Journey (06-12-62) 2-02. Starring The Saint (26-09-63) 2-04. Teresa (10-
10-63) 3-13. The Damsel In Distress (31-12-64)
Paul Williamason (Cast Member)
The Saint 5-11. Paper Chase (09-12-66)
Paula Byrne (Cast Member)
Interpol Calling 20. Game For Three Hands (01-02-60) 34. Dressed To Kill (06-05-60)
Man In A Suitcase 17. Why They Killed Nolan (17-01-67)
Paula Li Shiu (Cast Member)
Danger Man 3-25. Shinda Shima (26-02-67)
Pauline Challoner (Cast Member)
Public Eye 4-04. My Lifes My Own (20-08-69) 4-05. Case For The Defence (27-08-69)
Pauline Clifford (Cast Member)
The Saint 5-24. A Double In Diamonds (05-05-67)
Pauline Collins (Cast Member)
The Saint 5-09. The Better Mouse Trap (25-11-66)
Pauline Delaney (Cast Member)
The Avengers 2-19. The Golden Egg (02-02-63) 5-19. The £50,000 Breakfast (14-10-67)
Public Eye 2-02. Don't Forget You're Mine (09-07-66) 4-01. Welcome To Brighton? (30-07-69) 4-02.
Divide & Conquer (06-08-69) 4-03. Paid In Full (13-08-69) 4-04. My Life's My Own (20-08-69) 4-06.
The Comedian's Graveyard (03-09-69) 4-07. A Fixed Address (19-06-69)
Pauline Jameson (Cast Member)
Callan 2-04. The Little Bits & Pieces Of Love (29-01-69)
Undermind 02. Flowers Of Havoc (15-05-65)
Pauline Letts (Cast Member)
Danger Man 1-24. The Relaxed Informer (16-04-61)
Pauline Long (Cast Member)
Strange Report 06. REPORT 3906 COVER-GIRLS Last Years Model (26-10-69)
Pauline Loring (Cast Member)
Adam Adamant Lives! 13. The League Of Uncharitable Ladies (12-09-66)
Pauline Munro (Cast Member)
Adam Adamant Lives! 04. The Sweet Smell Of Disaster (14-07-07)
The Saint 5-25. The Power Artists (19-05-67)
Pauline Stroud (Cast Member)
Ghost Squad 2-04. The Golden Silence (08-06-63)
Pauline Yates (Cast Member)
Ghost Squad 2-20. P.G.7. (06-07-63)
Strange Report 16. REPORT 4977 Square Root Of Evil (11-01-70)
Pearl Catlin (Cast Member)
The Avengers 3-25. Espirit de Corps (14-03-64)

Pearl Prescod (Cast Member)
Danger Man 1-15. Colonel Rodriguez (18-12-60) 1-39. Deadline (20-01-62) 3-12. The Man On The Beach (16-12-65) 2-22. Parallel Lines Sometimes Meet (16-03-65)
The Saint 1-07. The Arrow Of God (15-11-62)
Peggy Ann Clifford (Cast Member)
Adam Adamant Lives! 04. The Sweet Smell Of Disaster (14-07-07)
Peggy Marsall (Cast Member)
The Avengers 2-14 Dead On Course (29-12-62) Ghost Squad 2-25 The Thirteenth Girl (27-4-63)
Peggy Scott Sanders (Cast Member)
The Avengers 4-04. Death At Bargain Prices (23-10-65)
Strange Report 03. REPORT 2641 HOSTAGE If You Won't Learn Die (05-10-69)
Penelope Horner (Cast Member)
The Avengers 6-18. The Morning After (29-10-69)
The Saint 3-15. The Set-Up (14-01-65) 5-03. The Russian Prisoner (14-10-66) 5-11. Paper Chase (09-12-66)
Penelope Keith (Cast Member)
The Avengers 4-07. The Murder Market (13-11-65) 5-14. Something Nasty In The Nursery (15-04-67) 6-23. Take Me To Your Leader (05-03-69)
Penelope Lee (Cast Member)
The Avengers 2-12. The Big Thinker (15-12-62)
Penny Bird (Cast Member)
The Avengers 5-20. Dead Man's Treasure (21-10-67)
Department S: 02. The Trojan Tanker (16-03-69)
Ghost Squad 2-23. The Menacing Mazurka (23-03-63)
Penny Brahams (Cast Member)
Randall & Hopkirk (Deceased) 16. When The Spirit Moves You (02-01-70)
Penny Service (Cast Member)
Strange Report 07. REPORT 3424 EPIDEMIC A Most Curious Crime (02-11-69)
Penny Spencer (Cast Member)
Man In A Suitcase 04. Variation On a Million Bucks Part 1 (18-10-67)
Percy Herbert (Cast Member)
Danger Man 1-21. The Conspirators (05-02-61) 3-06. The Mercenaries (04-11-65)
The Saint 1-03. The Careful Terrorist (18-10-62) 3-20. The Frightened Inn-Keeper (18-02-65)
Peter Arne (Cast Member)
The Avengers 2-18. Warlock (26-1-63) 2-19. The Golden Egg (2-2-63) 4-15. Room Without a View (8-01-65)
The Baron 26. The Long, Long Day (22-03-67)
The Champions 06. Operation Deep Freeze (30-10-68)
Danger Man 1-35. Find & Destroy (23-12-61) 2-03. Colony Three (27-10-64) 3-02. A Very Dangerous Game (07-10-65) 3-06. The Mercenaries (04-11-65)
Department S 10 Double Death Of Charlie Crippen (14-9-69) 28 The Soup Of The Day (4-3-70)
Man In A Suitcase 18. The Boston Square (24-01-67)
Man Of The World 1-05. The Frontier (27-10-62)
The Saint 3-05. The Revolution Racket (05-11-64)
Peter Ashmore (Cast Member)
The Saint 6-11. The Fiction Makers Part 1 (08-12-68)
Peter Badger (Cast Member)
Public Eye 4-06. The Comedian's Graveyard (03-09-69)
Peter Barkworth (Cast Member)
The Avengers 6-18. The Morning After (29-10-69)
Public Eye 1-02. Nobody Kill Santa Claus (30-01-65)
Undermind 06. Intent To Destroy (12-06-65)
Peter Bathurst (Cast Member)
Adam Adamant Lives! 18. Black Echo (07-01-67)
Peter Barkworth (Cast Member)
The Avengers 3-09. The Medicine Men (23-11-63) 5-09. The Correct Way To Kill (11-03-67)
The Protectors 10. The Deadly Chameleon (30-5-64)
Peter Bayliss (Cast Member)

The Avengers 4-07. The Murder Market (13-11-65) 6-32. Get-a-Way (14-05-69)
Peter Bennett (Cast Member)
Man In A Suitcase 10. All That Glitters (29-11-67)
Out Of The Unknown 1-11. Thirteen To Centauraus (13-12-63)
Peter Birrel (Cast Member)
Man In A Suitcase 13. The Bridge (20-12-67)
The Saint 5-21. Simon & Delilah (24-03-67)
Peter Blythe (Cast Member)
The Avengers 4-24. A Sense Of History (12-03-66) 5-22. The Positive Negative Man (4-11-67)
Callan 2-02. The Most Promising Girl Of Her Year (15-01-69)
Man In A Suitcase 07. Sweet Sue (08-11-67)
Peter Bowles (Cast Member)
The Avengers 3-08. Second Sight (16-11-63) 4-10. Dial a Deadly Number (04-12-65) 5-03. Escape In Time (26-01-67) 6-32. Get-a-Way (14-05-69)
The Baron 17. Time To Kill (18-01-67) 19. You Can't Win Them All (01-02-67)
Department S: 01. Six Days (09-03-69)
The Prisoner 03. A.B. & C. (13-10-67)
Out Of The Unknown 1-10. Some Lapse In Time (06-12-65)
The Protectors 02. The Bottle Shop (04-04-64)
The Saint 5-18. The Art Collectors (27-01-67)
Peter Brace (Cast Member)
The Baron 29. Countdown (12-04-67)
Danger Man 3-16. Dangerous Secret (13-01-66)
Man In A Suitcase 08. Essay In Evil (15-11-67) 18. The Boston Square (24-01-67)
The Prisoner 01. Arrival (29-09-67) 04. Free For All (20-10-67)
The Saint 5-05. The Helpful Pirate (28-10-66) 5-26. When Spring Is Sprung (02-06-67)
Peter Brayham (Cast Member)
Danger Man 3-16. Dangerous Secret (13-01-66)
The Prisoner 03. A.B. & C. (13-10-67)
Peter Brett (Cast Member)
The Baron 30. Farewell To Yesterday (19-04-67)
Department S: 06. The Man In The Elegant Room (13-04-69)
Peter Bromilow (Cast Member)
The Avengers 6-10. Noon Doomsday (27-11-68)
Department S: 01. Six Days (09-03-69)
Peter Burton (Cast Member)
The Avengers 4-16. Small Game For Big Hunters (15-01-65)
Man In A Suitcase 02. The Sitting Pigeon (04-10-67)
The Saint 5-23. The Gadget Lovers (21-04-67)
Peter Butterworth (Cast Member)
Danger Man 2-18. The Ubiquitous Mr Lovegrove (16-02-65)
Doctor Who 17. The Time Meddler: 4 Episodes (03-07-65)
Peter Cellier (Cast Member)
Callan 2-06. Heir Apparent (12-02-69)
Public Eye 4-02. Divide & Conquer (06-08-69) 4-03. Paid In Full (13-08-69)
Randall & Hopkirk (Deceased) 21. The Ghost Talks (06-02-70)
Strange Report 15. REPORT 4407 No Choice For The Donor (04-01-70)
Peter Clay (Cast Member)
The Avengers 5-24. Mission, Highly Improbable (18-11-67)
Peter Copley (Cast Member)
The Avengers 2-21. The White Dwarf (16-02-63) 6-08. All Done With Mirrors (13-11-68)
The Champions 24. Project Zero (12-03-69)
Danger Man: 2-01. Yesterday's Enemies (13-10-64)
Department S: 21. Death On Reflection (17-12-69)
Out Of The Unknown 1-03. Stranger In the Family (18-10-65)
The Saint 3-18. The Sign Of The Claw (04-02-65)
Peter Craze (Cast Member)
Doctor Who 15. The Space Museum: 4 Episodes (24-04-65)

Strange Report 03. REPORT 2641 HOSTAGE If You Won't Learn Die (05-10-69)
Peter Cushing (Cast Member)
The Avengers 5-17. Return Of The Cybernauts (30-09-67)
Peter Dennis (Cast Member)
The Avengers 5-10. Never, Never Say Die (18-03-67)
Peter Diamond (Cast Member)
The Avengers 4-03. The Cybernauts (16-10-65) 4-26. Honey For The Prince (26-03-66)
Doctor Who 12. The Romans: 4 Episodes (16-01-65)
Ghost Squad 2-19. Death of a Sportsman (26-01-63) 2-25. The Thirteenth Girl (27-04-63)
Out Of The Unknown 1-07. Sucker Bait (15-11-65)
The Saint 2-18. The Romantic Matron (16-01-64) 3-03. Jeannine (22-10-64)
Peter Dolphin (Cast Member)
Danger Man 1-28. Sabotage (14-05-61)
Peter Ducrow (Cast Member)
A For Andromeda 1-6. The Face Of The Tiger (07-11-61)
Adam Adamant Lives! 01. A Year For Scoundrels (20-06-66) 18. Black Echo (07-01-67) 29. A Sinister Sort Of Service (25-03-67)
Peter Duguid (Cast Member)
The Saint 2-06. Marcia (24-10-63)
Peter Dyneley (Cast Member)
Ghost Squad 1-09. Million Dollar Ransom (11-11-61) 2-11. A First Class Way To Die (13-07-63)
Interpol Calling 20. Game For Three Hands (01-02-60)
Man Of The World 1-03. Blaze Of Glory (13-10-62)
The Saint 1-03. The Careful Terrorist (18-10-62) 2-14. The Bunco Artists (19-12-63) 5-19. To Kill a Saint (24-02-67)
Peter Elliott (Cast Member)
The Avengers 5-13. A Funny Thing Happened On The Way To The Station (08-04-67) 5-20. Dead Man's Treasure (21-10-67) 5-21. You Have Just Been Murdered (28-10-67) 6-12. Have Guns Will Haggle (11-12-68)
Danger Man 2-16. A Room in The Basement (02-02-65)
Department S: 12. The Treasure Of the Costa Del Sol (08-10-69)
Ghost Squad 2-10. The Grand Duchess (11-05-63)
Randall & Hopkirk (Deceased) 16. When The Spirit Moves You (02-01-70)
The Saint 2-18. The Romantic Matron (16-01-64) 3-03. Jeannine (22-10-64) 5-08. The Man Who Liked Lions (18-11-66)
Peter Ellis (Cast Member)
The Saint 5-10. Little Girl Lost (02-12-66)
Peter Evans (Cast Member)
The Avengers 4-04. Death At Bargain Prices (23-10-65)
Peter Exposite (Cast Member)
The Saint 2-04. Teresa (10-10-63)
Peter Fontaine (Cast Member)
The Avengers 3-14. Dressed To Kill (28-12-63)
Out Of The Unknown 2-03. Lambda One (20-10-66)
The Saint 2-19. Luella (23-01-64)
Peter Forbes-Robertson (Cast Member)
The Baron 14. There's Someone Close Behind You (28-12-67)
Peter Fraser (Cast Member)
Ghost Squad 2-06. The Missing People (29-06-63)
Doctor Who 10. Dalek Invasion Of Earth (1964)
Out Of The Unknown 1-02. The Counterfeit Man (11-10-65)
Peter Gill (Cast Member)
City Beneath The Sea 1 episode (1962)
Danger Man 2-18. The Ubiquitous Mr Lovegrove (16-02-65)
Peter Graves (Cast Member)
Department S: 23. A Small War Of Nerves (21-01-70)
Peter Hager (Cast Member)
Man In A Suitcase 19. Somebody Loses, Somebody… Wins? (31-01-67)

Peter Halliday (Cast Member)
A For Andromeda 1-6. The Face Of The Tiger (07-11-61)
The Andromeda Breakthrough 6 Episodes (1962)
Avengers 6-10. Noon Doomsday (27-11-68)
Danger Man 3-07. Judgment Day (11-11-65)
Doctor Who 46. The Invasion: 6 Episodes (09-11-68)
Ghost Squad 2-11. A First Class Way To Die (13-07-63)
Man In A Suitcase 21. No Friend Of Mine (14-02-67)
Out Of The Unknown 3-03. The Last Lonely Man (21-01-69)
The Saint 5-04. The Reluctant Revolution (21-10-66)
Peter Henchie (Cast Member)
A For Andromeda 1-6. The Face Of The Tiger (07-11-61)
Peter Holmes (Cast Member)
Undermind 01. Instance One (08-05-65)
Peter Howell (Cast Member)
The Avengers 4-04. Death At Bargain Prices (23-10-65)
The Champions 13. Twelve Hours (18-12-68)
The Prisoner 06. The General (03-11-67)
Peter Hughes (Cast Member)
The Avengers 3-09. The Medicine Men (23-11-63) 4-22. What The Butler Saw (26-02-66)
Danger Man 3-12. The Man On The Beach (16-12-65)
Ghost Squad 2-06. The Missing People (29-06-63)
Randall & Hopkirk (Deceased) 08. Whoever Heard Of a Ghost Dying (09-11-69)
Undermind 09. Test For The Future (03-07-65)
Peter Hutchins (Cast Member)
The Baron 24. Long Ago & Far Away (08-03-67)
Peter Illing (Cast Member)
Danger Man 2-09. No Marks For Servility (08-12-64)
Interpol Calling 02. The Thirteen Innocents (21-09-59)
The Saint 1-02. The Latin Touch (11-10-62) 4-07. The Saint Bids Diamonds (12-08-65) 5-04. The Reluctant Revolution (21-10-66)
Peter Jeffrey (Cast Member)
Adam Adamant Lives! 12. Beauty Is An Ugly Word (15-09-66)
The Avengers 4-15 Room Without a View (8-1-65) 5-15 The Joker (22-04-67) 6-02. Game (2-10-68)
The Saint 2-22. The Invisible Millionaire (13-2-64) 3-22. The Crime Of The Century (04-03-65)
Strange Report 05. REPORT 8319 GRENADE What Price Change? (19-10-69)
Peter Jesson (Cast Member)
The Avengers 6-07. False Witness (06-01-68)
Danger Man 2-03. Colony Three (27-10-64)
Randall & Hopkirk (Deceased) 26. The Smile Behind The Veil (13-03-70)
Peter Jones (Cast Member)
The Avengers 4-18. The Thirteenth Hole (29-01-66) 6-19. The Curious Case Of The Countless Clues (05-02-69)
Man Of The World 1-06. The Sentimental Agent (03-11-62)
Randall & Hopkirk (Deceased) 09. The House On Haunted Hill (16-11-69)
Strange Report 14. REPORT 2493 Whose Pretty Girl Are You? (28-12-69)
Peter King (Cast Member)
A For Andromeda 1-6. The Face Of The Tiger (07-11-61)
Out Of The Unknown 3 -08. Little Black Bag (25-02-69)
Peter Kriss (Cast Member)
Man Of The World 2-01. The Bandit (11-05-63)
The Saint 2-24. Sophia (24-02-64)
Peter Kristof (Cast Member)
The Saint 6-15. Vendetta For The Saint Part 1 (05-01-68) 6-16. Vendetta For The Saint Part 2 (12-01-68)
Peter Laird (Cast Member)
Doctor Who 43. The Wheel in Space: 2 Episodes (11-05-68)
Peter Lawrence (Cast Member)

Department S: 04. The Pied Piper Of Hambledown (30-03-69)
Randall & Hopkirk (Deceased) 26. The Smile Behind The Veil (13-03-70)
The Saint 2-22. The Invisible Millionaire (13-2-64) 6-09. The House On Dragons Rock (24-11-68)
Peter Madden (Cast Member)
The Avengers 4-15. Room Without a View (08-01-65) 6-31. Pandora (30-04-69)
Danger Man: 2-01. Yesterday's Enemies (13-10-64) 2-08. The Battle Of The Cameras (01-12-64) 2-09. No Marks For Servility (08-12-64) 2-19. It's Up To The Lady (23-02-65)
Man Of The World 2-05. In The Picture (08-06-63)
Out Of The Unknown 1-05. Time In Advance (01-11-65)
The Prisoner 04. Free For All (20-10-67)
The Saint 5-01. The Queens Ransom (30-09-66) 6-15. Vendetta For The Saint Part 1 (05-01-68) 6-16. Vendetta For The Saint Part 2 (12-01-68)
Peter Murray (Cast Member)
Danger Man 1-09. The Sanctuary (06-11-60)
Peter Myers (Cast Member)
Department S: 11. Who Plays The Dummy (01-10-69)
Peter Perkins (Cast Member)
The Saint 2-27. The Saint Sees It Through (19-03-64)
Peter Porteous (Cast Member)
The Avengers 3-23. The Charmers (29-02-64)
Peter Purves (Cast Member)
Doctor Who 17. The Time Meddler: 4 Episodes (03-07-65) 18. Galaxy 4: Air Lock (25-09-65) 21. The Daleks' Master Plan: 3 Episodes (20-11-65) 23. The Ark: 4 Episodes (05-03-66) 24. The Celestial Toymaker: The Final Test (23-04-66) 25. The Gunfighters: 4 Episodes (30-04-66)
Peter Reynolds (Cast Member)
Department S: 06. The Man In The Elegant Room (13-04-69)
Peter Russell (Cast Member)
Doctor Who 17. The Time Meddler: 4 Episodes (03-07-65)
Peter Sallis (Cast Member)
The Avengers 3-17. The Wringer (18-01-64)
Danger Man 1-35. Find & Destroy (23-12-61)
Peter Sanders (Cast Member)
Doctor Who 15. The Space Museum: 4 Episodes (24-04-65)
Peter Sinclair (Cast Member)
Man Of The World 1-07. The Highland Story (10-11-62)
Peter Stephens (Cast Member)
The Avengers 6-21. Love All (19-02-69)
Danger Man 1-16. The Island (01-01-61) 3-22. The Paper Chase (31-03-66)
Doctor Who 24. The Celestial Toymaker: The Final Test (23-04-66)
Out Of The Unknown 1-05. Time In Advance (01-11-65)
Randall & Hopkirk (Deceased) 10. When Did You Start To Stop Seeing Things? (23-11-69)
Peter Swanwick (Cast Member)
The Avengers 6-09. Legacy Of Death (20-11-68)
Danger Man 1-11. The Key (20-11-60) 3-22. The Paper Chase (31-03-66)
Man In A Suitcase 30. Night Flight To Andorra (17-04-67)
The Prisoner 01. Arrival (29-09-67) 02. The Chimes Of Big Ben (06-10-67) 06. The General (03-11-67) 10. Hammer & Anvil (01-12-67) 12. A Change Of Mind (15-12-67) 16. Once Upon a Time (25-01-67) 17. Fall Out (01-02-68)
Peter Thomas (Cast Member)
The Avengers 4-16. Small Game For Big Hunters (15-01-65) 5-18. Death's Door (07-10-67) 6-08. All Done With Mirrors (13-11-68)
The Baron 06. Masquerade (Part 1) (02-11-66) 07. The Killing (Part 2) (09-11-66)
Department S: 12. The Treasure Of the Costa Del Sol (08-10-69)
Peter Thornton (Cast Member)
Danger Man 1-04. The Blue Veil (02-10-60)
Out Of The Unknown 1-03. Stranger In the Family (18-10-65)
Peter Vaughan (Cast Member)
Adam Adamant Lives! 10. The Doomsday Plan (01-09-66)

194

The Avengers 6-28. My Wildest Dream (07-04-69)
Interpol Calling 08. Diamond S.O.S. (02-11-59)
Man In A Suitcase 08. Essay In Evil (15-11-67)
Randall & Hopkirk (Deceased) 04. Never Trust a Ghost (12-10-69)
The Saint 3-06. The Saint Steps In (12-11-64)
Strange Report 07. REPORT 3424 EPIDEMIC A Most Curious Crime (02-11-69)
Peter Welch (Cast Member)
Callan 2-05. Let's Kill Everybody (05-02-69)
Danger Man 1-34. The Deputy Coyannis Story (16-12-61)
Out Of The Unknown 3-03. The Last Lonely Man (21-01-69)
Strange Report 10. REPORT 8944 HAND A Matter Of Witchcraft (30-11-69)
Peter Whitaker (Cast Member)
Doctor Who 35. The Faceless Ones: Episode 1 (08-04-67)
Peter Williams (Cast Member)
City Beneath The Sea All episodes (1962)
Ghost Squad 1-02. Bullet With My Name On It (16-09-61)
Man In A Suitcase 21. No Friend Of Mine (14-02-67)
Pathfinders In Space (1960) 7 Episodes
Pathfinders To Mars 1 Episode (1961)
The Protectors 11. Who Killed Lazoryck? (6-6-64)
Public Eye 1-02. Nobody Kill Santa Claus (30-01-65)
Peter Wyngarde
Department S All Episodes (1969)
The Prisoner 09. Checkmate (14-11-67)
The Saint 5-08. The Man Who Liked Lions (18-11-66) 5-27. The Gadic Collection (22-06-67)
Peter Woodthorpe (Cast Member)
Man In A Suitcase 30. Night Flight To Andorra (17-04-67)
Peter Wyatt (Cast Member)
Ghost Squad 2-22. The Magic Bullet (16-03-63)
Peter Wyngarde (Cast Member)
The Avengers 4-21. A Touch Of Brimstone (19-02-66) 5-11. Epic (25-03-67) The Baron 10. The Legends of Ammak (30-11-66) The Champions 02. The Invisible Man (02-10-68)
Petra Davies (Cast Member)
Ghost Squad 1-03. Ticket For Blackmail (09-09-61)
Out Of The Unknown 2-08. Tunnel Under The World (01-12-66)
Phil Brown (Cast Member)
Interpol Calling 03. The Money Game (28-09-59)
Phil Oxnam (Cast Member)
Ghost Squad 2-17. Mr Five Per Cent (06-04-63)
Phil Parkes (Cast Member)
The Saint 6-12. The Fiction Makers Part 2 (15-12-68)
Philip Anthony (Cast Member)
The Avengers 3-03. Man With Two Shadows (12-10-63) 3-22. The Outside-In Man (22-02-64)
The Saint 2-06. Marcia (24-10-63)
Philip Becker (Cast Member)
The Avengers 2-03. The Decapod (13-10-62)
Philip Bond (Cast Member)
The Avengers 6-14. The Interrogators (01-01-69)
The Champions 04. The Experiment (16-10-68)
Doctor Who 02. The Daleks: 5 Episodes (21-12-63)
Man In A Suitcase 14. The Man Who Stood Still (27-12-67) 23. Web With Four Spiders (28-02-67)
The Saint 2-05. The Elusive Elishaw (17-10-63)
Philip Brack (Cast Member)
Public Eye 4-07. A Fixed Address (19-06-69)
Philip Dunbar (Cast Member)
The Avengers 6-18. The Morning After (29-10-69)
Philip Guard (Cast Member)
The Avengers 2-07. The Mauritius Penny (10-11-62)

Ghost Squad 2-26. Sabotage (20-04-63)
Phillip James (Cast Member)
Randall & Hopkirk (Deceased) 10. When Did You Start To Stop Seeing Things? (23-11-69)
Philip Johns (Cast Member)
The Avengers 4-07. The Murder Market (13-11-65)
Philip Latham (Cast Member)
The Andromeda Breakthrough 2 Episodes (1962)
The Avengers 2-21. The White Dwarf (16-02-63) 4-15. Room Without a View (08-01-65)
Danger Man 1-01. View From The Villa (11-09-60)
The Saint 2-05. The Elusive Elishaw (17-10-63) 3-04. The Scorpion (29-10-64)
Undermind 08. Puppets Of Evil (26-06-65)
Phillip Lennard (Cast Member)
Randall & Hopkirk (Deceased) 14. Who Killed Cock Robin? (21-12-69)
Philip Levene (Cast Member)
The Avengers 5-16. Who's Who (29-04-67)
Ghost Squad 2-05. The Retirement Of The Gentle Dove (30-03-63)
Philip Locke (Cast Member)
The Avengers 1-15. The Frighteners (27-11-61) 3-18. Mandrake (25-01-64) 5-01. From Venus With Love (14-01-67)
The Baron 29. Countdown (12-04-67)
The Champions 21. The Body Snatchers (19-02-69)
Department S: 18. The Perfect Operation (26-12-69)
The Saint 6-11. The Fiction Makers Part 1 (8-12-68) 6-12. The Fiction Makers Part 2 (15-12-68)
Philip Madoc (Cast Member)
The Avengers 2-03. The Decapod (13-10-62) 2-25. Six Hands Across a Table (16-03-63) 3-05. Death Of a Batman (26-01-63) 5-09. The Correct Way To Kill (11-03-67) 6-28. My Wildest Dream (07-04-69)
The Baron 14. There's Someone Close Behind You (28-12-67)
The Champions 22. Get Me Out Of Here (26-02-69)
Doctor Who 47. The Krotons: 4 Episodes (28-12-68)
Man In A Suitcase 19. Somebody Loses, Somebody…Wins? (31-01-67) 27. Who's Mad Now (27-03-67)
Public Eye 1-12. The Morning Wasn't So Hot (10-04-65)
Randall & Hopkirk (Deceased) 04. Never Trust a Ghost (12-10-69)
The Saint 5-20. The Counterfeit Countess (03-03-67)
Philip Mosca (Cast Member)
The Avengers 2-18. Warlock (26-01-63)
Philip Needs (Cast Member)
The Saint 1-12. The Charitable Countess (20-12-62)
Philip O'Flynn (Cast Member)
The Saint 2-25. The Gentle Ladies (05-03-64)
Philip Ray (Cast Member)
Doctor Who 48. The Seeds Of Death: 6 Episodes (25-01-69)
Ghost Squad 1-02. Bullet With My Name On It (16-09-61) 2-05. The Retirement Of The Gentle Dove (30-03-63)
Interpol Calling 01. The Angola Bright's (14-09-59)
Philip Ross (Cast Member)
The Avengers 5-02. The Fear Merchants (21-01-67)
Strange Report 11. REPORT 1553 RACIST A Most Dangerous Proposal (07-12-69)
Philip Ryan (Cast Member)
Adam Adamant Lives!: 02. Death Has a Thousand Faces (30-06-66)
Callan: 1-06. You Should Have Got Here Sooner (12-08-67)
Philip Stone (Cast Member)
The Saint 2-06. Marcia (24-10-63)
Philip Voss (Cast Member)
Doctor Who 44. The Dominators: 5 Episodes (10-08-68)
Out Of The Unknown 1-05. Time In Advance (01-11-65)
Philippa Gail (Cast Member)

Man In A Suitcase 21. No Friend Of Mine (14-02-67)
Philippe Monnet (Cast Member)
The Avengers 5-19. The £50,000 Breakfast (14-10-67)
Philo Hauser (Cast Member)
Interpol Calling 07. You Can't Die Twice (26-10-59)
Man Of The World 2-03. Double Exposure (25-05-63)
The Saint 3-09. The Death Penalty (03-12-64) 5-18. The Art Collectors (27-01-67)
Phyllis Montefiore (Cast Member)
The Baron 20. The High Terrace (08-02-67)
The Saint 5-08. The Man Who Liked Lions (18-11-66)
Pippa Steel (Cast Member)
Department S: 28. The Soup Of The Day (04-03-70)
Polly Perkins (Cast Member)
The Avengers 3-01. Brief For Murder (28-09-63)
Powys Thomas (Cast Member)
Callan 1-01. The Good Ones Are Dead (08-07-67)
Priscilla Morgan (Cast Member)
Man In A Suitcase 09. The Girl Who Never Was (22-11-67)
Prudence Drage (Cast Member)
The Saint 6-08. The Master Plan (17-11-68)

Q

Quinn O'Hara (Cast Member)
The Saint 5-02. Interlude In Venice (07-10-66)

R

Rachel Gurney (Cast Member)
The Saint 2-15. The Benevolent Burglary (26-12-63)
Rachel Herbert (Cast Member)
The Champions 30. Autokill (30-04-69)
Danger Man 3-13. Say It With Flowers (23-12-65)
Man In A Suitcase 29. Castle In The Clouds (10-04-67)
The Prisoner 04. Free For All (20-10-67)
Rachelle Miller (Cast Member)
Man In A Suitcase 24. Which Way Did He Go, McGill (06-03-67)
Raf De La Torre (Cast Member)
The Avengers 4-06. The Master Minds (06-11-65)
Ghost Squad 2-24. Gertrude (13-04-63)
Raiken Ben-Ari (Cast Member)
Danger Man 3-07. Judgement Day (11-11-65) 3-17. I Can Only Offer You Sherry (20-01-66) 3-22. The Paper Chase (31-03-66)
Ralph Ball (Cast Member)
The Avengers 6-25. Who Was That Man I Saw You With (19-03-69)
Ralph Michael (Cast Member)
The Avengers 6-25. Who Was That Man I Saw You With (19-03-69)
Danger Man 2-10 Man To Be Trusted (15-12-64) 3-14 The Man Who Wouldn't Talk (30-12-65)
Man In A Suitcase 23. Web With Four Spiders (28-2-67) 21. No Friend Of Mine (14-02-67)
Ralph Nossek (Cast Member)
The Avengers 2-02. Propellant 23 (06-10-62)
Ghost Squad 2-12. Quarantine At Kavar (01-06-63)
Undermind 07. Song Of Death (19-06-65)
Ralph Tovey (Cast Member)
The Avengers 1-15. The Frighteners (27-11-61)
Ralph Truman (Cast Member)
Danger Man 1-29. The Contessa (21-05-61)
Ralph Watson (Cast Member)
Doctor Who 41. The Web Of Fear: 5 Episodes (03-02-68)
Ram John Holder (Cast Member)
Strange Report 11. REPORT 1553 RACIST A Most Dangerous Proposal (07-12-69)
Randal Kinkead (Cast Member)
Danger Man 1-03. Josetta (25-09-60)
Raoul Alkazzi (Cast Member)
Danger Man 2-01. Yesterday's Enemies (13-10-64)
Ghost Squad 2-26. Sabotage (20-04-63)
Raoul Skinner (Cast Member)
Public Eye 4-03. Paid In Full (13-08-69)
Ray Armstrong (Cast Member)
Department S: 04. The Pied Piper Of Hambledown (30-03-69)
Strange Report 07. REPORT 3424 EPIDEMIC A Most Curious Crime (02-11-69)
Ray Austin (Cast Member)
The Avengers 4-02. The Gravediggers (09-01-65) 4-09. The Hour That Never Was (27-11-65)
Ghost Squad 2-21 Polsky (2-3-63) 2-23 The Menacing Mazurka (23-3-63) 2-26 Sabotage (20-4-63)
The Saint 2-01. The Fellow Traveler (19-09-63) 2-09. The King Of The Beggars (14-11-63) 3-13. The Damsel In Distress (31-12-64) 5-05. The Helpful Pirate (28-10-66)
Ray Barrett (Cast Member)

The Avengers 2-22. Man In The Mirror (23-2-63)
Doctor Who 11. The Rescue: 2 Episodes (02-01-65)
Ghost Squad 2-21. Polsky (02-03-63) 3-01. An Eye For An Eye (22-02-64)
Man Of The World 1-07. The Highland Story (10-11-62)
The Saint 3-07. The Loving Brothers (19-11-64)
Ray Brooks (Cast Member)
The Avengers 6-10. Noon Doomsday (27-11-68)
Danger Man 3-05. Loyalty Always Pays (28-10-65)
Randall & Hopkirk (Deceased) 15. The Man From Nowhere (28-12-69)
Ray Browne (Cast Member)
The Avengers 2-09. The Sell Out (24-11-62) 2-12. The Big Thinker (15-12-62) 3-04. The Nutshell (19-10-63) 3-05. Death Of a Batman (26-01-63)
The Saint 5-20. The Counterfeit Countess (03-03-67)
Ray Chiarella (Cast Member)
The Saint 5-21. Simon & Delilah (24-03-67)
Ray Grover (Cast Member)
Doctor Who 37. The Tomb Of The Cybermen: 4 Episodes (02-09-67)
Ray Lewis (Cast Member)
Man Of The World 1-09. The Mindreader (24-11-62)
Ray Lonnen (Cast Member)
The Saint 5-13. Flight Plan (23-12-66) 6-13. The People Importers (22-12-68)
Ray Martine (Cast Member)
The Avengers 4-17. The Girl From AUNTIE (22-01-66)
Ray Marioni (Cast Member)
Department S: 11. Who Plays The Dummy (01-10-69)
Ray McAnally (Cast Member)
The Avengers 5-22 Positive Negative Man (4-11-67) 6-13 They Keep Killing Steed (18-12-68)
Man In A Suitcase 23. Web With Four Spiders (28-02-67)
Strange Report 01. REPORT 5055 CULT Murder Shrieks Out (21-09-69)
Ray Roberts (Cast Member)
Danger Man 3-01. The Black Book (30-09-65)
Raymond Adamson (Cast Member)
The Avengers 2-03. The Decapod (13-10-62) 3-10. The Grandeur That Was Rome (30-11-63) 6-23. Take Me To Your Leader (05-03-69)
The Baron 14. There's Someone Close Behind You (28-12-67)
Danger Man 2-05. Fair Exchange (10-11-64) 2-11. Don't Nail Him Yet (22-12-64)
Ghost Squad 1-07. Still Waters (21-10-61)
Randall & Hopkirk (Deceased) 07. Murder Ain't What It Used To Be (02-11-69)
The Saint 2-11. The Saint Plays With Fire (28-11-63) 2-15. The Benevolent Burglary (26-12-63) 5-03. The Russian Prisoner (14-10-66)
Raymond Burke (Cast Member)
The Avengers 6-31. Pandora (30-04-69)
Raymond Clarke (Cast Member)
Adam Adamant Lives! 07. To Set a Deadly Fashion (11-08-66)
Raymond Graham (Cast Member)
Strange Report 02. REPORT 0649 SKELETON Let Sleeping Heroes Lie (28-09-69)
Raymond Hardy (Cast Member)
Adam Adamant Lives! 16. D Is For Destruction (13-06-66)
Out Of The Unknown 2-04. Level Seven (27-10-66)
Raymond Hodge (Cast Member)
The Avengers 2-07. The Mauritius Penny (10-11-62)
Raymond Huntley (Cast Member)
The Baron 11. Samurai West (07-12-66)
Danger Man 1-23. The Gallows Tree (09-04-61)
Interpol Calling 23. Payment in Advance (22-02-60)
Raymond Llewellyn (Cast Member)
Doctor Who 39. The Ice Warriors: 4 Episodes (11-11-67)
Raymond Ray (Cast Member)

Man Of The World 2-01. The Bandit (11-05-63)
The Saint 1-05. The Loaded Tourist (01-11-62) 2-24. Sophia (24-02-64)
Raymond Smith (Cast Member)
Man In A Suitcase 09. The Girl Who Never Was (22-11-67)
Raymond Young (Cast Member)
Callan 2-02. The Most Promising Girl Of Her Year (15-01-69)
Danger Man 1-01. View From The Villa (11-09-60)
Randall & Hopkirk (Deceased) 13. But What a Sweet Little Room (14-12-69)
Rebecca Dignam (Cast Member)
Danger Man 1-35. Find & Destroy (23-12-61)
Redmond Bailey (Cast Member)
The Protectors 09. The Pirate (23-05-64)
Redmond Phillips (Cast Member)
The Avengers 5-17. Return Of The Cybernauts (30-09-67)
Danger Man 2-15. Whatever Happened To George Foster (19-01-65)
The Saint 3-15. The Set-Up (14-01-65) 5-05. The Helpful Pirate (28-10-66)
Reed De Rouen (Cast Member)
The Avengers 2-06. The Removal Men (03-11-62)
Interpol Calling 19. Act Of Piracy (25-01-60)
Man In A Suitcase 30. Night Flight To Andorra (17-04-67)
Reg Cranfield (Cast Member)
Adam Adamant Lives! 16. D Is For Destruction (13-06-66)
Reg Lye (Cast Member)
The Champions 25. Desert Journey (19-03-69)
Ghost Squad 2-03. Sentences Of Death (04-05-63)
The Protectors 04. No Forwarding Address (18-04-64)
Randall & Hopkirk (Deceased) 16. When The Spirit Moves You (02-01-70)
The Saint 3-07. The Loving Brothers (19-11-64) 4-04. The Smart Detective (22-07-65) 4-09. The Old Treasure Story (26-08-65)
Reg Pritchard (Cast Member)
The Avengers 4-26. Honey For The Prince (26-03-66) 5-08. The Hidden Tiger (04-03-67)
Doctor Who 14. The Crusade: 2 Episodes (27-03-65)
The Saint 6-09. The House On Dragons Rock (24-11-68)
Reg Whitehead (Cast Member)
The Avengers 6-13. They Keep Killing Steed (18-12-68) 6-20. The World Beater (09-02-69)
Doctor Who 39. The Ice Warriors: 4 Episodes (11-11-67)
Reggie De Beer (Cast Member)
Danger Man 2-08. The Battle Of The Cameras (01-12-64)
Reginald Barratt (Cast Member)
The Avengers 6-31. Pandora (30-04-69) Danger Man 3-16. Dangerous Secret (13-01-66)
Department S: 22. Last Train to Redbridge (14-01-70)
Doctor Who 09. Planet Of Giants: 3 Episodes (31-10-64)
Reginald Beckworth (Cast Member)
The Saint 2-22. The Invisible Millionaire (13-02-64)
Reginald Hearne (Cast Member)
Danger Man 1-23. The Gallows Tree (09-04-61)
Reginald Jarman (Cast Member)
Man Of The World 2-06. The Bullfighter (15-06-63)
Reginald Jessup (Cast Member)
The Avengers 6-19. The Curious Case Of The Countless Clues (05-02-69)
The Baron 08. The Persuaders (16-11-66)
The Champions 24. Project Zero (12-03-69)
Department S: 25. Spencer Bodily Is 60 Years Old (11-02-70)
The Saint 3-05. The Revolution Racket (05-11-64)
Reginald Marsh (Cast Member)
The Avengers 2-20. School For Traitors (09-02-63)
The Baron 15. Storm Warning (Part 1) (04-01-67) 16. The Island (Part 2) (11-01-67) 19. You Can't Win Them All (01-02-67)

The Champions 14. The Search (01-01-68)
Randall & Hopkirk (Deceased) 10. When Did You Start To Stop Seeing Things? (23-11-69)
The Saint 6-03. Legacy For The Saint (13-10-68)
Rene Sartoris (Cast Member)
Man In A Suitcase 28. Three Blinks Of The Eyes (03-04-67)
Renee Asherson (Cast Member)
Strange Report 10. REPORT 8944 HAND A Matter Of Witchcraft (30-11-69)
Renee Houston (Cast Member)
Man Of The World 1-04. The Runaways (20-10-62)
The Saint 2-25. The Gentle Ladies (05-03-64) 2-16. The Wonderful War (02-01-64)
Reuben Elvy (Cast Member)
Danger Man 3-19. Two Birds With One Bullet (10-03-66)
Rex Boyd (Cast Member)
The Corridor People 2 Episodes (1966)
Rex Everhart (Cast Member)
Man In A Suitcase 18. The Boston Square (24-01-67)
Rex Robinson (Cast Member)
Callan 2-09. Death Of a Friend (05-03-69) Ghost Squad 2-23. The Menacing Mazurka (23-3-63)
Rhoda Lewis (Cast Member)
The Avengers 2-22. Man In The Mirror (23-02-63)
Rhonda Ryan (Cast Member)
Danger Man 3-11. To Our Best Friend (09-12-65)
Rhys McConnchie (Cast Member)
Doctor Who 40. The Enemy Of The World: 6 Episodes (23-12-67)
Ric Felgate (Cast Member)
Doctor Who 48. The Seeds Of Death: 6 Episodes (25-01-69)
Ric Hutton (Cast Member)
The Avengers 3-06. November Five (02-11-63)
The Protectors 01. Landscape With Bandits (28-03-64)
Ric Young (Cast Member)
The Champions 01. The Beginning (25-09-68) 29. The Gun Runners (23-04-69)
Danger Man 1-22. The Honeymooners (02-04-61) 1-32. The Actor (11-06-61)
Ghost Squad 1-01. Hong Kong Story (23-09-61) 2-02. East Of Mandalay (09-02-63)
Man Of The World 1-05. The Frontier (27-10-62)
The Saint 3-03. Jeannine (22-10-64)
Strange Report 03. REPORT 2641 HOSTAGE If You Won't Learn Die (05-10-69)
Ricardo Cortes (Cast Member)
The Saint 1-10. The Golden Journey (06-12-62)
Ricardo Montez (Cast Member)
The Avengers 5-03. Escape In Time (26-01-67)
The Champions 22. Get Me Out Of Here (26-02-69)
Department S: 14. Les Fleurs Du Mal (22-10-69)
Man In A Suitcase 04 Variation On a Million Bucks Part 1 (18-10-67) 05. Variation On a Million
Bucks Part 2 (25-10-67) 14 The Man Who Stood Still (27-12-67) 30. Night Flight To Andorra (17-04-
67)
Man Of The World 1-06. The Sentimental Agent (03-11-62) 2-04. Jungle Mission (01-06-63) 2-06.
The Bullfighter (15-06-63)
The Saint 1-10. The Golden Journey (06-12-62) 2-04. Teresa (10-10-63) 3-05. The Revolution Racket
(05-11-64) 4-07. The Saint Bids Diamonds (12-08-65) 5-12. Locate & Destroy (16-12-66) 5-21. Simon
& Delilah (24-03-67) 6-16. Vendetta For The Saint Part 2 (12-01-68)
Richard Beale (Cast Member)
Doctor Who 25. The Gunfighters: 4 Episodes (30-04-66)
Richard Beaumont (Cast Member)
Strange Report 08. REPORT 2475 REVENGE When a Man Hates (09-11-69)
Richard Bebb (Cast Member)
The Avengers 4-15. Room Without a View (08-01-65)
Ghost Squad 1-04. Broken Doll (07-10-61)
Richard Bond (Cast Member)

The Champions 11. The Dark Island (04-12-68)
Richard Bradford (Cast Member)
Man In A Suitcase All episodes
Richard Burrell (Cast Member)
Ghost Squad 2-11. A First Class Way To Die (13-07-63)
The Third Man 2-02. One Kind Word (07-09-59)
Robert Butler (Cast Member)
Public Eye 1-12. The Morning Wasn't So Hot (10-04-65)
Richard Caldicot (Cast Member)
The Avengers 5-13. A Funny Thing Happened On The Way To The Station (08-04-67) 6-20. Wish You
Were Here (12-02-69)
Danger Man 2-15 Whatever Happened To George Foster (19-1-65) 3-08 The Outcast (18-11-65)
Department S: 09. Black Out (17-09-69)
Ghost Squad 2-24. Gertrude (13-04-63) 2-13. The Desperate Diplomat (18-05-63)
The Prisoner 07. Many Happy Returns (10-11-67)
Randall & Hopkirk (Deceased) 08. Whoever Heard Of a Ghost Dying (09-11-69)
Richard Carpenter (Cast Member)
The Baron 05. Enemy Of The State (26-10-66)
Strange Report 13. REPORT 4821 X-RAY Who Weeps For The Doctor (21-12-69)
Richard Cawdron (Cast Member)
Danger Man 1-06. The Girl In Pink Pyjamas (16-10-60)
Richard Clarke (Cast Member)
The Avengers 2-10. Death On The Rocks (01-12-62)
City Beneath The Sea 1 episode (1962)
Danger Man 1-20. The Vacation (29-01-61) 1-35. Find & Destroy (23-12-61)
The Saint 2-15. The Benevolent Burglary (26-12-63)
Richard Coe (Cast Member)
Man In A Suitcase 15. Burden Of Proof (03-01-67)
Strange Report 10. REPORT 8944 HAND A Matter Of Witchcraft (30-11-69)
Richard Coleman (Cast Member)
The Avengers 4-20. The Danger Makers (12-02-66)
Richard Curnock (Cast Member)
The Avengers 5-19. The £50,000 Breakfast (14-10-67)
The Protectors 07. It Could Happen Here (09-05-64)
Richard Cuthbert (Cast Member)
The Avengers 3-24. Concerto (07-03-64)
Richard Cuthbertson (Cast Member)
The Avengers 2-03. The Decapod (13-10-62)
Richard Dare (Cast Member)
Ghost Squad 2-01. Interrupted Requiem (02-02-63)
Richard Davies (Cast Member)
Out Of The Unknown 1-12. The Midas Plague (20-12-65)
The Saint 6-11. The Fiction Makers Part 1 (08-12-68)
Richard Dean (Cast Member)
Pathfinders In Space 7 Episodes (1960)
Richard Durden (Cast Member)
Department S: 24. The Bones Of Byrom Blain (28-01-70)
Richard Easton (Cast Member)
The Saint 3-14. The Contact (07-01-65)
Richard Franklin (Cast Member)
The Saint 6-11. The Fiction Makers Pt 1 (08-12-68) 6-12. The Fiction Makers Pt 2 (15-12-68)
Richard Gale (Cast Member)
Interpol Calling 19. Act Of Piracy (25-01-60)
Out Of The Unknown 1-10. Some Lapse In Time (06-12-65)
Richard Graydon (Cast Member)
The Avengers 4-26. Honey For The Prince (26-03-66)
Richard Heffer (Cast Member)
Department S: 25. Spencer Bodily Is 60 Years Old (11-02-70)

Richard Hurndall (Cast Member)
The Avengers 6-09. Legacy Of Death (20-11-68)
Richard Ireson (Cast Member)
Doctor Who 47. The Krotons: 4 Episodes (28-12-68)
Richard James (Cast Member)
Man In A Suitcase 03. Day Of Execution (11-10-67)
Richard Kerley (Cast Member)
Doctor Who 39. The Ice Warriors: 4 Episodes (11-11-67)
Randall & Hopkirk (Deceased) 16. When The Spirit Moves You (02-01-70) 18. Could You Recognise
The Man Again (16-01-70) 20. Money To Burn (30-01-70)
Richard Klee (Cast Member)
The Avengers 2-09. The Sell Out (24-11-62)
Ghost Squad 2-04. The Golden Silence (08-06-63)
Richard Leech (Cast Member)
The Avengers 2-11. Traitor In Zebra (08-12-62) 3-14. Dressed To Kill (28-12-63) 5-24. Mission,
Highly Improbable (18-11-67)
Danger Man 2-17. The Affair At Castelevara (09-02-65)
Ghost Squad 1-04. Broken Doll (07-10-61)
Interpol Calling 17. Mr George (11-01-60) 21. The Collector (08-02-60) 37. Pipeline (06-06-60)
Man Of The World 1-12. A Family Affair (15-12-62)
The Saint 5-15. The Persistent Patriots (06-01-67)
Richard Marner (Cast Member)
Danger Man 1-06. The Girl In Pink Pyjamas (16-10-60)
Richard Mathews (Cast Member)
The Baron 12. The Maze (14-12-67)
The Protectors 08. Freedom! (16-05-64)
Richard McNeff (Cast Member)
Doctor Who 10. Dalek Invasion Of Earth (1964)
The Saint 2-01. The Fellow Traveler (19-09-63)
Richard Neller (Cast Member)
The Avengers 3-10. The Grandeur That Was Rome (30-11-63) The Outside-In Man (22-02-64)
Richard O'Callaghan (Cast Member)
Out Of The Unknown 1-03. Stranger In the Family (18-10-65)
Public Eye 4-02. Divide & Conquer (06-08-69)
Richard O'Sullivan (Cast Member)
Danger Man 3-19. Two Birds With One Bullet (10-03-66)
Strange Report 14. REPORT 2493 Whose Pretty Girl Are You? (28-12-69)
Richard Owens (Cast Member)
The Avengers 5-19 £50,000 Breakfast (14-10-67) 6-25 Who Was That Man I Saw You With (19-3-69)
The Baron 13. Portrait Of Louisa (21-12-67)
The Champions 30. Autokill (30-04-69)
Danger Man 2-12. A Date With Doris (29-12-64) 3-01. The Black Book (30-09-65)
Man In A Suitcase 08. Essay In Evil (15-11-67)
Randall & Hopkirk (Deceased) 24. Vendetta For a Dead Man (27-02-70)
The Saint 5-22. Island Of Chance (07-04-67) 6-09. The House On Dragons Rock (24-11-68)
Undermind 11. End Signal (17-07-65)
Richard Pearson (Cast Member)
Danger Man 1-38. Dead Man Walks (13-01-62)
Richard Pescud (Cast Member)
The Avengers 2-11. Traitor In Zebra (08-12-62)
Randall & Hopkirk (Deceased) 11. The Ghost Who Saved The Bank At Monte Carlo (30-11-69)
Richard Poore (Cast Member)
The Saint 2-22. The Invisible Millionaire (13-02-64)
Richard Shaw (Cast Member)
Ghost Squad 1-02. Bullet With My Name On It (16-09-61)
The Saint 3-11. The Hijackers (17-12-64) 5-18. The Art Collectors (27-01-67)
Richard Stapley (Cast Member)
The Baron 14. There's Someone Close Behind You (28-12-67)

The Saint 3-13. The Damsel In Distress (31-12-64) 4-06. The Man Who Could Not Die (5-8-65)
Richard Thorp (Cast Member)
The Avengers 2-20. School For Traitors (09-02-63)
Danger Man 1-16. The Island (01-01-61)
Richard Turner (Cast Member)
The Avengers 3-02. The Undertakers (05-10-63)
Richard Vanstone (Cast Member)
Strange Report 06. REPORT 3906 COVER-GIRLS Last Years Model (26-10-69)
Richard Vernon (Cast Member)
The Avengers 2-07. The Mauritius Penny (10-11-62)
Department S: 04. The Pied Piper Of Hambledown (30-03-69)
The Saint 2-05. The Elusive Elishaw (17-10-63)
Richard Wardale (Cast Member)
Out Of The Unknown 3-03. The Last Lonely Man (21-01-69)
Richard Warner (Cast Member)
The Avengers 2-13. Death Dispatch (22-12-62)
The Baron 26. The Long, Long Day (22-03-67)
Man Of The World 1-12. A Family Affair (15-12-62)
The Saint 5-02. Interlude In Venice (07-10-66)
Richard Wattis (Cast Member)
The Avengers 6-17. Killer (22-01-69)
Danger Man 1-09, The Lonely Chair (30-10-60) 1-12. The Sisters (27-11-60) 1-17. Find & Return (08-01-61) 1-19. Name, Date & Place (22-01-61) 1-38. Dead Man Walks (13-01-62)
The Prisoner 02. The Chimes Of Big Ben (06-10-67)
Richard Wilson (Cast Member)
Danger Man 3-24. Koroshi (12-02-67)
Richard Young (Cast Member)
The Avengers 6-11. Look (Stop Me If You've Heard This One) But There Were These Two Fellers (04-12-68)
Richardson Morgan (Cast Member)
Doctor Who 41. The Web Of Fear: 5 Episodes (03-02-68)
Rick Jones (Cast Member)
The Avengers 3-16. The Little Wonders (11-01-64)
Undermind 07. Song Of Death (19-06-65)
Rio Fanning (Cast Member)
The Avengers 5-20. Dead Man's Treasure (21-10-67) 6-07. False Witness (06-01-68)
The Champions 13. Twelve Hours (18-12-68) 20. The Silent Enemy (12-02-69)
Ghost Squad 2-06. The Missing People (29-06-63)
Rita Davies (Cast Member)
Ghost Squad 2-25. The Thirteenth Girl (27-04-63)
Robert Arden (Cast Member)
Interpol Calling 07. You Can't Die Twice (26-10-59)
Man Of The World 2-07. The Prince (22-06-63)
The Saint 2-26. The Ever Loving Spouse (12-03-64)
Robert Ayres (Cast Member)
Danger Man 1-37. The Nurse (06-01-61)
The Saint 1-03. The Careful Terrorist (18-10-62) 5-02. Interlude In Venice (07-10-66)
Robert Beatty (Cast Member)
Doctor Who 29. The Tenth Planet: 3 Episodes (08-10-66)
Robert Bernal (Cast Member)
The Avengers 2-19. The Golden Egg (02-02-63)
Danger Man 1-03. Josetta (25-09-60)
Robert Bridges (Cast Member)
The Baron 20. The High Terrace (08-02-67)
The Saint 5-09. The Better Mouse Trap (25-11-66)
Robert Brown (Cast Member)
Interpol Calling 10. Dead On Arrival (16-11-59)
The Saint 2-11. The Saint Plays With Fire (28-11-63)

Robert Bruce (Cast Member)
The Saint 3-06. The Saint Steps In (12-11-64)
Robert Cartland (Cast Member)
Doctor Who 19. Mission To The Unknown (09-10-65)
The Protectors 03. Happy Is The Loser (11-04-64)
Robert Cawdron (Cast Member)
The Avengers 4-21. A Touch Of Brimstone (19-02-66) 5-23. Murdersville (11-11-67)
Interpol Calling 05. The Two Headed Monster (12-10-59)
The Saint 1-04. The Covetous Headsman (25-10-62) 2-07. The Work Of Art (31-10-63) 3-03. Jeannine (22-10-64) 4-02. The Abductors (08-07-65) 5-19. To Kill a Saint (24-02-67)
Robert Crewdson (Cast Member)
The Champions 09. The Iron Man (20-11-68)
The Baron 01. Diplomatic Immunity (28-09-66)
Man In A Suitcase 30. Night Flight To Andorra (17-04-67)
The Saint 5-03. The Russian Prisoner (14-10-66) 5-13. Flight Plan (23-12-66)
Robert Dean (Cast Member)
The Avengers 4-25. How To Succeed…. At Murder (19-03-66)
Danger Man 2-22. Parallel Lines Sometimes Meet (16-03-65)
The Saint 3-17. The Inescapable World (28-01-65)
Robert Dorning (Cast Member)
The Avengers 4-14. Silent Dust (01-01-66)
Robert Easton (Cast Member)
The Saint 1-02. The Latin Touch (11-10-62)
Robert Flemyng (Cast Member)
The Avengers 5-21. You Have Just Been Murdered (28-10-67)
Danger Man 1-11. The Key (20-11-60) Man Of The World 1-08. The Nature Of Justice (17-11-62)
Robert Gallico (Cast Member)
Interpol Calling 29. White Blackmail (11-04-60)
Robert Gillespie (Cast Member)
The Avengers 6-12. Have Guns - Will Haggle (11-12-68)
The Saint 5-19. To Kill a Saint (24-02-67)
Robert Hamilton (Cast Member)
Department S: 16. The Man From X (05-11-69)
Robert Harbin (Cast Member)
Danger Man 1-08 The Lonely Chair (30-10-60)
Robert Hardy (Cast Member)
The Baron 18. A Memory Of Evil (25-01-67)
The Saint 6-04. The Desperate Diplomat (20-10-68)
Strange Report 15. REPORT 4407 No Choice For The Donor (04-01-70)
Robert Harris (Cast Member)
The Avengers 6-21. Love All (19-02-69)
Robert Hartley (Cast Member)
The Avengers 2-17. Box Of Tricks (19-01-63)
Robert Hawdon (Cast Member)
Randall & Hopkirk (Deceased) 26. The Smile Behind The Veil (13-03-70)
Robert Henderson (Cast Member)
Danger Man 2-06. Fish On The Hook (17-11-64)
Ghost Squad 1-02. Bullet With My Name On It (16-09-61)
Robert Hunter (Cast Member)
City Beneath The Sea 1 episode (1962)
Doctor Who 08. The Reign Of Terror: 4 Episodes (08-08-64)
Interpol Calling 33. Eight Days Inclusive (09-05-60)
Robert Hutton (Cast Member)
Man In A Suitcase 27. Who's Mad Now (27-03-67)
The Saint 3-14. The Contact (07-01-65) 4-09. The Old Treasure Story (26-08-65) 6-02. Invitation To Danger (06-10-68)
Robert James (Cast Member)
The Avengers 3-13. Death a La Carte (21-12-63) 4-13. Too Many Christmas Trees (25-12-65)

6-11. Look (Stop Me If You've Heard This One) But There Were These Two Fellers (04-12-68)
Out Of The Unknown 1-11. Thirteen To Centauraus
Undermind 03. The New Dimension (22-05-65)
Robert Lankesheer (Cast Member)
The Avengers 3-03. Man With Two Shadows (12-10-63)
Robert Lee (Cast Member)
The Avengers 3-11. The Golden Fleece (07-12-63)
Danger Man 3-05. Loyalty Always Pays (28-10-65) 3-25. Shinda Shima (26-02-67)
Robert Mackenzie (Cast Member)
Interpol Calling 31. In The Swim (25-04-60)
Robert MacLeod (Cast Member)
Adam Adamant Lives! 08. The Last Sacrifice (18-08-66)
Man In A Suitcase 23. Web With Four Spiders (28-02-67)
The Saint 2-03. Judith (03-10-63) 3-17. The Inescapable World (28-01-65)
Robert Mill (Cast Member)
The Avengers 2-26. Killer Whale (23-03-63)
The Champions 27. Nutcracker (02-04-69)
Department S: 19. The Duplicated Man (03-12-69)
Public Eye 1-02. Nobody Kill Santa Claus (30-01-65)
Robert Morris (Cast Member)
The Avengers 3-18. Mandrake (25-01-64)
The Protectors 12. Channel Crossing (13-06-64)
The Saint 6-08. The Master Plan (17-11-68)
Robert Nichols (Cast Member)
The Saint 3-11. The Hi-jackers (17-12-64)
Robert O'Neil (Cast Member)
Danger Man 2-14. Such Men Are Dangerous (12-01-65)
The Saint 1-08. The Element Of Doubt (22-11-62)
Robert Perceval (Cast Member)
Man In A Suitcase 18. The Boston Square (24-01-67)
Robert Pitt (Cast Member)
Man In A Suitcase 24. Which Way Did He Go, McGill (06-03-67)
Robert Raglan (Cast Member)
Danger Man 1-06. The Girl In Pink Pyjamas (16-10-60)
The Saint 3-02. Lida (15-10-64)
Robert Rietty (Cast Member)
The Avengers 2-23. Conspiracy Of Silence (02-03-63)
Danger Man 3-11. To Our Best Friend (09-12-65)
Department S: 01. Six Days (09-03-69)
Ghost Squad 1-12. Princess (12-01-61)
Interpol Calling 08. Diamond S.O.S. (02-11-59)
Man In A Suitcase 12. Find The Lady (13-12-67)
Man Of The World 2-01. The Bandit (11-05-63)
Robert Russell (Cast Member)
The Avengers 6-32. Get-a-Way (14-05-69)
The Champions 19. The Mission (05-02-69)
Department S: 05. One Of Aircraft Is Empty (06-4-69)
Randall & Hopkirk (Deceased) 23. The Trouble With Women (20-02-70)
The Saint 5-08. The Man Who Liked Lions (18-11-66)
Robert Sansom (Cast Member)
The Saint 2-12. The Well Meaning Mayor (05-12-63)
Robert Shaw (Cast Member)
Danger Man 1-27. Bury The Dead (07-05-61)
Robert Shayne (Cast Member)
The Third Man 4-07. Diamond In the Rough (11-05-62)
Robert Sidaway (Cast Member)
The Avengers 6-08. All Done With Mirrors (13-11-68)
Doctor Who 46. The Invasion: 6 Episodes (09-11-68)

Out Of The Unknown 1-12. The Midas Plague (20-12-65)
Robert Tunstall (Cast Member)
Public Eye 1-02. Nobody Kill Santa Claus (30-01-65)
Robert Urquhart (Cast Member)
The Avengers 4-05. Castle De'ath (30-10-65) 6-20. Wish You Were Here (12-02-69)
The Champions 06. Operation Deep Freeze (30-10-68)
Danger Man 2-19. It's Up To The Lady (23-02-65) 3-09. English Lady Take Lodgers (25-11-65) 3-21. The Man With The Foot (24-03-66)
Department S: 19. The Duplicated Man (03-12-69)
Man In A Suitcase 03. Day Of Execution (11-10-67)
The Saint 4-02. The Abductors (08-07-65)
Robert Young (Cast Member)
The Avengers 3-01. Brief For Murder (28-09-63)
Robin Askwith (Cast Member)
Randall & Hopkirk (Deceased) 05. That's How Murder Snowballs (19-10-69)
Robin Bailey (Cast Member)
Man In A Suitcase 02. The Sitting Pigeon (04-10-67)
Robin Burns (Cast Member)
The Avengers 4-08. A Surfeit Of H2o (20-11-65)
Robin Hawdon (Cast Member)
Department S: 03. Cellar Full Of Silence (23-03-69)
Robin Hughes (Cast Member)
Ghost Squad 2-04. The Golden Silence (08-06-63)
The Saint 1-06. The Pearls Of Peace (08-11-62)
Robin John (Cast Member)
Adam Adamant Lives!: 02. Death Has a Thousand Faces (30-06-66)
Department S: 16. The Man From X (05-11-69)
Randall & Hopkirk (Deceased) 08. Whoever Heard Of a Ghost Dying (09-11-69)
Robin Phillips (Cast Member)
The Avengers 4-24. A Sense Of History (12-03-66)
The Saint 4-06. The Man Who Could No Die (05-08-65)
Robin Scott (Cast Member)
Doctor Who 33. The Moonbase: 2 Episodes (18-02-67)
Robin Tolhurst (Cast Member)
The Avengers 6-21. Love All (19-02-69)
Robin Wentworth (Cast Member)
The Avengers 2-04. Bullseye (20-10-62)
Rocky Taylor (Cast Member)
The Avengers 3-10. The Grandeur That Was Rome (30-11-63) 4-05. Castle De'ath (30-10-65) 5-03. Escape In Time (26-01-67)
Rod Beacham (Cast Member)
Doctor Who 41. The Web Of Fear: 5 Episodes (03-02-68)
Strange Report 12. REPORT 7931 SNIPER When Is Your Cousin Not? (14-12-69)
Rodney Burice (Cast Member)
Danger Man 1-25. The Brothers (23-04-61)
Rodney Bewes (Cast Member)
Man In A Suitcase 13. The Bridge (20-12-67)
Roger Avon (Cast Member)
Danger Man 2-20. Have a Glass of Wine (02-03-65)
Department S: 05. One Of Aircraft Is Empty (06-04-69) 22. Last Train to Redbridge (14-01-70)
Doctor Who 14. The Crusade: 2 Episodes (27-03-65)
Ghost Squad 2-10. The Grand Duchess (11-05-63)
Randall & Hopkirk (Deceased) 20. Money To Burn (30-01-70)
Roger Bizley (Cast Member)
Callan 2-14. Nice People Die At Home (09-04-69)
Roger Booth (Cast Member)
The Avengers 4-09. The Hour That Never Was (27-11-65) 5-03. Escape In Time (26-01-67)
Roger Croucher (Cast Member)

Out Of The Unknown 1-07. Sucker Bait (15-11-65)
Roger Delgado (Cast Member)
The Avengers 6-22. Stay Tuned (26-02-69)
The Champions 25. Desert Journey (19-03-69)
Danger Man 1-36. Under the Lake (30-12-61)
Ghost Squad 1-13. Death From a Distance (04-11-61) 2-18. The Heir Apparent (09-03-63) 2-12. Quarantine At Kavar (01-06-63)
Man In A Suitcase 15. Burden Of Proof (03-01-67)
The Protectors 08. Freedom! (16-05-64)
Randall & Hopkirk (Deceased) 11. The Ghost Who Saved The Bank At Monte Carlo (30-11-69)
The Saint 1-10. The Golden Journey (06-12-62) 5-12. Locate & Destroy (16-12-66)
Roger Hammond (Cast Member)
The Avengers 5-17. Return Of The Cybernauts (30-09-67)
The Corridor People Victim as Black (1966)
Doctor Who 16. The Chase: 6 Episodes (22-05-65)
Roger Jessup (Cast Member)
Danger Man 1-36. Under the Lake (30-12-61)
Roger Maxwell (Cast Member)
The Avengers 2-08. Death Of Great Dane (17-11-62)
Danger Man 2-14. Such Men Are Dangerous (12-01-65)
Roger Moore (Cast Member)
The Saint All Episodes
Roger Snowdon (Cast Member)
Out Of This World 02. Little Lost Robot (07-07-1962)
Roger Worrod (Cast Member)
Danger Man 3-09. English Lady Take Lodgers (25-11-65)
Roland Bartrop (Cast Member)
Interpol Calling 08. Diamond S.O.S. (02-11-59) 10. Dead On Arrival (16-11-59) 18. The Thousand Mile Alibi (18-01-60) 26. Trial At Cranby's Creek (21-03-60)
Roland Brand (Cast Member)
The Baron 15. Storm Warning (Part 1) (04-01-67) 16. The Island (Part 2) (11-01-67)
Ghost Squad 1-08. Assassin (28-10-61)
The Saint 1-09. The Effete Angler (29-11-62)
Roland Culver (Cast Member)
The Avengers 6-04. You'll Catch Your Death (16-10-68)
Roland Curram (Cast Member)
The Avengers 4-26. Honey For The Prince (26-03-66)
Public Eye 1-12. The Morning Wasn't So Hot (10-04-65)
Randall & Hopkirk (Deceased) 18. Could You Recognise The Man Again (16-01-70)
Romo Gorrara (Cast Member)
The Prisoner 09. Checkmate (14-11-67)
Randall & Hopkirk (Deceased) 08. Whoever Heard Of a Ghost Dying (09-11-69)
The Saint 5-14. Escape Route (30-12-66)
Ron Blackman (Cast Member)
Danger Man 2-04. The Galloping Major (03-11-64)
Ron Hutchinson (Cast Member)
Ghost Squad 2-20. P.G..7. (06-07-63)
Ron Moody (Cast Member)
The Avengers 4-26. Honey For The Prince (26-03-66) 5-05. Bird Who Knew Too Much (11-02-67)
Ron Pember (Cast Member)
The Avengers 6-33. Bizarre (21-05-69)
Department S: 26. The Ghost Of Mary Burnham (18-02-70)
Randall & Hopkirk (Deceased) 24. Vendetta For a Dead Man (27-02-70)
The Saint 6-13. The People Importers (22-12-68)
Strange Report 06. REPORT 3906 COVER-GIRLS Last Years Model (26-10-69)
Ron Pinnell (Cast Member)
Doctor Who 33. The Moonbase: 2 Episodes (18-02-67)
Ron Randell (Cast Member)

Man In A Suitcase 04. Variation On a Million Bucks 1 (18-10-67) 05. Variation On a Million Bucks 2 (25-10-67)

Ron Welling (Cast Member)
The Saint 4-04. The Smart Detective (22-07-65)

Rona Anderson (Cast Member)
Interpol Calling 33. Eight Days Inclusive (09-05-60)

Ronald Adam (Cast Member)
The Avengers 3-08. Second Sight (16-11-63)

Ronald Allen (Cast Member)
The Avengers 3-19. The Secrets Broker (01-02-64)
Danger Man 1-15. Colonel Rodriguez (18-12-60) 1-22. The Honeymooners (02-04-61)
Doctor Who 44. The Dominators: 5 Episodes (10-08-68)

Ronald Fraser (Cast Member)
The Avengers 4-02. The Gravediggers (09-01-65)
Danger Man 1-25. The Brothers (23-04-61)

Ronald Hines (Cast Member)
The Avengers 5-23. Murdersville (11-11-67)
The Baron 08. The Persuaders (16-11-66)
Out Of The Unknown 2-08. Tunnel Under The World (01-12-66)
The Saint 5-11. Paper Chase (09-12-66)

Ronald Howard (Cast Member)
Danger Man 1-14. The Traitor (11-12-60) 3-24. Koroshi (12-02-67)

Ronald Ibbs (Cast Member)
The Saint 2-20. The Lawless Lady (30-01-64) 3-17. The Inescapable World (28-01-65) 4-02. The Abductors (08-07-65)

Ronald Lacey (Cast Member)
The Avengers 5-15. The Joker (22-04-67) 6-09. Legacy Of Death (20-11-68)
Department S: 28. The Soup Of The Day (04-03-70)
Randall & Hopkirk (Deceased) 01. My Late Lamented Friend & Partner (21-09-69)

Ronald Leigh-Hunt (Cast Member)
The Avengers 4-03. The Cybernauts (16-10-65) Danger Man 1-35. Find & Destroy (23-12-61)
Department S: 18. The Perfect Operation (26-12-69)
Doctor Who 48. The Seeds Of Death: 6 Episodes (25-01-69)
Ghost Squad 1-03. Ticket For Blackmail (09-09-61) 2-03. Sentences Of Death (04-05-63)
Interpol Calling 25. The Girl With The Grey Hair (14-03-60)
The Saint 1-07. The Arrow Of God (15-11-62) 3-04. The Scorpion (29-10-64) 6-10. The Scales Of Justice (01-12-68)

Ronald Lewis (Cast Member)
Out Of The Unknown 1-10. Some Lapse In Time (06-12-65) 2-03. Lambda One (20-10-66)

Ronald Mansell (Cast Member)
The Avengers 3-22. The Outside-In Man (22-02-64)

Ronald Mayer (Cast Member)
The Avengers 2-20. School For Traitors (09-02-63)

Ronald Pickup (Cast Member)
Doctor Who 08. The Reign Of Terror: 4 Episodes (08-08-64)

Ronald Radd (Cast Member)
The Avengers 2-04. Bullseye (20-10-62) 3-22. The Outside-In Man (22-02-64) 5-24. Mission, Highly Improbable (18-11-67)
Callan 1-01. The Good Ones Are Dead (08-07-67) 1-06. You Should Have Got Here Sooner (12-08-67) 2-13. The Worst Soldier I Ever Saw (02-04-69) 2-14. Nice People Die At Home (9-4-69)
The Champions 22. Get Me Out Of Here (26-02-69)
Danger Man 2-12. A Date With Doris (29-12-64) 3-03. Sting In The Tail (14-10-65)
Department S: 18. The Perfect Operation (26-12-69)
The Prisoner 09. Checkmate (14-11-67)
Randall & Hopkirk (Deceased) 06. Just For The Record (26-10-69)
The Saint 2-02. Starring The Saint (26-09-63) 5-21. Simon & Delilah (24-03-67) 6-17. The Ex-King Of Diamonds (19-01-68)

Ronald Russell (Cast Member)

The Avengers 3-02. The Undertakers (05-10-63)
Ronald Wilson (Cast Member)
The Avengers 3-11. The Golden Fleece (07-12-63)
The Saint 1-09. The Effete Angler (29-11-62) 2-03. Judith (03-10-63)
Ronan O'Casey (Cast Member)
Danger Man 1-16. The Island (01-01-61)
Ronnie Barker (Cast Member)
The Avengers 5-08. The Hidden Tiger (04-03-67)
The Saint 5-09. The Better Mouse Trap (25-11-66)
Ronnie Stevens (Cast Member)
The Avengers 4-04. Death At Bargain Prices (23-10-65)
Rory MacDonald (Cast Member)
The Avengers 2-15. Intercrime (05-01-63)
Danger Man 1-21. The Conspirators (05-02-61) 2-13. That's Two Of Us Sorry (05-01-64)
The Saint 3-09. The Death Penalty (03-12-64)
Rosalie Crutchley (Cast Member)
The Prisoner 09. Checkmate (14-11-67)
Rosalind Atkinson (Cast Member)
Strange Report 10. REPORT 8944 HAND A Matter Of Witchcraft (30-11-69)
Rosalyn Hooker (Cast Member)
Undermind 05. Too Many Enemies (05-06-65)
Rose Alba (Cast Member)
The Saint 6-06. The Double Take (03-11-68)
Rosemarie Dunham (Cast Member)
The Avengers 3-16. The Little Wonders (11-01-64)
Rosemarie Reede (Cast Member)
The Saint 3-08. The Man Who Liked Toys (26-11-64)
Rosemary Chalmers (Cast Member)
The Avengers 2-03. The Decapod (13-10-62)
Rosemary Dexter (Cast Member)
The Saint 6-15. Vendetta For The Saint Pt 1 (5-1-68) 6-16. Vendetta For The Saint Pt 2 (12-1-68)
Rosemary Donnelly (Cast Member)
The Avengers 6-13. They Keep Killing Steed (18-12-68)
Department S: 16. The Man From X (05-11-69)
Randall & Hopkirk (Deceased) 10. When Did You Start To Stop Seeing Things? (23-11-69)
The Saint 6-20. The World Beater (09-02-69)
Rosemary Dorken (Cast Member)
Ghost Squad 2-08. The Man With The Delicate Hands (22-06-63)
Undermind 03. The New Dimension (22-05-65)
Rosemary Johnson (Cast Member)
Doctor Who 09. Planet Of Giants: 3 Episodes (31-10-64)
Rosemary Leach (Cast Member)
Strange Report 08. REPORT 2475 REVENGE When a Man Hates (09-11-69)
Rosemary Nicols (Cast Member)
Department S All Episodes (1969)
Man In A Suitcase 03. Day Of Execution (11-10-67)
Undermind All Episodes (1965)
Roshan Seth (Cast Member)
Strange Report 07. REPORT 3424 EPIDEMIC A Most Curious Crime (02-11-69)
Roslyn De Winter (Cast Member)
Doctor Who 13. The Web Planet: 6 Episodes (13-02-65)
Ross Drinkwater (Cast Member)
The Saint 6-02. Invitation To Danger (06-10-68)
Ross Hutchinson (Cast Member)
The Avengers 6-13. They Keep Killing Steed (18-12-68)
Ghost Squad 2-17. Mr Five Per Cent (06-04-63)
Ross Parker (Cast Member)
The Saint 2-03. Judith (03-10-63)

Rowena Gregory (Cast Member)
The Avengers 2-16. Immortal Clay (12-01-63) 3-15. The White Elephant (04-01-64)
Roy Beck (Cast Member)
The Saint 2-03. Judith (03-10-63) 4-07. The Saint Bids Diamonds (12-08-65)
Roy Boyd (Cast Member)
The Saint 6-12. The Fiction Makers Part 2 (15-12-68)
Roy Denton (Cast Member)
The Avengers 2-06. The Removal Men (03-11-62)
Roy Desmond (Cast Member)
Randall & Hopkirk (Deceased) 20. Money To Burn (30-01-70)
Roy Dotrice (Cast Member)
Public Eye 2-02. Don't Forget You're Mine (09-07-66)
Roy Evans (Cast Member)
Doctor Who 21. The Daleks' Master Plan: 3 Episodes (20-11-65)
Roy Gunson (Cast Member)
The Avengers 2-18. Warlock (26-01-63)
Roy Hanlon (Cast Member)
Adam Adamant Lives! 10. The Doomsday Plan (01-09-66)
The Baron 28. The Man Outside (05-04-67)
Department S: 17. Dead Men Die Twice (12-11-69)
The Saint 6-11. The Fiction Makers Part 1 (8-12-68) 6-12. The Fiction Makers Part 2 (15-12-68)
Roy Herrick (Cast Member)
Danger Man 3-15. Somebody Is Liable To Get Hurt (06-01-66)
Doctor Who 08. The Reign Of Terror: 4 Episodes (08-08-64)
Roy Hills (Cast Member)
Out Of The Unknown 1-11. Thirteen To Centauraus (13-12-63)
Roy Kinnear (Cast Member)
The Avengers 3-25. Espirit de Corps (14-03-64) 4-09. The Hour That Never Was (27-11-65) 5-04. The See Through Man (04-02-67) 6-33. Bizarre (21-05-69)
Roy Marsden (Cast Member)
Danger Man 3-14. The Man Who Wouldn't Talk (30-12-65)
Roy Patrick (Cast Member)
The Avengers 5-06. The Winged Avenger (18-02-67)
The Saint 1-02. The Latin Touch (11-10-62) 4-09. The Old Treasure Story (26-08-65)
Roy Purcell (Cast Member)
The Avengers 2-23. Conspiracy Of Silence (02-03-63)
Roy Spencer (Cast Member)
Doctor Who 23. The Ark: 4 Episodes (05-03-66)
Roy Stewart (Cast Member)
Adam Adamant Lives! 12. Beauty Is An Ugly Word (15-09-66)
The Avengers 6-12. Have Guns - Will Haggle (11-12-68)
Doctor Who 37. The Tomb Of The Cybermen: 4 Episodes (02-09-67)
Out Of The Unknown 1-01. No Place Like Earth (04-10-65)
Roy Vincente (Cast Member)
Man In A Suitcase 09. The Girl Who Never Was (22-11-67)
Royston Farrell (Cast Member)
The Avengers 4-09. The Hour That Never Was (27-11-65)
Royston Tickner (Cast Member)
The Avengers 2-17. Box Of Tricks (19-01-63)
The Baron 11. Samurai West (07-12-66) 12. The Maze (14-12-67)
Ruddolph Offenbach (Cast Member)
Danger Man 1-18. The Girl Who Likes G.I.'s (15-01-61)
Ghost Squad 2-15. The Last Jump (23-02-63)
Rufus Cruikshank (Cast Member)
Interpol Calling 04. The Sleeping Giant (05-10-59)
Rupert Davies (Cast Member)
The Champions 24. Project Zero (12-03-69)
Danger Man 1-32. The Actor (11-06-61)

Interpol Calling 01. The Angola Bright's (14-09-59)
Man In A Suitcase 14. The Man Who Stood Still (27-12-67)
The Third Man 2-02. One Kind Word (07-09-59)
Russell Hunter (Cast Member)
Callan 1-01. The Good Ones Are Dead (08-07-67) 1-06. You Should Have Got Here Sooner (12-08-67) 2-01. Red Knight, White Knight (08-01-69) 2-02. The Most Promising Girl Of Her Year (15-01-69) 2-04. Little Bits & Pieces Of Love (29-01-69) 2-05. Let's Kill Everybody (05-02-69) 2-09. Death Of a Friend (05-03-69) 2-13. The Worst Soldier I Ever Saw (02-04-69) 2-14. Nice People Die At Home (09-04-69)
Russell Napier (Cast Member)
Man In A Suitcase 17. Why They Killed Nolan (17-01-67)
Russell Waters (Cast Member)
The Avengers 4-05. Castle De'ath (30-10-65) 6-27. Thingamajig (16-04-69)
The Champions 04. The Experiment (16-10-68)
Interpol Calling 20. Game For Three Hands (01-02-60) 38. The Absent Assassin (13-06-60)
The Saint 2-17. The Noble Sportsman (09-01-64) 3-17. The Inescapable World (28-01-65)
Ruth Dunning (Cast Member)
The Avengers 3-06. November Five (02-11-63)
Undermind 10. Waves Of Sound (10-07-65)
Ruth Lodge (Cast Member)
Ghost Squad 2-23. The Menacing Mazurka (23-03-63)
Man Of The World 1-07. The Highland Story (10-11-62)
Ruth Trouncer (Cast Member)
Adam Adamant Lives! 07. To Set a Deadly Fashion (11-08-66)
The Avengers 5-02. The Fear Merchants (21-01-67)
Strange Report 03. REPORT 2641 HOSTAGE If You Won't Learn Die (05-10-69)

S

S. Ghosal (Cast Member)
The Third Man 2-10. Toys Of The Dead (03-11-59)
Saeed Jaffrey (Cast Member)
Callan 2-13. The Worst Soldier I Ever Saw (02-04-69)
Strange Report 07. REPORT 3424 EPIDEMIC A Most Curious Crime (02-11-69)
Sally Bazely (Cast Member)
Danger Man 1-22. The Honeymooners (02-04-61)
The Saint 1-03. The Careful Terrorist (18-10-62)
Sally Douglas (Cast Member)
Danger Man 2-19. It's Up To The Lady (23-02-65)
Sally Faulkner (Cast Member)
Doctor Who 46. The Invasion: 6 Episodes (09-11-68)
Sally Geeson (Cast Member)
Man In A Suitcase 03. Day Of Execution (11-10-67)
Strange Report 14. REPORT 2493 Whose Pretty Girl Are You? (28-12-69)
Sally-Jane Spencer (Cast Member)
Department S: 16. The Man From X (05-11-69)
Sally Nesbitt (Cast Member)
The Avengers 5-15. The Joker (22-04-67) 6-33. Bizarre (21-05-69)
Salmaan Peerada (Cast Member)
The Saint 5-13. Flight Plan (23-12-66) 6-13. The People Importers (22-12-68) 6-15. Vendetta For The Saint Part 1 (05-01-68)
Strange Report 07. REPORT 3424 EPIDEMIC A Most Curious Crime (02-11-69)
Sam Chowdhary (Cast Member)
Danger Man 1-32. The Actor (11-06-61)
Ghost Squad 1-01. Hong Kong Story (23-09-61)
Sam Kydd (Cast Member)
Man In A Suitcase 17. Why They Killed Nolan (17-01-67)
Out Of The Unknown 1-12. The Midas Plague (20-12-65)
Sam Wanamaker (Cast Member)
The Baron 19. You Can't Win Them All (01-02-67)
Danger Man The Lonely Chair (30-10-60)
Man Of The World 2-01. The Bandit (11-05-63)
Samantha Eggar (Cast Member)
Ghost Squad 2-09. Hot Money (25-05-63)
The Saint 2-06. Marcia (24-10-63)
Sandor Eles (Cast Member)
The Avengers 3-24. Concerto (07-03-64) 5-22. The Positive Negative Man (4-11-67)
The Baron 04. Red Horse, Red Rider (19-10-66) 27. Roundabout (29-03-67)
Danger Man: 3-22. The Paper Chase (31-03-66)
Department S: 28. The Soup Of The Day (04-03-70)
The Saint 4-02. The Abductors (08-07-65) 5-03. The Russian Prisoner (14-10-66) 6-14. Where The Money Is (29-12-68)
Strange Report 12. REPORT 7931 SNIPER When Is Your Cousin Not? (14-12-69)
Sandra Burville (Cast Member)
Man In A Suitcase 28. Three Blinks Of The Eyes (03-04-67)
Sandra Dorne (Cast Member)
The Avengers 2-23. Conspiracy Of Silence (02-03-63)
Interpol Calling 15. Last Man Lucky (28-12-59)
Sandra Tallent (Cast Member)
The Avengers 6-20. Wish You Were Here (12-02-69)
Sarah Brackett (Cast Member)
Danger Man 2-19. It's Up To The Lady (23-02-65) 2-20. Have a Glass of Wine (02-03-65)
The Saint 1-08. The Element Of Doubt (22-11-62) 3-12. The Unkind Philanthropist (24-12-64)
Sarah Branch (Cast Member)

Danger Man 2-13. That's Two Of Us Sorry (05-01-64)
Sarah Lawson (Cast Member)
The Avengers 4-25. How To Succeed…. At Murder (19-03-66)
Danger Man 1-02. Time to Kill (18-11-60)
Department S: 19. The Duplicated Man (03-12-69)
The Saint 3-22. The Crime Of The Century (04-03-65)
Sarah Marshall (Cast Member)
Strange Report 11. REPORT 1553 RACIST A Most Dangerous Proposal (07-12-69)
Sarah Maxell (Cast Member)
The Avengers 2-01. Mr Teddy Bear (29-09-62)
Scot Finch (Cast Member)
Man Of The World 1-13. Shadow Of the Wall (22-12-62)
The Saint 3-09. The Death Penalty (03-12-64)
Scott Forbes (Cast Member)
The Avengers 3-15. The White Elephant (04-01-64)
Scott Fredericks (Cast Member)
Strange Report 12. REPORT 7931 SNIPER When Is Your Cousin Not? (14-12-69)
Sean Arnold (Cast Member)
Out Of The Unknown 2-04. Level Seven (27-10-66)
Sean Kelly (Cast Member)
Man Of The World 1-11. Specialist For the Kill (08-12-62)
Sean Lynch (Cast Member)
Man In A Suitcase 02. The Sitting Pigeon (04-10-67)
Sebastian Breaks (Cast Member)
Out Of The Unknown 2-03. Lambda One (20-10-66)
Strange Report 01. REPORT 5055 CULT Murder Shrieks Out (21-09-69)
Shane Rimmer (Cast Member)
Danger Man 3-06. The Mercenaries (04-11-65)
Doctor Who 25. The Gunfighters: 4 Episodes (30-04-66)
Shane Shelton (Cast Member)
Doctor Who 29. The Tenth Planet: 3 Episodes (08-10-66)
Shaun Curry (Cast Member)
The Saint 6-12. The Fiction Makers Part 2 (15-12-68)
Shay Gorman (Cast Member)
Danger Man 1-09. The Sanctuary (06-11-60) 5-10. Little Girl Lost (02-12-66)
Sheena Marshe (Cast Member)
Doctor Who 25. The Gunfighters: 4 Episodes (30-04-66)
The Prisoner 15. The Girl Who Was Death (18-01-67)
Sheila Allen (Cast Member)
Danger Man 2-11. Don't Nail Him Yet (22-12-64)
The Prisoner 03. A.B. & C. (13-10-67)
Sheila Brennen (Cast Member)
Man In A Suitcase 16. The Whisper (10-01-67)
Sheila Burrell (Cast Member)
The Avengers 6-33. Bizarre (21-05-69)
Sheila Conner (Cast Member)
The Andromeda Breakthrough 2-1. Cold Front (28-06-62)
Sheila Fearn (Cast Member)
Adam Adamant Lives!: 02. Death Has a Thousand Faces (30-06-66)
The Avengers: 5-23. Murdersville (11-11-67)
Sheila Grant (Cast Member)
Adam Adamant Lives! 13. The League Of Uncharitable Ladies (12-09-66)
Shiela Hammond (Cast Member)
The Avengers: 6-23. Take Me To Your Leader (05-03-69)
Sheila Keith (Cast Member)
The Saint 6-03. Legacy For The Saint (13-10-68)
Sheila Raynor (Cast Member)
Man Of The World 1-13. Shadow Of the Wall (22-12-62)

Public Eye 1-02. Nobody Kill Santa Claus (30-01-65) 2-02. Don't Forget You're Mine (09-7-66)
Sheila Steafel (Cast Member)
Danger Man 3-16. Dangerous Secret (13-01-66)
Sheldon Lawrence (Cast Member)
Danger Man 1-22. The Honeymooners (02-04-61)
Ghost Squad 1-02. Bullet With My Name On It (16-09-61)
Sheree Winton (Cast Member)
Man Of The World 1-03. Blaze Of Glory (13-10-62)
Shirley Eaton (Cast Member)
Man Of The World 1-06. The Sentimental Agent (03-11-62)
The Saint 1-01. The Talented Husband (4-10-62) 1-09. The Effete Angler (29-11-62) 6-02. Invitation To Danger (06-10-68)
Shirley Cain (Cast Member)
Out Of The Unknown 1-04. The Dead Past (25-10-65)
Shirley Cooklin (Cast Member)
Doctor Who 37. The Tomb Of The Cybermen: 4 Episodes (02-09-67)
Shivaun O'Casey (Cast Member)
Man In A Suitcase 22. Jigsaw Man (21-02-67)
The Prisoner 09. Checkmate (14-11-67)
Shivendra Sinha (Cast Member)
Strange Report 07. REPORT 3424 EPIDEMIC A Most Curious Crime (02-11-69)
Sidonie Bond (Cast Member)
The Avengers 4-25. How To Succeed…. At Murder (19-03-66)
The Baron 11. Samurai West (07-12-66)
Undermind 07. Song Of Death (19-06-65)
Simon Barnes (Cast Member)
Randall & Hopkirk (Deceased) 05. That's How Murder Snowballs (19-10-69)
Simon Brent (Cast Member)
Danger Man 3-11. To Our Best Friend (9-12-65) 3-14. The Man Who Wouldn't Talk (30-12-65)
Man In A Suitcase 04. Variation On a Million Bucks Part 1 (18-10-67) 05. Variation On a Million Bucks Part 2 (25-10-67)
Simon Cain (Cast Member)
Doctor Who 40. The Enemy Of The World: 6 Episodes (23-12-67)
Simon Lack (Cast Member)
The Avengers 6-07. False Witness (06-01-68)
Danger Man: 3-22. The Paper Chase (31-03-66)
Ghost Squad 1-04. Broken Doll (07-10-61)
The Saint 5-12. Locate & Destroy (16-12-66) 6-05. The Organization Man (27-10-67)
Simon Oates (Cast Member)
The Avengers 5-21 You Have Just Been Murdered (28-10-67) 6-03 Super Secret Cypher Snatch (9-10-68)
Department S: 02. The Trojan Tanker (16-03-69)
Ghost Squad 2-25. The Thirteenth Girl (27-04-63)
Man In A Suitcase 23. Web With Four Spiders (28-02-67)
Simon Weers (Cast Member)
The Third Man 2-10. Toys Of The Dead (03-11-59)
Simon Williams (Cast Member)
Man In A Suitcase 13. The Bridge (20-12-67)
Skip Martin (Cast Member)
The Avengers 1-06. Girl On The Trapeze (11-02-61)
Sonia Fox (Cast Member)
Danger Man 2-15. Whatever Happened To George Foster (19-01-65) 2-17. The Affair At Castelevara (09-02-65)
Man In A Suitcase 26. The Revolutionaries (20-03-67)
The Saint 4-05. The Persistent Parasites (29-07-65)
Soo Bee Lee (Cast Member)
Danger Man 1-32. The Actor (11-06-61)
Spike Heatley (Cast Member)

The Avengers 2-17. Box Of Tricks (19-01-63)
Stan Jay (Cast Member)
The Saint 5-16. The Fast Women (13-01-67)
Stanley Ayers (Cast Member)
The Avengers 2-03. The Decapod (13-10-62)
Stanley Davies (Cast Member)
Adam Adamant Lives! 16. D Is For Destruction (13-06-66)
Stanley Hollingsorth (Cast Member)
Adam Adamant Lives! 29. A Sinister Sort Of Service (25-03-67)
Stanley Lebor (Cast Member)
Department S: 16. The Man From X (05-11-69)
Stanley Meadows (Cast Member)
The Avengers 5-08. The Hidden Tiger (04-03-67)
Out Of The Unknown 3-03. The Last Lonely Man (21-01-69)
The Protectors 07. It Could Happen Here (09-05-64)
Public Eye 4-04. My Life's My Own (20-08-69) 4-05. Case For The Defence (27-08-69) 4-06. The Comedian's Graveyard (03-09-69)
The Saint 2-06. Marcia (24-10-63) *2*-22. The Invisible Millionaire (13-02-64) 5-01. The Queens Ransom (30-09-66)
Undermind 08. Puppets Of Evil (26-06-65)
Stanley McGeagh (Cast Member)
Callan 2-05. Let's Kill Everybody (05-02-69)
Stanley Platts (Cast Member)
The Avengers 1-20. Tunnel Of Fear (05-08-61)
Stanley Stewart (Cast Member)
Callan 1-06. You Should Have Got Here Sooner (12-08-67)
Stanley Van Beers (Cast Member)
Danger Man 1-24. The Relaxed Informer (16-04-61)
Interpol Calling 25. Girl With The Grey Hair (14-3-60) 28. Slow Boat To Amsterdam (4-4-60)
Stanley Walsh (Cast Member)
Ghost Squad 2-04. The Golden Silence (08-06-63)
Stanley Watson (Cast Member)
Danger Man 3-08. The Outcast (18-11-65)
Stefan Gryff (Cast Member)
The Avengers 5-24. Mission, Highly Improbable (18-11-67)
The Saint 5-23. The Gadget Lovers (21-04-67)
Stella Bonheur (Cast Member)
The Saint 1-08. The Element Of Doubt (22-11-62) 1-10. The Golden Journey (06-12-62)
Stella Courtney (Cast Member)
Danger Man 2-02. The Professionals (20-10-64)
Stephanie Beacham (Cast Member)
Public Eye 4-04. My Life's My Own (20-08-69)
The Saint 6-03. Legacy For The Saint (13-10-68)
Stephanie Bidmead (Cast Member)
Adam Adamant Lives! 02. Death Has a Thousand Faces (30-06-66)
Doctor Who 18. Galaxy 4: Air Lock (25-09-65)
Stephanie Lacey (Cast Member)
The Avengers 3-21. Build a Better Mousetrap (15-02-64)
Stephanie Randall (Cast Member)
The Prisoner 01. Arrival (29-09-67)
The Saint 3-16. The Rhine Maiden (21-01-65)
Stephen Dartnell (Cast Member)
Doctor Who 07. The Sensorites: 6 Episodes (20-06-64)
Stephen Hancock (Cast Member)
The Avengers 2-25. Six Hands Across a Table (16-03-63)
Stephen Howe (Cast Member)
The Prisoner 15. The Girl Who Was Death (18-01-67)
Stephen Hubay (Cast Member)

The Avengers 6-26. Homicide & Old Lace (26-03-69)
The Saint 5-23. The Gadget Lovers (21-04-67)
Stephen Jack (Cast Member)
Danger Man 2-13. That's Two Of Us Sorry (05-01-64)
Stephen Whittaker (Cast Member)
Doctor Who 41. The Web Of Fear: 5 Episodes (03-02-68)
Strange Report 08. REPORT 2475 REVENGE When a Man Hates (09-11-69)
Stephen Yardley (Cast Member)
The Champions 07. The Survivors (06-11-68)
Danger Man 3-08. The Outcast (18-11-65)
Steve Cory (Cast Member)
The Avengers 2-24. A Chorus Of Frogs (09-03-63)
The Protectors 03. Happy Is The Loser (11-04-64)
Steve Forrest (Cast Member)
The Baron All Episodes
Steve Kirby (Cast Member)
Ghost Squad 2-17. Mr Five Per Cent (06-04-63)
Steve Morley (Cast Member)
The Avengers 4-08. A Surfeit Of H2o (20-11-65)
Steve Peters (Cast Member)
Adam Adamant Lives! 09. Sing a Song Of Murder (25-08-66) 18. Black Echo (07-01-67)
Doctor Who 48. The Seeds Of Death: 6 Episodes (25-01-69)
Steve Plytas (Cast Member)
The Avengers 2-16. Immortal Clay (12-01-63) 4-21. A Touch Of Brimstone (19-02-66)
The Champions 02. The Invisible Man (02-10-68)
Danger Man 2-02. The Professionals (20-10-64) 3-22. The Paper Chase (31-03-66)
Department S: 17. Dead Men Die Twice (12-11-69)
Doctor Who 29. The Tenth Planet: 3 Episodes (08-10-66)
Ghost Squad 2-24. Gertrude (13-04-63)
Interpol Calling 19. Act Of Piracy (25-01-60)
Man Of The World 1-06. The Sentimental Agent (03-11-62)
The Saint 5-11. Paper Chase (09-12-66) 6-16. Vendetta For The Saint Part 2 (12-01-68)
Steven Berkoff (Cast Member)
The Avengers 4-02. The Gravediggers (09-01-65)
The Champions 09. The Iron Man (20-11-68)
The Saint 6-18. The Man Who Gambled With Life (26-01-68)
The Third Man 2-10. Toys Of The Dead (03-11-59)
Steven Brook (Cast Member)
The Saint 5-07. The Angel's Eye (11-11-66)
Steven Scott (Cast Member)
The Saint 1-06. The Pearls Of Peace (08-11-62) 5-08. The Man Who Liked Lions (18-11-66)
Steven Scott (Cast Member)
The Avengers 3-08. Second Sight (16-11-63) 6-05. Split (23-10-68)
The Baron 17. Time To Kill (18-01-67)
Man Of The World 1-13. Shadow Of the Wall (22-12-62)
The Saint 1-06. The Pearls Of Peace (08-11-62)
Stewart Guidotti (Cast Member)
City Beneath The Sea All episodes (1962)
Pathfinders In Space 7 Episodes (1960)
Pathfinders To Mars 6 Episodes (1961)
Pathfinders To Venus 8 Episodes (1961)
Stewart Rose (Cast Member)
Danger Man 3-24. Koroshi (12-02-67)
Stratford Johns (Cast Member)
The Avengers 1-15. The Frighteners (27-11-61) 6-09. Legacy Of Death (20-11-68)
Department S: 06. The Man In The Elegant Room (13-04-69)
Ghost Squad 1-07. Still Waters (21-10-61)
Storm Durr (Cast Member)

The Avengers 2-09. The Sell Out (24-11-62)
Stratford Johns (Cast Member)
Interpol Calling 30. A Foreign Body (18-04-60)
Stuart Cooper (Cast Member)
The Saint 5-17. The Death Game (20-01-67)
Stuart Damon (Cast Member)
The Champions All Episodes
Man In A Suitcase 06. Man From The Dead (01-11-67)
The Saint 6-17. The Ex-King Of Diamonds (19-01-68)
Stuart Hoyle (Cast Member)
Randall & Hopkirk (Deceased) 05. That's How Murder Snowballs (19-10-69)
Stuart Hutchison (Cast Member)
Danger Man 1-34. The Deputy Coyannis Story (16-12-61)
Stuart Saunders (Cast Member)
Ghost Squad 2-03. Sentences Of Death (04-05-63)
The Saint 2-20. The Lawless Lady (30-01-64)
Sue Gerrard (Cast Member)
Department S: 20. The Mysterious Man In The Flying Machine (10-12-69)
Randall & Hopkirk (Deceased) 07. Murder Ain't What It Used To Be (02-11-69)
Sue Lloyd (Cast Member)
The Avengers 4-08. A Surfeit Of H2o (20-11-65)
The Baron 23 Episodes
Department S: 09. Black Out (17-09-69)
Randall & Hopkirk (Deceased) 20. Money To Burn (30-01-70)
The Saint 2-19. Luella (23-01-64) 5-22. Island Of Chance (07-04-67)
Sue McIntosh (Cast Member)
The Baron 26. The Long, Long Day (22-03-67)
Sue Vaughan (Cast Member)
Randall & Hopkirk (Deceased) 24. Vendetta For a Dead Man (27-02-70)
Surya Kumari (Cast Member)
Interpol Calling 35. Cargo Of Death (23-05-60)
Susan Broderick (Cast Member)
Department S: 04. The Pied Piper Of Hambledown (30-03-69)
Randall & Hopkirk (Deceased) 14. Who Killed Cock Robin? (21-12-69)
Susan Burnet (Cast Member)
Public Eye 1-12. The Morning Wasn't So Hot (10-04-65)
Susan Denny (Cast Member)
Department S: 21. Death On Reflection (17-12-69)
Susan Dowdall (Cast Member)
Public Eye 2-07. Works With Chess, Not With Life (13-08-66)
Susan Fleetwood (Cast Member)
Department S: 26. The Ghost Of Mary Burnham (18-02-70)
Susan Franklin (Cast Member)
The Avengers 2-18. Warlock (26-01-63)
Susan Hampshire (Cast Member)
Danger Man 3-10. Are You Going To Be More Permanent? (02-12-65)
The Andromeda Breakthrough 6 Episodes (1962)
Susan Jameson (Cast Member)
Strange Report 05. REPORT 8319 GRENADE What Price Change? (19-10-69)
Susan Richards (Cast Member)
Public Eye 4-03. Paid In Full (13-08-69)
Susan Sheers (Cast Member)
The Prisoner 10. Hammer & Anvil (01-12-67)
Susan Travers (Cast Member)
The Avengers 6-28. My Wildest Dream (07-04-69)
Danger Man 1-19. Name, Date & Place (22-01-61)
Interpol Calling 17. Mr George (11-01-60)
The Saint 6-13. The People Importers (22-12-68)

Susanna Carroll (Cast Member)
Doctor Who 18. Galaxy 4: Air Lock (25-09-65)
Undermind 10. Waves Of Sound (10-07-65)
Suzan Farmer (Cast Member)
Danger Man 2-09. No Marks For Servility (08-12-64)
Man In A Suitcase 01. Brainwash (27-09-67)
The Saint 1-02. The Latin Touch (11-10-62) 3-18. The Sign Of The Claw (04-02-65) 5-06. The Convenient Monster (04-11-66) 6-04. The Desperate Diplomat (20-10-68)
Suzanna Leigh (Cast Member)
The Saint 2-16. The Wonderful War (02-01-64)
Suzanne Lloyd (Cast Member)
The Avengers 4-07. The Murder Market (13-11-65)
The Saint 2-19. Luella (23-01-64) 2-22. The Invisible Millionaire (13-02-64) 3-05. The Revolution Racket (05-11-64) 5-08. The Man Who Liked Lions (18-11-66) 5-21. Simon & Delilah (24-03-67) 6-07. The Time To Die (10-11-68)
Suzanne Neve (Cast Member)
Man Of The World 1-13. Shadow Of the Wall (22-12-62)
The Saint 2-15. The Benevolent Burglary (26-12-63) 3-20. The Frightened Inn-Keeper (18-2-65)
Suzanne Vasey (Cast Member)
Department S: 26. The Ghost Of Mary Burnham (18-02-70)
Sydney Arnold (Cast Member)
Out Of The Unknown 1-12. The Midas Plague (20-12-65)
Sydney Dobson (Cast Member)
Public Eye 2-07. Works With Chess, Not With Life (13-08-66)
Sydney Tafler (Cast Member)
Danger Man 1-12. The Sisters (27-11-60)
Man In A Suitcase 29. Castle In The Clouds (10-04-67)
Sylva Langova (Cast Member)
The Avengers 2-07. The Mauritius Penny (10-11-62)
Man Of The World 2-07. The Prince (22-06-63)
Sylvia Bidmead (Cast Member)
The Avengers 2-25. Six Hands Across a Table (16-03-63)
Sylvia Coleridge (Cast Member)
The Avengers 4-17. The Girl From AUNTIE (22-01-66)
Out Of The Unknown 1-04. The Dead Past (25-10-65)
Sylvia Kay (Cast Member)
The Avengers 6-04. You'll Catch Your Death (16-10-68)
Strange Report 02. REPORT 0649 SKELETON Let Sleeping Heroes Lie (28-09-69)
Sylvia Syms (Cast Member)
The Baron 30. Farewell To Yesterday (19-04-67)
Danger Man 2-19. It's Up To The Lady (23-02-65)
The Saint 2-17. The Noble Sportsman (09-01-64) 3-03. Jeannine (22-10-64) 6-01. The Best Laid Plans (29-09-68) 6-11. The Fiction Makers Part 1 (08-12-68) 6-12. The Fiction Makers Part 2 (15-12-68)

T

T.P. McKenna (Cast Member)
Adam Adamant Lives! 29. A Sinister Sort Of Service (25-03-67)
The Avengers 3-21. Build a Better Mousetrap (15-02-64) 4-04. Death At Bargain Prices (23-10-65) 6-10. Noon Doomsday (27-11-68)
Danger Man 3-11. To Our Best Friend (09-12-65)
Man In A Suitcase 03. Day Of Execution (11-10-67)
The Saint 5-07. The Angel's Eye (11-11-66) 6-03. Legacy For The Saint (13-10-68)
Talfryn Thomas (Cast Member)
Adam Adamant Lives! 10. The Doomsday Plan (01-09-66)
The Avengers 4-08. A Surfeit Of H2o (20-11-65) 6-11. Look (Stop Me If You've Heard This One) But There Were These Two Fellers (04-12-68)
The Saint 6-09. The House On Dragons Rock (24-11-68)
Tania (Cast Member)
The Champions 16. Shadow Of The Panther (15-01-68)
Tanya Trude (Cast Member)
Public Eye 4-03. Paid In Full (13-08-69)
Teddy Kiss (Cast Member)
The Avengers 6-09. Legacy Of Death (20-11-68)
Tenniel Evans (Cast Member)
The Avengers 2-12. The Big Thinker (15-12-62) 3-11. The Golden Fleece (07-12-63) 6-08. All Done With Mirrors (13-11-68)
Out Of The Unknown 1-07. Sucker Bait (15-11-65)
Randall & Hopkirk (Deceased) 14. Who Killed Cock Robin? (21-12-69)
The Saint 5-15. The Persistent Patriots (06-01-67)
Undermind 04. Death In England (29-05-65)
Terence Alexander (Cast Member)
The Avengers 4-01. The Town Of No Return (2-10-65) 5-09. The Correct Way To Kill (11-3-67) 6-21. Love All (19-02-69)
The Baron 13. Portrait Of Louisa (21-12-67)
The Champions 23. The Night People (05-03-69)
Man In A Suitcase 25. Property Of A Gentleman (13-03-67)
Terence Bayler (Cast Member)
Doctor Who 50. The War Games: 10 Episodes (19-04-69)
Terence Brady (Cast Member)
The Avengers 6-24. Fog (12-03-69)
Terence Brown (Cast Member)
Doctor Who 47. The Krotons: 4 Episodes (28-12-68)
Terence Donovan (Cast Member)
Man In A Suitcase 07. Sweet Sue (08-11-67)
The Prisoner 09. Checkmate (14-11-67)
Terence Edmond (Cast Member)
The Saint 6-05. The Organisation Man (27-10-67)
Terence Fallon (Cast Member)
Man Of The World 1-13. Shadow Of the Wall (22-12-62
Terrance Hooper (Cast Member)
Danger Man 2-18. The Ubiquitous Mr Lovegrove (16-02-65)
Terence Lodge (Cast Member)
The Avengers 3-03. Man With Two Shadows (12-10-63) 3-17. The Wringer (18-01-64)
The Baron 05. Enemy Of The State (26-10-66)
The Protectors 13. Cargo From Corinth (20-06-64)
Undermind 03. The New Dimension (22-05-65)
Terence Longdon (Cast Member)
The Avengers 6-32. Get-a-Way (14-05-69)
Danger Man 1-21. The Conspirators (05-02-61) 2-06. Fish On The Hook (17-11-64)
Terence Maidment (Cast Member)

The Avengers 5-18. Death's Door (07-10-67)
Terence Morgan (Cast Member)
Out Of The Unknown 1-01. No Place Like Earth (04-10-65)
Terence Mountain (Cast Member)
The Avengers 4-05. Castle De'ath (30-10-65)
The Baron 15. Storm Warning (Part 1) (04-01-67) 16. The Island (Part 2) (11-01-67)
The Saint 5-20. The Counterfeit Countess (03-03-67)
Terence Plummer (Cast Member)
The Avengers 4-08. A Surfeit Of H2o (20-11-65) 5-12. The Superlative Seven (01-04-67)
Randall & Hopkirk (Deceased) 08. Whoever Heard Of a Ghost Dying (09-11-69)
The Saint 6-04. The Desperate Diplomat (20-10-68)
Terence Rigby (Cast Member)
Public Eye 4-02. Divide & Conquer (06-08-69)
The Saint 5-07. The Angel's Eye (11-11-66) 6-07. The Time To Die (10-11-68)
Terrence Sewards (Cast Member)
The Avengers 6-29. Requiem (16-04-69)
Terence Soall (Cast Member)
The Avengers 3-07. The Gilded Cage (09-11-63)
Terence Taplin (Cast Member)
Undermind 11. End Signal (17-07-65)
Terence Woodfield (Cast Member)
The Avengers 2-05. Mission To Montreal (27-10-62) 2-20. School For Traitors (09-02-63)
Terry Bale (Cast Member)
Doctor Who 08. The Reign Of Terror: 4 Episodes (08-08-64)
Terry Brewer (Cast Member)
The Avengers 2-26. Killer Whale (23-3-63) 3-08. Second Sight (16-11-63) 3-24. Concerto (07-03-64)
Terry Duggan (Cast Member)
Randall & Hopkirk (Deceased) 09. The House On Haunted Hill (16-11-69)
Terry Eliot (Cast Member)
The Avengers 6-07. False Witness (06-01-68)
Terry Richards (Cast Member)
The Avengers 4-07. The Murder Market (13-11-65) 5-17. Return Of The Cybernauts (30-09-67)
Terry Scully (Cast Member)
Doctor Who 48. The Seeds Of Death: 6 Episodes (25-01-69)
Terry Yorke (Cast Member)
The Avengers 5-18. Death's Door (07-10-67)
Man In A Suitcase 20. Blind Spot (07-02-67)
The Prisoner 03. A.B. & C. (13-10-67)
The Saint 4-08. The Spanish Cow (19-08-65) 5-14. Escape Route (30-12-66)
Tessa Wyatt (Cast Member)
Callan 2-13. The Worst Soldier I Ever Saw (02-04-69)
Public Eye 4-06. The Comedian's Graveyard (03-09-69)
Theodore Wilhelm (Cast Member)
The Avengers 2-07. The Mauritius Penny (10-11-62)
Ghost Squad 2-06. The Missing People (29-06-63)
Thomas Baptiste (Cast Member)
Danger Man 2-14. Such Men Are Dangerous (12-01-65)
The Saint 1-07. The Arrow Of God (15-11-62) 5-22. Island Of Chance (07-04-67)
Thomas Gallagher (Cast Member)
Danger Man 2-05. Fair Exchange (10-11-64)
Ghost Squad 2-17. Mr Five Per Cent (06-04-63)
Thomas Heathcote (Cast Member)
Ghost Squad 2-15. The Last Jump (23-02-63)
The Prisoner 12. A Change Of Mind (15-12-67)
Randall & Hopkirk (Deceased) 21. The Ghost Talks (06-02-70)
Thorley Walters (Cast Member)
The Avengers 4-22. What The Butler Saw (26-02-66)
Thors Piers (Cast Member)

Ghost Squad 2-19. Death of a Sportsman (26-01-63)
Tim Barett (Cast Member)
The Avengers 5-13. A Funny Thing Happened On The Way To The Station (08-04-67)
The Corridor People Victim as Birdwatcher (1966)
The Saint 4-01. The Chequered Flag (01-07-65) 5-24. A Double In Diamonds (05-05-67)
Tim Brinton (Cast Member)
The Avengers 2-01. Mr Teddy Bear (29-09-62)
Tim Condren (Cast Member)
Out Of The Unknown 1-07. Sucker Bait (15-11-65)
Tim Wylton (Cast Member)
Strange Report 07. REPORT 3424 EPIDEMIC A Most Curious Crime (02-11-69)
Timmy Gardner (Cast Member)
The Saint 4-09. The Old Treasure Story (26-08-65)
Timothy Bateson (Cast Member)
The Avengers 5-09 The Correct Way To Kill (11-3-67) 6-12 Have Guns - Will Haggle (11-12-68)
Man In A Suitcase 06. Man From The Dead (01-11-67)
Out Of The Unknown 2-08. Tunnel Under The World (01-12-66)
The Saint 2-25. The Gentle Ladies (05-03-64)
Timothy Benke (Cast Member)
Danger Man 1-21. The Conspirators (05-02-61)
Timothy West (Cast Member)
Randall & Hopkirk (Deceased) 24. Vendetta For a Dead Man (27-02-70)
Tina Packer (Cast Member)
Doctor Who 41. The Web Of Fear: 5 Episodes (03-02-68)
Tina Ruta (Cast Member)
The Saint 6-19. Portrait Of Brenda (02-02-69)
Tita Dane (Cast Member)
The Saint 5-02. Interlude In Venice (07-10-66)
Toby Robins (Cast Member)
Department S: 06. The Man In The Elegant Room (13-04-69)
Toke Townley (Cast Member)
The Avengers 3-15. The White Elephant (04-01-64)
The Champions 08. To Trap a Rat (13-11-68)
Department S: 15. The Shift That Never Was (25-10-69)
Ghost Squad 2-04. The Golden Silence (08-06-63)
Tol Avery (Cast Member)
The Third Man 4-07. Diamond In the Rough (11-05-62)
Tom Adams (Cast Member)
The Avengers 6-30. Take-Over (23-04-69)
Ghost Squad 1-05. High Wire (30-09-61)
Strange Report 02. REPORT 0649 SKELETON Let Sleeping Heroes Lie (28-09-69)
Tom Bowman (Cast Member)
Danger Man 3-06. The Mercenaries (04-11-65)
Ghost Squad 2-21. Polsky (02-03-63) 2-13. The Desperate Diplomat (18-05-63)
Man In A Suitcase 02. The Sitting Pigeon (04-10-67)
Randall & Hopkirk (Deceased) 20. Money To Burn (30-01-70)
Tom Busby (Cast Member)
Ghost Squad 2-07. Lost in Transit (15-06-63)
Tom Chatto (Cast Member)
Ghost Squad 2-03. Sentences Of Death (04-05-63)
Randall & Hopkirk (Deceased) 01. My Late Lamented Friend & Partner (21-09-69)
Tom Clegg (Cast Member)
The Saint 6-11. The Fiction Makers Part 1 (8-12-68) 6-12. The Fiction Makers Part 2 (15-12-68)
Tom Criddle (Cast Member)
Man In A Suitcase 24. Which Way Did He Go, McGill (06-03-67)
Out Of The Unknown 2-04. Level Seven (27-10-66)
Tom Gill (Cast Member)
The Avengers 4-16. Small Game For Big Hunters (15-01-65)

Danger Man 1-24. The Relaxed Informer (16-04-61) 2-14. Such Men Are Dangerous (12-01-65)
Man Of The World 1-10. Portrait Of a Girl (01-12-62)
Tom Kempinski (Cast Member)
The Avengers 6-28. My Wildest Dream (07-04-69)
Callan 1-01. The Good Ones Are Dead (08-07-67)
Tom Macaulay (Cast Member)
Adam Adamant Lives! 01 A Year For Scoundrels (20-06-66)
The Saint 5-09. The Better Mouse Trap (25-11-66)
Tom Naylor (Cast Member)
The Saint 2-07. The Work Of Art (31-10-63)
Tom Payne (Cast Member)
Ghost Squad 2-04. The Golden Silence (08-06-63)
Tom Sheridan (Cast Member)
Doctor Who 11. The Rescue: 2 Episodes (02-01-65)
Tom Watson (Cast Member)
Doctor Who 32. The Underwater Menace: 2 Episodes (21-01-67)
Tommy Ansah (Cast Member)
Man In A Suitcase 16. The Whisper (10-01-67)
Tommy Duggan (Cast Member)
Interpol Calling 26. Trial At Cranby's Creek (21-03-60)
The Saint 2-24. Sophia (24-02-64) 5-13. Flight Plan (23-12-66)
Tommy Eytle (Cast Member)
Danger Man 3-12. The Man On The Beach (16-12-65)
The Saint 5-22. Island Of Chance (07-04-67)
Tommy Godfrey (Cast Member)
The Avengers 2-23. Conspiracy Of Silence (02-03-63)
Department S: 22. Last Train to Redbridge (14-01-70)
The Saint 5-25. The Power Artists (19-05-67)
Tommy Yapp (Cast Member)
Danger Man 3-25. Shinda Shima (26-02-67)
Toni Gilpin (Cast Member)
The Avengers 2-10. Death On The Rocks (01-12-62) 6-14. The Interrogators (01-01-69)
Danger Man 1-12. The Sisters (27-11-60)
Tony Arpino (Cast Member)
The Saint 1-02. The Latin Touch (11-10-62)
Tony Beckley (Cast Member)
The Saint 2-06. Marcia (24-10-63) 2-11. The Saint Plays With Fire (28-11-63)
Tony Britton (Cast Member)
The Saint 6-05. The Organisation Man (27-10-67)
Tony Caunter (Cast Member)
The Avengers 5-23. Murdersville (11-11-67)
The Baron 19. You Can't Win Them All (01-02-67)
Doctor Who 14. The Crusade: 2 Episodes (27-03-65)
The Saint 6-05. The Organization Man (27-10-67)
Tony Cyrus (Cast Member)
Adam Adamant Lives! 05. Allah Is Not Always With You (21-07-66)
Man Of The World 2-04. Jungle Mission (01-06-63)
Tony Doonan (Cast Member)
Man In A Suitcase 23. Web With Four Spiders (28-02-67)
The Saint 5-14. Escape Route (30-12-66)
Tony Handy (Cast Member)
Doctor Who 32. The Underwater Menace: 2 Episodes (21-01-67)
Tony Harwood (Cast Member)
Doctor Who 39. The Ice Warriors: 4 Episodes (11-11-67)
Tony Jason (Cast Member)
Danger Man 3-17. I Can Only Offer You Sherry (20-01-66)
Tony Kemp (Cast Member)
Man In A Suitcase 28. Three Blinks Of The Eyes (03-04-67)

223

Tony Lambden (Cast Member)
The Avengers 3-25. Espirit de Corps (14-03-64)
Tony Lawrence (Cast Member)
Ghost Squad 2-24. Gertrude (13-04-63)
Tony Lee (Cast Member)
Danger Man 3-08. The Outcast (18-11-65)
Tony O'Leary (Cast Member)
The Avengers 4-01. The Town Of No Return (02-10-65)
Tony Quinn (Cast Member)
Undermind 03. The New Dimension (22-05-65)
Tony Robins (Cast Member)
The Saint 5-26. When Spring Is Sprung (02-06-67)
Tony Selby (Cast Member)
The Avengers 6-19. The Curious Case Of The Countless Clues (05-02-69)
Department S: 16. The Man From X (05-11-69)
Tony Steedman (Cast Member)
The Avengers 3-16. The Little Wonders (11-01-64) 6-07. False Witness (06-01-68)
The Champions 10. The Ghost Plane (27-11-68)
Department S: 01. Six Days (09-03-69)
Strange Report 01. REPORT 5055 CULT Murder Shrieks Out (21-09-69)
The Protectors 14. The Reluctant Thief (27-06-64)
Randall & Hopkirk (Deceased) 25. You Can Always Find a Fall Guy (06-03-70)
Undermind 01. Instance One (08-05-65)
Tony Sympson (Cast Member)
Ghost Squad 2-17. Mr Five Per Cent (06-04-63)
Tony Thawnton (Cast Member)
The Avengers 5-17. Return Of The Cybernauts (30-09-67)
The Baron 08. The Persuaders (16-11-66)
Danger Man 3-10. Are You Going To Be More Permanent? (02-12-65)
Department S: 07. Handicap Dead (20-04-69) 18. The Perfect Operation (26-12-69)
Randall & Hopkirk (Deceased) 05. That's How Murder Snowballs (19-10-69)
Tony Wager (Cast Member)
Out Of The Unknown 1-02. The Counterfeit Man (11-10-65) 2-03. Lambda One (20-10-66)
The Saint 2-08. Iris (07-11-63) 3-15. The Set-Up (14-01-65)
Tony Wall (Cast Member)
The Champions 16. Shadow Of The Panther (15-01-68)
Doctor Who 08. The Reign Of Terror: 4 Episodes (08-08-64)
Tony Wright (Cast Member)
The Avengers 6-06. Whoever Shot George Oblique Stroke XR40? (30-10-68)
The Saint 1-07. The Arrow Of God (15-11-62) 4-03. The Crooked Ring (15-07-65) 6-14. Where The Money Is (29-12-68)
Totti Truman Taylor (Cast Member)
The Baron 30. Farewell To Yesterday (19-04-67)
Tracy Reed (Cast Member)
The Avengers 6-19. The Curious Case Of The Countless Clues (05-02-69)
Man Of The World 1-01. Death Of a Conference (29-09-62) 1-02. Masquerade In Spain (06-10-62) 1-03. Blaze Of Glory (13-10-62) 1-04. The Runaways (20-10-62) 1-06. The Sentimental Agent (03-11-62) 1-07. The Highland Story (10-11-62) 1-11. Specialist For the Kill (08-12-62) 2-01. The Bandit (11-05-63)
Tracey Crisp (Cast Member)
Randall & Hopkirk (Deceased) 19. A Sentimental Journey (23-01-70)
Tracy Reed (Cast Member)
Man Of The World 8 episodes
Tracey Vernon (Cast Member)
The Protectors 08. Freedom! (16-05-64)
Trader Faulkner (Cast Member)
The Avengers 2-02. Propellant 23 (06-10-62)
Trevor Ainsley (Cast Member)

The Avengers 3-23. The Charmers (29-02-64)
Trevor Bannister (Cast Member)
The Avengers 5-14. Something Nasty In The Nursery (15-04-67)
The Saint 6-19. Portrait Of Brenda (02-02-69)
Trevor Baxter (Cast Member)
Adam Adamant Lives! 15. The Village Of Evil (06-10-66) 18. Black Echo (07-01-67)
Trevor Peacock (Cast Member)
Man In A Suitcase 17. Why They Killed Nolan (17-01-67)
Trevor Reid (Cast Member)
The Avengers 2-14. Dead On Course (29-12-62)
Interpol Calling 11. Air Switch (23-11-59) 31. In The Swim (25-04-60)
Tricia Chapman (Cast Member)
Randall & Hopkirk (Deceased) 18. Could You Recognize The Man Again (16-01-70)
Tricia Noble (Cast Member)
Danger Man 3-23. Not So Jolly Roger (07-04-66)
Trisha Mortimer (Cast Member)
Strange Report 13. REPORT 4821 X-RAY Who Weeps For The Doctor (21-12-69)
Tristian Jellinek (Cast Member)
The Saint 5-25. The Power Artists (19-05-67)
Trudi Nielson (Cast Member)
The Saint 5-23. The Gadget Lovers (21-04-67)
Tsai Chin (Cast Member)
Man Of The World 2-02. The Enemy (18-05-63)
Tudor Davies (Cast Member)
Danger Man 3-24. Koroshi (12-02-67)
Tutte Lemkow (Cast Member)
The Avengers 6-09. Legacy Of Death (20-11-68)

U

Ursula Howells (Cast Member)
Interpol Calling 27. Ascent To Murder (28-03-60)
Man In A Suitcase 17. Why They Killed Nolan (17-01-67)
Unity Grimwood (Cast Member)
Strange Report 06. REPORT 3906 COVER-GIRLS Last Years Model (26-10-69)

V

Valentine Dyall (Cast Member)
The Avengers 6-04. You'll Catch Your Death (16-10-68)
Valentine Palmer (Cast Member)
The Saint 6-18. The Man Who Gambled With Life (26-01-68)
Valantino Musetti (Cast Member)
The Avengers 2-03. The Decapod (13-10-62) 2-26. Killer Whale (23-03-63) 3-02. The Undertakers (05-10-63) 3-13. Death a La Carte (21-12-63) 3-19. The Secrets Broker (01-02-64) 3-22. The Outside-In Man (22-02-64) 3-26. Lobster Quadrille (21-03-64)
Doctor Who 14. The Crusade: 2 Episodes (27-03-65)
Public Eye 1-02. Nobody Kill Santa Claus (30-01-65)
Valerie Bell (Cast Member)
The Avengers 3-24. Concerto (07-03-64)
Public Eye 2-07. Works With Chess, Not With Life (13-08-66)
The Saint 5-16. The Fast Women (13-01-67)
Valerie Cockx (Cast Member)
The Avengers 4-09. The Hour That Never Was (27-11-65)
Valerie French (Cast Member)

The Prisoner 14. Living In Harmony (29-12-67)
Valerie Leon (Cast Member)
The Avengers 6-06. Whoever Shot George Oblique Stroke XR40? (30-10-68)
The Baron 29. Countdown (12-04-67)
Randall & Hopkirk (Deceased) 05. That's How Murder Snowballs (19-10-69)
The Saint 5-19. To Kill a Saint (24-02-67)
Valerie Sarruf (Cast Member)
The Avengers 2-13. Death Dispatch (22-12-62)
Valerie Stanton (Cast Member)
Adam Adamant Lives! 05. Allah Is Not Always With You (21-07-66)
The Avengers 2-03. The Decapod (13-10-62)
Valerie Van Ost (Cast Member)
The Avengers 5-20. Dead Man's Treasure (21-10-67)
Strange Report 16. REPORT 4977 Square Root Of Evil (11-01-70)
Valerie White (Cast Member)
Ghost Squad 2-05. The Retirement Of The Gentle Dove (30-03-63)
Valli Newby (Cast Member)
The Baron 10. The Legends of Ammak (30-11-66)
Vanda Godsell (Cast Member)
The Saint 2-09. The King Of The Beggars (14-11-63)
The Third Man 3-01. A Question In Ice (27-06-64)
Vanessa Thornton (Cast Member)
Public Eye 1-02. Nobody Kill Santa Claus (30-01-65)
Varley Thomas (Cast Member)
Public Eye 4-06. The Comedian's Graveyard (03-09-69)
Vera Cook (Cast Member)
Danger Man 2-19. It's Up To The Lady (23-02-65)
Vera Day (Cast Member)
The Saint 1-11. The Man Who Was Lucky (13-12-62)
Vernon Dobtcheff (Cast Member)
The Avengers 4-15. Room Without a View (08-01-65) 5-07. The Living Dead (25-02-67)
 6-27. Thingamajig (16-04-69)
The Protectors 08. Freedom! (16-05-64)
The Saint 5-23. The Gadget Lovers (21-04-67)
Vernon Duke (Cast Member)
The Avengers 2-17. Box Of Tricks (19-01-63)
Vernon Joyner (Cast Member)
Undermind 11. End Signal (17-07-65)
Out Of The Unknown 1-01. No Place Like Earth (04-10-65)
Vernon Morris (Cast Member)
Danger Man 3-24. Koroshi (12-02-67)
Veronica Carlson (Cast Member)
Department S: 10. Double Death Of Charlie Crippen (14-09-69)
Randall & Hopkirk (Deceased) 11. The Ghost Who Saved The Bank At Monte Carlo (30-11-69)
The Saint 6-18. The Man Who Gambled With Life (26-01-68)
Veronica Hurst (Cast Member)
The Baron 20. The High Terrace (08-02-67)
Man In A Suitcase 24. Which Way Did He Go, McGill (06-03-67)
Veronica Strong (Cast Member)
The Avengers 6-21. Love All (19-02-69)
The Baron 05. Enemy Of The State (26-10-66)
Veronica Turleigh (Cast Member)
The Saint 2-21. The Good Medicine (06-02-64)
Vic Chapman (Cast Member)
Danger Man 1-28. Sabotage (14-05-61) 2-08. The Battle Of The Cameras (01-12-64)
Vic Wise (Cast Member)
The Avengers 6-09. Legacy Of Death (20-11-68)
Ghost Squad 1-05. High Wire (30-09-61)

Public Eye 1-12. The Morning Wasn't So Hot (10-04-65)
Vicki Graham (Cast Member)
Department S: 21. Death On Reflection (17-12-69)
Vicki Woolf (Cast Member)
Man In A Suitcase 09. The Girl Who Never Was (22-11-67)
The Saint 5-14. Escape Route (30-12-66)
Vicky Hughes (Cast Member)
The Saint 5-09. The Better Mouse Trap (25-11-66) 5-21. Simon & Delilah (24-03-67)
Victor Baring (Cast Member)
Danger Man 1-10. An Affair Of State (13-11-60)
Man Of The World 1-03. Blaze Of Glory (13-10-62)
Victor Beaumont (Cast Member)
The Baron 27. Roundabout (29-03-67)
Ghost Squad 1-07. Still Waters (21-10-61)
Interpol Calling 16. No Flowers For Onno (04-01-59)
The Saint 3-16. The Rhine Maiden (21-01-65) 5-12. Locate & Destroy (16-12-66)
Victor Brooks (Cast Member)
The Champions 26. Full Circle (26-03-69)
Danger Man 2-20. Have a Glass of Wine (02-03-65)
Department S: 22. Last Train to Redbridge (14-01-70)
Man In A Suitcase 25. Property Of A Gentleman (13-03-67)
Out Of The Unknown 1-12. The Midas Plague (20-12-65)
Victor Chanet (Cast Member)
The Saint 1-08. The Element Of Doubt (22-11-62)
Victor Harrington (Cast Member)
The Avengers 3-10. The Grandeur That Was Rome (30-11-63) 3-24. Concerto (07-03-64)
Danger Man 2-18. The Ubiquitous Mr Lovegrove (16-02-65)
Ghost Squad 2-10. The Grand Duchess (11-05-63)
Victor Maddern (Cast Member)
The Avengers 4-18. The Thirteenth Hole (29-01-66)
The Baron 30. Farewell To Yesterday (19-04-67)
The Prisoner 10. Hammer & Anvil (01-12-67)
Randall & Hopkirk (Deceased) 19. A Sentimental Journey (23-01-70)
The Saint 5-16. The Fast Women (13-01-67) 6-10. The Scales Of Justice (01-12-68)
Victor Pemberton (Cast Member)
Doctor Who 33. The Moonbase: 2 Episodes (18-02-67)
Victor Platt (Cast Member)
The Avengers 4-02. The Gravediggers (09-01-65)
The Prisoner 09. Checkmate (14-11-67)
The Saint 2-14. The Bunco Artists (19-12-63)
Strange Report 02. REPORT 0649 SKELETON Let Sleeping Heroes Lie (28-09-69)
Victor Rietti (Cast Member)
Danger Man 1-29. The Contessa (21-05-61)
The Saint 1-12. The Charitable Countess (20-12-62)
Victor Spinetti (Cast Member)
The Saint 2-18. The Romantic Matron (16-01-64)
Victor Winding (Cast Member)
Doctor Who 35. The Faceless Ones: Episode 1 (08-04-67)
The Saint 5-19. To Kill a Saint (24-02-67)
Victor Woolf (Cast Member)
The Prisoner 10. Hammer & Anvil (01-12-67)
Viktor Viko (Cast Member)
The Saint 3-01. The Miracle Tea Party (8-10-64)
Vilma Ann Leslie (Cast Member)
The Saint 5-16. The Fast Women (13-01-67)
Vince Fleming (Cast Member)
The Avengers 4-11. Man Eater Of Surrey Green (11-12-65)
Vincent Ball (Cast Member)

Ghost Squad 2-04. The Golden Silence (08-06-63)
Man In A Suitcase 18. The Boston Square (24-01-67)
Vincent Charles (Cast Member)
The Avengers 2-10. Death On The Rocks (01-12-62)
Vincent Harding (Cast Member)
The Avengers 6-32. Get-a-Way (14-05-69)
Danger Man 3-20. I Am Afraid You Have The Wrong Number (17-03-66)
Ghost Squad 2-07. Lost in Transit (15-06-63)
The Saint 6-12. The Fiction Makers Part 2 (15-12-68)
Viola Keats (Cast Member)
The Champions 13. Twelve Hours (18-12-68)
Virginia Clay (Cast Member)
The Avengers 6-24. Fog (12-03-69)
The Saint 2-06. Marcia (24-10-63)
Virgina Maskell (Cast Member)
Danger Man 2-07. The Colonels Daughter (24-11-64)
The Prisoner 01. Arrival (29-09-67)
Virginia North (Cast Member)
Department S: 20. The Mysterious Man In The Flying Machine (10-12-69)
Virginia Stride (Cast Member)
The Avengers 3-22. The Outside-In Man (22-02-64)
The Baron 08. The Persuaders (16-11-66)
Public Eye 2-02. Don't Forget You're Mine (09-07-66)
Virgina Wetherell (Cast Member)
Doctor Who 02. The Daleks: 5 Episodes (21-12-63)
Vivian Pickles (Cast Member)
The Avengers 3-23. The Charmers (29-02-64)
Vivian Sherrard (Cast Member)
Callan 2-04. The Little Bits & Pieces Of Love (29-01-69)
Vivian Ventura (Cast Member)
The Saint 4-08. The Spanish Cow (19-08-65)
Vivienne Bennett (Cast Member)
Doctor Who 16. The Chase: 6 Episodes (22-05-65)
Vivienne Cohen (Cast Member)
Department S: 21. Death On Reflection (17-12-69)
Vivienne Drummond (Cast Member)
The Avengers 2-21. The White Dwarf (16-02-63)
Vivienne Martin (Cast Member)
Undermind 03. The New Dimension (22-05-65)
Vladek Sheybal (Cast Member)
The Baron 09. And Suddenly You're Dead (23-11-66)
Callan 2-04. The Little Bits & Pieces Of Love (29-01-69)
The Champions 11. The Dark Island (04-12-68)
Danger Man 2-06. Fish On The Hook (17-11-64)
The Saint 5-05. The Helpful Pirate (28-10-66)
Strange Report 12. REPORT 7931 SNIPER When Is Your Cousin Not? (14-12-69)

W

W. Thorpe Deverreux (Cast Member)
Interpol Calling 38. The Absent Assassin (13-06-60)
Wade Barker (Cast Member)
Strange Report 08. REPORT 2475 REVENGE When a Man Hates (09-11-69)
Wallas Eston (Cast Member)
Man In A Suitcase 16. The Whisper (10-01-67)
Walter Brown (Cast Member)
Ghost Squad 1-10. Catspaw (05-01-61)
The Saint 2-05. The Elusive Elishaw (17-10-63) 3-19. The Golden Frog (11-02-65) 4-03. The Crooked Ring (15-07-65)
Walter Gotell (Cast Member)
The Andromeda Breakthrough 4 Episodes (1962)
The Baron 22. Night Of The Hunter (22-02-67)
The Champions 06. Operation Deep Freeze (30-10-68)
Danger Man 1-29. The Contessa (21-05-61) 1-36. Under the Lake (30-12-61)
Interpol Calling 03. The Money Game (28-09-59) 23. Payment in Advance (22-02-60)
The Saint 3-11. The Hijackers (17-12-64)
Walter Horsbrugh (Cast Member)
The Avengers 4-01. The Town Of No Return (02-10-65)
The Baron 30. Farewell To Yesterday (19-04-67)
The Saint 5-14. Escape Route (30-12-66)
Walter Hudd (Cast Member)
The Avengers 2-12. The Big Thinker (15-12-62)
Walter Randall (Cast Member)
Danger Man 2-06. Fish On The Hook (17-11-64)
Doctor Who 14. The Crusade: 2 Episodes (27-03-65)
Ghost Squad 2-07. Lost in Transit (15-06-63)
The Saint 3-05. The Revolution Racket (05-11-64) 5-04. The Reluctant Revolution (21-10-66)
Walter Rilla (Cast Member)
Interpol Calling 03. The Money Game (28-09-59)
Walter Sparrow (Cast Member)
Adam Adamant Lives! 16. D Is For Destruction (13-06-66)
The Champions 23. The Night People (05-03-69)
Randall & Hopkirk (Deceased) 18. Could You Recognize The Man Again (16-01-70)
Walter Swash (Cast Member)
The Avengers 3-01. Brief For Murder (28-09-63)
Wanda Ventham (Cast Member)
The Avengers 4-02. The Gravediggers (09-01-65)
Danger Man 2-10. A Man To Be Trusted (15-12-64) 2-21. The Mirror's New (09-03-65)
Department S: 16. The Man From X (05-11-69)
Doctor Who 35. The Faceless Ones: Episode 1 (08-04-67)
The Saint 3-09. The Death Penalty (03-12-64) 5-14. Escape Route (30-12-66)
Warren Clarke (Cast Member)
The Avengers 6-16. Invasion Of The Earthman (15-01-69)
Warren Mitchell (Cast Member)
The Avengers 3-11. The Golden Fleece (07-12-63) 3-23. The Charmers (29-02-64) 4-12 Twos a Crowd (18-12-65) 5-04. The See Through Man (04-02-67)
Danger Man 1-10. An Affair Of State (13-11-60) 1-14. The Traitor (11-12-60) 1-17. Find & Return (08-01-61) 2-07. The Colonels Daughter (24-11-64) 2-20. Have a Glass of Wine (02-03-65) 3-17. I Can Only Offer You Sherry (20-01-66)
Ghost Squad 1-12. Princess (12-01-61) 2-19. Death of a Sportsman (26-01-63)
Interpol Calling 14. The Man's a Clown (21-12-59)
Man Of The World 1-01. Death Of a Conference (29-09-62)
The Saint 1-02. The Latin Touch (11-10-62) 1-12. The Charitable Countess (20-12-62)
Warren Stanhope (Cast Member)

The Baron 16. The Island (Part 2) (11-01-67)
The Champions 20. The Silent Enemy (12-02-69)
Department S: 25. Spencer Bodily Is 60 Years Old (11-02-70)
Man In A Suitcase 04. Variation On a Million Bucks Part 1 (18-10-67) 23. Web With Four Spiders (28-02-67) 05. Variation On a Million Bucks Part 2 (25-10-67)
Man Of The World 2-07. The Prince (22-06-63)
The Protectors 13. Cargo From Corinth (20-06-64)
The Saint 1-06. The Pearls Of Peace (08-11-62) 2-03. Judith (03-10-63) 6-02. Invitation To Danger (06-10-68) 6-14. Where The Money Is (29-12-68)
Waveney Lee (Cast Member)
Interpol Calling 14. The Man's a Clown (21-12-59)
Wendy Allnutt (Cast Member)
The Avengers 6-16. Invasion Of The Earthman (15-01-69)
Wendy Craig (Cast Member)
Danger Man 1-23. The Gallows Tree (09-04-61) 3-17. I Can Only Offer You Sherry (20-01-66)
Wendy Gifford (Cast Member)
Out Of The Unknown 1-05. Time In Advance (01-11-65)
Wendy Hall (Cast Member)
Man In A Suitcase 08. Essay In Evil (15-11-67) 19. Somebody Loses, Somebody… Wins? (31-01-67)
Wendy Johnson (Cast Member)
Out Of The Unknown 1-11. Thirteen To Centauraus
Wendy Padbury (Cast Member)
Doctor Who 43. The Wheel in Space: 2 Episodes (11-05-68) 44. The Dominators: 5 Episodes (10-08-68) 45. The Mind Robber: 5 Episodes (14-09-68) 46. The Invasion: 6 Episodes (09-11-68) 47. The Krotons: 4 Episodes (28-12-68) 48. The Seeds Of Death: 6 Episodes (25-01-69) 49. The Space Pirates: Episode 2 (15-03-69) 50. The War Games: 10 Episodes (19-04-69)
Wendy Richard (Cast Member)
Danger Man 2-11. Don't Nail Him Yet (22-12-64)
Wendy Ventham (Cast Member)
The Prisoner 11. It's Your Funeral (08-12-67)
Wendy Williams (Cast Member)
Danger Man 1-09. The Sanctuary (06-11-60)
Interpol Calling 23. Payment in Advance (22-02-60)
Wensley Pithey (Cast Member)
Danger Man 1-33. Hired Assassin (18-06-61)
Man Of The World 2-05. In The Picture (08-06-63)
The Saint 2-02. Starring The Saint (26-09-63)
Wesley Murphy (Cast Member)
Danger Man 1-25. The Brothers (23-04-61)
Weston Gavin (Cast Member)
Department S: 26. The Ghost Of Mary Burnham (18-02-70)
Wilfred Boyle (Cast Member)
The Avengers 3-21. Build a Better Mousetrap (15-2-64) 6-23. Take Me To Your Leader (5-3-69)
Wilfred Carter (Cast Member)
Ghost Squad 2-07. Lost in Transit (15-06-63)
Wilfred Grove (Cast Member)
The Avengers 2-14. Dead On Course (29-12-62)
Man Of The World 1-06. The Sentimental Agent (03-11-62)
Wilfred Lawson (Cast Member)
Danger Man 3-23. Not So Jolly Roger (07-04-66)
Will Stampe (Cast Member)
Man In A Suitcase 29. Castle In The Clouds (10-04-67)
William Buck (Cast Member)
The Avengers 2-05. Mission To Montreal (27-10-62)
The Baron 16. The Island (Part 2) (11-01-67)
The Saint 2-13. The Sporting Chance (12-12-63) 5-03. The Russian Prisoner (14-10-66)
William Corlett (Cast Member)
Danger Man 2-15. Whatever Happened To George Foster (19-01-65)

William Devlin (Cast Member)
The Avengers 3-22. The Outside-In Man (22-02-64)
William Dexter (Cast Member)
Adam Adamant Lives! 08. The Last Sacrifice (18-08-66)
Danger Man 1-29. The Contessa (21-05-61) 1-38. Dead Man Walks (13-01-62) 3-13. Say It With Flowers (23-12-65)
Man In A Suitcase 20. Blind Spot (07-02-67)
The Saint 2-09. The King Of The Beggars (14-11-63)
William Dysart (Cast Member)
Randall & Hopkirk (Deceased) 24. Vendetta For a Dead Man (27-02-70)
Strange Report 15. REPORT 4407 No Choice For The Donor (04-01-70)
William Ellis (Cast Member)
The Avengers 6-13. They Keep Killing Steed (18-12-68)
William Fox (Cast Member)
The Avengers 5-06. The Winged Avenger (18-02-67)
William Franklyn (Cast Member)
The Avengers 4-14. Silent Dust (01-01-66) 6-17. Killer (22-01-69)
The Baron 23. The Edge Of Fear (01-03-67)
The Champions 29. The Gun Runners (23-04-69)
Interpol Calling 28. Slow Boat To Amsterdam (04-04-60)
William Gaunt (Cast Member)
The Avengers 2-11. Traitor In Zebra (08-12-62)
The Champions All Episodes
 Ghost Squad 2-10. The Grand Duchess (11-05-63)
The Saint 5-13. Flight Plan (23-12-66)
William Greene (Cast Member)
Ghost Squad 1-02. Bullet With My Name On It (16-09-61)
The Saint 2-03. Judith (03-10-63)
William Hartnell (Cast Member)
Doctor Who all episodes (1963-1967)
Ghost Squad 1-05. High Wire (30-09-61)
William Holmes (Cast Member)
The Saint 5-06. The Convenient Monster (04-11-66)
William Hurndell (Cast Member)
Adam Adamant Lives! 04. The Sweet Smell Of Disaster (14-07-67)
Danger Man 2-19. It's Up To The Lady (23-02-65)
Doctor Who 25. The Gunfighters: 4 Episodes (30-04-66)
William Ingram (Cast Member)
Danger Man 3-18. The Hunting Party (27-01-66)
William Job (Cast Member)
The Avengers 4-11. Man Eater Of Surrey Green (11-12-65) 6-07. False Witness (06-01-68)
William Kendall (Cast Member)
The Avengers 6-11. Look (Stop Me If You've Heard This One) But There Were These Two Fellers (04-12-68)
Department S: 11. Who Plays The Dummy (01-10-69)
Randall & Hopkirk (Deceased) 09. The House On Haunted Hill (16-11-69)
William Lucas (Cast Member)
The Avengers 5-18. Death's Door (07-10-67) 6-16. Invasion Of The Earthman (15-01-69)
Danger Man 1-13. The Prisoner (04-12-60) 2-16. A Room in The Basement (02-02-65)
Ghost Squad 1-06. Eyes Of The Bat (14-10-61)
Interpol Calling 18. The Thousand Mile Alibi (18-01-60)
Public Eye 4-03. Paid In Full (13-08-69) 4-04. My Lifes My Own (20-08-69) 4-05. Case For The Defence (27-08-69)
The Saint 3-22. The Crime Of The Century (04-03-65)
William Lyon Brown (Cast Member)
The Avengers 5-18. Death's Door (07-10-67)
The Baron 02. Epitaph For a Hero (05-10-66)
The Prisoner 08. Dance Of The Dead (17-11-67)

William Marlowe (Cast Member)
The Avengers 6-25. Who Was That Man I Saw You With (19-03-69)
Ghost Squad 2-17. Mr Five Per Cent (06-04-63) 3-01. An Eye For An Eye (22-02-64)
The Saint 3-09. The Death Penalty (03-12-64)
William Marshall (Cast Member)
Danger Man 1-39. Deadline (20-01-62) 2-04. The Galloping Major (03-11-64)
William Maxwell (Cast Member)
The Corridor People All Episodes (1966)
William Mervyn (Cast Member)
Randall & Hopkirk (Deceased) 02. A Disturbing Case (28-09-69)
William Moore (Cast Member)
The Corridor People Victim as Red (1966)
Public Eye 4-03. Paid In Full (13-08-69)
William Russell (Cast Member)
Doctor Who 01. An Unearthly Child: 4 Episodes (23-11-63) 02. The Daleks: 6 Episodes (21-12-63) 05. The Keys Of Marinus: 6 Episodes (11-04-64) 06. The Aztecs: 4 Episodes (23-05-64) 07. The Sensorites: 6 Episodes (20-06-64) 08. The Reign Of Terror: 4 Episodes (08-08-64) 09. Planet Of Giants: 3 Episodes (31-10-64) 10. Dalek Invasion Of Earth: 6 Episodes (21-11-64) 11. The Rescue: 2 Episodes (02-01-65) 13. The Web Planet: 6 Episodes (13-02-65) 15. The Space Museum: 4 Episodes (24-04-65) 16. The Chase: 6 Episodes (22-05-65)
William Squire (Cast Member)
The Champions 27. Nutcracker (02-04-69)
Randall & Hopkirk (Deceased) 19. A Sentimental Journey (23-01-70)
William Sylvester (Cast Member)
The Baron 30. Farewell To Yesterday (19-04-67)
Danger Man 1-13. The Prisoner (04-12-60)
Ghost Squad 1-13. Death From a Distance (04-11-61)
The Saint 3-23. The Happy Suicide (11-03-65) 5-02. Interlude In Venice (07-10-66)
William Wilde (Cast Member)
The Avengers 6-32. Get-a-Way (14-05-69)
Department S: 13. The Man Who Got a New Face (15-10-69)
The Saint 6-20. The World Beater (09-02-69)
Undermind 07. Song Of Death (19-06-65)
Willie Payne (Cast Member)
Danger Man 2-04. The Galloping Major (03-11-64)
Ghost Squad 2-25. The Thirteenth Girl (27-04-63)
Willie Shearer (Cast Member)
The Avengers 2-23. Conspiracy Of Silence (02-03-63)
Willoughby Goddard (Cast Member)
The Avengers 1-15. The Frighteners (27-11-61) 6-27. Thingamajig (16-04-69)
The Baron 23. The Edge Of Fear (01-03-67)
Danger Man 1-26. The Journey Ends Halfway (30-04-61)
Ghost Squad 2-06. The Missing People (29-06-63)
Out Of The Unknown 1-04. The Dead Past (25-10-65)
The Saint 6-17. The Ex-King Of Diamonds (19-01-68)
Willoughby Gray (Cast Member)
The Avengers 6-04. You'll Catch Your Death (16-10-68)
Winifred Evans (Cast Member)
Department S: 19. The Duplicated Man (03-12-69)
Windsor Davies (Cast Member)
Doctor Who 36. The Evil Of The Daleks: Episode 2 (27-05-67)
Wolf Frees (Cast Member)
The Champions 28. The Final Countdown (16-04-69)
The Saint 5-23. The Gadget Lovers (21-04-67)
Wolfe Morris (Cast Member)
The Avengers 2-03. The Decapod (13-10-62) 4-12. Twos a Crowd (18-12-65)
The Champions 29. The Gun Runners (23-04-69)
Department S: 27. A Fish Out Of Water (25-02-70)

232

Ghost Squad 2-02. East Of Mandalay (09-02-63)
Doctor Who 39. The Ice Warriors: 4 Episodes (11-11-67)
Man In A Suitcase 15. Burden Of Proof (03-01-67)
The Saint 2-24. Sophia (24-02-64) 5-12. Locate & Destroy (16-12-66)

Y

Yashar Adem (Cast Member)
Danger Man 3-07. Judgement Day (11-11-65)
Yemi Ajibade (Cast Member)
Danger Man 3-05. Loyalty Always Pays (28-10-65)
Yoko Tani (Cast Member)
Danger Man 3-24. Koroshi (12-02-67) 3-25. Shinda Shima (26-02-67)
Man In A Suitcase 04. Variation On a Million Bucks Part 1 (18-10-67) 05. Variation On a Million
Bucks Part 2 (25-10-67)
Yolande Turner (Cast Member)
The Avengers 4-17. The Girl From AUNTIE (22-01-66) 5-19. The £50,000 Breakfast (14-10-67)
Department S: 10. Double Death Of Charlie Crippen (14-09-69)
The Saint 2-07. The Work Of Art (31-10-63) 5-24. A Double In Diamonds (05-05-67)
Yole Marinelli
The Avengers 5-19. The £50,000 Breakfast (14-10-67)
Yootha Joyce
The Avengers 5-14. Something Nasty In The Nursery (15-04-67)
The Saint 5-03. The Russian Prisoner (14-10-66)
Yuri Borienko (Cast Member)
Adam Adamant Lives! 03. More Deadly Than The Sword (07-07-66)
Yutte Stensgaard (Cast Member)
The Saint 6-04. The Desperate Diplomat (20-10-68)
Yvette Herries (Cast Member)
Man In A Suitcase 28. Three Blinks Of The Eyes (03-04-67)
The Saint 5-24. A Double In Diamonds (05-05-67)
Yvonne Furneaux (Cast Member)
The Baron 06. Masquerade (Part 1) (02-11-66) 07. The Killing (Part 2) (09-11-66)
Danger Man 3-02. A Very Dangerous Game (07-10-65)
Yvonne Lime (Cast Member)
The Third Man 4-07. Diamond In the Rough (11-05-62)
Yvonne Marquand (Cast Member)
Danger Man 2-21. The Mirror's New (09-03-65)
Yvonne Mitchell (Cast Member)
Out Of The Unknown 2-01. The Machine Stops
Yvonne Romain (Cast Member)
Danger Man 1-28. Sabotage (14-05-61)
Yvonne Shima (Cast Member)
The Avengers 2-24. A Chorus Of Frogs (09-03-63)

Z

Zed Zakari (Cast Member)
Interpol Calling 12. The Chinese Mask (07-12-59)
Zena Marshall (Cast Member)
Danger Man 1-17. Find & Return (08-01-61) 1-29. The Contessa (21-05-61) 2-06. Fish On The Hook (17-11-64)
Man Of The World 1-01. Death Of a Conference (29-09-62)
Zena Walker (Cast Member)
The Prisoner 13. Do Not Forsake Me Oh My Darling (22-12-67)
Zeina Merton (Cast Member)
Strange Report 07. REPORT 3424 EPIDEMIC A Most Curious Crime (02-11-69)
Zeph Gladstone (Cast Member)
The Avengers 4-25. How To Succeed…. At Murder (19-03-66)
The Baron 08. The Persuaders (16-11-66) 22. Night Of The Hunter (22-02-67)
Zeynep Tarimer (Cast Member)
Danger Man 3-03. Sting In The Tail (14-10-65)
Zia Mohyeddin (Cast Member)
The Avengers 4-26. Honey For The Prince (26-03-66)
The Champions 16. Shadow Of The Panther (15-01-68)
Danger Man 1-38. Dead Man Walks (13-01-62) 2-07. The Colonels Daughter (24-11-64) 2-14. Such Men Are Dangerous (12-01-65) 3-06. The Mercenaries (04-11-65) 3-15. Somebody Is Liable To Get Hurt (06-01-66)
Man In A Suitcase 30. Night Flight To Andorra (17-04-67)
Zoe Zephyr (Cast Member)
Danger Man 2-07. The Colonels Daughter (24-11-64)
Zorenah Osborne (Cast Member)
Danger Man 3-06. The Mercenaries (04-11-65)
Zulema Dene (Cast Member)
The Avengers 6-21. Love All (19-02-69)

i

ii

235

Printed in Great Britain
by Amazon

14133946R00133